EVERY NIGHT IS LADIES' NIGHT

 *An Imprint of* HarperCollins*Publishers*

EVERY NIGHT IS LADIES' NIGHT

S T O R I E S

MICHAEL JAIME-BECERRA

HarperCollins books may be purchased for educational, business, or sales promotional use. For information, please write: Special Markets Department, HarperCollins Publishers Inc., 10 East 53rd Street, New York, NY 10022.

FIRST EDITION

Designed by Shubhani Sarkar

Printed on acid-free paper

Library of Congress Cataloging-in-Publication Data
Jaime-Becerra, M. (Michael)
    Every night is ladies' night : stories / by Michael Jaime-Becerra.—1st ed.
      p.   cm.
    Contents: Practice tattoos—Every night is ladies' night—The corrido of Hector Cruz—Lopez Trucking Incorporated—George and Wanda—Riding with Lencho—Gina and Max—Media vuelta—La fiesta brava—Buena Suerte Airlines.
    ISBN 0-06-055962-4 (acid-free paper)
    1. United States—Social life and customs—Fiction.   2. Hispanic Americans—Fiction.   I. Title.

PS3610.A38E94 2004
813'.6—dc21   2003054814

04 05 06 07 08 DIX/QW 10 9 8 7 6 5 4 3 2 1

FOR MY FAMILY AND FRIENDS

CONTENTS

ACKNOWLEDGMENTS

I am most pleased to thank Geoffrey Wolff and Michelle Latiolais. Their warmth, wit, and candor have been continual sources of inspiration. Their support is the chief reason I now have this book in my hands.

I am equally pleased to thank Ann Patchett, who generously gave her time and energy to this project, and Lisa Bankoff, who called when she said she would, and did so to share great news. They are the two chief reasons why you now have this book in your hands.

Thank you, René Alegria and Dan Menaker, for your enthusiasm and keen editorial eyes.

It is good to have smart friends. I'm lucky to have many at Irvine, and I'm especially grateful for those who saw these stories first. Arielle Read also deserves special recognition, as her dedication to the students in the program is a rare and valuable thing. Thank you, Adam Meave, for helping me with cars. Thank you, Maurya and Susan, as well as Barton and Robert, for helping me get started.

It is good to have family, a father who takes pride in his work, a mother who looks closely at things, a sister who is tough and funny.

Thank you also, Patrick and Anthony. Gracias a toda la familia Seáñez en Chihuahua, y la familia García en Juárez. Thank you, Tía Connie, for helping ensure that what I said in Spanish was actually what I meant to say. Thank you, Tía Angie, for inviting me East to read.

Lastly, I am happily indebted to Elizabeth, my dearest darling, the one who makes the hard things easier, the one who makes the good things brighter.

My most sincere thanks go to you all.

EVERY NIGHT IS LADIES' NIGHT

If I make seven free throws in a row, Violet Cervantes will like me. I've made ten straight before, but now the rim is hard to see because it's late and the courts at Kranz have no lights. It feels like I've been out here for a couple of hours, but still I don't wanna go home because my mom and Gina were fighting over Gina's boyfriend when I left. Knowing my mom, she won't get over this guy Max having his ears pierced. I shoot the ball and miss. It bounces left to another court, the rim on this one all crooked and bent from someone hanging on it. Okay, if I make six in a row, Violet will like me.

I shoot and make it. Then two. Three. Four in a row. I'm about to make number five, but I stop because I hear yells and the smash of a bottle from the other end of the grass field by the basketball courts. It's probably cholos. Even though my mom makes me go to church with her twice a week because she says I make her feel safe, I'm so skinny that there's no way I could stop a bunch of drunk cholos from killing me if they wanted to. I turn around and shoot at the rim way on the other side, thinking of Violet, hoping the shot goes in. When the ball misses, I run after it and wonder where to go next.

GINA'S DRAGGED THE PHONE into her room to talk to Max, laughing loud and making lots of noise because our parents aren't home. The cord's stretched straight from the phone jack by the couch, down the hall, under the door to her room. It looks like a tightrope, and I step on it, arms out for extra balance. One step and the cord pops out from the wall. Something bangs on the other side of Gina's door. I close my eyes, keep my arms stretched, and imagine that I'm falling, that a net will be there to catch me before I hit the ground. I open my eyes and Gina's staring at me, puppy dog slippers on her feet, green towel around her head like a genie. She calls me a fuckin' weirdo, then slams the door to her room.

I'm weird? I'm not the one with black nail polish on my toes. The one whose friends all think they're punk rock Draculas. I mean Gina's boyfriend, Max, all he wears is black. His pants are all tight and he always wears a leather jacket like it's glued to his back. Last month, when we went to see *Beverly Hills Cop*, I saw him and his friends pushing his green Tercel at the mall. It was almost summer, and the bus I was on had air-conditioning. Just looking at him pushing that car out in the heat and wearing that stupid jacket made me sweat. Max is weird, but at least he's not Junior, Gina's last boyfriend.

Junior always scratched and picked at his face. He was super-skinny too. One time I saw him with his shirt off and his stomach was all caved in like it was trying to eat itself. Him and my sister were together for like six months. For Gina that was like six years. When he would come and pick up my sister it was always a big deal. Gina said it was because Junior lived over in Pico Rivera and he had to take three buses to see her. I remember him biting his lip as he waited by the door for my sister.

Junior always had this shitty, pissed-off look on his face, like he just came from a fight he had started and lost.

The last time anybody talked about Junior was also the last time I saw my mom drive the car. Math homework was kicking my ass that night. My mom answered the phone and listened for a few seconds before saying Junior's name and making the sign of the cross. She took the pencil from my hand, suds dripping onto my book as she leaned over to write in the margins. The dishes stayed in the sink, and my mom had me recopy her sloppy directions as she looked for the car keys and her purse. My mom's always been afraid to drive, but there she was, going fast and crazy, running a red light and honking at the screeching cars like it was their fault they were in our way.

We flew through Whittier Narrows and got to the bowling alley in about ten minutes. The big signs advertising 36 LANES and THE SLO-POKE LOUNGE colored everything red. My mom drove around the packed parking lot, and I went inside to look. The place was chilly from too much air-conditioning. I went up to the front desk, and before I could talk, the guy behind the counter put down the pair of shoes he was spraying and told me to get in line. Instead, I checked the pay phones and thought a couple times about going into the ladies' room. I wandered down to one end of the building, bumping into people while I looked for Gina's face. A bowler hollered in a lane nearby and kicked at the air like a ninja as the people around him laughed. I said Gina's name over and over as I tried to remember what she had on when she left the house.

After a while I went back outside and walked around the building. I could hear my mom before I even saw the two of them. The car was in front of an orange Dumpster, driver door open, engine still running. One of the headlights shone on Gina. She was plopped on the ground, and it looked like the Spanish words flying from my mom's mouth were punches that kept my sister from lifting her head out of her hands.

My mom finally stopped her yelling when she saw me standing behind her.

She told Gina to get in the car, and we both sat in the back and didn't say anything. Gina had mascara stripes down her face and she kept her hand tucked tight against her neck. Her eyes followed the cars that passed us as our mom drove home. We stopped at a signal, and the bright lights from the Mobil station by our house flooded the car. Gina took her hand from her neck, and I could see blood on her palm, a dark shiny spot the size of a dime. My mom stepped on the gas and I tried to mind my own business as the car ducked under a freeway overpass. Later on, I found out this was Gina's last fight with Junior, that he had used her neck as an ashtray before dumping her at the bowling alley. The car groaned from my mom's foot, and Gina stared at her hand, sorta smiling before rubbing it into the sleeve of her shirt.

THIS IS WHAT I KNOW ABOUT VIOLET CERVANTES:

1. Her dad owns Paisano's Pizza. Every day she goes straight there after school. When I pass by on the way home, she's already working.
2. Her, Yvette Valdez, and Isabel Zaragoza got caught smoking in the girls' bathroom right before Christmas vacation.
3. Last year she was going around with Sal Torres, but she broke up with him. Rico told me she slapped him across the face at Yvette's party because Sal stuck his hand up her shirt and everybody saw.
4. Sometimes, mostly on Fridays, she wears these blue socks that have white stars on them.
5. She sits across from me in Clack-clack's class. In Mrs. Aispuro's class, she sits in the front row by the chalkboard. Violet pays attention and writes a lot of stuff down.

6. She's way better than me at math. Whenever we take tests, the people who get A's get their picture taken. The photos are pinned to a wall covered in red construction paper with a sign of a cartoon pencil saying GREAT JOB! One time I got an 89 on a test. Mrs. Aispuro said to try harder next week, but that's the best I ever did. The next time Violet gets her picture taken, I think I'm going to steal it.

GINA HAS PURPLE HAIR! She's standing in front of me, putting on her makeup, with this purple fuckin' hair. Max is outside, honking the horn on his piece-a-shit car. I ask where's she going and she says to tell Mom she went to the movies with her friends. Yesterday Gina was all excited because she won tickets to a concert off the radio. I ask if she's going to see one of her stupid KROQ groups. Gina says the name of the band, and I say, "Social who?"

She looks up from the dark lipstick in her hand and repeats herself real slow, like I'm an idiot for not knowing what she's talking about. "Social. Distortion. They're opening for the Jesus and Mary Chain."

"Mom'll love that one," I say, but Max honks again.

Gina kisses a Kleenex, throws her makeup in her bag, and mumbles something about Max needing to calm down. She checks herself in the mirror one last time. I tell Gina she looks like a Muppet and she tells me to fuck off.

I POUR A GLASS OF WATER and reach into the freezer for ice cubes. I drop three into the glass and rub one on the back of my head until it starts to melt between my fingers. Tomorrow I'll probably have a bump from that foul, but at least I made the basket and we won the last game. My dad tells me to turn off the light in the kitchen because he's watching

TV. I pick up my ball, and as I start to my room, I stop and listen. Besides the television, I can hear Gina's voice in the bathroom. She's explaining about her hair, how it isn't that big a deal, that it'll probably wash out in a week. Two at the most.

"Besides," she tells my mom, "tú también te lo pintas."

I sorta laugh at that one and walk closer to the half-open bathroom door. My mom does get her hair dyed black every two weeks at Brenda's Hair Salon. The color's so dark I always imagine Brenda painting it on with a brush, the dye thick and steaming like the tar my dad uses to stick roofs to people's houses. My mom tells Gina it's not the same thing. She says she doesn't come home looking like a monster.

Gina says, "God, it's no big deal," and then I hear a smack.

"Don't bring God into this," my mom says. "Ni digas el nombre de Dios con esa greña."

The faucet turns on and I can hear water splashing in the bathtub. There's the sound of people pushing and Gina whining. Someone slams someone else against one wall before bouncing them to the other. Gina screams and my mom keeps shouting in Spanish, you're not my daughter, looking like this you're not my daughter. There's the big crash of bodies falling, and my dad yells to keep it down. I step into the bathroom and they both look up at me. My mom's on top of Gina, teeth clenched, one hand on my sister's neck, her other one trying to push the crown of purple suds on Gina's head under the running water. The faucet is pointed toward the wall, and water splashes all over, and blood is coming from Gina's forehead. The blood mixes with the dye and the suds from the spilled shampoo, making this kind of syrup on the rim of the tub, and some of it hits me when my mom points and tells me to shut the door.

I STEP OUT of the confessional and my mom takes my place inside. The door closes behind her with a thud. It's Monday night and the church is empty. It's only us, the priest in the other half of the confession box, and a nun who's sweeping up around the altar. The priest gave me a short penance, and I kneel to start my first Our Father. Halfway through I stop. If we had come on Thursday like normal, I wouldn't be missing the Laker game right now. I start praying the names of the Lakers instead, calling out the starting lineup in my head. I say their names over and over, faster and faster. Each name speeds up in my brain until all the players become a blur of whispered words and uniform numbers.

I get up and slide back against the pew. After a while I start counting the stations of the cross. I squint and make out seven candles around the altar. I throw my head back and count sixteen iron lamps hanging from the ceiling. I take out my wallet, inspect my three dollars, and re-arrange the papers and cards inside. The nun has started sweeping the pews across from where I'm sitting. She looks at me and I smile, all embarrassed like she caught me doing something nasty. The door to the confessional opens. My mom kneels and does a quick sign of the cross. She adjusts the black leather bag on her shoulder, pulling out a yellow scarf. She uses it to wipe at her eyes, then ties it around her head, hiding her face as she hurries outside.

I DRIBBLE WITH MY LEFT and carry my trophy in my right hand as me and Rico walk into Paisano's Pizza. It's Saturday, and both Violet and her older sister Leti are working. I put the trophy on the counter and hold the ball with my foot. Violet's filling tiny plastic containers with Parmesan cheese. Leti's talking on the phone. There's a sign that says WE ONLY USE FRESH INGREDIENTS behind them. Violet takes Rico's order, and I smooth my wrinkled money on the counter, the bills damp from being in my shorts the whole tournament. Rico gets three pepperoni slices and a root beer. I ask for cheese pizza, two slices, and I make sure to say please. When Rico sees that I don't have a drink, he says he'll lend me the money so I can buy a Coke. I tell him thanks and take his money and pretend to read the menu on the wall because my face has turned red.

Violet gives me my change and I sit with Rico at one of the two tables facing the street. Leti hangs up the phone and gives the order to her dad. Mr. Cervantes reads the slip of paper before shoving it into his apron. He tells Leti to write neater as he slides a pizza in the oven, closing the heavy steel door before going back to the kitchen. A few seconds later, two cholos walk in. One is big and tall, like six-foot-something. He looks like a bear standing on its back legs. The other one is tall too, only thinner. His head is shaved and his nose points out like a Doberman's. As they stand at the counter, I can read the tattoos that branch out from their tank tops and stretch across their shoulders. The Bear orders two Cokes with extra ice. The Doberman taps a cigarette on the counter while Violet gets the drinks. Leti takes their money. She says there's no smoking in here, and the Doberman smiles and tells her to relax.

Mr. Cervantes comes back out from the kitchen carrying a stack of cardboard. He drops it on the counter and stares at the cholos as they take their drinks, his eyes practically pushing them out the door. The cholos leave without saying anything, probably because Mr. Cervantes looks like he could pick up the pizza oven and throw it at them. Mr. Cervantes tells Leti to bring our food, then tells Violet that those delivery boxes aren't going to fold themselves. Violet pulls her hair into a ponytail and wipes her hands on her apron. Leti brings our plates of pizza, then sits next to Violet, and thin white boxes start to form between them.

Rico folds two of his slices together to make a sandwich. He takes a big bite and fans air into his mouth because it's hot. He swallows and starts talking about the Laker game and I answer without paying attention. I listen to Leti ask Violet if she liked either of those guys, if she saw all those tattoos, if she thought the Doberman was cute. I take a bite of my pizza, but don't chew. Violet shrugs and says I guess. Both of them giggle at the same time and I want to leave.

THE DOOR PLAYS "La Cucaracha" when Gina opens it, and she dances past a wall of fish tanks as I step inside. The place smells like one of the animals had an accident and the owner just covered the floor with straw instead of mopping the mess up. We're there because she says Max picked up a stray dog and she wants to buy it a collar, a cool one with spikes so the dog can look punk. Gina needs money. She said she'd take me to Max's house if I lent her the cash to buy a collar for the stupid dog because Max has a tattoo gun, and she can talk him into doing me for no charge.

The man working has a thin mustache that reminds me of the guy who controls the Tilt-A-Wheel at the Epiphany carnival. He says hi and to let him know if we need any help, then goes back to scooping fish out of a tank. There's a big brown iguana in an aquarium by the cash register. He scratches lazy at the glass like he hasn't accepted that he's going to spend the rest of his life behind it. A radio plays salsa music and the guy working starts singing to the fish as he chases them around in the water with his blue net. He pours them into plastic bags, fills them with a squirt of air from a big green tank, and spins them around with his hand like miniature dance partners.

Gina finds the collars. She calls me over to decide between a black leather one with silver spikes and a brown one that's thicker and decorated with studs.

"Get whichever one's cheaper," I say.

I don't tell her that I've been saving this money for two weeks, skipping lunches and washing our neighbors' cars. Gina picks the black one, looks at its price tag, and asks me for twenty bucks. I give her the money, and she presses the spikes against my cheek and says, "See, they're not even sharp."

Gina tells the guy working that she thinks she's ready, and he turns the knob on the air tank and spins another bag of fish before he heads to the cash register. As my sister pays, I wonder if that tank has the kind of air that makes your voice all squeaky and high. The guy's not looking, so I stick the tube in my mouth and turn the knob. My cheeks puff with air and I can feel it push down my throat and burst through both my nostrils. I cough and drop the tube. It lands in a bucket of sawdust and I have to cover my eyes as it clouds up around me. The guy yells and Gina starts laughing and we both run out the door. I sprint all the way down to the liquor store where I start walking, popping my ears until Gina catches up. She tells me I should of thought of that sooner, that maybe we coulda got the collar for free.

MAX LIVES IN A RENTED GARAGE. There's a bed and a dresser, a radio with tapes piled on top, and a long couch that's so dirty it looks like it's covered in camouflage. There's a table with a glass top held together by stickers and strips of duct tape. I sit on an aluminum beach chair, and Max is across from me, his chair creaking as he flips through a notebook full of scribbles. He isn't wearing a shirt, probably to show off the practice tattoos he's been giving himself, or maybe to give them air so they can heal. There's a skull on Max's chest that's either laughing or shouting. It's hard to tell because the ink is dark and the skin around it is all raw and red.

I ask Max about his dog, and he looks up from his notebook and says, "Ask your sister. She's the one who left the gate open."

Gina gets up off the couch and leans over Max. "Again, for the thousandth time, I'm sorry. Besides, you didn't really want him anyway," she says, kissing Max on the neck. She traces her finger across Max's tattoo. He flinches and pushes her away, then he says that he's sorry. He grabs my sister's hand and pulls her close for a quick kiss. After that, Gina walks away and turns on the TV. She twists the knob through a few channels and takes a bag of Polly seeds from her purse, sticking a few in her mouth before sitting on the couch.

"Is this how you want it?" Max asks. The page he shows me has Violet's name written out in curly letters, the V in that style you see on diplomas. It's a little big, longer than my hand, but I still tell Max yeah, and reach behind my shoulder and say, "Put it right here."

"Who's this Violet girl anyway?" Gina asks. I tell her she's my girl-friend. Gina splits a seed in her mouth and picks the small shell apart with her fingers. "If Violet's your girlfriend, how come she never calls the house?"

I tell Gina that Violet can't get through. "You're always on the fuckin' phone."

Max tells me to take off my shirt and to sit on the floor near the couch. I do both. Gina's watching channel 34, an old Mexican movie about a charro who wears a wrestling mask. Max sits behind me, and the charro shoots about ten shots from a revolver, killing all the bad guys except for the one holding his girlfriend hostage. I can't really tell what happens next because Max tells me to put my head down. He rubs my shoulder with alcohol and it's so cold that I get chills. He wipes me with a towel, then starts to draw an outline on me with a marker. He tells me not to move. I can feel the tip of his pen curving up and down my shoulder blade as the movie goes to a commercial. The marker tickles, but I make myself concentrate on the ads to keep from laughing. When the charro comes back, Max says that I'm ready.

I lift my head and the charro is singing on his horse. The horse rears up, hoofs kicking at the air, and some lady hugs herself and says for him, she'll wait forever. Max pushes my head back down and turns his tattoo gun on. It makes this angry mechanical buzz like Max is holding a metal bee. "Hold still," he says, and I think of Violet giggling, and right before the needle touches me I scoot away.

Max asks what's wrong, and my sister laughs. She flicks a shell to the small mess on the floor. "I knew you wouldn't do it."

"He's just nervous," Max says. He turns the gun off, goes to his dresser, and comes back with a bottle. It's dark brown with a train on the front. "For relaxation," he says before taking a long drink to help me believe him.

I THINK I'M GOING TO DIE right here, on the sidewalk, coming home from church. I want to sleep. My head is pounding. All through mass, when the people were singing, I wanted to take two pillows and stuff them in my ears, lean over on the pew, and close my eyes. Now my mom wants to stop at La Dulzura, the bakery over on Penn Mar. This morning I told her I was sick, that I ate something bad at Rico's house, that his mom can't cook, because it always makes my mom feel good to know she's better than other parents.

La Dulzura smells like sugar and flour, and the heat from the oven in back hugs you when you walk in. My mom takes a number and we wait. All the pan dulce actually looks good, probably because I didn't have breakfast and last night, when he drove us home, Max had to pull over three times so I could puke. Afterwards Gina gave me some gum and called me a lightweight. This morning my mom woke me up fifteen minutes before she wanted to leave. Time to brush my teeth and comb my hair. I grabbed the only clean church shirt I could find, my white one from like two years ago that fits me all tight.

The lady calls our number and my mom gets half a dozen bolillos to make my dad sandwiches for work. Then she starts picking pan dulce.

She gets two empanadas for herself, a concha with yellow sugar on top and another one with chocolate. She gets one of those pink things with raisins and coconut that Gina likes. My mom tells me to pick something, and I look in the glass case for one of those Neapolitan cookies. I lean over, and my shirt gets all tight like it's going to rip apart. I ask the lady if they have any cookies de tres colores. She says no, so I get an elote instead.

My mom pays and we leave, and when we get outside she tells me to take my shirt off. I swallow and ask, "What?"

Her voice gets loud and slow. "Quítate la camisa."

I try to laugh and start walking, but my mom grabs me.

I unbutton my shirt and look around. Two guys sitting outside the liquor store across the street watch me. Even though I didn't get the tattoo, the outline Max drew is still there. I'm standing with my shirt in my hands, my chest getting all goosepimply from the cool morning air. My mom gasps and makes the sign of the cross. I'm about to explain, but she slaps me across the face. Her nail scratches my eyelid. I rub the pain a few seconds. When I take my hand away, the guys across the street are blurry, but I can still tell that they're laughing.

The rest of the walk home is quiet, and I stay behind my mom the entire way. I don't bother explaining because she won't listen to anything now, and besides, no matter what I say, I'm fucked once we get home. When we come to our street, I'm surprised to see Max's green piece-a-shit parked where he left it last night, and even more surprised that my mom doesn't notice. She unlocks the front door, we step inside the house, and we both hear the same noises. It takes her a few seconds to figure out that they're coming from Gina's room. My mom leaves her purse in the doorway, keys in the knob, and marches down the hall, switching both bags of bread to her left hand before opening the door. I look over my mom's shoulder, and Gina's right there in the middle of the floor, on the carpet, naked. Max's face is between her legs and she's groaning, one foot turning a slow circle in the air, the other playing with the waistband to Max's chones.

"Oh shit," I say, and Max turns around, his eyes big with surprise, his chin all wet with drool. Gina screams and pulls the sheet off her bed to cover up. My mom jumps on top of them, swinging the plastic bags of bread to beat them apart. Max reaches for his jacket. Its zippers scrape against the wall and the pictures wobble as he squeezes past me and heads for the door wearing only his boxers. My mom yells about rape and calling the police. She hurls the bolillos for my dad's lunch at Max and they bounce off him like those fake rocks in Godzilla movies.

My mom and Gina argue inside the house, but I follow Max outside. He's trying to get the Tercel started, but it just coughs and whines. He gets out and starts to push it into the street. Gina comes outside wearing shorts and a T-shirt, the laces to her monkey boots untied and dragging. She carries some clothes that she throws in Max's car. My mom's right behind her as Max gets it rolling. The engine catches and they get in. I'm waiting for my mom to stop her, but instead she stays at the curb like she's chained to the house, quiet like our street is someplace unknown and dangerous.

So I go after them, racing at full speed and staying close enough to read the numbers off Max's license plate until they reach Parkway. By then the car's exhaust is choking me. I run through the intersection and there's the squeal of brakes and I turn as a gold Cadillac skids to a crooked stop right in front of me, smoke coming up from its tires as it rocks backwards. The driver jams his hand against the horn, but instead of moving, I turn back toward Fineview, where Max is driving Gina away. The air around me stinks of burned rubber, the Tercel a shrinking green dot. I yell my sister's name, but the Cadillac keeps honking, the horn so loud that Gina couldn't hear me if I was riding in the back seat. The scratch over my eye burns.

1 9 8 5

My tía Ruby quits telling me how much money she saved by getting her medication in Ensenada with her friend Alicía, instead of buying it over here. "But look at this, Lily," she tells me. "This is the real bargain." She pushes her bottles of medication aside and grunts when she lifts a cardboard carton onto the kitchen table.

"These are for Jairo," she says. "You know, with Fourth of July coming next week and everything."

I sit down and pull the box open. It's filled with blue bricks of firecrackers and bundles of skyrockets. The skyrockets' stems are almost a foot long, wrapped in pink paper and silver ribbon, like little sticks of dynamite dressed for prom.

"These turistas were lighting them," my tía says. "They'd shoot them off the beach and the sky would light up, reds and greens shining on the water. The turistas were loud and rowdy, and those borrachos mensos left this whole box right there on the beach."

She calls Jairo over, but he's so glued to Bugs Bunny in the living room you'd think he was deaf. I go in there and turn off the TV. "Look at someone when they talk to you," I tell him.

"I know," he says, his voice hard with attitude. "I know."

Jairo's too young to talk to me like this. I prod him toward the kitchen, where my tía shows him one of the skyrockets. Jairo handles it like an inspector. He picks at the ribbon and tugs at the fuse. He smells the end and starts to pull at the paper as if unwrapping a lollipop. Me and my tía reach at the same time. She takes the rocket and I tell Jairo no.

"Look, mijito," my tía Ruby says. "You do it like this." She pours the rest of her beer down the sink, and we all go out on the balcony of our apartment. My tía takes out her cigarette lighter. She balances the bottle on the rail with the rocket inside and lights the fuse. It sparks and hisses and takes off—*FWISH*—and my tía throws up her arms and smiles in the second of quiet. Then there's the *BOOM* and all three of us jump a little. Silver sparkles fall over the cars parked on the street, and the bottle wobbles a moment before dropping down to the sidewalk.

Jairo puts his hands over his ears. He starts to cry really hard. His whole body shakes as he hugs me, arms around my waist, face digging into my stomach. Jairo's been afraid of thunder ever since he was five, since the time a couple years ago when lightning hit the tree in front of the old house on Parkway. The tree split in pieces, part falling on the street, part taking out a power line, part crashing through the window where Jairo and I were sleeping. Our bedsheets caught fire. Tío José was still with us at the time, and he smothered the flames with a blanket, which made things worse until my tía brought wet towels from the bathroom. The four of us beat the mattress to keep the fire from spreading, and orange sparks glowed in the dark bedroom, turning to ash before they hit the floor.

I SLOW DOWN AND PULL the truck over because there's a bunch of boys chasing me. When they catch up, only one approaches the truck. The others stay by the curb, sulking in the shade of a big tree. They busy themselves by stripping the low-hanging branches of their leaves, scattering them in the air. Some kick at water in the gutter, and two trade slugs to the other's shoulders, wincing then smiling then wincing again. I lower the music and head back to the coolers, where I slide open the side window. This kid looks about fourteen, slightly cross-eyed and all out of breath. His tank top is dirty, his brown cut-offs unraveling. "Are you the ice cream lady that sells cuetes?" he asks.

"Maybe," I say.

"How much for a brick of firecrackers?"

I tell him ten and right away he pulls two five-dollar bills from his back pocket. They're crisp and new, no marks besides the folds in the middle. The boy stares at the bills like they're the last ones in the world. I poke my head out the window to check around for any other grown-ups, or, even worse, any police. Satisfied, I take his money. I get a brick from the carton, one of three left. All week, I've kept the carton stashed under a towel, hidden between the generator and the wheel-well. I put the firecrackers in a plain paper bag. "Be careful," I say. The boy tells me thanks and his friends crowd around him as he walks away.

When I put the truck into gear, the clutch is a soft wet sponge. First gear eventually catches, and someone whistles, a cholo across the street. He leans on the handlebars of a bicycle, resting under the shade of another tree, and he nods when I look at him, eyes following me as I drive away. Before I get to the corner, there's a burst like gunshots. My foot stamps on the brake and the cholo ducks down behind his bike. The boys scream and laugh in my side mirror, jumping around tiny clouds of smoke and shredded bits of paper. Hidden dogs bark behind fences and gates, and I turn the music up as I move back into the street.

JAIRO'S DAD WAS NAMED RAY. On March 17, 1979, my RayRay was found in the riverbed with an ice pick buried in his head. The police said someone wanted his wallet and whatever was in his lunch pail, but they never found out for sure. This was two months before Jairo was born. The guys at the funeral home didn't do a real good job, because when you walked by my RayRay's body you could still see dents in his forehead. I guess you get what you pay for. When I had Jairo in the hospital, it was just him and me and a nurse telling us to breathe. I stayed home with him while my tía Ruby and tío José went to work. Jairo was a quiet baby, though if he saw me cry, he'd start too. Sometimes I'd wrap him in the woolly orange blanket Ruby made him, roll his crib in front of the TV, and lock myself in the bathroom.

My RayRay started working at the Kerns plant after dropping out halfway through his senior year. He made jelly. Huge copper vats of grape and strawberry, boysenberry and raspberry when they were in season. With seeds and without. Some nights I'd take the bus to meet Ray when his shift ended. Across the street from the plant was a warehouse where wrecked and repossessed cars were auctioned off. We'd walk past the lot and pick out the ones we'd drive one day. Ray liked this one maroon Monte Carlo with a shattered windshield, and once I showed him a white and shiny Cadillac, the wire wheels twinkling for me.

The night I think I got pregnant, a bunch of junked buses were left in the Auto Auction parking lot. They looked tired leaning against one another, the sides crumpled in from collisions. Ray ran toward them, smacking the windows like he was trying to wake passengers still sleeping inside. Ray said he wanted to show me something, something amazing, and as he pulled me along with him, my skirt caught and tore on a snarled bumper. I followed him inside one of the buses, stepping careful around cracked seats and panels missing from the floor. We walked down the aisle to the row of seats in back, the Kerns plant whistling and gushing steam behind us. I sat on Ray's lap and asked what the big deal was as I wiped a smudge from the dimple in his cheek. He kissed me instead of answering, and when I kissed him back, my RayRay smelled like strawberries and tasted like salt.

Afterwards we walked to Joey's for hamburgers and fries, and I stopped halfway across the bridge on Valley, searching through my purse for a safety pin to fix the tear in my skirt. Ray leaned against the rail, looking at the dry riverbed below, and I held the pin in my lips, pulling the torn fabric together. The concrete trembled beneath us as cars zoomed by. Ray talked about how, after a big storm, all the rain in the city would wash through here.

"The river will be full of this rusty-colored water," he said, "and there'll be tree branches, tires and trash tumbling like in a giant washing machine." Ray pulled me close and the pin fell from my mouth into the darkness below. I was seventeen and wasn't even thinking about getting pregnant, about having a kid and raising him. The rest of the way I complained to Ray about my skirt being ruined, my safety pin tiny and small among the dry rocks of the riverbed, waiting for the water to come and take it away.

OSCAR POUNDS THE PHONE on his desk and slams the door as he leaves his office. Today hasn't been a good day for him. In the hour I've been here loading up, I've overheard all his conversations. One of his suppliers keeps calling about an unpaid balance, the owner of the Tidy-Rite Cleaners is giving him a hard time about his window, and the guys at the salvage yard don't have two doors to replace the ones on the truck Sylvia crashed.

Sylvia's route was on the north side, over by the Chuck E. Cheese and

Norwood Village. Yesterday she was backing up when the truck hit the curb. She floored the gas instead of the brake, and went up on the sidewalk, knocking over a tree and smashing the storefront to the Tidy-Rite Cleaners. I wasn't surprised. Sylvia drinks. I've seen her stumble around the warehouse, and after work we've had talks about her boys, Franco and Francisco, where her words slurred and didn't make any sense. Sylvia wears a lot of eyeliner, and I can picture her face streaked with makeup as she begs Oscar not to fire her. Then again, I can just as easily see Sylvia parking the truck crooked in the warehouse, throwing the keys at Oscar and telling him to go fuck himself.

Oscar sighs and runs his hand through his hair. One of the other drivers left out the pallet jack. He sets down his clipboard and sighs again, a deep sigh this time, like someone is pressing the life out of him. He starts to drag the yellow jack back to the other end of the loading dock, then suddenly turns around as if he forgot something important. He hurries toward my truck, pulling the pallet jack with him, breathless when he asks how I'm doing.

"I'm probably better than you are right now," I say, tossing some empty boxes aside and shutting the back door of the ice cream truck.

Oscar sort of smiles. The wrinkles around his eyes make him look older than twenty-seven. He pumps the handle on the pallet jack and the metal arms slowly rise. "We're still on for tomorrow night, right?"

I never really thought about Oscar in that way, romantically I guess, until he asked me out on Monday. A drink after work, maybe dinner. "It'll be ladies' night at La Parranda," he said. "We should probably go."

Without answering, I get in the truck. It's only the two of us in the warehouse. Oscar follows me, and, as I slip on my seatbelt, I look hard at him and wonder. Guys like Oscar always have someone waiting for them at home. Outside, the sun is bright. The glare makes the open door to the warehouse look like a giant white block. I start the truck up and wiggle the gear shift, trying to find first. "You get this clutch fixed, and I'm all yours."

OSCAR'S CAMARO WON'T START. The engine whines in La Parranda's parking lot and Oscar apologizes. "This almost never happens," he says, reaching under the steering wheel. The hood pops and Oscar gets out of the car. The Camaro rocks back and forth as he messes with something, and after a few minutes he asks me to start it up. I reach over and turn the key. Now the ignition just clicks. I don't know a lot about cars, but I can tell this isn't good.

Oscar gets back in. He's sweating and he hits the steering wheel with his hand, honking the horn and leaving a grease mark. The horn sounds loud and I jump. We both laugh, then just sit there. I point to Oscar's hand and he reaches into the back seat, grabbing an old T-shirt to wipe his palm clean. Oscar sighs, the same kind of exasperated sigh he lets out at work. "Let me make a quick phone call," he says.

"Okay," I say. "I'll keep an eye on the car."

Oscar smiles and jogs back to the restaurant where the glow of red lights and the sounds of mariachis escape as he steps inside. Alone, I check my face in the rearview mirror. It's slick and oily, even though I checked it in the restaurant bathroom before we left. I do my best with my compact, then get out of the car to smoke a cigarette. When Oscar comes back he tells me something about his insurance and him being out of towing mileage as he tries to start the Camaro again. The ignition keeps clicking until Oscar gives up. "I'm really sorry," he says. He jams his hands into his pockets like he's embarrassed by them instead of his dead car. "Let me get you a cab."

"Don't worry about it," I say. "I can walk home." I point at the Camaro and smile. "Besides, it looks like you need your money for other things."

"Hey," Oscar says. "It's ladies' night." He points to the banner hung over the door advertising two-dollar Budweisers and half-priced appetizers. "Money is no object."

"Better yet, why don't you walk me home? Make sure I get there safe." I toss my cigarette into the street. "It's not that far."

The headlights of the passing cars stretch our shadows like rubber bands across the sidewalk, snapping them into the darkness as they go by. After two or three blocks I start sweating, the night air thick and wet. The sky is crowded with clouds, gray as wet cement, oversized and heavy with rain. Oscar tells me that it looks like it's going to pour. He tells me about spending his summers in Arizona as a kid, about monsoon season in the desert. "Sometimes, the sky would rip open with rain," he says. "There'd be wind and sometimes hail. You couldn't drive because you couldn't see anything. My cousin had this old Mustang that would stall, and the leaky floorboards would fill with water, and then it would all be over. I mean *over*. You'd be sitting there, your shoes and socks soaked, and not a cloud in the sky."

We come to a signal, and, as we wait for it to change, I take off my shoes because the heels have started to kill me. The street feels warm against my bare feet as we cross the intersection. We pass a used car lot on Garvey. The cars aren't anything fancy, but they're clean and polished, and they shine under the white lights, orange price tags pasted across their windshields. Gold, red, and green streamers are tied from a tall pole in the middle to posts at the corners of the lot. A semi roars by and the streamers shake like leaves and sway like a giant spider web.

"Those look nice," I say.

"Yeah, they do."

Oscar steps over the chain at the edge of the lot. He walks to the pole in the middle and starts climbing, springing upward like a monkey. I tell him he's crazy and walk a circle on the sidewalk, looking around to see if anyone is watching. Oscar reaches the top and starts to grab at the streamers, yelling as he rips a gold line that falls across a row of pickups. I shake my head as I watch him slide back down the pole, then tear off a section of the streamer. Oscar walks toward me, his pants and shirt ruined with dirt. He wraps the gold streamer around me like a scarf. Some cars race by and Oscar has to talk loudly over their roaring engines. "To match your earrings," he says. My skirt rustles in the breeze and the streamer's fringe tickles my face like dozens of delicate golden fingers.

THE OTHER DAY I thought I saw you. You were over on Rush, across from the bakery and Magaña's taco stand. It was around lunchtime and you were wearing dirty gray coveralls, walking with a plastic bag, sipping on a white Styrofoam cup. You weren't dead. You hadn't been missing from my life for the last five years. You were right there on the corner, checking your watch and looking tense, jabbing at the button for the crosswalk like you were trying to make something explode.

As I waited for the signal to change, I thought of Oscar asking me out. Of me saying yes. Of you knowing. I put the truck into gear and my left foot slid off the clutch. The right one flooded the engine with gas and the truck stalled in the intersection. Behind me, cars honked and I just stared at the steering wheel, sure you would turn around and spot me. The engine roared and lurched forward when I started the truck again, and behind me I could hear the ice cream bars shifting in the coolers and candy falling from the shelves.

You were walking fast. I kept the truck slow, giving myself the chance to decide if I wanted to know if it really was you. You disappeared into one of the factories, a warehouse with a sign for wrought iron. Sections of fences and rusty iron screens were laid against the wall where I parked. I stepped out of the truck, the engine still running, feeling like I'd been sawed in half by some awful magician, my legs barely connected to the rest of my body, the noises from inside the factory getting louder as I neared the open warehouse door. I stayed close to the abandoned fences, and held on to one of the bars as I searched for you inside. A forklift beeped as it backed up, arms raised and stacked with steel rods. This guy welding two pieces of steel was nodding to the cumbia blaring out of the radio next to him, sparks scattering all over the floor.

A short guy in the same gray coveralls was looking up at you and yelling. You agreed with every single word he said. Your eyes were smaller and forced away from each other. Your face was smooth, your nose straight. It wasn't you. I rushed back to the truck and jammed it in reverse and my hands shook as I backed out of the driveway. I wiped them on my jeans and bit my lip when they left orange smears of rust across my thighs. I drove as fast as I could, and, between peeks at the road, I looked at my pants and hoped that the marks wouldn't stain.

ROSA JAMS ON THE BRAKES and the truck screeches to a stop. Things fall off the shelves behind us and slide across the floor. I can smell the skid she left on the church's empty parking lot. She's laughing. Rosa brushes away the hairs caught at the corners of her mouth. Last week she told me how she moved up to dye jobs in her tía Brenda's hair salon, all excited because her tía says she can work there full-time if she graduates next year. Rosa turns the truck around. She promised to dye my hair the same shade of brown as hers for tomorrow night if I would show her how to drive. I grab the wheel. "I think you got it," I say.

We trade seats and I turn the truck out onto Michael Hunt. We head over to the park by Shively, and nobody's there except for a guy on a tractor mowing one end of the field and some kids playing baseball at the other. I stop the truck. Rosa says the floor looks like a piñata exploded. There are bags of chips everywhere and all the candy on the two shelves above the cooler has toppled to the ground. The cigar box with all the money is also at my feet, the box flipped over, the bills spread everywhere, nickels and dimes under the freezers and trapped in the seams of the floor. I gather the bills and Rosa grabs some Doritos. She opens the bag and seems unconcerned when I tell her that I don't remember how much money was here.

"Can't you figure it out?"

"I guess I can."

Rosa seems content to watch me work, taking a break from the chips to point at the guy throwing the ball and tell me he looks fine. The guy's wearing a purple baseball cap, a tank top and dark jeans. The next pitch he throws gets smacked high in the air. The ball vanishes in the sunlight and everyone playing starts to run in different directions.

After a while, they come over. I'm recounting the day's money, seventeen dollars in cash, six seventy-five in change. Rosa's guy asks for a Coke and I whisper fifty cents to Rosa as I hand her the can. He pays and Rosa steps to the end of the truck. She opens one of the back doors and sits on the bumper. Rosa's guy goes over. I can't hear everything they talk about, but Rosa tells him she goes to Mountain View and that she's a junior. Rosa's guy picks at the stickers on the unopened door and Rosa laughs like they were old friends.

The truck creaks as I stoop over to reach under the counter for some packs of gum. I stand up and find a few candy rings in the corner, the sugar jewels gleaming through their cellophane. I put them back and go to start the truck up. Rosa ties her hair back into a ponytail and looks at me like she wants me to go away. I start the engine anyway. Rosa comes back inside, shutting the door, stomping toward the passenger seat. The guy follows her over. Rosa grabs her purse from the dashboard, taking out an eyebrow pencil. She tells her guy to hold his hand out. She giggles. He smiles and looks up at me as she starts writing. Her phone number starts on his wrist and stretches to the bend in his elbow.

TOO MANY SONGS HAVE GONE BY. I know that one day Oscar would like to quit this job and study to become a chef, that he makes better salsa than his mother but refuses to tell her the recipe, that he hates frozen vegetables and feels guilty for loving Slim Jims. His favorite color is blue. Dark blue. "Like a clear sky at midnight," he says.

When I talk about my life, I talk about how I miss my tío José more than my parents because he's the one who raised me, how me and my tía Ruby always catch *The Love Boat* when it's on, and how we pretend to be on vacations where fancy things happen to us. I don't talk about Jairo, about how in yesterday's Little League game he jumped in front of a pitch because my tía Ruby promised to take him to Chuck E. Cheese if he got on base. I don't mention him, even though Oscar must know, must've heard me talking about him with the other drivers. But the moment is like the moment before I sit down to balance my checkbook and figure out what's left in my account—things are so much easier when you don't really know.

A slow song comes on and Oscar pulls me close. We get up off the loading dock and dance, moving slower and slower until we're not moving at all. I can smell the musk behind Oscar's failing deodorant, the smell of dust behind that. Dust on the floor, on the dock, on the freezers and empty pallets. Layers on top of layers up in the rafters. It's as if Oscar's part of the warehouse, like he's lived here his entire life. I can feel the sweat on the side of his head. He kisses me once. Twice. The third kiss stretches on and on, as though we'd both suffocate if our lips came apart, and it's then that I let him back me up behind the trucks in a dark corner of the warehouse.

THE TRUCK IS PARKED in front of the Community Center and all the kids coming from their swimming lessons are crowded around it. I can hear their tiny hands slapping against the sides as they point to the different pictures of ice cream. The truck shakes a little and somehow the licorice whips hanging by the window get tangled in my hair. There's a scream, high-pitched and girlie, followed by a huge splash that sounds like someone dropped a refrigerator into the pool.

A viejito buys his little girl a Sno-Cone, and makes me feel old when he calls me "señora." The girl's face looks soft and white, her black hair dripping onto the red towel wrapped around her shoulders. I count out the old man's change, and the girl tears open the Sno-Cone's wrapper with her teeth. She immediately puts her hand up to her mouth and starts crying. The viejito asks what's wrong, then stoops over to pick something off the sidewalk. He shows it to me. A tooth. He takes a brown bandanna from his back pocket, and then has the girl stare up at the sky while he dabs at her mouth, checking for blood and explaining about lost teeth being good luck.

I spend the rest of the afternoon digging Big Sticks and Ice Tickles and Drumsticks from their frosty boxes in the freezer. I sell gum and candy and bag after bag of potato chips. I help the little ones sort out sticky amounts of exact change. By three o'clock the truck's nearly empty. When I start it up, a big kid runs out from the tennis courts. He's about twelve or thirteen, his face red with pimples. He asks if he can buy a 7-UP. I leave the motor running, step back to the cooler, and the icy water inside bites my hand as I reach around for a green can. I flick my wet fingers at the picture of Jairo taped inside the window, blessing him the way priests do in church. The kid comes around to the side, and I watch brown leaves blow across the grass as he digs in his pockets for fifty cents. The leaves stick to the chain-link fence surrounding the pool, looking like hands caught in a net. The kid gives me a quarter and counts out three dimes, then asks if I have any skyrockets.

I TAKE ALL THE MONEY from my purse. The last of Jairo's fireworks sold today. Just a couple weeks and now they're gone. I've counted forty,

forty-two, forty-four dollars. It's all in small bills. A few fives. A few ones. Stacks and stacks of change that I sort according to size. There's probably enough here for that new dress I saw with Rosa at Fashion Girl. It's there in the window, maroon and sleeveless, little flowers embroidered around the neckline, the mannequin with one hand on her hip and the other pointing at something far away. I ask my tía Ruby about borrowing the money and she stops stirring her té de limón and turns down the burner on the stove. She picks up the bills and starts counting without answering my question.

"Tomorrow I'm taking Jairo to Sears," she tells me, "to buy a suit, and maybe to Tres Hermanos for a good pair of shoes if I have enough left. This year I don't want Jairo looking amolado when they take his picture for the school."

I tell her it doesn't matter what Jairo wears because they only take the pictures from his chest up. Ruby waves her hand to stop me from talking. She plucks her cigarette from the ashtray and takes a long drag before she speaks. "Do you remember what he wore in last year's photo?"

The picture's right there in my purse, stuck between baby pictures and portraits and every other photo Jairo's in since preschool. There's another copy framed on my dresser and there's the one in the truck. Right now, Jairo is asleep on our bed in the other room. He had macaroni and cheese for dinner, two servings, and he left his green beans untouched. This afternoon he got a bloody nose at the recreation center from running around in the heat. Yesterday my tía took him to church with her, and this I know because I just found a crumpled card with the Virgin Mary in his pocket when sorting his laundry for the washer. I know all this, but that photo's a blank spot in my head. "A white dress shirt," I say, guessing.

"My poor Jarrito was wearing Levi's, those old Levi's he outgrew the year before. He had on a white shirt that *I* got him from the Salvation

Army. He had on a clip-on-tie *I* borrowed from Mini, Hector's old one that she was donating to the veterans."

Ruby sits down next to me and inhales deep on her cigarette. Her tea is simmering on the stove. I need something nice for my date with Oscar this Saturday. It's not my fault I get paid every two weeks. I'll return the money. My tía folds the bills and sticks them in her pack of cigarettes. She sweeps the piles of change into her apron pocket. "Tomorrow," she says. "Tomorrow we go shopping."

I get up and grab the key to the laundry room. I ask my tía for fifty cents for the dryer, and leave when she gives it to me. Outside, I'm running outfits through my mind, something that will look and feel new this weekend, when a screen pops off one of the windows in the apartments across the courtyard. The screen sends up a small cloud of dust when it hits the floor. That's Rosa's room. Someone climbs out of her dark drapes. The guy from the park. He puts the screen up on the window, leaving it crooked, and walks toward the stairs, toward me, looking back like he left something behind. He seems to recognize my face as he passes, but he doesn't say hello. Instead, he goes down the stairs and, in one quick motion, he hops over the wrought iron fence surrounding our building.

THERE'S ONE LIGHT hanging over the door, its orange extension cord poking through a hole in the window screen. The light is bright, and it makes me squint as we move through the people dancing on the lawn. I bump into someone who turns out to be one of Oscar's cousins. The music from the party is so loud that Oscar yells when he introduces me to him. "This is Lily," he says. "Lily, this is Lupe." I smile and shake Lupe's hand, then this girl Evelyn's too. Evelyn's wearing a dress, and even though Oscar's told me I look great, I suddenly feel underdressed in my blue blouse and jeans.

Inside the house, we walk past kids crowded around a TV in the living room. They're playing a video game, and when Oscar asks who's winning they point to an older kid with big glasses and bigger eyes, his fingers scrambling over the controller in his hand. Something blows up on the TV and all the kids cheer.

The kitchen floor's covered with pink and green confetti. Oscar walks to the sink, and gives the chubby viejita washing dishes a hug and a kiss on the cheek. He introduces me to his nina and, before she shakes my hand, she wipes hers on a dingy towel. Her hands are warm and damp, shapeless as fresh masa. She offers us food, but Oscar lies and says that we already ate and asks for beers instead. She points to the patio, to a table filled with liquor bottles, and Oscar walks out to the bar. I start to follow him, but this girl wearing a pink dress made entirely of ruffles runs screaming through the kitchen. A boy wearing the paper head of a donkey piñata follows her. He crashes into the table, then sits on the floor crying. "Kids," Oscar's nina says, taking the boy in her arms and smiling at me like she has to.

I follow Oscar's laugh out to the patio. He's looking through all these half-empty liquor bottles, shaking them like he can't see how much is left inside each one. I pinch his side and he turns around. "What are you drinking?" he asks.

"Whatever."

Oscar offers to make me a margarita, promises that even though there's no salt, this will be the best margarita I've ever had. He takes a red plastic cup and scoops some ice from a plastic bag, the bag ripped open and dripping onto the floor.

"Don't worry," Oscar says, "if you get hungry, we can stop and get something later. I don't like my nina's food because she always gets distracted when she cooks. Everything she makes comes out burned. Tamales, sopa, tortillas. Everything. I didn't want you getting stuck with a plate you wouldn't eat."

I nod and wait quietly while Oscar makes my drink. When he finishes, the margarita I get tastes stronger than I like them. "It's good," I tell him, the sip burning in my throat.

We work our way back to the front yard, passing through the garage where the DJ is set up, meeting more people and shaking more hands. A song comes on that I haven't heard since forever, the one about weekends being made for fun. I leave my drink in a pot of flowers and drag Oscar by the arm to make him dance with me. I slip off my shoes, putting them on the grass with my purse. Oscar dances stiffly, nodding his head and bobbing to the beat of the music. I move around him, the grass tickly and cool between my toes, the light over the door making our shadows so long they stretch into the street and look scary, like giants fighting.

By midnight, most of the people have gone home. Oscar's nina and his cousin Lydia or Luisa, I can't remember which, are in the kitchen cleaning up, wrapping slices of birthday cake in tin foil and stuffing the refrigerator with food. Lydia or Luisa's kids are asleep, their bodies stretched out and drooling on the couches and chairs. I sit with Oscar and his nino in the patio, the three of us smoking and flicking the ashes into the ashtray Oscar's nino has balanced on his knee. Oscar's nino is big and round and crammed into his wheelchair. He looks sad, even when he smiles, his tired face sagging away from his skull as he talks. "Seven kids and thirty-two years later here we are," he says, calling Oscar's nina and blowing her a kiss. She smiles and waves back.

Oscar's nino stubs out his cigar and sets the ashtray on the table. Oscar finishes his beer and tells him that we've got to go.

"Are you guys driving?" Oscar's nino asks.

"Yeah," Oscar says, "but Lily lives not too far from here."

Oscar's nino tells us we shouldn't drink and drive. "Look at your cousin Joey. The pendejo gets his license, then two weeks later he crashes your tía Maria's station wagon." Oscar's nino slams his hand so hard on the table that some of the bottles jump and fall over. "Take the bike," he says, pointing to a rusty beach cruiser leaning against the garage.

I can't believe we're actually doing this. Oscar's nino waves to us from the curb, and as Oscar starts to pedal away, I can hear the motor of his nino's wheelchair rolling him back to the house. I'm holding the foil-covered paper plate of leftover carne asada and birthday cake with one hand, and grabbing onto the handlebars with the other, trying not to fall because Oscar's riding all swervy. We coast real close to the curb, and I tell Oscar we're going to crash. Dogs bark and I scream and the plate slips and falls onto the street.

A few blocks later, the handlebars are hurting my butt, but the cool air feels good against my face as we start to go faster. Oscar's standing up, pedaling hard, and I smile as he breathes on my neck. We cross Durfee and the streetlights start to lose their brightness. They get dimmer and hazy, hiding from us behind trees, flickering on and off as we ride by. When we start down my street, a car I don't know passes us. One of the passengers throws an empty beer can that rattles across the asphalt into the gutter, the car honking wildly as it drives away.

As we near my building, Oscar stops pedaling. He leans forward and starts kissing my neck and ear. I squirm. I giggle like a little girl and lose my balance, almost falling off. Oscar's laughing and I start laughing too, as we get off and walk the beach cruiser around some parked cars. He starts to drag the bicycle up the stairs, but the pedal gets stuck in the rail. Oscar pulls and pulls, and each time the bike bangs against the rail, he shushes it quiet with his finger. Finally Oscar leaves the bike there. By the time he walks up the stairs, I've got my apartment door open.

My tía Ruby's asleep on the couch, a copy of *Vanidades* open over her face. I turn out the lamp and wave Oscar in. It's like I'm back in high school, sneaking Ray in the house. We go to the bedroom, walking slow and trying not to make any noise. Oscar tries to grab me, but the hand I knock away isn't his. I open the bedroom door and turn on the light. Jairo's standing between us. I sigh and sit on the bed. Oscar walks around him and sits next to me.

Jairo's quiet and when I ask him what's wrong he doesn't answer. Instead he looks at me like he wants to say something, like he's trying to but the words are glued together in his brain. I tell him to sleep in the other room. That his tía Ruby will wake up and pull the bed out of the couch. Jairo doesn't move. Oscar slips his hand up the back of my blouse. He finds one of the scars on my back, then my bra straps. Again I tell Jairo to leave, trying not to giggle because Oscar's working his fingers around to my chest.

I look around the room, wondering what my tía will say if she finds us here. To get Jairo to leave, I tell him he's got to sleep in the closet if he wants to stay here. "Your mommy's friend is tired and we want to go to bed," I say.

Instead of leaving, Jairo pushes back one of the closet doors, looking at us as he clears away a pile of Ruby's shoes. He sits back against the wall, head disappearing in the folds of hanging dresses and pants.

"Shouldn't you give him something?" Oscar asks.

Oscar kisses me and he holds me tight and the feeling gives my body a second electric skin that's glowing and wonderful and warm. We'll be quiet and Jairo will be fine. Oscar gets up, taking the comforter and pillow I hand him. He turns out the light, tossing the items into the dark closet before pulling the door closed. As my eyes get used to the blackness, I see Oscar pull off his shirt. He unties his shoes and sets them neatly beside one another. He lies down and things are silent as I slide on top of him.

I GET OFF THE PHONE with the lady at 911, and Jairo answers the door, opening it slowly, carefully, as if by some magic the ambulance has arrived before I could hang up the phone. Oscar comes in carrying two plastic bags. His hair is crooked and stiff and the shirt he wore last night is wrinkled. Fresh bolillos fall out of one bag as he sets it on the table. From the other bag comes a small Styrofoam pail that steams when he takes off the lid. "Menudo for everybody," Oscar says, tearing a chunk of bread and stuffing it into his mouth.

I stare at my tía. The expression on her face is stubborn and angry. My hands shake as I take the copy of *Vanidades* and set it on the end table with her stack of magazines. Oscar looks through our cupboards until he finds a small pot. "Is this the biggest one you have?" he asks.

"My tía Ruby's dead."

The words make me dizzy. Oscar puts down the pot and walks over to my tía, calling her name loudly as if she might wake up. He pokes her in the ribs.

"Stop it," I say. "She's really dead." Oscar stares at the body, shoving a hunk of bread in his mouth like he's trying to plug up a hole. I tell him I called the police. "They'll be here soon."

Oscar walks over to me, slowly crossing the living room as if there'd be no floor beneath the rug. He pulls me toward him, his body tense, the hug so awkward I might as well be hugging a mannequin. We stand like this until I pull the rest of the orange blanket covering the couch over my tía Ruby's body. The holes in our couch are visible, and even though I don't want Oscar to see them, I make sure that my tía's face is covered. The blanket is short. My tía's white feet stick out, so I tell Jairo to bring another one.

Jairo trudges to the bedroom and I go to the kitchen, where Oscar's busy jingling silverware. I'm about to tell him that he's looking in the wrong drawer, when he tells me maybe he better leave.

"You should probably be alone, you know . . . with him and everything." Oscar nods toward the bedroom. He turns a spoon in his hands and sets it on the table. He grabs another bolillo and gives me another crooked hug. "I'll call you later," he says. I let him out and his feet pound their way down the stairs as I lock the door.

Jairo's sitting on the end of the couch. He's covered my tía Ruby with the comforter, and he stares at her body and picks the stuffing out from one of the couch's holes. I tell him to stop. "Come here," I say.

I should be giving him this big talk about what it means when people die, about his tía Ruby going to a better place, and angels watching us from their clouds in the sky. We sit at the table, Jairo across from me. He starts to tear a bolillo apart, and I watch him mash it between his fingers as I figure out how to begin.

THE CORRIDO OF HECTOR CRUZ

1 9 8 4

It's three in the morning and Hector Cruz is out of his apartment, waiting behind an old vaquero and his date at a lunch truck parked over on
Durfee. The vaquero's black cowboy hat is pulled down tight, his face
slick with sweat, a damp dark oval spread across the back of his pale
blue shirt. His feet shift as if trapped in boots half a size too small. The
woman with him is busy reading the menu painted on the side of the
truck, her makeup sloppy, her green dress wrinkled. She's wearing ny-
lons with unshaven legs. In places, her leg hair curls through the beige
fabric and the stockings sag and bunch around both ankles like shack-
les. In June, Hector went to a party for Mini's abuelita, and they made
quiet jokes after noticing that all the viejitas in her family dressed the
same way.

Mini's pregnant, three months pregnant, and twenty minutes ago
she woke Hector up to talk about chorizo, how the same grandma with
hairy legs used to make her chorizo with potatoes instead of with eggs
because the eggs would give her asco.

"When I was a kid," Mini said, "just the idea of eating anything with eggs made my stomach do flip-flops."

His head still heavy with sleep, Hector rolled in the warm sheets toward Mini's voice and waved his hand out into the darkness to stop her. The way the morning sickness has been hitting Mini lately, she might've thrown up right there in their bed, sick from simply thinking about a breakfast from fifteen years ago.

A wind blows by, cool enough to make Hector miss his sweatshirt, but the vaquero's standing here sweating. After they order, he tells his date a joke, something in Spanish about the devil taking the souls of three drunks. The vaquero waves his arms as he mimics each drunken character, pausing a moment to pound a burp out of his chest. When he gets to the punchline, they both burst with laughter that develops immediately into a long hug and a wet crooked kiss.

When Hector reaches the front of the line, he steps up to the small window and talks before the teenage girl has her pencil in hand to write anything down. When the girl's ready, he repeats Mini's order: one chorizo burrito, no eggs, can you please put potatoes instead. The girl nibbles on the pencil eraser and looks at him as though he's asked them to substitute egg shells. "Es para mi esposa," he explains. "Está embarazada."

The girl smiles. Before giving Hector the total, she walks the yellow order slip over to the cook flipping corn tortillas on the grill. The girl talks in his ear and the cook nods, the grill steaming as he sorts sizzling things with his spatula. Hector pays and takes his change, folding the bills carefully into his wallet.

He waits against a telephone pole. From there he spots a boy, about five or six years old, sitting in the lunch truck's driver's seat. The boy works his hands across the steering wheel, and his mouth makes a motor that roars loudly, spit flying as he tears down some road somewhere. He beats on the horn and the girl yells in the direction of the cab. The boy giggles and the honking stops.

The vaquero's order gets called, and his date picks up the food, grabbing two inches of napkins, half of which blow out into the street as she walks back to the vaquero's rusty orange Rambler. They put the food on the hood and the vaquero reaches inside to turn on the radio. A ranchera blares from the open door as they each grab at the plate of tacos, the date adding salsa, the vaquero only salt. He shoves the taco into his mouth and grabs his woman. He pulls her close, spins her wildly so that her hair whirls and gets caught on her face. The vaquero brushes it aside, kisses her a second time, and they dance with a big bite in each of their mouths. They keep going once the song ends, one arm reaching for food, one arm holding each other close.

Hector yawns. He doesn't know how many more trips he'll have to make in the months Mini has left. One night last week she wanted pastrami, not a sandwich, just the meat with some mustard on the side. Another night it was fresh-brewed jamaica. This morning it's chorizo with potatoes. Tomorrow it'll be frozen fish sticks, or ice milk, or taquitos and homemade guacamole, Hector smashing the avocados in their kitchen as the sun comes up. The vaquero moves his old lady across the sidewalk, and Hector knows that the details of Mini's appetite don't matter. He'd drive to Alaska for ice cubes if she asked him to. A few minutes pass and Mini's order gets called. The girl holds on to the hefty brown bag for an extra moment, hinting that, out of the thousands made in this truck, the burrito Hector's holding is special.

GEORGIE HAS HECTOR RESTACKING a row of car doors that stink of dog piss and rust. They stand for a second, but the last door starts to slip, then the one before it, and before Hector can do anything, they're all screeching and sliding across the concrete. Fuck. Hector takes a deep breath and begins restacking the doors, reminded of *That's Incredible*, and how last week they showed some guy who lined up thousands of dominos for some kind of world record. The dominos were in perfect order so that when they started falling, the reaction made this soft whirring click like a fine machine had been set in motion. Hector swallows a yawn. Who has the free time to think up that shit?

Hector's body feels like it could shut down right here and sleep through the weekend. Still, last night and all the others like it are worth the effort. When Mini told Hector she was pregnant again, he was so surprised that he asked her what she meant. She scooted across the bed and rubbed her hand on his neck. She made her voice serious and started talking about how sometimes these things happen when a daddy and a mommy are in love. Hector half laughed. He asked his wife if she was sure, and Mini said yes. He told her that this baby would make it, and Mini said she knew it would. They kissed and hugged so long that when Hector finally looked at the clock on the nightstand, Mini was late for work.

The intercom cracks on to call Hector to the office. He takes off his gloves and stretches his back. As Hector passes the service area, Benny slides out from the '81 Cutlass he's working on to say "Oooooh," like Hector's headed for the principal's office. Hector balls up the rag in his back pocket and tosses it at Benny. Hector walks through the stockroom to the office, past shelf after shelf of rebuilt alternators, generators and steering columns, the old wood warped from their weight.

Georgie's sitting behind the counter, talking on one phone and twirling a spark plug around in his fat fingers. Hector asks him what's up and Georgie points the plug at the other phone on his desk and mouths, line two. Nobody ever calls Hector at work. Line two flashes, and he thinks of Mini and slips into the other rickety chair with his fingers crossed. He picks up the phone and says hello. The man on the line asks if the person speaking is Hector Cruz. Hector answers yes and the man asks for his social security number in order to confirm Hector's identification.

"Can't you just tell me what's the matter?" Hector asks.

"This is just procedure," the man says, and Hector takes out his wallet, finds the card just to be sure, and reads him the numbers. Georgie starts to argue with his customer over the price of a distributor cap, and to escape the racket of Georgie's haggling, Hector takes the phone into the stockroom as far as the cord will let him. Hector stares at the grimy tag hanging from the ignition to a '78 Camaro and waits for heavy words to come.

"Does the name Felix Cruz sound familiar?"

Hector tells him that Felix is his brother, but that Felix passed away fifteen years ago. "What does this have to do with my wife?" he asks.

"I don't know," the man says. He tells Hector that his name is Jim. Hector goes back into the office to get a pen from Georgie because this seems important enough to copy down. Part of him unwinds after Jim explains that he's calling long-distance from a boys' home in Solano County, but this same part clenches back up into a hard, tense ball when he mentions the name Lencho Cruz.

MERCED IS HECTOR'S OLDER BROTHER who's in prison and Felix is his oldest brother who's dead. Felix was on the job, dragging pallets of stock into position so the forklift could raise them to the second floor of the warehouse, when one of the hydraulic seals blew on the forklift. The pallet of piping raised over him came crashing down and that was it. The next day the plant manager went to his apartment. He had his wife, Teresita, sign a contract full of hidden clauses that allowed the plant to pay for the funeral. Felix was buried two days later in Merced's blue tie and his scuffed work shoes that Hector painted black with a marker. A collection was taken from the employees at the plant to buy Felix a suit for his funeral. Teresita bought a gray suit with pants the wrong size, and Felix's legs shot out from the cuffs. Amá complained until the day she moved back to Rosarito that if Teresita had given her the money, Felix would be wearing a good suit right now, that her mijito wouldn't be shuffling around the afterlife in high-waters, looking like the last link in a hand-me-down chain.

Hector misses his brother. Sometimes when he gets run down from work, his tired muscles bring Felix to mind. Felix had started off at Spectrum Industrial Rubber making little test tube stoppers when he was seventeen. He worked nine to five, six days a week, and once in a while his supervisors would give him overtime on Sundays. There were other times when Felix would work eighteen-hour shifts. He'd come home exhausted and beaten, and Hector would imagine laboratories and college classrooms filled with people in lab coats, their bubbling experiments on hold until Felix's stoppers arrived.

Felix soon smelled like a pile of new tires. It lingered on him, after he stripped off his rubber-coated pants, after the Cruz family shower ran out of hot water. Felix had worn a heavy leather apron when he first started, but he lent it to Teresita because somebody stole hers from her locker. At work, excess rubber would be pressed out from the molds Felix operated. The rubber oozed off the machines and soaked into Felix's clothes where it cooled and hardened, leaving his legs slick and shiny as a wetsuit. Hector once asked Felix if the melted rubber burned, if it hurt him, and Felix said, "No. Not anymore."

Soon Felix started going places after work and staying out later in his rubberized clothing. Teresita was nineteen at the time, and occasionally she took night classes at Valle Lindo because she hadn't made it through high school. She was from Sonora, and Felix said her family had a bumper sticker with a Mexican flag on the door to their trailer that said so. They were one of those couples that looked good together in a fucked-up sort of way. They matched. Teresita's nose looked more like a beak, and she was real skinny like Felix, the two of them tall. They both had terrible teeth. When Hector thought of Teresita kissing Felix, he always imagined a sound like the couple was eating broken dishes.

That year Valle Lindo had a winter formal a few weeks before Christmas, a prom for people who missed it the first time around, and Teresita was going with Felix. Hector's brother had been letting his hair expand into a dull brown afro, and he borrowed a light blue tuxedo with a frilly shirt from their neighbor Javier. Felix said that Teresita had bought some nice material and her mom was sewing a dress. The night of the dance, Amá began to urge Felix not to see Teresita anymore. She saw things forming between Felix and Teresita that no one else had noticed.

Felix was shaping his hair with a pick, dancing in the mirror and ignoring the claims that Amá was making. She called Teresita a wetback and said she probably didn't have a green card or a work pass. "I'll bet ten dollars to your one that not one of the huevones in that girl's family has any kind of papers," Amá said. She leaned in close to Felix. "That girl's talking about love and weddings and marriage, isn't she, mijo?"

Felix's smile stayed unchanged, his mind someplace else, and Hector was sure his brother felt he and Teresita were the only two people in the city. Felix brushed Amá off and resumed shaping his hair with his palms.

"She's just using you Felix," Amá said.

Felix stepped away from the mirror. "You're wrong."

He slipped the pick in his back pocket and grabbed Javier's powder blue jacket. He buttoned it tight, and the ruffles from his shirt bunched up and burst out from his chest like flowers forced to bloom.

HECTOR HEADS HOME, where he waits for Mini and makes lunch. Mini's shift usually ends at one o'clock, and at one fifteen she comes in the door. She looks surprised and asks what Hector's doing home.

She kisses him on the forehead, tosses her keys on the coffee table, and heads straight to the bathroom before he can answer. Mini asks Hector if he needs anything from the mall, before shutting the bathroom door. Hector stares at the knob and says, "Minerva, we gotta talk about something."

"Can it wait two minutes?"

Hector tells her yeah, then walks back to the living room and collapses on the couch.

Mini's five-two, but whenever people ask how tall she is, she always tells them she's five-four. She's looked the same forever, same short black hair, thin as a child. She's only started to show in the last month. She's due in February, but Mini can't weigh more than a hundred, a hundred and ten pounds. Hector's never really known her exact weight. They'd been together about two years when she was pregnant the first time. Mini would get on the scale after taking a shower, but she wouldn't let Hector see. For her it was top-secret stuff. That baby's not something they talk about anymore.

There are times when Hector thinks Mini still wants to save the world. When he first met her, she was working at the McDonald's on Valley, and had just started taking classes at Rio Hondo because she eventually wanted to be a pediatrician. Mini still has a sticker on her Corolla that says HUGS NOT DRUGS. A few weeks after Mini lost the first baby, her boss offered her the job as morning shift manager. Mini dropped her classes and has worked full-time ever since.

The toilet flushes and Mini comes out wearing the concerned face she makes whenever she thinks something is wrong with her husband. She sits on the couch and puts her hand on Hector's shoulder. "What's going on?"

Hector asks if she remembers him telling her about his brother Felix, the one who died a long time ago.

"Yeah," she says. "Of course I do."

He asks if she remembers him mentioning his son.

Mini says no and Hector explains the morning's phone call, concentrating and talking slow to make sure he gets everything straight. He tells Mini that Lencho Cruz is his nephew, that after Felix died, his wife moved up north with some family she had there.

"She took Lencho with her, but left for Mexico over some trouble, and Lencho was on his own for a year. He's a gang member. No, he *was* a gang member, and was caught breaking into some guy's apartment. Lencho's seventeen now, and for the last two years he's been living in a boys' home. Now they're trying to place him with a relative. Merced and I are the only family Lencho has left. Everyone on Teresita's side is undocumented." Hector says that Lencho's going to have to stay with them.

Mini sits up and starts asking the questions Hector anticipated. Is he violent? What about school? Has he graduated? Is he going to work?

Hector doesn't know.

"We don't have room," Mini says. "Where's he going to sleep?"

"I don't know. I'll help him get a job."

Mini leans back on the couch. She stays quiet for a few seconds and looks around the room. Hector can tell that she's rearranging their furniture. She takes a deep breath and pats the couch cushion and says, "I guess he can sleep here."

THERE'S BEEN NOTHING but green fields and cows for the last hour. Once in a while, Hector will drive past a mountain of worn-out tires, but that's about it. He figures this must be the place where old whitewalls and radials go to die. His left leg has started to fall asleep. He squirms in his seat and yet again he wishes that Mini's Corolla had cruise control. The coffee he bought this morning has turned cold and bitter, but he takes a sip in hopes that it'll help him focus on the highway.

He perks up when he sees Sundown Road, the exit the directions tell him to follow, and after driving down a long stretch of bumpy asphalt, he finally sees the first sign for the Watershed Boys Home. The asphalt turns to gravel, and Hector follows the signs to the main office. The only available parking space is next to a Solano County Sheriff's cruiser. Hector parks, gets out, and stretches his tingling leg. When he steps into the office, he walks like he's crippled. A deputy is talking to the secretary and they both look up. The deputy rests his hand on his holster and the secretary finishes telling him about this kid being the fourth to go AWOL this year.

"I'm here to pick up my nephew," Hector says.

He gives her Lencho's name and the receptionist says, "Honey, you need to see Jim Holsworth." She stands and points. "Just head on down this hall here, and it'll be the third door on the right."

Hector thanks her and nods at the deputy as he moves toward Jim's office. The hallway is brightly lit, making the pictures on the wall stand out. In the first photo, there's a group of kids standing around crates of oranges, two of them holding shovels. Their hair hangs down to their shoulders and they glare at the camera. The next photo is older, black-and-white. The kids in it have short hair and are unloading a flatbed truck full of Christmas trees. To Hector it feels as if he's going backwards in time, the last picture old enough that the kids in it appear as if they should be on a corner shining shoes or selling newspapers with headlines about America entering the war.

The third door on the right is half open, but Hector knocks anyway. Jim Holsworth reaches over the mess of papers on his desk to shake Hector's hand and Hector takes the seat he's offered. Holsworth asks about the drive up, adjusting his thick glasses, and asking if Hector made good time. Hector tells him it was all fine, and gets directly to business by asking about Lencho. He tells Holsworth that he's got to get out of here, that he's due back at work by two, even though Georgie gave him the day off. Holsworth says, "Sure, sure," and gives Hector a clipboard with a few forms to fill out. On these, Hector writes more neatly than usual. He reads all the small print and wishes Mini was here to do this. When he signs at the bottom, Hector feels like he just bought a home way out of his price range.

"You know," Holsworth says, "Lencho's come such a long way in the time that he's been here." Holsworth flips through some papers in a manila folder, occasionally pulling one out and tracing his finger along as he reads. "If you saw him when he started, you wouldn't believe it."

Hector hands back the clipboard, and Holsworth tells Hector about Lencho and the auto repair program. "That nephew of yours, he's developing into an ace mechanic," he says.

Holsworth lowers his voice as though he's about to share a grand secret. "It's a shame about Lencho's mother abandoning him and running back to Mexico." Holsworth says they called every agency they could think of looking for her. Hector nods as Holsworth tells him that it's terrible that Lencho's case is so common. "That's the biggest problem most of these kids face," he says. "The parents just don't care."

Hector says yeah and folds his hands, and Holsworth repeats his last sentence like he's trying to get it right. He skims over Hector's information with a pen.

Holsworth makes a few calls and asks that Hector wait in his office while he finds Lencho. The last time Hector saw Lencho was at Felix's wake. Hector was nine and Lencho couldn't have been more than two years old. Hector can't imagine what Lencho's going to be like now. Lencho Cruz the gang member. Lencho Cruz the drug-addict burglar. Lencho Cruz, Felix's seventeen-year-old son, who's now his responsibility.

Lencho turns out to be big. He's about four inches taller than Hector and he takes up most of the space in the doorframe. Lencho's wearing baggy blue pants and a white T-shirt with the Watershed insignia on the pocket. His hair is black and short and he has his mother's nose.

Hector's uncertain as to whether he should hug him or shake hands. He makes sure that he's smiling, and sticks out his hand, but Lencho yanks them together, smothering Hector in his arms. They hug and Hector sees that Lencho has CRUZ tattooed in black ink on one side of his thick neck. When Lencho lets go, Hector notices the crucifix inked into his nephew's right forearm. Lencho's voice sounds deep and comes slow, like it has to travel a long way before getting out of his body. "I thought I was going to see my Nino Merced," he says, and Hector tells him no, Merced's in prison for first-degree murder.

They both sign some more papers and Holsworth comes from around his desk to shake Lencho's hand. "I hope things go well for you," he says. Lencho has a small duffel bag, which Hector failed to notice when he came in. He offers to take it, but Lencho says no, and the two men leave. They go back down the hall, and in the waiting room Lencho waves good-bye to the secretary, the deputy gone.

Outside, they walk over to Mini's Corolla.

"Nice car," Lencho says.

"It's not that nice a car," Hector says. They both chuckle. "It's my wife's car, your tía Mini."

They get in and Hector finds Lencho hunched over, knees up against the glove compartment, his head an inch from the ceiling. "It's four hours to El Monte," he tells him. "Unless you want to sit like that the whole way, you might want to put the seat back."

"Sure," Lencho says, smiling. "Okay."

He reaches under the seat, and, once he finds the lever, he scoots it as far back as the rails will let him. The gravel road crunches against the Corolla's tires as they head to the freeway. Lencho rolls down his window. He looks hard at the trees going past as if he's trying to memorize them. He's quiet. Hector's quiet. This goes on until they hit Sundown Road, and then Lencho rolls up his window and says, "Thank you, Tío Hector. Thank you."

"Sure. No problem." Hector keeps his eyes on the road. He asks Lencho what he wants to do tonight and Lencho says he doesn't know.

"Stay home, I guess. I don't really have any money."

Hector tells him that Mini's planning dinner, but he's not sure what it is. It occurs to him that Lencho doesn't know what Mini looks like. Hector has Lencho hold the wheel while he fishes out his wallet. He shows Lencho the photo of Mini he keeps with him, one taken at a wedding a few years ago, Hector in his suit and Mini in her best dress, dark blue with tiny white flowers.

"She's pretty," Lencho says. "She's little too."

Hector nods, then changes lanes to get around a truck piled high with green produce. When the bride tossed her bouquet that night, Mini bumped and pushed all the other women trying to get it. They'd been dating four months at that point, and even though Mini's taller cousin grabbed the flowers, Hector remembers feeling certain that with this girl good things would happen.

Hector and Lencho make mismatched conversation about cars and music, Lencho punching the buttons on the radio trying to find a good station between the country music, traffic reports, and plain awful static. Lencho says he'd like to get a car, any car of his own.

"What would you get?"

Lencho says a Monte Carlo or maybe a Regal. "Something I could drop, something I could put some nice rims on. I could do it, you know, if I had a job."

Hector tells Lencho that he'd been thinking about that, and he tells him about Georgie. "What do you think about working with me?"

"I'd like that a lot. I'm pretty good at fixing cars. You know, I once overhauled a transmission on a '79 Accord, and I can do all kinds of other stuff." Lencho turns in his seat. He reaches into his bag and brings out a candy bar. He peels the orange wrapper and offers some to Hector, but Hector declines.

"I've always liked cars," Lencho says. He breaks off a section of chocolate and holds it in his hand. "Before, I'd be up all night on speed, and I'd run around my high school. It was close by. I took auto shop for a quarter there, and our teacher was this old guy, real old, and sometimes he'd forget to lock the back door to his office. I'd let myself in because I had nothing else to do, and take apart whatever I could find until the sun started coming up. They were like these greasy puzzles to me. I'd screw or click the different parts into place and it would be the best feeling in the world."

"We'll talk to Georgie," Hector says.

The word "speed" imposes a silence, makes him think of Merced. Lencho munches on his chocolate, but after a minute he must guess that this kind of quiet is a bad thing.

"That's in the past," he says. He folds the wrapper into a neat and shiny square. "I mean, I still like to fix cars, but that other stuff, all that was really a long time ago."

MERCED'S TROUBLE STARTED when he was ten. Merced was first busted at the TG&Y for stealing three Butterfingers along with a small sack of marbles. Hector could understand his brother taking the candy bars, but he didn't see why Merced grabbed the marbles, since he never played with them at school. Merced had stuck the bag down the front of his pants, shoved the candy bars in his back pocket, and they were almost out the door when they were stopped by a cashier. Merced's T-shirt was caught on a Butterfinger, its bright yellow wrapper in full view. The cashier grabbed his arm, the marbles shifted, and Hector stood helpless as they spilled out of his brother's pants and scattered across the floor.

Hector watched his abuelo beat Merced a hundred times with every belt in his closet, but the beatings didn't make any difference. In junior high, Merced was taking bicycles, riding them home and leaving them on the lawn. By high school, he was taking car stereos. He spent his sophomore year in Juvenile Hall for assault. When Merced returned home, it seemed to Hector that his brother's eyes opened a little wider, that his head jerked quickly at every other sound. Hector told Felix that Merced seemed different to him, but Felix was too busy being in love to notice. Merced seemed to do everything with a new urgency, like there would be drastic consequences that went along with every little task. Merced now acted as if his skeleton had been removed and replaced by bolts of lightning.

At sixteen, Merced carried a small tire iron to smash people's windshields and take the rosaries hanging from their rearview mirrors. Hector saw a report on a mystery thief in a news broadcast, and later connected it to Merced after seeing the growing collection he kept in a shoe box under his bed. The box of rosaries had been painted black with spray paint and Merced used a gold marker to write SALVATION LIES WITHIN on the lid in clumsy-looking letters.

Hector was certain that he was the only one to see that shoe box, to chart the change in Merced. While Amá was nearly psychic with Felix, she acted as if she knew nothing about Merced's habits, and even now there are times when Hector wonders if he could have stopped her from turning a blind eye on her middle son, if this would have made a difference. Merced would come home after being gone for two or three days, stinking sour with sweat. Merced's hands would have dried crusts of blood on them, his knuckles purple with scabs. Hector thought of approaching him, of asking him what was going on. He wondered if Merced had begun stealing other things from people, and he imagined his brother beating strangers for whatever money was in their pockets. Once, Hector had worked up the will to ask his brother about all this, and when he sat next to Merced, Hector's brother looked raw with desperation and greed. In the end, it was easier for Hector to believe that

Merced's hands bore scars from reaching through smashed windshields and picking rosaries from bits of broken glass. When confronted with these options, Merced's collection seemed to be a petty vandalism, constructive by comparison, as if Merced had been busying himself by picking aluminum cans out of other people's garbage.

GEORGIE'S ONE OF THE LAST white people living in El Monte. His shop has been there for years. There's a picture of him and his wife, Wanda, standing in front of the old Kuluzni Auto Repair and Salvage sign when the shop first opened on Ramona in 1964. Georgie was thin then, and he still had his hair. The old place was bigger, but after Wanda died, Georgie let some people go and moved to a smaller shop on Peck. Wanda had handled most of the books, because there was a while when Georgie would just pay Hector and Benny in cash. Hector didn't mind. He was sixteen and the only one in the family making real money.

When Abuelo gave Hector his truck, Georgie let the young mechanic bring it in after work and he helped him restore the entire machine from the inside out. Georgie told Hector that he bought a beater like that back in '52 with the money he won racing stock cars around California. According to Georgie, he was pretty good, but there's only one trophy from back then in the office, an ancient cup that's so rusted you can't read the name on the base.

Georgie's got connections with other salvage and wrecking yards and places all over. At first, Hector wanted to keep the entire truck stock, but Georgie convinced him to rebuild it with a Chevy engine, because parts for flathead Fords were pretty rare, and the ones Georgie could find would cost an arm and a leg. When Hector pulls into work on Friday morning, he knows Georgie's going to help him out with Lencho.

Georgie's sitting on the couch, in his spot under the wall covered with old license plates, reading one newspaper, then comparing it to another. He looks like a giant lump of dough stuffed into blue coveralls and topped off with a greasy yellow Pennzoil cap. Hector fills out his time card and Georgie asks him what "humo" means. Hector tells him, "Smoke," and Georgie says, "Oh." Wanda was Mexican, born on this side. She knew Spanish, and for the last twenty years Georgie's been trying to learn her language by buying copies of La Opinion and the Times, then comparing the cover stories. Georgie puts down the newspapers and asks Hector if he's going to finish up the '77 Buick today. Hector tells him, "Yeah, soon as those gaskets get here." He pours a cup of coffee, and, as he looks for the sugar, Georgie asks what happened with his nephew yesterday.

"It's funny that you'd bring that up. I was going to ask you, Georgie, what do you think about hiring him for around here?"

Georgie shifts uncomfortably in his seat. He sticks out his arm, and Hector helps him up from the couch. Hector reminds him that besides the two of them, there's only Manny and Benny. "And between the two of us," he says, "I think Benny does some pretty shitty work."

Georgie paces a small circle before walking behind the counter and sitting by the telephone in his wooden chair. Hector tells him about Lencho being in the Auto Repair program and Holsworth saying that Lencho's turning out to be a real ace.

"What kind of record does this kid have?"

Hector knows that Georgie's getting old, that he doesn't like working the way he used to. He tells Georgie that Lencho's a good kid. Sure, he's had some problems, but that's all behind him. "He's at home right now. He could start today," Hector says. "Maybe he could clean up around the yard, do an oil change or two, maybe help Manny out in the body shop."

Georgie looks at the telephone on his desk like he wishes it would ring. He takes off his cap and rubs his hand over his face, groaning as though Hector has wrenched his body into some improbable position.

HECTOR DOESN'T WANT TO DO THIS. In the eight years that Merced's been at Vacaville he's only received two letters from Hector, and both of them were sent a long time ago. Hector and Mini talk about it while she gets ready to take Lencho to the mall for lunch and some new clothes. She thinks Merced should know about Lencho being with them. She's probably right. "After all," Mini says, "Merced is Lencho's godfather."

It takes Hector a while, but eventually his pencil starts moving. He begins by telling Merced that he's sorry for not writing very often, that things have been busy and that he hopes his brother is well. He writes about Lencho staying with him and Mini, what Lencho looks like now and where he came from. He includes a few words about Lencho's conviction for breaking and entering. Hector tells Merced that he's got Lencho a solid chance at a job, that, starting Monday, Georgie's given Lencho two weeks to prove himself.

Hector writes about Mini, that he'll be a father sometime around Valentine's Day, and after that there isn't much else to say, so he writes "Keep your fingers crossed" and gets up to look for Merced's address. It isn't in the junk drawer by the phone, so Hector goes to the bedroom. There he starts rethinking the letter as he paws through the papers in his nightstand. Hector pictures a teenage Merced pacing in a gray prison cell, eyes closed, fingers crossed. He goes back to the table and erases the last line. Whatever luck Merced has, there are probably better things to use it on.

The image in Hector's head comes from Lencho's baptism, a day that found Merced incredibly nervous. Hector thought that his brother wanted to be someplace else, anywhere but inside the church. Felix had asked Merced to be his son's godfather as a sign of confidence, in hopes that Merced's delinquency was a phase he'd quickly outgrow. They stood in the church lobby and Felix leaned over, complaining of a hangover, asking Hector to find him some aspirin. The priest led the family to the front of the church, to the pool on the side of the altar. Felix held Teresita's hand tight and stared at the priest. Teresita remained quiet, but Hector could easily tell how she felt. Her scowl was constant, and it fixed on Merced when it was his turn to dunk Lencho. Merced approached the little pool carefully, measuring his steps as if the water inside might rise up and wash the two of them away.

BY THE SMELL in the apartment, Hector can tell that Mini is cooking sopa and carne asada, one of the five meals she knows how to make well. Lencho heads for the bathroom and Hector pours out the cold coffee in his thermos. He checks the pan of sopa simmering on the stove, certain that Mini put in the perfect amount of garlic. Hector's washing his hands when she walks in carrying a plate of carne asada, the meat prepared the way he likes it, smoking and black around the edges. Mini kisses him on the cheek and tugs at the zipper to his coveralls. "Nice uniform," she says, nodding at Lencho.

Lencho's on the couch in Hector's extra set of coveralls, the long tear on the thigh stitched up. Lencho says thanks and Mini asks how his first day went. She tells him to sit at the table.

Lencho takes the seat by the window. "Okay, I guess."

"It was better than 'okay,' " Hector says. He takes the tortillas from the fridge. "Georgie loved him, Mini. He took one look at Lencho's tattoos and said the work on them was beautiful." Mini checks on the sopa and Hector tosses a tortilla on the adjacent burner. "You should've seen it. At lunch Georgie unzipped himself right there in the office and rolled down his coveralls to compare his one tattoo with Lencho's. Ten years I've been working there and I've never seen Georgie outside those coveralls."

Hector tells Mini about Wanda's name under a pair of checkered flags on Georgie's upper right arm, the ink green and the letters smudged. Lencho finishes the rest of the story. He tells Mini how Georgie got the tattoo a long time ago, in Long Beach on his second date with Wanda, and how he said he was lucky that eventually the two of them got married.

Mini smiles and asks again, "So everything went good?"

Lencho groans and says, "Yeah."

Hector nods. He wraps the smoking tortilla in a dry dishcloth and tosses a fresh one on the burner. He fixes his stare at the blue flames coming from the stove. Hector doesn't tell Mini about Lencho, their ace mechanic, botching his first job, an oil change where he forgot to screw the drain plug back into the oil pan. When Lencho poured in the new oil, all four quarts ran right out in a golden puddle, and it took them three bundles of rags and a roll of paper towels to sop up the mess before Georgie could notice.

Mini puts the carne asada on the table and takes a big orange bowl from the cupboard. She goes to the stove and starts talking to no one in particular. "Did I tell you guys about that birthday party we had at work yesterday?"

Hector wraps a few more tortillas in the towel and tells Mini no as he sets them on the table.

"Some of the kids at this party were pushing a boy so fast on the merry-go-round in McDonaldland that he flew off and landed on the AstroTurf. I even think he was the birthday boy. He couldn't have been more than six years old. Maybe seven.

"Something snapped when he landed. It sounded like a pencil breaking. His eyes rolled back and he fell over when he saw his hand pressed against his wrist, the carpalia ready to rip through the skin. The poor thing went into shock." Mini says that someone called an ambulance and she knelt with the mother as she slapped at her son's face, telling her again and again how terrible she felt, that she was so sorry this happened.

"What's a carpalia?" Lencho asks, but Mini keeps right on talking and scooping sopa out of the pan. Her voice gets tense and the words start coming out like she's trying to say everything in one breath.

"I wanted to do something. I wished for smelling salts. A bandage. A splint. Anything. I wanted to take his small crooked hand and work my fingers over those bones until they regained their normal shape. I needed to help. You know what I mean?"

Mini comes to the table and Hector hugs her from the side, the bowl in the way. He tells Mini that she did help. "You did the best you could," he says.

September 3rd, 1984
Hector,

Fuck you and your wife and your unborn fucken child. You don't write me one word for eight fucken years and the first thing I read from you is that my brother wants to feel sorry for me? When did I ask you to? Besides, it's a little late for that now, isn't it? I'm happy that Lencho is staying with you, that you're trying to give him a home. I am well aware that I'm still his godfather and even though there will be little I can do for him over the next twenty-five years to life, I am still concerned. I hope that job deal you've set up works out for Lencho. If it doesn't, you make it work out. You get him that job. You put a roof over his head, maybe get him back into school. You owe Felix that much and even more to me. I still remember your precious truck and I know that the word "family" doesn't carry much weight with you. I'll leave things between us at that.

Merced

MERCED'S LETTER STAYED with Hector most of the week, memories stomping around his head like they were mad at the neighbors downstairs. This morning, Hector was installing new struts on a Civic, and he set down his torque wrench to watch Lencho for a long minute as his nephew cleaned the window over the outside sink. Hector recalled leaving a greasy handprint there on Tuesday, knew exactly where it was on the glass. He could see that Lencho had missed the smudge with his rag. He wanted to point it out, but the compressor hose was hissing too loudly around him, and so he stood there, holding his breath until Lencho reached over and finally wiped up the spot.

There have been many moments like this. If Lencho's feeling any pressure, he isn't acting very nervous. He hasn't said anything to Hector. At work, Lencho's spent his first couple of days visiting other yards and picking up parts with Georgie. He's done three more oil changes without any problems. This morning, Georgie had Lencho help Benny replace both the front and rear brakes on a '79 Coupe de Ville, then had him yank out a worn water pump with Hector. Hector was under the chassis, calling out tools and replacement parts, and Lencho said, "Yes, Doctor," and handed his uncle the right thing every time.

At home, Lencho smokes. No particular brand, whatever he can bum off Benny or Manny, and he's good about keeping it out of the apartment. He brings home Georgie's old newspapers, the ones in English, and reads them in the kitchen, tracing his hand across the paper until his fingertips turn black.

Yesterday, Mini kept the food section, and Lencho helped her prepare strange-tasting dishes with ingredients they bought at the Vietnamese market: spicy chicken and green bean stir-fry, Khmer fish stew with lemon grass. Twice this week he's gone with Hector to get food for Mini, egg rolls on Sunday night, doughnuts from the same place on Tuesday. When he went grocery shopping with Mini, Lencho came back with a copy of the *Auto Trader*. He sat on the couch and circled the photos of Monte Carlos and Regals he liked.

A couple of the cars were nearby, and Lencho asked Mini for directions to them when Hector was in the shower. Lencho went walking, and that was three hours ago, and now Mini's gone off to bed and Hector's alone and waiting. Lencho will get his first paycheck next Friday, and Hector feels good about Georgie deciding to keep Lencho on. Today, on the way home, Lencho promised to give Hector some of his check no matter what. "For rent and food," he said. Hector told his nephew not to worry about it, but still he got the sense that, come this Friday and next Friday and the Friday after that, Lencho will press the cash into his hand anyway, and when he does, Hector looks forward to setting this money aside and watching it accumulate into a down payment on a car.

There have been times when Hector's been with Mini and seen people with their kids and wondered if it's in him to be a parent. On their third date, Mini and Hector were at the movies, in the lobby waiting to buy popcorn, and this girl—she couldn't have been more than three years old—was crying, wailing hard and loud, her face red and wet as a boiled tomato. Her mother kept telling her to be quiet, and, after a few minutes, the mother slapped the daughter and the daughter calmed down. Hector remembers feeling relieved and thinking the mother had done the right thing, but Mini recoiled in horror. Her grip tightened in Hector's hand. "That's something I'd never do," she whispered in his ear.

Hector often goes back to that moment, to how wrong and backward his impulses seem when compared to Mini's. But then there are times like this. Times when he has a right idea, like the down payment, and it's all his own. These times usually go by quick, but they give him the sense that he'll be a good father, the father he never had. When these moments come, everything feels right. The doubt that rattles and knocks about inside him is replaced by a confidence that he likens to the sound made by a good engine. Smooth. Even. Perfectly tuned.

HECTOR HAD JUST COME HOME and it was late. He stood in the kitchen, looking in the refrigerator for a beer, when Amá came in to tell him Merced had been arrested. "This time the police said they got him breaking into someone's house."

Hector opened a can of Bud, flipped the pull-tab into the trash, and sighed as he sat at the table. This was Merced's fifth arrest as an adult.

"Your brother's in jail," Amá said. Her job at the grocery store kept the lights on and the water running. Abuelo had no money. His check from the government barely took care of his dialysis. Felix was out starting a family of his own. Hector paid rent and that money put food in the fridge. Amá sat next to her youngest son and placed her hand on his. "Would you put the truck up for Merced's bail?"

She said when Merced called, he told her that any bondsman would take the title and they could have him out by morning. Hector took a long drink of his beer. The papers had been in his name for less than a month. Besides a few pieces of clothing, the truck was the only thing he considered his own.

"Mijito, it's your brother. You know that there's no way he could do all those things. The police might have him confused with someone else. You know how the police are. They see one Mexican and they think we're all the same." Amá got up and walked into the other room, raising her voice. "He's innocent. You know Merced."

Hector did know Merced. He knew his brother didn't break into that house the same way he hadn't been stealing from Amá's purse since they were kids, the same way he hadn't roamed around half the San Gabriel

Valley smashing windows and swiping rosaries. Merced couldn't have done any of that, yet Hector was certain that Merced would probably steal whatever he could get his hands on. The last time Hector saw him, Merced was busy hopping up and down and telling his brother about being up for a week straight. Merced was changing his shirt and his ribs looked like two sets of fingers inside him, like the hands of something meaner and stronger trying to rip its way out. Talking with his brother that day had left Hector with the feeling that Merced would beat Hector's head open if he thought there was a dollar in his brother's skull.

Hector remained seated and ran his fingers through his hair and drank his beer. Amá came back into the kitchen carrying the phone book and the telephone, the cord dragging behind her. She started flipping through the Yellow Pages, and, after finding the right listing, she pushed the book toward Hector like he knew which bondsman to call. Hector was positive his brother was a thief, and sitting in the back of his head, resting and waiting to be called upon, was the conviction that Merced would always be a loser. Hector stood and pushed his chair back in. He took his keys from the table and said, "No." He stepped over the telephone cord and walked out of the room.

GEORGIE OFFERED TO BUY LUNCH if Lencho and Hector would pick it up. Joey's is busy, clogged with the lunchtime crowd, and Hector waits in the long line. Lencho immediately slides onto the bench of an orange table, even though a girl's already sitting there. Lencho says hello, eyes big, smile wide, arms on the table displaying his tattoos. The girl says, *"Whatever,"* disgust in her voice, hands up in the air, a pair of exclamation points. She stands and joins the two girls waiting before Hector. They whisper and sneak dirty looks at Lencho. When one girl notices that Lencho and Hector are in the same blue coveralls, coveralls with the same logo on the back, they all quiet down and get their food to go.

Hector orders Georgie's two chili dogs when he reaches the cashier. He orders Georgie's fries and his extra large Diet Coke, then three cheeseburger specials, onions for Benny, none for him and Manny. Lencho comes over, hands in his pockets, and asks, "What should I get?"

"Whatever you want. Georgie's paying."

Lencho orders a Coke, then, after a moment of careful contemplation, adds a fish sandwich. "Onion rings, too." He nods his head as he says it. Hector pays and both men return to the table.

"I haven't had onion rings for the longest time," Lencho says. "At Watershed all they had were these fucked up potatoes they called home-style fries." Lencho checks his hair, patting a spot where it's grown shaggy. "They'd serve you these dry hamburgers, and I swear they'd cut a potato in four pieces, fry it for two seconds so the centers were still raw and hard, then call them home fries." He shakes his head, then says, "Fuck all that shit."

"Still," Hector says, a smile on his face, "that sounds better than that stuff Mini cooked the other night." Lencho doesn't laugh. For a while they both just stare out the window. The girls have left and are standing on the corner, sucking on their sodas as they wait for the signal to change. Lencho stares at them, and Hector wonders on which of the three his nephew's focusing. Hector tries to remember their faces and is disappointed when he can't. The signal changes, and the girl in the middle turns around. She looks back at the window and smiles before turning to cross the street. Lencho grins.

Lencho was alive a week before his father told anyone about him. When he did, Hector and Merced couldn't believe the news. Instead, they posed silly questions. Hector asked, since both parents still worked at the Spectrum plant, if the baby came out all rubbery and soft, like a chew toy for dogs. Merced laughed and asked if Lencho had a bell inside his stomach, one that jingled when you picked him up.

When Felix told Amá and Abuelo that night, there was the screaming all three brothers expected. Felix had already tossed his clothes in a trash bag. He left, the black bag over his shoulder like Santa Claus, the screen door bouncing off it before slamming behind him. Not a minute later, Abuelo burst into the room Hector shared with Merced. Abuelo's left hand grabbed Hector's T-shirt. His right hand wrapped around the boy's neck. Hector's feet left the floor as Abuelo pressed him to the wall, and the boy felt for a second that the breath inside him had to last forever. Abuelo's eyes were wet. "Bring home any more mouths to feed, and you'll be out on your ass too," he said, and Hector did his best to nod, even though matters like sex, love, and childbirth were strange and hazy mysteries.

The cashier calls their number and Hector hands Lencho one of the bags while he waits for ketchup and chiles. When he meets up outside with Lencho, his nephew's already going through the bag. He digs out his onion rings, their paper pouch gray with grease. Lencho selects the fattest onion ring Hector's ever seen. It's the size of a deep-fried piston ring, two fingers thick, shining in the sunlight. Lencho quickly gulps down half, then blows on the rest.

"Still hot," he says. "Probably just out of the fryer."

They head back to the shop, Lencho lagging a few steps behind. Hector tells him to forget about those girls, but Lencho is so busy looking for them that he's practically walking backwards. He tries to take another bite of the onion ring. It slips from his fingers and falls to the ground, but Lencho grabs it off the sidewalk, barely brushing away the dirt before cramming it in his mouth.

TODAY MAKES THREE STRAIGHT DAYS that Lencho's ordered onion rings for lunch. He's brought the *Auto Trader* to work, and between bites he flips a few pages back and forth, comparing two ads. Manny enters the office with his lunch pail and collapses on the sofa next to Lencho, his skinny frame spread out as if he'd fallen through from the second floor. Manny rubs his eyes and groans and smoothes back his greasy black hair. Lencho offers him an onion ring, but Manny says no thanks, opening his beaten gray lunch pail instead. Manny's lunch always looks like he stole it from a third-grader: two peanut butter and jelly sandwiches and a thermos full of red Kool-Aid. "I'm gonna need some help on that Falcon if it's gonna be done by Friday," he says.

Georgie puts down his newspaper and rolls out from behind his desk, the wooden chair creaking as it slides across the worn linoleum. "What's the problem?"

The problem is that the Falcon's for one of Georgie's buddies, this guy who owns a wrecking yard over in Irwindale. It's a birthday present for the guy's daughter, sweet sixteen with a driver's license straight from the DMV, the whole bit. But Hector knows that there's also three other cars parked around the body shop that Manny has to get to, cars with owners that are paying business, not free favors.

"There's a lotta work back there," Manny says.

"Paint the Falcon first," Georgie says. "Lencho'll help you with the sanding after lunch." Georgie slides back to his desk and picks up his newspaper. "That Falcon's gotta be primered before either of you go home today."

Manny sighs and looks over at Lencho and they both say, "Right."

Later, Georgie asks Hector what "osadía" means, and Hector tells him that he's never heard the word before.

Benny comes into the office with a small plastic bag and a bottle of Coke. He grabs an empty chair, turns it around, and rests his arms on its back. *"Osadía?"* he asks. "That's like bravery," he says, snapping his fingers before remembering the exact definition. "Like courage or daring."

Georgie nods his head but doesn't tell the mechanics about the newspaper story to which the word's related. Benny starts in on his lunch, laying out four store-bought tamales, cold store-bought tamales since there isn't a microwave or a hot plate in the office. Still, Benny unwraps the first small bundle and eats half of it in his first bite, chewing hungrily, licking the red grease off his fingers as if he were new to the basic pleasures of the outside world. "Already buying a car?" he asks Lencho.

"Just looking," Lencho says.

Benny asks him what he'd like and Lencho passes the magazine to Manny who passes it to Benny. "I saw that one last night and it looked pretty clean," Lencho says. "New paint. New tires."

Benny takes the *Auto Trader*, wiping his mouth with his sleeve. "Why you want a Regal?"

"I don't know. I guess I like the sound of the name. The way it'll look dropped with some good rims."

Benny uncaps his Coke, and takes a drink as he reads the ad Lencho's circled. He puts the bottle down and shakes his head. "Man, that's too many miles. Way too many for that kind of money. Didn't your uncle over there tell you this?" Benny unwraps his second tamale, apparently forgetting about the other half of the first one, crumbling the oily wax paper wrapper. "Hector, that's nothing but problems waiting to happen."

"How many miles does it have?" Georgie asks.

Benny reads the ad aloud, stressing the number—185,000—and everyone laughs, even Lencho, who smirks as if he knew this all along.

"Oh no," Georgie says. "That's no good, Lencho. You don't want that much mileage on a used car. Jesus, Hector. What're you thinking, letting him consider buying a car like that? Anything over a hundred thousand and the motor'll be likely to fall apart soon as he backs out the driveway."

Hector knows this, but Lencho didn't ask him about this or any car. Lencho didn't seek his tío's advice. When Lencho came back last night, he didn't even bother to wake Hector up, and Hector stayed sleeping with his head on the kitchen table. Lencho asks Manny what he thinks, and Manny rubs his eyes and yawns. "Let me take a look," he says. Something fails inside Hector, and from this fissure spreads a hot black shame. Hector reaches over and intercepts the *Auto Trader* to redeem himself, but Georgie doesn't allow him the chance.

"Listen, Lencho," Georgie says, "forget about all the junk in that rag." The old mechanic takes the magazine and tosses it into the clutter on his desk. "There's nothing but wackos selling wrecks in that thing. You don't need somebody else's headache. Once you get some money saved up, you let me know. I'll make a few calls and I'll see what I can do."

HECTOR WAKES UP TO THE SOUND of Mini laughing. She's in the other room, and he gets out of bed and stands in the hall just out of sight. She's pulled a chair up to the kitchen window and is talking to an empty screen, a mug of her manzanilla tea in her hand.

"I'm happy that you're here," Mini says. She blows at the steam rising from the mug and lifts out the tea bag with a spoon. "I'm happy that you're safe."

The front room is covered in the blue light of dawn. Lencho's bed is unmade, the sheets tossed to the side, the couch cushions crooked. A pack of Marlboro reds is open on the coffee table. Hector can't see Lencho, but the morning is quiet enough that he can hear his low voice outside. He asks Mini what it's like being pregnant, if she'd rather have a boy or a girl, and Mini looks down and says it doesn't really matter. "Hector wants a boy," she says. She takes a sip of her tea. "Deep down, he *really* wants one. Me, I just want the baby to be healthy."

"Do you know what it's going to be?"

Mini smiles. "Yes, but I'm not telling anyone, especially Hector." Lencho asks why and Mini stares out the window for a long time. Hector can hear birds chirping in the courtyard downstairs. Someone starting their car. He forces himself to remain still, as if not moving would somehow make him invisible. "I was pregnant once before," she tells Lencho. "But it didn't work out right."

"What do you mean?"

Mini tells Lencho about her first baby with Hector. Lencho says he's sorry and Mini says, "I'm sorry too." She takes a big drink of her tea, then sets the mug on the counter. "We didn't know what the first baby was, but I had my doctor tell me this time. Of course, I don't want what happened before to happen again, but if it does, I think it'll be easier on Hector if he didn't know. If he couldn't picture the baby the way I can. He's lost enough people already. I won't let him lose one more."

Lencho goes quiet.

Mini closes her eyes, and, after a few seconds, she tells Lencho goodnight. "You can light that cigarette now," she says. Mini sighs a bit as she stands and lumbers back toward the bedroom. Hector's heart slows. His wife approaches, and his heart pounds hard, the blood pumping sluggishly as if it had been replaced by mercury. Part of Hector wants to hide, but whatever stealth he possessed has been negated by a sudden heaviness inside him. The best he can do is retreat a few steps into the darkness of the bedroom. Mini enters the bathroom, walking past Hector without noticing that her husband stands less than five feet away. The bathroom door closes and the light goes on inside. The scale makes small squeaks. When the light goes off, Hector slips back into bed. The words in his mind are birds afraid to leave their cage. They withdraw to his fingers, and when Mini gets under the covers, Hector curls up behind her, his heart still emitting laborious and rhythmic thumps, his hand over hers. Hector looks at their alarm clock, and for the next forty-two minutes he pretends that he's asleep.

HECTOR'S ABUELO HAD BEEN IN KOREA for the war. He was a marine and he would tell Merced and Hector his stories about crawling in the freezing mud and men losing fingers and toes to the cold. On Hector's eighth birthday, Abuelo unearthed his old helmet from the trunk he kept packed in the back of his closet. The camouflage canvas covering the helmet was torn in spots around the rim, and when Abuelo gave it to Hector, the boy said it smelled bad and passed it on to his brother. For the next few weeks, the Cruz household was centered on the 38th parallel. Merced would attack the furniture to take his family hostage, then release them and shoot enemies that only he could see.

One day Hector caught Merced digging through Abuelo's closet. The boys were alone in the house, a new occurrence at that point. Before Felix started seeing Teresita, Hector and Merced were never left by themselves. Merced's fists shook with excitement as Hector pulled him away from the trunk. "Look at this," he said, his right hand opening, a silver medal resting in his palm. The medal dangled from a ribbon, white with light blue stripes, the words KOREAN SERVICE circling a gateway. Merced pinned it to his shirt. Hector had never seen the medal before, and, because Abuelo had never shown it to him, he knew this was something secret neither of them should be touching. This was a clear and immediate truth for Hector, like the sun in the sky and water being wet, but he didn't know what to say. That was Felix's job. Felix could speak to Merced. He knew how to get him to do things.

What Hector did do was take the medal back. He asked at first, and Merced ignored these requests and soon the brothers were wrestling, a match that ended quickly, Merced pinned to the floor, overpowered and breathless, Hector sitting atop his chest. "You can't have this," Hector said, and Merced let out a small and desperate squeal as Hector undid the clasp, the medal cold in his hand. He let Merced up, and there was a rotten look on his older brother's face. Merced was always chiple as a child, so, before he returned the medal, Hector waited until Merced tightened the strap on the helmet and ran out to the shadowy command post he kept under Abuelo's broken-down truck.

Hector had no idea as to where in the trunk the medal should go. He recalled Abuelo showing him his money clip once, being instructed to always keep his big money, his tens and twenties, hidden under his one-dollar bills. "This don't go on top," he'd told Hector as he folded some ones around a twenty. "Things like this you hide." The memory made Hector confident. He placed the medal at the bottom, below a thick stack of papers and a green sweater made from scratchy wool. He made sure the clasp was closed, the ribbon smooth, and he knew he had done something good, something right.

Later, he heard Merced yell. It was a high-pitched scream, shrill with fear, and Hector rushed outside to find his brother rocking from side to side, his head shaking, the helmet rattling against the door of the truck. He held out his right arm and said, "Snake." Then he collapsed. Hector shook Merced and told him to wake up. When he didn't answer, he ran to the front house and called Javier. When Hector showed him his brother, a bruise had started around the bite marks in Merced's arm. Javier took a penknife from his back pocket and sliced an X over the dark mark. He started sucking and spitting. Javier's mouth quickly became a red mess and the blobs he spit made little clumps in the dirt around them.

Javier yanked off his belt and tied it around Merced's arm. He wiped his mouth on his sleeve and told Hector to grab his brother's feet. Hector grabbed Merced by the ankles and Javier took him by the armpits.

Javier drove a '65 Impala and they put Merced in the back. Hector sat with him, using his T-shirt to wipe the oozing blood, slapping him lightly on the cheek and begging him to wake up. As Javier sped through the streets, he tapped one hand on the steering wheel to the beat of the radio. He was so relaxed, they could have been making a beer run. Hector's dying brother in the backseat didn't seem to matter. Before the song was over, the Impala screeched to a stop before the emergency room doors. Merced's arm had turned white. As the nurses took him away, Hector thought his brother's arm was dead, that the poison was just waiting to take the rest of his brother once the doctor untied Javier's belt.

Javier returned home and left Hector in the emergency room to think of the best possible way to tell Amá and Abuelo that Merced had died. He examined the change in his pockets and watched the faces of the people using the row of pay phones. He wondered where the nurses had put Merced and he looked at the people coming through the doors. There were coaches from El Monte High with a kid in a basketball uniform, his face stretched in a scowl, his knee encased in ice packs. He saw a bloody couple from a car accident, and a man who had been stabbed, the knife firmly planted in his leg as he grimaced and limped past. All these people looked like they would live and Hector wondered what made them so special.

Amá and Abuelo finally came. They went straight to the nurses' desk where Amá cried out Merced's name. Everyone watched Amá run down the hall, stopping to look in every room. When Hector saw her enter one, he closed his eyes and counted to ten before looking. He stood and hoped that the right words would come. He walked to the room and found Amá holding Merced. His arm was wrapped in white bandages, and a tired smile was on his face. The nurse from the front desk advised Amá to let the boy stay the night, but Abuelo told her they couldn't afford such things. Afterwards, as Amá signed the release forms, the nurse told them how lucky they were. She called Merced a longshot, a thousand to one, and asked for the numbers in the boy's birthday so she could take them to Vegas.

THE BAND IS SETTING UP when they get to La Parranda. Mini's already in the bar, sitting alone and sipping a 7-UP. Hector sneaks up behind her and kisses her head. He hugs Mini sideways so he won't get her dress dirty. Mini looks at her husband, then her nephew, and frowns. "I would've brought you guys extra clothes if I knew you were still in your coveralls," she says.

Hector feels bad for a moment, but this feeling goes away when Benny arrives wearing his dingy coveralls, and Georgie wobbles into the restaurant in a grubbier blue uniform.

Even though the men are plainly underdressed and the place is busy with the dinner crowd, Georgie still manages to get them a booth in the corner. There's a little boy in the adjacent booth, and Mini waves to him as she scoots over to the middle, Georgie and Benny sitting on one end, Hector and Lencho on the other. Their waitress comes with waters and menus and chips and salsa, and the men start off with Budweisers. Mini gets another 7-UP, and Lencho gets carded. Lencho shrugs at this and Hector asks the waitress for an extra glass. When she returns with their drinks, Benny tells her that they need a few more minutes to order, that he's waiting for another person. Hector pours half of his beer into the glass and slides it across the table to Lencho. Mini nudges him in the ribs. "It's okay," he tells her. "It's Friday and we're celebrating."

Georgie raises his bottle. "To the new member of Kuluzni Auto Repair and Salvage," he says.

Lencho looks at the floor and pokes holes in his napkins with his fork. Mini slaps his arm. "Don't be shy," she says. "This is great. You should be proud. You should smile."

Lencho looks up, a wide, honest grin on his face. Mini takes his wrist and lifts his glass for the toast. Some of Lencho's beer spills and the group's bottles and glasses clink over the center of the table. The mechanics all take long pulls off their beers, Benny taking the longest, so that his bottle's half-empty when he sets it down. He checks his watch. "Marie shoulda been here by now." He asks if anyone has a quarter and goes to the pay phone near the bathrooms after Mini fishes one from her purse.

Georgie pushes the basket of chips aside and reaches over to hold Mini's hand. Mini gives him a kind smile when he tells her how good it is to see her. "You should drop by the shop more often," Georgie says. "Someone like you could really brighten the place up." Lencho nods at Georgie's old, leathery hand over Mini's, and looks at his uncle like he should be worried. Hector shakes his head. He knows that Georgie's just being Georgie.

"I'll try to stop by," Mini says. "You never know. Once I have this baby, the two of us could be there so much you'll have to order him some coveralls and put a third Cruz on your payroll." Georgie laughs. He lets go of Mini's hand and takes another drink of his beer.

It's a boy.

At that moment, Hector hears Benny slam the pay phone so hard that the change inside it rattles. He sees Benny walk back and slide into the booth, jamming his cigarettes and lighter in his chest pocket. The waitress stops by and asks if they're ready to order. Everyone picks and points at different things on the menu, and, when the waitress looks at Hector, he says, "Carne asada," because it's the first thing that manages to surface in the sudden flood of happiness filling his mind. The waitress asks if Hector wants corn or flour tortillas, but the decision is impossible. Tortillas don't matter. Not when Mini is carrying his first son.

Georgie says, "Give him the corn ones, señorita." The waitress seems both rushed and annoyed as she jots this on her notepad. She turns away before Georgie can continue, but Benny gets her attention by tugging at the knot on her apron. Georgie shows the waitress his bottle. "And keep these coming."

Hector sits. He puts his hand on Mini's thigh and squeezes gently, as though Mini were blind and needed reassurance of her husband's presence.

Benny grumbles. He picks a big chip from the basket and dips it carefully into the salsa.

"What happened with Marie?" Lencho asks.

"Ahh," Benny says, "it's not even worth talking about." The chip crunches in his mouth and he looks away at the musicians taking the stage. The first song starts, a norteño that blares loudly. Food comes halfway through the third or fourth song, the plates clunking heavily when the waitress sets them on the table. Hector cuts into his carne asada and Mini points to the tall and thin bass player on the far right. The musician's face is red, his eyes narrow with concentration. He can't be a day over sixteen. "That guy's so young," Mini says.

Hector nods and chews and smiles as he swallows. A boy. His boy.

People at other tables let loose with piercing, drunken gritos, and the band responds to the wild shouts by repeating the up-tempo tune. A few couples leak out onto the dance floor. Hector can feel Mini shifting in her seat. "Dance with me," she says over the music.

"Yeah," Georgie says. "Dance with her."

Mini tugs on his arm, then leans over and puts her mouth to his ear. Her voice is clear, her breath warm. "Dance with me," she whispers. "Please."

Hector's dancing is about as good as Georgie's Spanish, but even still he wants to get out there, to make a fool of himself, because he's with Mini. This urge is something new, and Hector stays in the booth to enjoy the moment, this feeling of overwhelming joy, his half-eaten plate quickly going cold.

Benny wipes his mouth with his napkin and tosses it on the table. "Shit," he tells Mini, "I'll dance with you if Hector won't." Benny grabs Mini's arm and they go out to the middle of the floor where Benny pulls Mini close. He holds her face against his chest and bumps his way back and forth across the dance floor. Benny isn't really dancing with Mini. It's more like he's sweeping the floor with her.

Lencho moves aside, letting Hector out of the booth. Hector picks his way through the dancing couples, his pulse pounding in his ears as he taps Benny on the shoulder. "I think I'll finish this song out," he says.

"Hey man," Benny says, "we just got started."

"Well I'm not in the mood for any more of this," Mini says. She squirms to get away but Benny's hand is firm on her waist.

Benny looks down at Mini. "You and me, we're just dancing here," he says. Benny bobs his shoulders to the music. "You know, doing a little cha-cha-cha."

"I'm done dancing with you," Mini says. She squirms and Benny loosens his grip.

"Fine," he says, nudging Mini toward Hector.

"Hey, take it easy." Lencho's standing behind Hector, been standing behind him since he left the table.

"Take it easy yourself, kid." Benny lights a cigarette as though he were alone on a street corner, taking his time, enjoying the smoke spreading through his lungs. The band stops playing and Benny flips his lighter shut with a slow and deliberate click. Hector asks Mini if she's okay and she says yes, and they walk back toward the booth together, hand in hand, the other couples frozen around them.

Benny follows them and bumps into Lencho, shoulder to shoulder, as if he expected to walk right through him. Lencho pushes Benny back. Benny turns around and Hector jumps between them, telling both of them to relax.

Benny shoves Lencho. Lencho slips to the floor, and, when he gets up, he gets up swinging. His face is red and the first punch he lands pops off Benny's chin. It snaps the mechanic's head back, but it doesn't knock him down. Benny throws a right that crunches against Lencho's nose. The dancers and other patrons close around the two men, and even the waitresses set down their trays to join the wall of spectators. Hector can't see the fight, can only hear the sounds of the crowd, and in those seconds everything inside him drains away, each cheer a puncture, each whistle a perforation, leaving Hector empty, his spirit porous as a colander.

Hector forces his way through the gathered people, and when he gets to the empty space, Lencho's fist strikes Benny square in the jaw, leaving Benny panting, his balance so shaky that he stumbles back against the stage, banging into the legs of the accordion player, knocking the shiny red instrument out of the musician's hands. Half of the accordion hangs from the stage, and the instrument wheezes like a smashed harmonica before falling to the floor.

Hector grabs Lencho's sleeve and hauls him outside. Mini follows the men to her car. Lencho keeps telling Mini that he's sorry, that he didn't mean for this to happen, that he was just trying to help. Lencho's lower lip is split. Parts of his face are starting to get puffy. He keeps saying, "For reals Mini. I wanted to help you, for reals." Hector asks Mini to get Lencho home, to stay there with him, and he gives her a quick kiss before he goes back into the restaurant.

Benny is sitting in the booth. When he sees Hector, he pops up like he was touched by a live wire. Georgie holds him back and Hector pats Benny on the shoulder and sits down. He assures the host that he has nothing to worry about. "It's over," Hector says. "He's gone." The host tells the musicians to get back on the stage. Hector apologizes to Benny, a convincing apology even though he knows he has nothing to apologize for. "Both of you were out of line," he says, "and for Lencho's part in this, I'm sorry." Georgie nods and Hector grabs at the waitress. "Bring three more Buds over here, one for me and one for him and an extra cold one for this guy right here." Benny scowls and Hector tells him not to worry. "This round's on me."

HECTOR FINDS THE APARTMENT DARK AND QUIET. He sets his keys and wallet on the kitchen table, and finds Mini in their bed, on her side facing the wall, asleep. He doesn't bother with the lights. Instead, he watches over his wife, over the shadows, their dark shapes on her resting body. Lencho's not home. Hector reenters the living room, harboring inside him the vague and childish hope that Lencho might magically appear. Hector sits on the couch and takes off his shoes, leaving his socks on, stretching his toes on the carpet. Lencho's sheets and blanket are folded neatly just to the side of the couch with his pillow and his bag of toiletries. Hector rises and heads to the bathroom. He stands before the toilet, and when he can't go, Hector flushes it anyway. He brushes his teeth vigorously, trying to remove the taste of beer from his mouth. He goes back to the bedroom, where he changes out of his coveralls, leaving them in a heap atop the dirty laundry stacked in his hamper.

"He said he was going for a walk, and then he just left, and he hasn't returned."

Hector sits on the bed. "Do you think he'll come back?"

"I asked him that, and he said he would, and because he said he would I let him go."

Hector yanks off his socks and quietly pulls on an old pair of shorts. "He's gone, isn't he?"

"It might look that way," he says. Hector closes his eyes even though he knows that tonight he won't sleep.

"I'm sorry," Mini says.

Hector tells her that he knows, and they stay that way, together and unmoving.

In the weeks after his eighteenth birthday, just before Lencho was born, Felix disappeared. Amá had always told the Cruz boys that they were to stay in the house until they were married because that's the way her family was and that's the way it should be. "A man's got no business living with a woman if they aren't married," she'd say. This was usually followed by "A man's not a man unless he's got a wife."

Amá had begun standing on the porch when Felix's shifts were supposed to be over, waiting for him to come home. She'd pretend to be checking the mailbox or doing something in the yard, but Hector knew she was waiting. She'd wait and wait, sometimes for hours, and sometimes Felix would come home and sometimes he wouldn't. One night Amá waited long after nightfall. She swept the porch twice, and, with the light of a full moon above her, she picked all the weeds from the cracks in the walk. She collected the trash that had blown against Javier's chain-link fence, but none of her chores brought Felix home that day, or the day after, or the day after that.

The fear in those days was the worst that Hector had ever known. Worse than knowing his older brother might die from a snake bite. Worse than the feeling he would soon have watching his older brother walk off with his possessions in a trash bag. When Merced was hospitalized, a sense of finality overcame Hector that left him more sad than scared. But when Felix disappeared, matters were different. More than the grim and morbid scenarios that his imagination conjured up, it was the not knowing, the inability to say where Felix was that scared Hector, that kept him awake, his mind fueled by a white and chilling fright.

Mini taps Hector on the shoulder. "This might sound silly," she says, "but I'm hungry."

"Really?"

"Yeah. You know what would be good right now? Lasagna and bread with olive oil, good bread, the kind that's hard on the outside and soft on the inside. Hot chocolate too."

Hector checks the alarm clock and it's later than he thought, close to midnight. He tells Mini it's too late to find lasagna. "Anything I'd get right now would be frozen."

"That's fine," Mini says.

Hector gets out of bed and changes back into his coveralls. "What brand do you want?" he asks.

"Any kind, as long as it's got lots of cheese."

Hector can't find his socks, and, rather than get a fresh pair from his dresser, he walks out into the living room and puts on his work shoes, their leather insoles sticky and cold against the bottoms of his bare feet. His eyes adjust to the darkness and he sees that the front door's cracked open, a pale sliver of light dividing Hector's face as he leans forward. He goes outside and Lencho's leaning against the rail, looking out into the courtyard. He's smoking. "My tía Mini's hungry?" he asks.

"She is."

"For what?"

"You should get some rest," Hector says.

"Why bother?"

Hector tells him that he talked to Georgie. "We've both got work to-morrow," he says.

Lencho nods. "The Alpha Beta's open until two." He sets his ciga-rette on the rail. "If you want, I'll go. Just tell me what I need to buy."

The two men go inside the apartment and Hector turns on the kitchen light to write down the things Mini wants. He gives Lencho a twenty, but the money is refused.

"I cashed my check," he says. "I can get this one."

Hector passes his nephew the keys to his truck. "Mini's car doesn't have gas," he says, even though he filled the tank two days ago and the Alpha Beta's five minutes away.

"Sure," Lencho says. "Okay."

Hector listens to Lencho's steps pounding down the stairs. Outside, he listens to the truck starting in the parking lot, the engine echoing under the metal carport, the sound fading as Lencho drives away.

Hector goes to the kitchen and pours some water into a small saucepan, setting the saucepan on the stove and giving it a medium flame. He finds Mini's mug in the cupboard, the ChocoMilk on the shelf beneath it, way in the back. He loosens the dense powdered chocolate with a spoon. He turns toward the light to read the suggestions on the side of the jar. The water gets tossed out and the milk is taken from the refrigerator. Hector pours two cups in the saucepan, more than enough, and replaces the pan on the stove. There's nothing but quiet, a good, satisfying quiet, just the stirring of milk and the gas going blue into flame. Occasionally, Hector tests the milk by pressing the spoon to his lips. He doesn't want it too hot. He just wants to take away the chill.

1 9 8 5

Evelyn's going nuts in the passenger seat because Mario still isn't done with her wedding dress. My sister's too nervous to drive, and since I'm the only one home, I'm taking her for her fitting. Evelyn's wedding is in four days, on Saturday, and she's the kind of person who plans everything in her life, from buying wrapping paper for next year the day after Christmas to ordering all her keys by color and size. She gets her craziness from our mom, and while I've had sixteen years to get used to it, Lupe's only had two.

Mom's Tercel stalls at the signal on Durfee. My sister's holding a clip in her mouth, working her long black hair into a ponytail. She stomps the floor, and, through her clamped teeth, she tells me she'd probably be better off walking there. I start the car up again and give the engine some gas, and Evelyn lets out a deep breath when the car starts moving. Evelyn was this freaked out two years ago, just before her high school graduation, and she left the house five minutes late and totaled my dad's car running a red light. She spent six months in the hospital wrapped like a mummy, so there's no driving for her this week.

Evelyn fidgets and changes the radio station. "Double Dutch Bus" comes on, and she tells me it used to be her favorite song. She starts to sing along but gets the lyrics all mixed up and changes the station to something else I don't recognize.

I shift into second, then into third, and the tires squeal as I make a left turn onto Valley. I pull up to Mario's, and there's no parking on the street, so I drop Evelyn off. She disappears into the shop with her list of alterations and crumpled *Bride* magazines, the ones with every other page marked by a color-coordinated tab. I park the car in the lot for the tortilleria, then walk over to the dress shop. Mario's glass door has been boarded up with cardboard, and I have to push hard to get inside.

The stuffy shop is two small rooms, one in back with a changing booth, one in front with white silk and mannequins everywhere. I flip through the thick binder of sample photos and clippings from magazines that Mario keeps bolted to the counter. Mario's a little old guy. He's not a midget or anything, but there are small wooden boxes and milk crates in front of the different mannequins pinned with bright, half-sewn dresses. Evelyn's in the back room, changing behind a curtain, telling Mario in Spanish that the left sleeve is a little too loose and that the right one is too tight. My mom had Mario make Evelyn's dress against Evelyn's will because he made one for a girl my mom works with at the market. Mom looked at the pictures of this other girl's dress, and besides the fact that it was "just gorgeous"—her words, not mine—she was surprised to find out how affordable the whole thing was.

Mario handles my sister with the patience of a monk. His teeth are full of pins that he spits into his hand to talk. Mario answers some question about Belgian lace and looks over at me and smiles and says, "Pues, todo tiene que ser perfecto para la señorita."

I nod in agreement.

Mario shakes his head and rubs his balding scalp in a way that makes me think there are bigger things for him to worry about. He checks on a few other details, then tells her to be careful taking the dress off. Still, Evelyn comes out with a section torn at her right shoulder and a long red scratch on her arm. Mario apologizes. He says he'll get a Band-Aid, but he comes back from his bathroom with a long strip of toilet paper that he dabs on Evelyn's arm.

I'M ELEVEN YEARS OLD AGAIN when I hear those sounds Wednesday morning. There's the gurgling motor, the brakes' high squeal, the heavy creak of axles coming to rest. I get out of bed and look through the window. Grandpa Lopez's rig is against the curb, looking pretty much the same as the last time I saw it. The red paint has faded a little, but the chrome trim shines bright in the morning light. The windshield is topped with a chrome sun visor, the glass split down the center so it looks like eyes, like the rig's studying our house. When I was a kid, Grandpa Lopez's rig made me think of a dragon creeping down the road. Even now, without the trailer, the long hood still reminds me of a snout, the exhaust pipes chugging black smoke as though a great fire is burning in the cab. On the rig's door, LOPEZ TRUCKING INCORPORATED is painted in handwritten yellow script. You'd think my grandpa was the head of a huge operation, but far as I know, Lopez Trucking Incorporated has always been him and only him. The engine cuts off and I have no idea why he's here.

Grandpa Lopez climbs down from the cab and looks around before walking across the green grass to the house. He's wearing a short-sleeved plaid shirt, dark jeans, and pointy black cowboy boots wicked with polish. When he knocks on the door, I notice that his face is rounder and his cheeks have sagged. Though his hair has thinned on top, what's left is combed up into an inky wave that glistens with pomade. He's still got those tinted eyeglasses on, the ones with thick black frames that always made me think he should be strumming a guitar and singing "Pretty Woman."

I debate opening the door. I mean, I don't really know Grandpa Lopez too well. The only person in the family who does is Grandma Josefina, but just mention Ramiro Lopez and she'll spit Spanish curses like the blood inside her has soured to vinegar, her bones turned to salt. Grandpa Lopez knocks again. We haven't seen him in six, maybe seven years, and it's this excitement that makes me answer the door.

Grandpa Lopez smiles. "Look at you," he says, "You're almost a man."

"Hey," I say. "Come on in."

Grandpa Lopez shakes my hand as he enters, making it a point to squeeze hard, the muscles coming out on his forearm like he's trying to press my fingers into a new shape. He follows me into the kitchen and refuses the seat I offer.

"I've been on my butt for the last five hours," he says. "The last thing I want to do is sit down." He leans over and looks down the hall to the bedrooms like someone might be hiding there. "Where's everybody?"

"Mom and Dad are at work."

"What about my Evelyn?"

"She's out running errands with one of her friends."

Between me and Evelyn, my sister's always been Grandpa's favorite. She might not admit it now, but when she was a kid, Evelyn wanted to be a truck driver too. She wore little cowboy boots and wrote reports on truck driving for school. We would pass a rig on the freeway, and Evelyn would stick her head out the window, my mom reaching over with one hand trying to pull her back inside. Evelyn would check every time to see if the guy behind the wheel was Grandpa, her hair blowing around as she pulled the chain to an imaginary air horn to get the driver to honk. This was before the divorce, when Grandpa Lopez was around more often and our family was still talking to him.

"How's your mom?"

I tell him she's fine. "She's still at the market, still working hard."

"And your grandma?"

"Okay," I say.

Grandpa taps his finger on the table like he wants to ask more about Grandma, but he doesn't. "School?" he asks. "How's that?"

I tell Grandpa I'll graduate in two years.

He coughs and nods, then says, "Wow."

I offer him coffee and sort through the cupboard, looking for the jar of instant my mom keeps for guests willing to drink it. I ask how he's been, if he's been busy, and listen to him talk about running surplus piping from Phoenix to Galveston and bales of cotton from Lubbock for processing in Las Cruces.

"Sounds like a long way out," I tell him, brushing the dust from the jar of Folgers, wondering if coffee goes bad.

"Well," Grandpa says, "you go where the work takes you."

I'm about to ask if he knows about the wedding when he starts coughing, heaving hard. His breathing comes quick and sounds like a pair of bricks scraping in his chest. Grandpa reaches into his back pocket and takes out a handkerchief and a purple envelope. He blows his nose and hacks into the hanky. I know that envelope. I know it's made of heavy handmade paper with yellow rose petals pressed into the pulp, that the lettering on the front was done by a calligrapher in Arcadia who charged Evelyn three dollars per address.

ONCE, WHEN THEY WERE STILL MARRIED, right before the divorce, my grandma Josefina came over unexpected and drunk. She shivered in our doorway, her gray hair pasted to her face, drenched from walking from the bus stop to our house in a heavy rain. She clenched a pistol in one hand, her cane in the other. I wondered if I should put my arms up, if this was a joke and she was pretending to rob me. She pressed the gun into my hands and took some bullets from her purse. The bullets were different sizes and different lengths, and she said she couldn't get any of them to fit. "But you're smart," she said. "You do good in school, so I know you can figure it out."

It was the first and only time I've held a real gun. The weight surprised me and when my mom came to the door and took the pistol away, my hands felt light and hollow. She pulled Grandma inside and made me get her a towel. I ran and grabbed the only one hanging on the rack in the bathroom. I ran back and sat as my grandma patted her damp forehead and rubbed her arms.

"What's the matter?" my mom asked.

"It's your father, mijita. He's out on the road right now, probably pulled over on the highway, or in some motel room, or probably in the sleeper of that damn rig, parked at some truck stop, fucking his gringa whore." Grandma let go of her cane and grabbed my mom by the shoulder, reaching for the gun my mom held above her head. "I know he's your father, mijita, but when I find them, I'm going to kill them both."

I never met the woman that came between my grandparents. The only pretty white women I knew in El Monte were in the underwear sections of the Sears catalogue and the weekly ads from Kmart. I imagined her having big blond hair, wearing nothing but white boots and a cowboy hat, an older member of the Dallas Cowboy cheerleaders. I imagined him sitting with her at a bar, the two of them tinted by the dim green light of a jukebox, the woman giggling at the sweet and nasty things my grandpa whispered in her ear. This while my grandma sat next to the CB unit on the nightstand in their bedroom, drinking beer as she scanned the channels, listening for her husband's voice in the distorted mix of radio waves.

GRANDMA JOSEFINA, MY MOM, and Evelyn are all sitting around the kitchen table. They're filling little plastic champagne cups with chalky mints, wrapping them in white lace, and tying them with custom-made ribbon that reads *Guadalupe Peña Negrete and Evelyn Peña Salazar—April 12, 1985*. My mom's telling Grandma how Evelyn made Mini drive to five different shops for that customized ribbon until finally they found a place in Norwalk that could spell *Peña* instead of *Pena*. My grandma grabs her cane, limps over to the kitchen sink, and lights a cigarette. Evelyn holds up a finished cup as my grandma blows smoke in the air. "That's beautiful, mija," my grandma says before taking a second drag.

I'm looking for my house keys so I can leave for work, and Evelyn grabs me by the arm.

"You're still taking me later," she says.

"Where?" Mom asks. "Where're you taking her?"

I don't know what to say, so I stay quiet until Evelyn says it for me.

"Grandpa Lopez is here," she says. "He stopped by this morning, but I missed him."

My mom looks over at me. "No. No way, Max. You're not taking her anywhere."

Grandma puts down her cigarette. "How did he know Evelyn's getting married?" She stubs out the barely smoked Marlboro, glaring at me like my mentioning of Grandpa ruined it.

"Don't look at me," I tell her. "I didn't mail the invitations."

My mom and my grandma sigh at the same time.

"Oh Evelyn," Grandma says, "how could you invite that man?"

"It's my wedding." She slides a finished champagne glass with the others on the table. "I'll invite who I want to."

EVELYN'S NEXT TO ME, double-checking the list of places we still gotta hit today. We've already been to the truck stop by the 605 where Grandpa told me he was staying, but his rig wasn't there. We have to go to Mario's for another fitting, the florist over on Garvey to confirm the flower arrangements, Mini's place to make sure her shoes were dyed the same shade of lavender as the dress. Then there's the stationery store at the mall to get thank-you cards for the wedding gifts Evelyn hasn't even received yet, and the camera shop for film, since, even though they've hired two photographers, Evelyn wants her own camera nearby. The list goes on forever. We're on Penn Mar, waiting for the light to change, and Evelyn tells me to pull over because the bakery's across the street. While we're here we can make sure the cake'll be ready on time.

Evelyn's cake isn't supposed to have strawberry custard, it's supposed to have strawberry cream. My sister says this in Spanish to the girl behind the counter. The girl puts her finger up and says one minute. She tells Evelyn that she'll check with the owner and disappears behind the plastic curtain to the room of ovens and the smell of baking bread. Evelyn leans on the glass counter like she's about to collapse. She looks at me.

"Are you going to look like this at my wedding? You think you might get a better haircut?" Evelyn reaches into her purse and gives me a ten and a twenty. "I know you have a tie," she says. "Just buy a jacket or something."

I start telling Evelyn that I have my own cash, but the girl comes back. Evelyn pushes the money in my pocket, and groans when the girl says, "Pues la señora todavía no llega."

Disgust comes over my sister's face. She asks when the owner will be here, and when the girl says one o'clock, my sister grabs me by the arm and we leave.

The whole drive over to Mario's, Evelyn complains about how last Thursday the owner was around. "Why isn't she there now?"

This time there's parking in front of the dress shop, and Evelyn gets out before I turn off the engine. Inside, Mario's eating his lunch, poking a fork into an open Styrofoam container that has stunk up the whole shop like chile rellenos. He says "Buenas tardes," wipes his hands, and points to the mannequin wearing Evelyn's wedding dress. Evelyn walks over, circling the dress and inspecting it like a boxer checking an opponent for weakness. Mario washes up in his bathroom, and, before he finishes, Evelyn calls him back. He's drying his hands as Evelyn lifts the arm of the dress. "This isn't what I wanted. This isn't what I told you to do."

Mario has sewn the wrong lace around the cuffs and the neckline. Evelyn's tone shrinks a few inches off the dressmaker. I know it's a big deal. I can see how she'd be mad. But as Evelyn snaps at Mario, I'm embarrassed by the fact that I'm related to her. I don't want to watch this. Evelyn goes behind the brown curtain while Mario starts taking the dress off the mannequin. I tell her I'll be back in a while, that I'm going to look for a suit. Evelyn pops her head out from the curtain, and, before she can say anything, I tell her I'll be back in thirty minutes.

I drive three blocks to the Salvation Army. The store is crowded, so crowded that I have to wait as this older guy goes through the sports jackets and blazers. I flip through the assortment of wide and bright polyester ties, not really interested. The ones that slip from the rack I leave on the floor. When I look through the suits, I find one made of faded black pinstripe material that feels soft as an old dollar bill. I check my watch and fifteen minutes have already gone by. The jacket fits okay when I try it on, but, just by looking, I can tell the pants are way too big.

Both my legs could fit into one. I could wear the jacket with my black Dickies and my black tie. My sister might not mind seeing me in something like this. I go through the rest of the suits and find nothing better. I hold up the jacket and check for stains or tears. I smell it, and up close I notice a peasized white mark on the lapel. This could be covered with that Misfits button I have. I want to take a second look at the ties, but my half hour's running out. With the way my sister's acting about everything, I wonder if she's more in love with the idea of being married than with Lupe himself. I check my watch again and pick up the ties that are on the ground. It's time Evelyn learns how to wait.

EVELYN'S NEARLY PACKED UP ALL HER STUFF. In her room there's a stack of empty apple boxes that Mom brought home, but Evelyn's collection of stuffed animals, her TV, most of her furniture and most of her clothes are already at Lupe's apartment in Baldwin Park. A collage of my sketches and Evelyn's photos covers one wall of my sister's room. It's among the last things to go. Evelyn owns three cameras. You'd think she'd be good at taking pictures, but she's not. She's always snapping shots of everything, and they usually come back from the camera shop crooked and out of focus, too dark or too light. Birthday parties look like they were held in caves. Evelyn's friends blink like she's trying to blind them with her flash. She always blames the camera. She takes three different shots and hopes one will turn out.

Of all the stuff on Evelyn's wall, my favorite photo is of us when I was four and Evelyn was eight. It's one of my first memories, sitting with her on the cold metal steps of Grandpa's rig, me in fuzzy red corduroys, Evelyn in pink overalls with the legs tucked in her cowboy boots, both of us smiling for the camera. There's a hand in the corner of the photo, Grandpa's hand.

I stare at this picture and wonder where Grandpa Lopez is right now.

Maybe he's doing his laundry, watching it circle and turn. Maybe he's alone in the rig, smoking a cigar and reading a paperback western. Is he driving around the city, looking for the places he used to go? Maybe he's at the Horseshoe Club or the Jester's or the Mexicali Bar, drinking beer and telling the stories he's told me about driving high on Hundred Mile Coffee and White Crosses, roaring from Wyoming to California without giving the snow on his roof a chance to melt. Maybe he's at the supermarket where Mom works, standing in line, yanking the knots in his stomach tighter as the piles of groceries and the line of customers dwindle, bringing him closer to saying hello. Maybe he's by his old house, wondering who lives there now. Does he know that Grandma moved to the Holy Cross Seniors' Apartments over on Tyler, that after the divorce she went back to using her maiden name? Maybe he's by a pay phone right now, twirling a quarter in his fingers, scanning the White Pages, column after column of names where Grandma's number might be listed.

THURSDAY NIGHT I TAKE EVELYN BACK to the truck stop. The lot is full of big rigs that look even bigger up close, and make me feel like I'm behind the wheel of a toy. Mom's Tercel gets lost in the shadows of the trailers as we drive between them. We go around behind Linda's Restaurant, and there's the rig we're looking for. It looks pink coated in polish. Grandpa's standing on the front bumper, wiping down the hood. I honk as we get closer. He turns and looks at the car, and doesn't recognize us until Evelyn sticks her head out the window and yells his name. I park and we get out. Grandpa climbs off the rig and hugs Evelyn, lifting her off the ground. Grandpa's jeans are dirty, and his T-shirt is limp with sweat. He leaves my chest damp when I hug him, and I can hear him breathe when he lets me go.

My sister's voice gets all high and chirpy when she tells Grandpa how happy she is to have him here. "I can't believe we're talking," she says. "I can't believe that it's you."

"I should say the same thing. I can't believe my little Evelyn's getting married." He jams the rag into his back pocket and puts his arm on Evelyn's shoulder. He leans in close to her, almost whispering in her ear, like he's describing a faraway mountain. "I'm sorry, mija, but I can't stay for your wedding. I've got to leave Saturday morning. There'll be a load waiting for me at a mill in Scottsdale, and to be there by six o'clock, I've got to leave here by ten."

Evelyn looks down, and Grandpa tells her not to worry. "I'll drop by the house before I go."

Evelyn nods. "All right," she says. "I just wanted you to be there."

My sister has one of her Kodaks with her, and she has me take a few pictures of her with Grandpa. My grandpa finishes polishing the driver side of the rig, and they lean against the grill, Evelyn with both arms around his waist, squinting at the camera.

"Stand right there," she says. "No, more over to the right."

I take one shot, then Evelyn has me take a second and a third. She looks up at Grandpa and says, "Just in case."

Grandpa goes back to wiping down the rig. We follow him around to the passenger side of the truck. "So tell me more about this Lupe. What's he really like?"

"He's great," Evelyn says. "He works at a bank. He's going to be a loan officer soon."

"But what's he really like?"

"He's good, Grandpa. He loves me."

"Are you sure?"

"Yes," Evelyn says. She holds out her hand, then takes off her engagement ring, twin gold bands, a diamond the size of a pinhead where the bands intersect. She gives the ring to Grandpa, and it seems smaller in his hand. "Lupe saved for three months to get it," she says. "Of course I'm sure."

Grandpa returns the ring and gets back to his truck, to the corners and tight spots still dull with polish. He says marriage is a big deal. "Look at me," he says, patting the rig's fender. "I've had all twenty gears and 456 horsepower for the last eighteen years. This is the only thing I depend on. I've cared more for this baby than any of the women I've been with in my entire life." Grandpa looks at Evelyn and smiles. "Well, except your grandma."

I GIVE EVELYN AND MY MOM all the telephone messages I took while they were at the Holy Cross—Mario checking the type of stitching Evelyn wants for the veil, my cousin Freddy saying he can't make it to the church but he'll be at the reception, my tía Julieta and tío Ramón calling from Guaymas to offer their congratulations.

"You should see the lasso your grandma's making," my mom says.

"Is she still using fake pearls and plastic orange blossoms?" I ask.

"Don't talk like that," my mom says. "It's coming out nice."

"Really," Evelyn says. "It looks good."

I ask if it'll be done by tomorrow, because at the rate Mario's going, the dress will be ready when Lupe and Evelyn get back from their honeymoon.

"I'm trying not to think about it," Evelyn says. She sits at the kitchen table and sighs. She rubs her arm where it was scratched.

"Watch," I tell her. "Tomorrow you'll be at the church, kneeling with Lupe before the altar, Lupe in his tux and you in your blue jeans when Father Albert puts the lasso on your shoulders."

GRANDPA'S GOT BOTH EYES ON LUPE. It's late and we're at La Parranda with Evelyn, who wants her fiancé to meet Grandpa Lopez before the wedding. Except for a few people at the bar, the restaurant is empty, and, even though our food is bad, I make a taco of the rubbery carnitas my grandpa ordered.

Grandpa turns to Evelyn and Lupe and asks the happy couple how they met. Lupe's got his arm around my sister. She looks back at him and smiles. "It was at the bank, after he screwed up one of my deposits. He credited my account with only a hundred dollars when my paycheck was for five hundred."

Lupe laughs. "I'd noticed Evelyn at the bank for a while. Always on Monday mornings. Always at nine o'clock just as my manager opened the doors. I was dating two other girls when I went out with Evelyn the first time." Lupe gazes at my sister. "We had our ups and downs, but two months later, it was only Evelyn in my life."

"What do you mean 'ups and downs'?" Grandpa asks.

An awkward smile comes across Lupe's face. "Well—

"Let's just say that it took him a little longer than me to figure out we were meant for each other," Evelyn says. She pats Lupe on the cheek and gives him a quick kiss.

"Hey, I made the right choice, right?"

Grandpa Lopez nods.

He should've been at our house earlier tonight. Lupe and his family came to dinner after the rehearsal. My mom made steak picado, and Lupe took out the chiles. My sister plucked them from his plate and popped them in her mouth. Lupe's parents were quiet most of the time, the father with the same nose as his son, flat and wide like a link of chorizo somebody stepped on. I don't know what Lupe's parents think of Evelyn, but my dad likes Lupe because he's got a steady job and a paycheck that'll put a roof over Evelyn's head. My mom seems to like him because he wants to have a big family, even though Evelyn's said a million times that she doesn't want kids. Lupe says that they'll work it out later.

Lupe has one story that he shares with people the way mothers talk about their babies and holy rollers rattle on about God. Grandpa Lopez hasn't heard it though, and he listens closely, Evelyn grabbing Lupe's arm as if he's about to win her a stuffed animal. In his senior year, Lupe hit a home run for Mountain View that sent the team to the Valley finals. First time in the school's history. Next game they lost, though. Lupe couldn't play because some kids from Bassett had followed him off the field the week before. These guys kicked his ass in the parking lot, hit him with bats, broke his ribs and his right arm. They popped his left eye out of its socket.

Nobody reacts to any of this. Lupe starts to look nervous, like he's not quite sure of his place, like maybe he's said too much and has offended someone. Things are quiet and I do my part to let them stay that way. Lupe picks at the carnitas and asks Grandpa what it's like driving such a big truck.

"It's hard and lonely," Grandpa says. "Your arms vibrate from the engine, even when you pull over to rest. You spend the whole day bouncing in your seat from potholes in the road, maybe talking to some people on the radio, and after a while everything starts to look the same, the highways, the food, the people."

My grandpa then reaches for his denim jacket, pulling out a small flat box from the inside pocket. For a second I hoped it might be one of his cigar tubes. When we were kids, he'd send us glass cigar tubes from wherever he was on the road, sometimes full of pennies, sometimes with dimes. To keep them from breaking, he'd pack them in boxes stuffed with truck-stop napkins, old maps, and newspapers. They'd come postmarked from far off places like Corpus Cristi, Texas, and Bellingham, Washington, and Missoula, Montana. One year, a tube of pennies was wrapped in a newspaper all the way from Elmira, New York, and I went to school early the next day to look at the giant map in our classroom. I stuck thumbtacks in the cities I could find in the packing sent over the year, hoping I could see which direction Grandpa was headed, hoping he'd reached the end of the country and was on his way back.

Evelyn opens the box. Inside is a horseshoe. "For good luck," Grandpa says. He moves the salt and pepper shakers together and takes them apart. "See, I was hauling a double load of steel beams from Texarkana to El Paso, and I got into this poker game at a truck stop just outside Dallas." Grandpa stops a second and looks like the story in his brain has to catch up with his mouth. "To make a long story short, by the time the sun started coming up, I had won a horse. Quarter horse named Something for Nothing. Beautiful animal. Evelyn, I never saw many horses up close. I mean real close, so that you can see their eyes and the look on their faces. They're like people. I couldn't keep him, of course, but afterwards I went straight out to the rig and grabbed a mallet and a screwdriver from my toolbox. I had the guy pry the shoes off that horse right there in the parking lot, then I hit the road behind schedule, fighting to stay awake.

"I'm not thirty miles away from the stop, when I swear I see your grandma standing in the middle of the road. I tugged on the air horn and pumped the brake pedal, but she wouldn't move. I panicked and jammed the brake to the floor, feeling all the weight of that steel behind me. I plowed right through the spot where she was standing. For a second, all fifteen tons were about to slide off the first trailer and level the cab. I closed my eyes and thought, *Victor Lopez, this is it.* I took one hand off the wheel, looking for the cross hanging from my neck, and there's those horseshoes sitting in my chest pocket. My tires were burning against the asphalt, and I opened my eyes and in my mirror that second trailer starts to whip around. It breaks away from the first one and flips over. The beams come loose. They're tumbling and plowing through the asphalt like it's frosting on a cake. Tearing up everything in their way. My rig slowed down and stopped, and I sat there in my seat, breathing in the smoke around me.

"I'll tell you, losing half that load was a miracle from somewhere. I shouldn't be sitting here with you tonight. The way I see it, those horse-shoes are the luckiest things I own. There's only four of them, and I want you and your future husband here to have one."

THERE'S THIS BAND FROM CANADA called the Subhumans. I'm mentioning them because at La Parranda, Grandpa Lopez asked if I had ever been in love and I lied.

"I'll bet you're a real heartbreaker," Grandpa said.

He said this, having had many conquests with women. He said it in front of my sister and Lupe, and I sat there feeling like a penguin at a table of peacocks. The conversation screeched to a standstill. It seemed they were about to fall in my lap waiting for me to answer. I could see my sister looking away, fiddling with her ring as if she just noticed it on her finger. It was just easier to say no than to try and explain what happened with Irene.

I met Irene Rosales last summer, between freshman and sophomore year. She was eighteen when she sat next to me on the bus coming back from the paper tube factory where I had just started working. I was dirty, in work clothes, and listening to my Walkman when she got on. Irene was wearing a black leather jacket with the left sleeve painted green and the Subhumans' logo painted down the other. She asked what I was lis-tening to and we started talking about our favorite Ramones songs, school, and anything else I could think of. Irene had a thin face and hair dyed purple. Her smile made me go home and practice mine in the mirror.

Later, Irene told me she stole the jacket from an old boyfriend when she lived with her brother in Ventura, that the spikes around the cuffs and fake leopard skin on the collar were things she added herself. Irene was living with an older sister named Sandra. Sandra worked three jobs, so I only saw her once, between naps and uniforms, her face pale and gray. Sandra was almost never home, so Irene and I usually had her place to ourselves.

I found myself over there almost every day. The first time I went to Irene's apartment was early in July when she had just dyed her hair pink. We bought twenty dollars worth of fireworks and lit them in the street. I would find the fuses, Irene would light them, and, holding hands, we'd run from the hissing behind us. When there were no more fireworks, we lit the box the fireworks came in, then leaves and scraps of paper from the gutter. When we ran out of things to burn, we went upstairs to her room. Sex was new for me, but I didn't tell her this. I smiled and tried not to make any noise. When Irene started to moan, I did too.

Afterwards, we shared a glass of water, sweating through the sheets because the apartment didn't have air-conditioning, and I thought for the first time that this is what it's like when someone really cares for you. Irene's hair was a wig of cotton candy, and I imagined taking a bite until I kissed her ear and caught a stiff whiff of the chemicals from the dye.

She didn't work that summer. She spent most of her free time either messing with her hair or trying to fuck with mine. I watched her dye her hair four or five different shades. The purple when we met went to Bubble Gum Pink, which turned to Stinkbug Black, then to a red called First-Degree Murder.

We split up not long after that, Irene saying something about me being around too much. A few months ago I saw her. She was driving a Honda that had been in so many accidents it looked like the body was made out of orange foil. I was buying cigarettes at Road Runner Liquor when the Honda bounced into the lot, screeching and bumping into the concrete bar separating the parking space from the one in front of it. Irene got out. Her hair was brown and short. She was wearing a yellow visor and a brown vest for the Happy Donut. As I waited for the bus, I watched her work. Irene was a cashier. She plucked donuts from the racks and smiled as she poured coffee and when she handed customers their change, Irene looked completely ordinary.

EVELYN SLAMS THE PHONE DOWN. "The dress will be done in twenty minutes," she says. My sister and my mom have been working in the bathroom since eight, and Evelyn's makeup is perfect, her hair freshly curled. She sits across from me wearing sweats and an old shirt, the bottom buttons missing and the collar spotted with green paint. Evelyn looks like a princess hiding among the people she'll one day rule. She fans her hands in front of her eyes. "Okay, okay, okay," she says. "Calm down. You're not going to cry."

The wedding's at Saint John's in an hour, and the priest wants everybody there at least half an hour before, because we're the first of three other weddings in the church today. I mess with my tie. I fold and refold my coat. Evelyn calls Mini to see if she'll pick up the dress, my sister counting the number of times that the phone rings. "If it rings ten times, the answering machine will turn on," she says. Her eyes light up. "Hello? Hello, hello, hello? Mini are you there? Hector?"

There's no answer, so my dad says he'll go to Mario's and Mom can get Evelyn to the church.

"What about my mother?" my mom asks. Grandma's another problem. There's only two cars, and going to the Holy Cross means half an hour on the other side of town.

More calls are made, and it turns out that everyone in our family, all our invited friends, seem to be doing what we should already be doing, getting to Saint John's. I go outside and let my parents figure things out, and there at our curb is Grandpa's rig. He climbs down from the cab, and I wave and lean in the door to call Evelyn outside.

I shake Grandpa's hand, then hug him. Evelyn comes out and hugs him too, and Grandpa asks if she's ready for the big day. Evelyn explains about the dress, then stops midsentence.

"Can you pick it up?" she says. "Don't worry, the place isn't far and the dress is already paid for." She points to me. "Max can go with you. He knows how to get there."

Grandpa says, "Sure mija, whatever you need."

Evelyn runs inside, and a few seconds later my mom comes to the door. Grandpa says hello, but he doesn't bother to move toward her. My mom just stares and stays quiet. I can hear the Tercel starting in the garage, and soon after my dad joins my mom at the door, his hand on her shoulder.

"We've gotta go," he says.

"Yeah, I'll see you there," I say.

The rig smells like old smoke and salty leather. Sitting on the dashboard is a statue of the Virgin Mary and a yellow clay ashtray in the shape of Texas that I remember Evelyn making for Grandpa in the third grade. It's been cracked and glued back together a few times. The passenger seat is big and soft. It feels like I'm sitting in a catcher's mitt until Grandpa starts the engine and everything begins to vibrate—the seat, the Texas ashtray, the teeth in my head and the fillings in my teeth. Grandpa pulls on a pair of black leather gloves and works the gearshift. We begin moving.

"Where we headed?"

"Go down a block, then make a left."

Taped to Grandpa's sun visor is a black-and-white photo of my mom and dad in the patio of our house just after they were married. My dad's sitting on a bench, his arms resting on his knees, and Mom's reclining in a chair holding a glass in her hand, pregnant with Evelyn. In the chair next to her, Grandpa's sitting with his legs crossed, his arm around my mom. My grandma's standing, pulling the tab off a can of Budweiser and looking right at the camera like she's facing a firing squad.

"Go left on Klingerman," I say, talking loud over the engine. "Go right on Durfee, left on Valley."

Grandpa asks if Evelyn's nervous.

"I don't think she's eaten much of anything since the rehearsal dinner," I say.

There are wallet-sized pictures of me and my sister taped in different spots around the cab. The backgrounds are different, red leaves for fall, green leaves for spring, and there we are in kindergarten, first and second and third grades, my hair flat and parted straight down the center, Evelyn bucktoothed and grinning like she's sitting on a five-dollar bill. The pictures stop there, and it seems as if we suddenly stopped growing too. In Grandpa's mind, we've been the same age for the last seven years.

At Mario's I climb out and leave Grandpa and the rig running in the middle of the street. Mario has the dress ready in a big white box with a cellophane window on the lid.

"Dile a la señora Evelyn que me dispense," Mario says as he fixes a detailed receipt to the box with an inch of tape. I take the box, the dress heavy inside it, and Mario holds the door as I walk back out to the rig. The passenger door is open and I hand the dress to Grandpa, then get inside. Grandpa holds the box a few seconds before reaching back and placing it on the mattress in the sleeper.

"Go up to Ramona, then make a right."

Grandpa nods, and we go a few blocks and wait at a red light. When the light turns green, the truck doesn't move. Cars behind us honk, and Grandpa looks back at the dress for a few seconds.

"Uh, you can go," I tell him.

My grandpa stares at the gearshift like he forgot which way to move it. He reaches back and pulls the receipt off the box. He inspects the amounts on it and whistles a slow, sad whistle. He folds the paper in half and hands it to me.

"I think you should get out." Grandpa Lopez checks his side mirror and I check mine as if I didn't hear him. "Tell Evelyn, tell her I'm sorry, tell her I love her and because I love her, I can't let her do this." My grandpa sticks his arm out his window to wave cars around him. "She's too good for this Lupe guy. He's not the one."

I pass the receipt between my hands. I think of Evelyn waiting at Saint John's and I stay put. I love my sister too.

"Mijo, get out."

I smooth the crease in the folded slip of paper and picture Evelyn in the future, in a couple of years, little Evelyns and Lupes running around her, and I think of Irene arranging sprinkled donuts on a silver tray, and I open the door and climb down to the street without saying good-bye. The rig shudders and black puffs spout from the smokestacks as the rig goes into the first of many gears. I dodge a car and get to the sidewalk. The receipt gets folded into a small square, and I put the square in my wallet. I walk the opposite direction down Valley, afraid to look back at Grandpa's rig, certain that I'll chase after him if I do.

My arms and legs feel weak, like I've been strapped in a roller coaster, and the feeling reminds me of last year, of the earthquake that happened in the first week of school. I was by the basketball courts when the ground started to rumble and the backboards started to sway. It was in the morning, before first period, and afterwards everyone in the school gathered on the soccer field. While the teachers took roll and waited for news reports, I sat and felt the ground ripple underneath me as the aftershocks continued. I sat until noon, when parents started to come for their kids and the school day was officially canceled. No one came for me, and eventually I decided to walk home. Out front, the signals weren't working and Father Albert was in the intersection, directing traffic. Crossing the street, I felt a similar intense shaking, and for a second I couldn't tell if my body had begun to tremble or the ground was getting ready to crack open and swallow me whole.

GEORGIE AND WANDA

1956

Georgie winces as he walks into Walt's Barber Shop. He steps toward the short row of red folding chairs facing the sink and mirrors, a deep sigh escaping his chest when he sits down. The bruise is spread across his ribs, but other, smaller pains shoot through his arms and legs, nagging him with stinging bursts when he moves. Walt looks up from the gray-haired old-timer he's working on to say good morning, and Georgie only manages to grunt a response. He tries to sit still and wonders if this is what his body will feel like when he gets old. He closes his eyes and listens to the quiet sounds of Saturday morning, the snipping of Walt's shears, and the country music coming from the Motorola. The old man hums along with the radio. There's only one part in the song that he seems to know, the chorus which he sings softly, "Go cry your heart out, don't come cryin' to me."

Georgie's own heart is beating in odd places. His head pumps and the foot in his right boot pulses. In the ring and pinkie fingers on his right hand, his heart throbs as if last night's crack-up had shattered it, sending its pieces to the most remote parts of his body. Underneath his blue T-shirt, a black arc curves across his chest. The bruise is deep and it marks the place where he was rammed into the roadster's steering wheel. Georgie wonders if he's fractured anything, if any of his ribs are cracked, if something broken keeps the little bones in his right hand from making a complete fist. Last night, his roadster's restraints held loosely and Georgie was flung forward fast and hard. Somewhere in the fogginess, he told Link he'd have been better off strapping himself down with rubber bands.

He hasn't slept or showered. He smells of smoke, and his T-shirt and jeans are stiff, marked in places with chalky blotches of dried sweat. After the crack-up, Georgie spent much of last night with the roadster, watching Link and some people from the other crews douse it with water, only to have the flames flare up from the engine a few minutes later. Georgie watched from the infield as his '32 Ford burned and died, fire truck sirens approaching, the other roadsters rumbling on the dirt track around him.

When Walt finishes with the old-timer, he slaps the red barber chair with a rag. Since Georgie was a child, his hair's been cut every two weeks on a Saturday morning. Georgie's father is a barber in Joliet, Illinois, a pincher of cheeks and a giver of lollipops, who always told Georgie that there's no greater shame than a handsome man who lets a good haircut grow out.

The old man hands Walt a few dollars and nods as he shuffles past. Walt tells Georgie, "Okay champ! You're next." In the five years that Walt has cut Georgie's hair, he's always called him "champ," and this morning more than ever, the nickname makes him uneasy. He shifts in his seat and takes a deep breath. Even though he's done well enough with racing, moving from the amateur ranks to A Class in just a few years, Georgie has yet to prove himself a true champion of anything.

Last night was only his third time in Gardena, but he was sure his tires would hold if he went into turn three with the throttle open, sure that the dirt of Carrell Speedway wouldn't betray him. Georgie saw this track as he saw all tracks, the same simple ring with the promise of wide open space for the man brave enough to trade the most paint with his opponents. Everyone racing in A Class had one of four engines under their hoods, and sure the engine made you fast, but it was the driver who won the race. Georgie started this racing season by placing fifth at the Highway 99 in Modesto. In Bakersfield he took third, and just last week, at the Orange Bowl in San Bernardino, he finally walked away with a kiss on the cheek from Etiwanda Andrade, the Mexican-American beauty queen who appears at each race in a bathing suit and sunglasses to hand out the day's only trophy.

That kiss turned into a conversation, which turned into a phone number. Last Wednesday night, Georgie made plans with Etiwanda over the telephone. He promised her a win, and besides a second kiss on the grandstand, she agreed to have dinner somewhere afterwards. Georgie can't decide which is worse, wrecking his car or missing out on his date with Etiwanda, and he quickly arrives at the conclusion that both are nothing but bad, bad news.

Walt ties the apron around Georgie's neck and starts to spray his hair. He asks Georgie if he's been keeping cool, for it's been an unseasonable September. Smog has hazed the city, and the normally hot temperatures have soared into the hundreds and have stayed parked. As Walt begins cutting Georgie's hair, the mercury is close to ninety. In four hours, it's expected to peak in the San Gabriel Valley at 108 degrees.

Walt asks Georgie about last night's race and Georgie tells him it isn't worth talking about. "It was going good," he says. "My only competition was a guest entry from Tucson who was holding a shaky lead going into lap ninety-five." Walt sprays Georgie's hair with more water. When he cocks Georgie's head to catch the right light, Georgie winces and stops talking.

Last night, behind the wheel of the roadster, Georgie told himself there was no reason why he couldn't push a hundred going into turn three. Out of fear, no one else was breaking ninety miles an hour in Gardena's third turn. With four laps to go in the race, Georgie saw himself whipping ahead of the pack, emerging from turn three with nothing ahead of him but empty space and that second kiss from Etiwanda. As the pack of roadsters reverberated with downshifting, Georgie pictured his leg made of steel, his foot carved from stone. The gas pedal remained flat against the floorboard, and Georgie was certain, from his head to his gear box, that he couldn't be stopped by physics.

SEÑORITA ETIWANDA ANDRADE, REINA DE CHURUBUSCO, Queen of the Black and White Ball. For the duration of this summer's racing season, Georgie kept a picture of Etiwanda Scotch-taped between the fuel and speed gauges on his dashboard. The picture came from a newspaper clipping cut from Section II of the *Times,* one day after her coronation in mid-May. In the photo, the tiara on Etiwanda's head is tilted at an angle, her hands holding her trophy by its heavy wooden base. There have been nights, long nights spent alone in the shop, when Georgie has sat in his roadster and has done nothing more than smile back at Etiwanda, pretending that their eyes are locked, her gaze fixed on him. Once at a timing meet in Russetta, dehydrated from racing and dizzy from the vibrations of the crankshaft under his seat, Georgie swore that she nodded to him as the roadster flew across the hard desert floor. However, he has kept all of this to himself.

The accompanying article is taped to the lamp on Georgie's nightstand. Beginning in May, and all through June, he spent his nights memorizing the small gray square of text, running the four sentences through his mind until they replaced the heat and the smell of motor oil to send Georgie off to sleep:

QUEEN PRESENTED WITH TROPHY

A stately 22-year-old El Monte señorita is the proper and fitting queen of Southern California's bevy of Latin-American beauties. Señorita Etiwanda Andrade, of 11335 Medina Court, reigned at the 16th annual Black and White Ball at the Los Angeles Breakfast Club, sponsored by Stoltz Lincoln. Her selection was based on beauty, personality, education, and personal appearance from a field of eight candidates by a board of judges, which included the Cuban consul, four Los Angeles newspapermen, one of Mexico's movie queens, and Bill Stoltz, owner of three Southern California Lincoln dealerships. As queen, Señorita Andrade's primary responsibility will be to represent Stoltz Lincoln at regional California Racing Association events.

It's the beginning of the second sentence that Georgie has studied closest. He's turned the numbers of Etiwanda's address and the name of her street over and over in his mind, but he's too afraid to actually go and see the place. Each time that he's considered visiting Medina Court, a series of new and childish fears envelopes him: What if she's already seeing someone? A girl like that's gotta be seeing someone. What if she sees me and recognizes me? What if she doesn't? What do I do then? The questions spring open like a set of trapdoors, and Georgie falls through one after another after another.

Much of this spring was spent sitting on his lumpy mattress, eyes closed, content to imagine Etiwanda's address in three huge dimensions, to study it from different angles and pretend as though Etiwanda would be hiding in the curves and crevices of the type if only he looked closely enough. Since his win in July, Georgie has raced all over the state with her in his mind. Thoughts of Etiwanda rode with him at Huntington Beach Speedway, Gilmore Stadium, Bonnelli Stadium in Saugus, and the S.C.T.A. time trials at El Mirage. Georgie sees himself standing on the winner's podium again, close enough to catch the shine on her lips, to simply smell her. Once at Sears, Georgie went through the women's department and sniffed all the perfumes, fruitlessly looking for the one he remembered as hers.

In the races before winning the Orange Bowl, Georgie did well with the exception of Huntington, where his radiator blew a hose, and he was forced to drop out early in a mad gush of steam. Even with oven mitts on, Link couldn't replace the torn hose because of the hot engine, and Georgie spent the rest of the afternoon on the tailgate of Link's truck, looking out into the parking lot for the blue Lincoln that brings Etiwanda to each event. In the other two races, Georgie came in second. He was beat by thirty-two hundredths of a second at Saugus, and by twenty-six hundredths at Bonnelli. Before San Bernardino, Georgie's guts had turned to sauerkraut in these moments. He made his way to the winner's podium, and looked at his boots when Etiwanda passed him to plant one on the cheek of Bill Paterson or Larry Soto or whoever happened to be this week's lucky man.

AFTER WALT'S, GEORGIE STOPS by the Woolworth's to buy some aspirin. He opens the jar while waiting in line, and he starts chewing a handful of the bitter pills as the cashier hands him his change. He takes a long drink from the water fountain to help him swallow the pasty mixture. From there, Georgie walks down Atlantic Boulevard, back toward Link's Speed Shop, the place he's lived the last four years.

Link Kelly has been Georgie's mechanic since Georgie left his brothers in an Illinois storm window factory to race professionally in California where the weather was warm and the prize money was big. Link's father was a Baptist who started preaching in the Texas badlands after the first World War and didn't stop until he talked his way clear out to Los Angeles. The way Link tells it, Old Man Kelly thought his son was a connection between the divine hands of Jesus and the wretched people here on Earth, and that's how he was named. Link has also told Georgie that sitting in church and listening to all the holy songs and sermons was like having someone throw pennies at his head for an hour.

In the Army, Link not only learned how a motor works, but he figured out different ways to improve its operation. Link owns five patents and no Bibles. Georgie's been working for him for six years, but it wasn't until two seasons ago that Link started turning the wrenches on Georgie's roadster. Right away, Georgie noticed the way it performed. Among other things, Link machined custom gears and piston rings. The differences with the new parts were small, but they were important. That first race with Link in the pits was the first time Georgie's roadster truly sounded the way the other cars sounded, and Georgie felt for the first time that he was competing on a level field.

Today the ten-minute walk back to the shop takes Georgie twenty, the sun beating down all the way. Georgie steps into the office, and, despite the heat, Link is behind the counter pouring what, most likely, isn't the morning's first mug of coffee. "There you are," he says. Link is tall and thin, with arms and legs that seem to be made of pipe cleaners, and a blond flattop that looks like he's trying to grow a broom. Some of the coffee spills out of his mug as he talks, and he steps back to avoid it. "The way you disappeared this morning, I thought you got hit by a car or captured by a flyin' saucer." Link sits on his stool and slaps the counter like he just told a joke. "How'd you like that for luck? You survive a crackup and then, *pow!*, you get kidnapped by little green Martians."

"I just been out walking," Georgie says, "walking and thinking."

"For three hours?" Link asks. "That musta been some walk."

The phone rings and Link answers. He takes a pencil and licks the tip and starts quoting prices and writing things down. He holds his hand up so Georgie will wait, but Georgie ignores him. He grabs one of the waiting room chairs and drags it into the warehouse through the doorway on his right, stopping a foot from the charred roadster. Even with three industrial fans blowing and the doors wide open, the warehouse is steaming and still smells of burned rubber and metal. It seems to Georgie as if his car is still burning, as if some part of it, some chamber inside the engine's core, is still on fire. Georgie sits and stares and takes a long, hard look. Because of the stink, he covers his mouth with his hand.

Georgie's been racing since he was fourteen, piloting midgets up and down the streets of suburban Chicago. He's been in a few crack-ups before, but this is the first car he's ever totaled. Halfway through the turn, Georgie could feel his tires slipping, the roadster sliding up the embankment toward the retaining wall as if someone on the other side was reeling him in. The rear of the car was put to the wall first, the force of the collision nearly tearing the rear axle away from the frame. Georgie vaguely remembers spinning light and a large flash as the roadster ricocheted, the other axle cracking when the front end hit the wall. This second impact lifted the car sideways and sent it rolling into the infield on two wheels. The other cars swerved, and, in the moment before Georgie reached the grass, he was inches away from striking the roadster running in second place.

Here in Link's garage, the roadster rests on four sad, misshapen rubber stumps. The tires' tread was torn away in the collision, the sidewalls collapsing in the fire, the steel belts now exposed in dull silver patches. Both the roadster's grille and nerfing bar are missing, along with the body panels on the right side. The left side of the body is crumpled. Fortunately for Georgie, the gas tank riding in the seat next to him was thrown clear, and the doors that took Link two days to weld shut had come loose in the impact. Georgie unbuckled himself and fell from the car when it stopped rolling. As someone pulled him away, the air he had just been breathing fed a burst of flame. Now, the steering wheel droops toward the ground and there is nothing left of the seat except the charred springs. The wooden floorboard is burnt away. The glass in all the gauges is cracked, the numbers blackened with soot, each exposed needle curled like an eyelash. Etiwanda's photo is gone.

The fans hum heavily, Link to Georgie's right, both men staring. A passing car honks emphatically, but they don't bother to look away.

"This came for you a little while ago," Link says.

Georgie takes the yellow telegram from Link's hand, sees the return address of the C.R.A. offices downtown, and shoves the envelope in his back pocket without bothering to open it. Whatever's inside can't be good.

"The car's gotta go out back until we can figure out if we can keep anything from it," Link says.

There are customized pieces in this hulk that Georgie still owes money on, pieces that probably welded together in the fire, forming a fused chunk of intricately carved steel. Georgie will be working until Christmas just to pay this chunk off. He watches Link roll the engine hoist over, and passes the thick three-quarter-ton chain back after Link slides it under the roadster and turns the hydraulic crank. Both men are quiet as the roadster slowly comes off the ground.

"Goddamn," Link mutters, his voice somber as if he's somehow seeing the roadster for the first time. "When they come apart on you, they really come apart."

"Yup," Georgie says.

He has given the last six years of his life to this car. He bought it from a widow in Pomona for thirty-five dollars. It belonged to her husband, but he died somewhere in Europe during the war, and she felt more comfortable riding the bus. The roadster wobbles slightly as they push it toward the lot of old hulks and broken parts that Link has out back.

The muscles ache in Georgie's back and shoulders, and with each step he hopes the aspirin he chewed earlier will kick in.

MOST OF THE '54 SEASON was spent running around with a girl named Ruthie Lee. Georgie was still banging around with the weekend racers in "C" class when he met her. Ruthie Lee was from Pasadena, and hung around the pit area of the Glendale Fairgrounds like they were handing out twenty-dollar bills. A looker with big black hair and a purse full of French cigarettes, Ruthie Lee liked to drink. Don't get Georgie wrong, he's been shit-faced and wall-eyed plenty of times, but Ruthie Lee really liked to drink. When Georgie thought back, he couldn't remember a time when her lips didn't taste like some kind of booze.

Ruthie Lee also liked to smoke reefers and sometimes she shared her occasional funny cigarette with Georgie. He already had a tendency to worry, but Ruthie Lee's reefers made him downright paranoid. There were races at Glendale where Georgie suspected that every last nut and bolt on his roadster was loose, that the engine would somehow drop from the chassis as Link pushed the car off the starting line. Pit stops turned into full-blown tune-ups. One time Georgie got out of the car, took off his driving gloves, and overtightened the carburetor manifold, stripping half the nuts. Link had to yank the wrenches from his hands, and shove him into the car to get it back in the race. His knuckles had been seared by the engine. He could barely hold the wheel, and eventually pulled out of the race, blowing a thin lead, but a lead nonetheless.

The ride back to the shop that afternoon was a quiet one, no radio. Link drove and Georgie alternated his hands in a small bucket of ice water. When they pulled in the Speed Shop's driveway, Link cut the engine and sat for a moment with his large ring of keys in his lap.

"Pull another bonehead stunt like that, and you'll be on your own." He didn't look at Georgie as he said this, but his tone was cold and clear, and for Georgie that flagged the end of things with Ruthie Lee.

GEORGIE DOESN'T HAVE MUCH BESIDES the knife in his boot and the twenty-three dollars in his wallet. Link doesn't have a second car he might race, and even if he did, the C.R.A. has suspended Georgie's racing license for the remaining five weeks of the season. The telegram that arrived earlier termed Georgie "a reckless hazard and a menace to the good name of stock car racing." He's also a couple hundred dollars in the hole to Link, and for all Georgie knows he might end up in the hospital with internal bleeding. Georgie's heard of guys getting into crack-ups, and two or three days later keeling over right on the street. Still, twenty-three dollars can buy dinner for two, and maybe a movie, or maybe a rock 'n' roll show at the Legion Stadium. Georgie knows that if he loses track of Etiwanda now, if he doesn't get on the phone and call her, he'll probably never have a reason to see her up close again.

He's got the number memorized—KLondike 9-8216. Georgie decides to use the phone in the office, because he can't hear anything in the garage over the droning of the fans. Georgie dials. The phone buzzes once and it buzzes again and as it buzzes a third time, Georgie can feel himself starting to sink inside. Someone picks up on the fourth buzz, and Georgie holds his breath and says, "Hello."

The girl on the line's other end says "Yeah," instead of "Hello." She sounds clearly annoyed, sounds as if Georgie had spoken another language where "Hello" meant "Fuck you." Georgie asks for Etiwanda and the girl asks, "Who's this?"

"It's Georgie. Georgie Kuluzni. I'm a friend of hers from the racetrack."

"Hold on." Georgie hears the girl put the phone down. He flips on a small desk fan that blows warm air in his face. Georgie closes his eyes and rubs a spot of soreness in his neck.

"Yes." Etiwanda's voice is the complete, comforting opposite of the first one, soft and cool as melting ice cream. In a perfect world, it would be a capsule for Georgie's aches and pains.

"Etiwanda? It's Georgie."

"Georgie? Oh Georgie, how are you?"

"I'm fine." Georgie winces as he switches the telephone to his other ear. "Just some bumps and bruises."

"My God, you're lucky to be alive. I saw the whole thing. It was awful. They didn't stop the race, and the other cars didn't even slow up, and when I tried to get down to the track to see you, the guards wouldn't let me through."

"I don't remember seeing you come down," Georgie says. "In fact, I don't remember too much of the whole thing."

Georgie tells Etiwanda some of what he's pieced together from last night. He was out cold for almost an hour, and when he woke up, the race was long over. Most of the people were gone, except for the gawkers who gathered around the smoldering roadster. Link borrowed a winch from one of the other crews and pulled the hulk onto the trailer and drove it back to the shop. Georgie tells Etiwanda that he couldn't sleep, but he doesn't tell her about sitting up the rest of the night with a fifth of Dixie Belle and a fire extinguisher in case the car should flare back up, about jabbing his knife into the soft rubber of the deformed tires, and kicking the body panels until he collapsed. Georgie was never prone to weeping, but last night he came close.

Georgie asks Etiwanda who won, and she says she doesn't remember the guy's name. "He was the guest entry from Tucson. Number 229, I think."

Georgie nods and swallows, his ability to make conversation, good and interesting conversation, slipping from him. "Yeah. Well listen, I was wondering if you still wanted to get together. Maybe tonight, if you don't already have plans." Georgie stares at the silver blur of the fan blade, and though it hurts, he wraps the phone cord around his fingers.

"I'm sorry Georgie, but I already have an engagement." Georgie wants to bang his head on the counter as Etiwanda tells him she's busy with Crawford's Supermarket's Fall Festival. "I'm supposed to pull the curtain on something called The Big Cheese. They tell me it's a two-ton block of cheddar."

Georgie recovers a bit, and asks if she'd like to go to dinner before that. "I'll pick you up," he says.

"Should you even be driving right now?"

"I'm fine," Georgie says. " I could pick you up at six or seven o'clock. Whenever you're ready."

"I don't know, Georgie. You wouldn't have much fun just sitting there, watching me smile and sign autographs for people. And what about the car? Having the Lincoln with me at events is part of my contract, and it's not like either one of us is on the list of approved drivers. Maybe we could get dinner some other time. Right now, the whole thing sounds too complicated."

"I'd really like to see you tonight," Georgie says. "It doesn't have to be complicated."

Things get quiet. There's the oppressive droning of the fans, and Link hosing the black smudges left on the warehouse floor by the roadster. The distant sound of a rooster crowing comes through the receiver in Georgie's hand, but there's nothing else, nothing important, until Etiwanda says, "Let me check on something, and I'll call you back in five minutes."

Georgie gives her the number to the shop, and he doesn't hang up the phone until he hears the click on the other end.

Not long after Ruthie Lee, Georgie met a woman named Claudette. Claudette was a typist in the advertising department of the *San Gabriel Tribune*. Link ran an ad for the Speed Shop in their sports section, and Georgie met Claudette when he dropped in to pay for the month's advertisements. He told her a joke and made her laugh, and they met for dinner that night. They made plans for Saturday and that turned into six months of lunch dates. When it was sunny they'd go to Almanzor Park, or they'd stop by The Hat for pastramis and soggy French fries, or sometimes they'd stay and brown-bag it, eating Claudette's homemade tuna salad sandwiches on the benches in front of the *Tribune's* office.

Against Link's advice, Georgie was still driving the roadster around town, risking the impound for breaking the vehicle code. Whenever Georgie took Claudette anyplace, she would tie bright scarves over her hair that matched her skirt and her shoes. Georgie would tap the gas pedal, and the engine would rumble, and Claudette would recoil as though a wild animal was clawing its way through the firewall. Georgie couldn't go over forty-five miles an hour with her in the car. Claudette would watch his speedometer as he drove, following the needle and gripping the seat so firmly with her bare hands that her nails left marks. When Georgie told Link about this, Link laughed and told Georgie to make her wear mittens so she wouldn't ruin the leather.

Georgie couldn't get very far with Claudette. She was saving herself, and each time things managed to get interesting, they were quelled by Claudette's talk of rings and wedding dresses and honeymoon suites in Hawaii. Claudette was fond of reading the society section of the newspaper on Mondays and sighing at the pictures of the brides who were married over the weekend.

All of Claudette's pent-up energy went into the one thing she enjoyed most: dancing. Claudette knew the bunnyhop and the mambo, the stroll and the walk, the jitterbug and the cha cha cha. Her favorite song was something called "The Woodpecker Rock," and on Friday nights she'd bug Georgie for nickels to call KFWB so that the disk jockey would get it on the radio. Georgie never really went for music in a big way. Whenever music was playing—if there was a radio around, if something she liked came on the jukebox, or a car went by blaring— Claudette's foot would start tapping and Georgie would get nervous.

LINK IS DRYING HIS HANDS on his shirt when he comes into the office. Georgie waits until he's refilled his coffee mug before asking if he can borrow his car that night. Link drives an emerald-green '48 Chevy, a two-door with shaved handles, a bull-nosed hood and custom black-and-white leather upholstery. Link takes a sip of his coffee, and gives Georgie a quizzical look. "Why?"

Even though Link knows what Georgie had planned for last night, Georgie explains the current situation with Etiwanda in careful detail. Link listens and shakes his head. "I'm sorry, Georgie, but after last night, you could have a date with Lana Turner, and I still wouldn't loan you my car."

The telephone rings as Link steps out of the office. Georgie says hello and he listens for a few moments and says that six sounds great, that he'll pick her up, no problem, that he's got a great restaurant in mind for dinner. He copies down some directions and smiles as he hangs up the phone.

Link is watching from the doorway. "Okay," he says, "you can take the truck." He takes a long sip of his coffee, then nods toward the pick-up parked out front, the '46 Ford with its faded and flaking yellow paint, the old machine smudged with hundreds of greasy handprints. The hinges on its driver door are rusted shut, the cab steeped in sweat and gasoline, but its engine is as sturdy as a Clydesdale. "It won't be towing anything in the near future."

AFTER CLAUDETTE CAME MISS PEARL. Miss Pearl was older, Italian and widowed. She owned a hair salon over on Las Tunas, and the rumor was that Miss Pearl had poisoned her husband with the same chemicals she used to make curly hair straight and straight hair curly. Georgie met Miss Pearl at the bar during a fellow racer's wedding reception. She insisted that he call her "Miss," and she dangled her fingers in front of him and said, "See, no rings."

After Georgie bought her a few Greyhounds, they went back to her apartment in Alhambra. Miss Pearl had pillows stuffed with down and a mattress that cupped Georgie like a nest. She kept a large picture on the dresser across from the bed, a portrait of her late husband, Harold, wearing an expression so serious that it appeared carved from fine wood. Midway through the act, Georgie opened his eyes and saw Miss Pearl's gaze fixed on Harold. Afterwards Miss Pearl and Georgie slept, and Georgie dreamt that there were ducks squawking in Miss Pearl's living room, that her mattress was indeed filled with feathers, that Miss Pearl sat with a bird at the foot of the bed, and yanked them out one by one.

In the daytime, Miss Pearl wore a green uniform with her name embroidered in white stitching, and no matter how much she scrubbed, her hands still smelled like chemicals. Georgie told her about the regularity of his haircuts, and she insisted on trimming his hair from that point forward. When he wouldn't let her, they squabbled over Georgie's greasy, curly crown. The fight escalated, Miss Pearl first hurling her half-finished highball at Georgie's head. Then came a glass ashtray. If it was ever in Georgie to hit a woman, Miss Pearl would have been the one. She accused him of not trusting her, and, rather than give her the honest answer, he left.

He stopped at a diner where he ordered an early breakfast, scrambled eggs and sausage with sourdough toast, orange juice with extra ice. He flipped through a rumpled newspaper while he waited, and ran into the article with Etiwanda. It was the photo that immediately struck Georgie. He studied Etiwanda carefully, the substantial bouquet and her heavy-looking trophy, the way her smile eclipsed the twinkling crown on her head. Something in the plain and simple joy of the moment displaced all thoughts of Miss Pearl, of Claudette and Ruthie Lee and all the other women Georgie had known in between.

Georgie tore out the article, and, sitting there at the diner counter, after reading and rereading the caption and knowing Etiwanda Andrade would be there this Saturday and every Saturday for the next twenty-two weeks, Georgie found his purpose in racing renewed. The season's starting race was in two weeks at the Speed Bowl in Porterville. The prospect of winning it consumed Georgie so immediately that his hunger subsided and he left his eggs and sausages untouched. He took the toast and the paper with him, and when Link came to work the next morning and raised the warehouse doors, he found Georgie tinkering with the roadster to secure every last fraction of speed.

GEORGIE CAN'T TELL IF THE HEAT or his nerves are making him sweat. The fifteen-minute drive from Link's Speed Shop in San Gabriel to Etiwanda's house in El Monte has taken him half an hour because he couldn't stay on the expressway. Georgie's running late, ten minutes late at this point, and though he's worried about the time, his chest was seized with a choking fear when he checked his mirror and saw the traffic thrusting toward him. It was as if God had placed Georgie in His hand and squeezed like King Kong. As the cars zoomed past, horns blaring, the truck running out of on-ramp, Georgie felt like the engineer of an antique locomotive, the equipment in his hands and at his feet suddenly unfamiliar, their operations confusing and foreign. Georgie exited quickly, and even though he's complained about the truck's poor performance every time he's driven it, even though Etiwanda's probably tapping her toe and checking the clock, Georgie doesn't mind going slow tonight.

Georgie doesn't have any change on him to call Etiwanda. It wouldn't look good to call her collect, and even if there was a nickel in his pocket, Georgie's not about to tell her about this new phobia. To make up some time, Georgie decides to go down Valley Boulevard instead of taking Garvey into El Monte. The banks and movie theaters and department stores with shiny display windows give way to thrift stores and feed shops with gold pyramids made of hay, the buildings progressively dilapidated as Georgie nears Medina Court.

Georgie's done his best to improve the truck. Though he was too sore to give it a decent cleaning, he covered the bench seat's stains and splotches with a clean bedsheet. He also swiped a few air fresheners from the shop. Somewhere along the way, Georgie pulls over to change into his maroon, short-sleeve shirt that's been dangling behind him on a hanger to keep it clean and crisp. Multiple flashes of pain ignite, especially in his shoulders, his left side shuddering as he straightens his collar in the rearview mirror. He puts the truck into gear and adjusts his hair with a comb, waiting for the traffic to dissipate. Georgie's fingers become tacky from his pomade, and he wipes them on the bedsheet as the truck eases onto the street.

Medina Court is a narrow road, some houses more ramshackle than others, with dead brown lawns and the occasional thin, sickly tree. There are no curbs and no sidewalks. Georgie spots Etiwanda's blue Lincoln in a driveway, and he drives past it, turning the truck around. He parks across the street. A tough bunch of Mexican kids a few houses down stop smoking their cigarettes and guarding their mailbox, and Georgie can feel their gaze evaluating him as he walks up to Etiwanda's house. 11335 Medina Court is a small blue house, light blue that's chipped away in spots to show the white plaster underneath.

Georgie presses the doorbell, but it doesn't ring. He knocks once, then he knocks again. He can hear something going on behind the door, and, when it finally opens, the young Mexican woman standing before him is so small that it takes Georgie a second to discern that she's not a child. It takes him two more seconds to figure out that the black patch over the woman's right eye is real.

"Hi," Georgie says. "I'm here for Etiwanda."

The woman looks up at him and uses her hand to shield her good eye. "Yeah," she says. "Of course you are."

Georgie steps inside. The woman shuts the door and goes back to a couch that sits in the center of the living room. On the coffee table, along with some scissors, envelopes, and a sheet of stamps, is a stack of newspapers. The woman ignores Georgie and picks up a paper, resuming the project he apparently interrupted. She casts the first section aside, and Georgie recognizes its headline from the day following Etiwanda's coronation—9 "PACHUCOS" HELD IN BIZARRE MURDER CASE. The woman turns to Section II and begins cutting.

Had Georgie been welcomed, he might've asked her for a copy, a replacement for the one he lost last night, but he wasn't, and so he just stands there, forcing a smile. Earlier he thought about buying flowers, but in recalling the oversized bundle of roses Etiwanda had held in the newspaper photo, Georgie's pride convinced him that any bouquet he might scratch together on his thin twenty-three-dollar budget would be pointless, practically an insult. Now he wishes he'd stopped for a simple rose of his own to keep him from feeling so purposeless. Georgie stretches the ache in his left shoulder. He jams his hands in his pockets, and stares at the pile of newspapers as longingly as a man possibly can.

"They're for the family in Mexico."

Georgie looks up and there she is.

"Those newspapers have been sitting there for five months and we're just getting around to sending them to the little fan club my tías have started down there." Etiwanda's wearing a red blouse, a charcoal skirt, and matching red heels. Her curly hair is pinned up, piled atop her head like an assortment of dark exotic seashells. Georgie apologizes for being late and Etiwanda squeezes his arm and tells him it's all right. "It's really good to see you," she says. Along with her purse, she takes a white sash hanging from a hat rack, its words printed in black letters: SEÑORITA DE LAS AMERICAS.

She tells the woman that she might be home late. "I'll bring you a piece of cheese," Etiwanda says, and, without looking up from the envelope she's addressing, the woman tells her, "Don't do me any favors."

Georgie steps aside to let Etiwanda shut the door. "Would you believe that she's my sister?" she says. "I have to pay her to do this."

They walk out to the truck, Etiwanda's heels clicking on the concrete as they pass the blue Lincoln. Georgie asks how she got out of the obligation with the car dealership, and Etiwanda points to the tires and tells Georgie that she let the air out. "You can't drive a car with four flats," she says with a smile. "And it's not my fault if Mister Stoltz can't get someone out here to change them in time. Besides, Jorge will be grateful for the night off." Etiwanda explains that her cousin Jorge usually drives the Lincoln for her. "Jorge's seventeen and he's barely learned how to drive, but I lied and told Mister Stoltz that he's twenty-two. He's a good kid. Sometimes, I'll bring my case of 45s and Jorge will play them. He'll drive slow so the record won't skip, and I'll sit in the back and pretend that I'm a starlet." Etiwanda laughs and puts her hand over her mouth, looking around after she says this.

They get to the truck and Georgie explains about the driver door not opening. He slides across the seat and Etiwanda looks at the sheet skeptically before getting in. When she does, Georgie starts up the truck. The motor catches and Georgie puts both hands on the wheel. Before pulling away from the curb, he takes a deep breath that jabs a needle into his chest. He looks at Etiwanda, smiling and hoping she didn't notice. They drive past the tough guys on the corner, and one of them whistles. Another says something in Spanish that Georgie can't understand. Etiwanda blushes.

It's still hot when Etiwanda and Georgie arrive at a dimly lit restaurant on Rosemead Boulevard. The place is called The Chuck Wagon, and the hostess seats them in back, in a brown leather booth with a glass table laid over a wooden wagon wheel. A waitress arrives with menus, and Georgie orders a Pabst. Etiwanda gets ice water. A few minutes later, Georgie gets winter food despite the heat, meat loaf with mashed potatoes and green beans on the side. Etiwanda decides on a Coke and a salad and the chicken-fried steak.

Alone, they sit silently in the racket of clanking dishes and other people's chatter. Etiwanda looks around. She shifts, apparently uncomfortable in her seat.

"What's wrong?" Georgie asks.

"I just noticed something," Etiwanda says. "Take a look at this place."

Georgie glances around The Chuck Wagon and doesn't see anything unusual. Their waitress is wiping the table two booths down. Across from them, a baby girl in a high chair throws a biscuit, striking the mural of smiling cowboys that runs the length of the restaurant. The baby claps with delight, oblivious to her scolding parents. The other waitress is busy behind the counter, filling the glass case with slices of cherry pie, and joking with the hostess who's changing the roll of paper in the cash register.

"What is it?"

It didn't occur to Georgie that everyone in the restaurant would be white, that there might be places in this world where you might not take a Mexican, even if she is a beauty queen.

"Never mind," Etiwanda says. "It's just me." She takes a sip of her water, and uses her napkin to carefully wipe away the lipstick print left on the glass. "I'm a little tired of all these official events." Etiwanda tells Georgie about her other obligations besides the Big Cheese and C.R.A. races. "The worst are the appearances at supermarkets and department stores," she says. "Every time I go to one of these functions, there will be some—" Etiwanda looks at Georgie and pauses to find the right word, "some person, some housewife or a group of teenage boys, someone who talks to me like I shouldn't understand English. When I answer them, they're always surprised. Last week, this old woman actually congratulated me on spelling her name right." Etiwanda laughs a little. "I guess I'm happy this whole 'Señorita' thing is only temporary."

Georgie asks what she plans on doing when it's all over. Etiwanda smiles and cocks her head as though a photo of her future is framed on the wall. "I think going to school would be nice."

"To study what?" Georgie asks.

"I'm not sure. I've always been good with numbers. Maybe business? Maybe accounting? All I know," she says, giving Georgie a quick glimpse of the tiara in her purse, "is that this won't last forever."

Georgie nods, and, in doing so, notices that Etiwanda is wearing the same silver necklace that she had in her newspaper photo. The necklace catches the light and he offers Etiwanda a drink of his beer, but she declines.

"I want you to call me Wanda," she says. "See, when we were kids, my family moved all around Riverside, and my dad named us for the different streets in the city because he was so happy to be in the States. Maggie's whole name is Magnolia, and we had a younger sister, God rest her soul, whose name was Madison."

Wanda makes the sign of the cross when she finishes. "Maggie's really jealous of all this beauty queen stuff," she says. "Maggie wanted to be the beauty queen in the Andrade family. She had won a title—Miss Teenage Casablanca—when she was sixteen. The year after, though, Maggie fooled around with this guy and his fiancée came after her with a bicycle chain. That's how she lost her eye."

Georgie says, "Ouch," and, in trying to make a joke, he manages to remind himself of his own pain. He takes two of the six aspirin in his shirt pocket and follows them with a swallow of beer. Wanda asks if he's all right and Georgie says, "Yeah, it's just the bruises from the crack-up. I'll be okay."

Wanda smirks.

"What?" Georgie asks.

"You and your 'crack-ups.' You're just like all the other guys."

Georgie can't recall the moment when the term entered his vocabulary, who exactly he learned it from. All he knows is that for as long as he's been behind the wheel, he's never used the word "accident" for any scrape he's been involved with.

"One of the first things you learn," Georgie says, "is that if anything bad happens, it's always the car's fault. Calling something an 'accident' says that things are out of your hands. It says that whatever happened wasn't what the driver intended to do. But drivers can't be wrong. You can't say you made a wrong decision on the track, because you'll start second-guessing yourself. It'll make you think too much, make you think about traveling that fast, make you think about how soft your body really is compared to everything else around it." Georgie goes quiet. He stares at the napkin dispenser and taps it with his fingernail. When he speaks, his mood is tainted, indignant. "You let that happen and you'll be too afraid to stick the key in the ignition."

"So the car always breaks down? Never the driver?" Wanda looks around the table as if the cowboys in the murals are eavesdropping. She leans in close to Georgie and moves the napkin dispenser aside, lowering her voice to a whisper. "Was it the car that drove into the wall last night? The car that was trying so hard for first place?"

Georgie slides back to his side of the booth and fights the urge to crawl under the table. Wanda takes his hands in hers. She rubs the rough calluses, the scars and burn marks on Georgie's hands. "Just between the two of us, is that what really happened?"

Georgie looks up. He shakes his head sheepishly.

"You ask me, I think you did the right thing," Wanda says. "The whole time I was up in the grandstands, I was hoping the winner would be you."

When the waitress brings the bill for dinner, Wanda asks her the time. It's a quarter to eight. Wanda gathers her things and Georgie pays, not bothering to wait for any change. Outside, the sun has almost finished setting. They get in the truck and Georgie fumbles with the names and directions of different surface streets until Wanda declares that the fastest way from the Chuck Wagon to Crawford's Market is on the expressway.

Down the street there's an entrance, and what little glare is left from the sundown finds its way into Georgie's eyes as the truck curves up the on-ramp. He presses the gas pedal hard and pumps the clutch to move the truck through its first few successive gears. The truck shudders, lurching forward as if someone yanked on the grille, and Georgie apologizes. Wanda simply smiles. Georgie checks his mirrors as the expressway approaches. He hangs his arm out the window to signal, and he sticks out his head to judge the space behind him.

Georgie merges into the first lane while Wanda removes her lipstick and compact from her purse. She holds the round mirror in her palm and works her lipstick with a calm and steady hand. She kisses a tissue and crumples it into a tiny ball, and she shows no signs of tension, no nervousness, no wringing fingers, nothing. In fact, Wanda's only annoyance seems to be the temperature. She rolls down her window, then turns the knob on the smaller one in the corner, pushing the small triangle of glass outward so that cool evening air begins to fill the cab.

The needle on the speedometer rises as the truck moves among the other automobiles. Sixty-five. Seventy-five. Eighty-five miles per hour. The engine is laboring under Georgie's foot and the steering wheel shudders in his hands. He closes both sets of fingers and ignores the pain by telling himself to hold on. Georgie had a crazy-son-of-a-bitch uncle named Leonard, a marine who returned from the South Pacific with a piston tattooed on the length of each forearm. Leonard taught Georgie to drive in the narrow and bumpy roads that separated the nearby fields. His chief advice to young Georgie was basic. "You let go of that wheel, and all hell will break loose. You hold on and you can beat anybody." Georgie recalls the fragrant tomatoes and the short trees filled with apples, recalls how it felt to have command over the machine slicing the green blur of the outside world in two. These are Georgie's earliest recollections of speed, of the tremendous burst of pleasure that surges through him when he knows he's faster than anyone else.

The Valley Boulevard exit approaches, less than a quarter mile away. Wanda takes her carefully folded sash from her purse and holds the band of white silk in her lap. Georgie changes lanes without looking, cutting left around a moving van, cutting right to avoid a slow-moving station wagon. He can tell exactly where the other cars are, remembers their positions around him, how fast they're going, and how much faster he needs to be, the calculations immediate and natural. Georgie can feel the engine working, the compression in each cylinder, the pistons rising and falling, falling and rising. He can feel the valves' delicate pitter-patter, the intake closing, the exhaust opening, each instantaneous and explosive stroke happening over and over and over again. Georgie's secured the truck's toil in his grip. He's not reckless. He's driving, and he's certain Wanda won't be late.

RIDING WITH LENCHO

1 9 8 9

My buddy Lencho has another problem. He thinks the thermostat on his Regal is shot, so we've been driving for the last hour with the heat on full blast to keep the needle down on the temperature gauge. We work in the body shop at Kuluzni Auto Repair and Salvage over on Peck, but Lencho's been collecting disability checks since his old lady Josie got pissed at him for always being tired. I don't know the whole story, but while he stayed with me, I found out most of the big parts. Between working full-time, night classes twice a week, and Josie's little girl, Mayra, Lencho was a pretty busy guy. One night Josie was yelling about something, and, in the middle of getting crazy, she knocked over the coffee maker and the boiling coffee burned him. The way he was sleeping at the table, Lencho's hands and arms got the worst of it.

Lencho pulls the car over but leaves it running. He gets out and walks to the edge of the cliff, stretching and yawning before undoing his belt to piss on the beach below. The ocean is on our side of the highway, on the other a wide empty field that leads to some low foothills. The heat in the car has made me sleepy, and I've been drifting in and out since somewhere around Camp Pendleton. Crossing the border is the last thing I remember, Lencho nudging me with his elbow as he nodded and smiled at the Mexican policemen guarding their booths with oversized hats and chests full of bright medals.

I get out and piss too. "Where we at?" I ask.

"Somewhere between Tijuana and Rosarito," Lencho says. "About twenty minutes to go."

We turn back onto the highway when I finish, the road curving away from the ocean after about a mile. As thanks for letting him stay at my place, Lencho invited me to the house that used to be his grandma's for a weekend of partying. He's had his bandages off a few weeks now, and he said he's been wanting to get out of town, promising beer and women so I'd come along. If I knew ahead of time about the thermostat and riding with the heat on, I definitely would have said no. We come up on some small roadside houses and a bonfire burning a big pile of trash. The flames crackle in the twilight, feeding a thick black tail of smoke that stretches across the highway. We go through it and roll the windows up to keep the smell out, but some of the smoke still manages to get in the car. I hold my breath, drops of sweat rolling down my chest, wetting my tank top, the heat feeling worse to me than before.

I don't see how Lencho can stand to keep his thermal on. It's long-sleeved and navy blue, the material around his neck and armpits darkened with sweat and circled with white salt rings. I know that, since the accident, Lencho doesn't like to show his arms or hands, but staying covered up in this heat is ridiculous. When we get away from the fire, I roll down my window and Lencho takes one hand off the wheel to crank his down too. He's wearing gloves. They're the mesh kind, black with the fingers cut off, his fingers pink as a baby's.

LENCHO CAME TO WORK WITH US about five years ago. Things had been busy around the shop, and Lencho's uncle Hector made a deal with Georgie to get me the extra help. Lencho had been in some boys' home, and he was still cut with the muscles he'd developed while he was away. The first time we talked, he told me about keeping a shortened, daily version of the workout he followed there. Lencho had tattoos, a few on each arm, but on his neck was the one that made him proudest of handling the pain. His last name had been inked in inch-high letters just to the right of his Adam's apple, so that when Lencho had his coveralls on, his name would peek out from the collar of his undershirt.

Georgie's business was going good at the time. There were cars waiting to be primered and painted, fenders to be fixed, doors with dents to be pounded out. Lencho figured out his way with a slide-hammer and a disk sander real quick, and that September the work was just falling into our laps.

In the winter, things slowed down. I remember Lencho and I having contests to see who could work the point of a screwdriver around our fingers the fastest. One day, he started taking spare parts that were lying around with the idea of putting together a little man. He called it a mascot. Lencho used a muffler for a body, and sections of old tailpipes for the arms and legs. The legs were heated and bent to make feet that were welded to an old rim for a base. Lencho brazed lug nuts to an oil filter for a head with a nose and a pair of eyes. I held each piece in place for him with pliers, my eyes closed to the sparking white light. Even though the pliers' handles were coated with rubber, I could feel the heat from the blue flame in my hands as Lencho worked his way around each attachment, and it was a relief every time he put the torch down to admire his work.

WE GET BACK ON THE STRIP, and I tell Lencho that the next two crates of beer will be on me. He says sure, making a right turn onto another paved street where the windshield turns bright with the sunset glare. Even with the visors flipped down and our hands over our eyes, it's hard to see. The vents are still blowing hot air, and it feels like our destination's by the sun instead of by the ocean. When we reach the end of the street, I can see the water, but Lencho turns the car away from the beach, up a new road. He stops, groaning as he looks at the muddy street ahead of us. Lencho parks the Regal even though the houses don't start for another twenty yards.

I get out and pull off my tank top and enjoy the ocean breeze. I tuck my shirt into the waistband of my Dickies, and notice what Lencho was groaning about. The street is wet, not from the ocean, but from the gushing of a busted water pipe in the middle of the road, about eight houses down. "That thing's been cracked almost every time I've been here," Lencho says.

He unlocks the trunk and I grab the cooler with the block of ice we just bought. He gets both crates of beer, and, between the empty lot and his uncle's house, the asphalt under our feet turns to thick and slippery mud.

The locals have set out some wooden planks and strips of plywood by the left side of the road. I follow Lencho to Hector's place, which turns out to be the first house we get to. It's made of yellow and brown bricks the color of bananas and fudge. There's a concrete driveway, and a small yard that's bare except for a mound of dirt and a tall braid of cactus growing off in one corner. The place is surrounded by a low stone wall topped with sections of wrought iron. Lencho looks for the right key to the front gate, and I notice the difference between this place and the houses around us.

The neighboring homes are all run-down and pieced together, with dingy, faded paint and broken or missing windows. Instead of a front door, the house across the street has a section cut from a Carta Blanca billboard, half of the red-and-gold logo swinging open on a squeaky hinge. Lencho's uncle's house looks like a part-time home compared to the others, somewhere for summer vacations, not daily life. The only visible damage to the place is on the wrought iron, the paint bubbled from rust just like an old fender or a floorboard. Lencho unlocks the gate and black chips come off in my hand, the metal underneath them orange and corroded from the mixture of water and salt in the ocean air.

When we get inside, Lencho flips the light switch and nothing happens. He walks to the kitchen and flips another one. Nothing. Lencho goes outside, around to back of the house. His shadow glides past the living room window and the lights go on as I hear a switch being thrown in the fuse box. I pick up the cooler and set it on the floor in the kitchen.

Hector's house smells musty, like everything in here's been wet for a long time. The floor's made of the same cement as the driveway, and there are plenty of small rugs and mats trying to cover up the grayness. There's a TV, and at the far end of the living room is a door that probably leads to one of the bedrooms. I go back to the kitchen, and, through the open doorway at the other end, I see another bed. When Lencho comes back, he checks the stove for a pilot light. "No gas," he says. Lencho looks behind the front door, where there's a silver propane tank that's almost as tall as me, a crescent wrench sitting on top of it. Lencho puts the wrench in his pocket and we carry the heavy tank outside to the back of the house.

"Does Hector come down here much?" I ask, the base of the tank nearly cutting into my hand.

"Not too often," Lencho says. "We came a few times with Mini and Peter in the summer when the water was warmer." Lencho nods in the direction of the ocean.

Between the house and the stone wall, there's about two feet of space. We set the tank down near some fixtures and a water heater covered with cobwebs and orange padding. From here I can look into the neighbor's living room, where an old woman is watching Felix the Cat cartoons on a tiny black-and-white television. Lencho hooks the tank up with the crescent wrench. He turns the knob with his gloved hand and gas rushes into the house's pipes.

Lencho then takes a book of matches from his pocket and lights the pilot on the water heater. "Now we can shower," he says, stretching his hand, opening and closing his fist. "Let's get the sleeping bags. After cleaning up, we'll grab some tacos and head to a few bars I know on the strip."

We walk back to the house and I point to the crates of Bohemia. "We should probably put some of that beer on ice."

Lencho agrees. We bring the beer inside, and Lencho looks through the kitchen drawers for an ice pick. I start putting some bottles in the fridge and there's nothing inside but warm air, a bottle of Peñafel mineral water, and a shriveled lemon that looks like a walnut and vibrates from the sound of the fridge's motor working hard.

Lencho starts to break the block of ice apart with a screwdriver he's found. Sharp wedges crack off and fly from the rim of the cooler, shooting to different corners of the kitchen, until Lencho jumps up. He drops the screwdriver and runs to the sink. His eyes are shut. His jaw's clamped. I expect blood, but there's nothing coming from his hand but clear running water. Lencho yanks his right glove off and rubs the pink skin fiercely. I ask if he's okay and Lencho says yeah, adjusting the faucet handle with his left hand, trying to get the water to just the right temperature.

"Sometimes I can't hold things too tight for too long," he says. "It's pretty random. The nerves in my hand just go nuts and there's nothing I can do about it."

A YEAR AGO, I met a fine-ass girl named Marisol. We were at a party her boyfriend was DJ-ing, and she looked bored with him. She told me she had gone to Rio Hondo and was transferring to UCLA in the fall. Marisol gave me her number, and two days later I registered at Rio Hondo so we'd have something to talk about when I called her, something to fill the big spaces I imagined our conversations having. I was twenty-five at the time and hadn't picked up a book in eight or nine years.

I waited in a long line of other people registering late. They gave us these tiny golf pencils to fill out the one registration form. I wrote my name and filled in the appropriate bubble for each letter. The only courses that were still open were College Algebra One and World History One. I signed up for the algebra, the first part of a year-long course, and spent three bucks on a notepad with RIO HONDO on the front and fifty-some dollars on a used textbook. When I got home, I flipped through the pages. I had chosen math because history was naptime, and I could always balance my checkbook when I sat down to write out my bills once a month. Sitting on my couch, I became dizzy from all the shifting numbers in the examples. When I called Marisol that night, the answering machine I got had a different girl's voice.

I left my first message and started going to class. College Algebra One was in a room the size of a small theater, and I sat in the back. I can't honestly say that I tried, because I soon discovered that algebra was a tangle of numbers whose knots would get tighter when I started moving the figures around in my brain. After three classes and three unanswered messages on what I hoped was Marisol's machine, I looked at my book and wondered what the hell I was thinking. At work the next day, I told Lencho about it and he laughed.

"You should finish the class anyway," he said. "If you want, I'll come down and check it out with you."

The next night, me, Lencho, and Mayra sat in one of the front rows, Mayra scribbling in a coloring book, Lencho writing things down, and me trying to keep up. They started coming with me and getting more out of it than I was. By Halloween I had decided to drop out. When I told Lencho, he offered to buy my book. He gave me twenty bucks and I took it and threw in the notepad for free.

I WAKE UP AND EVERYTHING is orange and stuffy. The material from the sleeping bag sticks to my face. I get up and find the bathroom and piss. I stumble around, looking for my toothbrush, the throbbing bump on my head making the big teddy bear in the corner of the room seem weirder, especially since I don't remember either from the night before. I brush my teeth and thank God for the jar of aspirin in the medicine cabinet. In the kitchen, I get a beer from the fridge to wash down a few white pills, and try to piece last night together.

I remember eating tacos from a stand where the guy cooked carne asada on a grill in front of you and chopped it to pieces on an old wooden board. His wife warmed the tortillas and filled them with meat and salsa and onions. The tacos were small and cheap, fifty cents each, and me and Lencho must've spent twenty dollars there. Then we were at this bar, I can't remember what it was called. I was talking broken Spanish to this local girl with a ribbon in her hair. She would try out some of her English on me and we would laugh about the funny way our words came out. American music was playing, and I remember chasing tequila shots with Tecate, and hearing the Beastie Boys once or twice. Then things turn hazy until I get to the part where me and Lencho were thrown out after the Stray Cats came on and I flung my beer mug at the jukebox.

I go back to the bedroom and put on my pants, wishing I could remember that girl's name as I look around the house for Lencho. He's not in the other bedroom. His sleeping bag's unrolled on the bed, but it's zipped up and flat like his body never touched the mattress. There's also nothing to eat. I finish half of my beer and pour out the rest before putting on my shoes and walking outside. The Regal's in the driveway, mud sprayed all over the door and fender. I leave the front door unlocked and hope that Lencho isn't far. Out in the street, water isn't coming from the pipe like yesterday, but the dirt road still feels like a giant Hershey bar left in the sun. There are smooth skidmarks in the set of tire tracks that lead to the gate, and puddles of water where Lencho must've floored the Regal to make it through the mud.

I find a couple dollars in one of my pockets, and I go to the corner store, where a bag of chicharrones costs two hundred and twenty pesos. I ask the cashier if I can pay with a dollar. He nods sure and starts pushing buttons on a calculator to figure out the change. On the counter there's a jar of pigs' feet floating in cloudy water with jalapeños and slices of carrot, and my stomach does an odd, nauseous turn just looking at them. I tell the cashier not to bother with my change. From there I walk down to the beach, taking my shoes off when I reach the sand, cramming the rest of the chicharrones in my mouth and putting the bag in my pocket.

The sand is buzzing with flies. I don't know what time it is, but because there's no one on the beach except a bunch of seagulls and some old men with fishing poles, I'm guessing it's still pretty early. I wander for a while, and farther down the shore I hear Lencho call my name. He's standing in the water, the foam rushing around his ankles, and he's waving like a castaway trying to flag down a plane. "Hey Manny," he yells. "Come here. You gotta check this out."

I walk over on the hard, wet sand, and Lencho's picked up this dead fish and he's holding it by the tail, shaking the small gray and blue thing back and forth like it's swallowed something very small and very valuable. "Do you know what this is?" he asks.

"Man, I've always hated fish," I tell him.

"Not me," Lencho says. "Me and my tía Mini cook fish all the time. I could make you a caldo de pescado that would change your mind." Lencho smiles and kisses his fingertips to show me just how delicious this soup would be. He hurls the fish at the ocean and we walk back to the house, past the pack of squawking seagulls, past the old men who throw their lines at the waves and reel up empty hooks from the white foam.

JOSIE WASN'T HAPPY WITH LENCHO when he got serious about going back to school. She said Lencho had no reason to learn all that fancy math, especially when it meant keeping Mayra out until ten o'clock on school nights. Josie and Lencho rented a small house over by the duck farm with a separate bedroom for Mayra, even though Lencho told me that Josie's daughter usually slept curled up with him. Josie worked at the Horseshoe Club over on Valley, a hole-in-the-wall with peanut shells that crunched when you walked in. She worked most nights from six to closing, one or two A.M. during the week, sometimes later on the weekends. Josie had long black hair and a big mouth. She was the kind of person that laughed too hard at beer commercials and bad jokes about wetbacks.

Josie wasn't exactly pretty either, but she had done some modeling once for a personals advertisement when she worked at the Pennysaver. Late one night at the Horseshoe Club, Josie showed me a folded copy of the ad. She pointed to her picture and said that she would still have her figure from six years ago if it wasn't for Mayra. Josie liked to wear bad jewelry too. Big plastic bangles hung from her wrists, matching the color she had picked for the season. Last year it was green, another year it was lavender, and all of Josie's outfits would have to match.

A while back, Lencho dropped by and we went to the Horseshoe Club for a beer. Lencho had just gotten an A– on his College Algebra

Two final. It was crowded for a Thursday, and as Nick the bartender poured us a couple of beers, I saw that Josie wasn't as impressed with Lencho's grade as he was.

"So what," she told Lencho. "So what. Where's Mayra?"

Lencho told Josie that she was across the street, asleep in the back seat of the Regal, and that was the first time I saw them fight in public. Josie yelled at Lencho and he yelled right back. It went on for a good ten minutes. When they were finished, things had turned so quiet that you could hear Lencho shift on his stool and Josie's steps as she walked away.

There are no windows in the Horseshoe Club, so Josie had to open the door to check on the Regal. She watched from the doorway for a few seconds, then walked back to the stool where I was sitting, waiting for Nick to finish pouring my second beer. "You started all this higher education bullshit," she said. "You took Lencho to that school. You gave him your fuckin' book."

Nick put the mug in front of me, and I slapped my money on the bar as Josie wedged herself between the stools.

"Do you know that Lencho cares more about that book than he does about me?"

"Hey, leave him alone," Lencho said.

But Josie turned her back on him and got so close that I could count her eyelashes.

"That's fine," she said. "I can deal with that. But I'll tell you what, Manny. You better drink that beer fast, because if anything happens to Mayra out there, I'll consider it your fault."

I GET BACK FROM THE STORE to find the Regal with its hood up, the front end raised on the emergency jack. Lencho hasn't finished flushing the radiator and replacing the thermostat. He's put two big soup pots under the car, the radiator dripping the last of the fluid into the larger one. Lencho found an auto parts store while I was sleeping this morning. When I came across him on the beach, it was later than I thought, about one in the afternoon. We came back, and after I took a quick shower, he asked me to find us some lunch while he worked on the Regal.

That was three hours ago. A job like this would take me an hour, maybe an hour and a half. Someone going by the instructions on the back of the thermostat's packaging could do it in two. The Regal's old thermostat sits next to the rubber outlet housing on the open lid of Lencho's toolbox. The copper valve is clogged, the round aluminum attachment bent where Lencho must've pried it off. I watch as he scrapes the old gasket away with a razor, nudging the blade, then flinching as the blade clatters between the parts of the engine. "Need some help?" I ask.

Lencho looks up from his work, his face sweating. "No," he says.

I tell him I got saltines and cheese, a small box of Frosted Flakes and some bottled water. Lencho says fine, not paying any attention. He comes up with the razor and continues his scraping. He checks the pots and screws the drain plug back in the radiator. One pot is full of green anti-freeze and the other is full with the lighter, flushed fluid.

I ask Lencho again if he needs any help.

He shakes his head. "Go ahead and relax," he says. "I'll be done in a minute."

I head inside with the food, turn on the television, and watch the dubbed version of a movie where Burt Reynolds plays a stuntman. It's pretty good. I check on Lencho during the commercials and go back outside an hour after the movie ends. I find him taking Mayra's picture off the Regal's dashboard. The picture's all curled up, probably from being taped next to the air vents, from exposure to all the heat. In the picture, Mayra's wearing a green cap and gown. It's her kindergarten graduation two years ago. There's some gasket sealant left, and Lencho spreads some of the thick brown glue across the back of the picture. This time he sticks it to his wallet, pressing on it with his palm until the sealant takes hold.

IN THE WEEKS AFTER HIS ACCIDENT, before Lencho started renting that extra room over on Delnice, he stayed with me. Hector had invited him back into his apartment, but Lencho knew there really wasn't any room for him there. He didn't want to return to Josie's, and I couldn't blame him. During his stay in the hospital, Josie didn't come to say she was sorry. Lencho didn't get to see Mayra. So Lencho spent almost a month at my place. The Regal collected dust and bird shit on the street until the metal braces that kept Lencho's arms from moving were taken off, along with the bandages on his left hand, which had been burned less than the right one. He took pain medication, and every two days I drove him to a treatment center before I went to work.

Each time I offered to wait, and each time Lencho said no. Either he took the bus or walked home, but somehow he made it back. The place was in Duarte and there Lencho got cream applications and clean bandages. The doctors at the treatment center would put this cream on Lencho, silver sulfa-something, and he swore that he could feel the medication working its way into his arms and hands and fingers, that he could feel the new cells multiplying underneath all the gauze. He had lost four fingernails on his right hand, and each one itched like crazy as it grew back.

"It's not like a cast where you can stick a pencil in there and scratch away," he said. "I got blisters and infections to worry about."

I let Lencho borrow some clothes. All of his were at Josie's, and, except for the coveralls, the things of Hector's that Mini brought him were too small. He took a pair of my sweats, a second pair of coveralls, and a few old shirts that he cut up. They all fit him pretty tight, but that didn't matter because, except for his treatments, he hardly ever left. I offered him keys, but Lencho insisted on using the spare ones I kept taped to the top of my security door in case I was ever locked out.

At night Lencho would stay up late. I wondered if he was afraid to go to sleep, afraid of waking up with his hands burning. He asked that I bring Georgie's newspapers home from work, only the ones in English. I took them when I remembered, and stopped at the liquor store when I didn't. I'd wake up at three or four in the morning, and find Lencho reading the paper, sitting on my living room floor with the different sections spread across the carpet. Before I'd head to work, over toast and coffee, he'd tell me weird stories from the back pages, stories about chimpanzees that took prize-winning photographs and nuns who made chocolate in the Hollywood hills.

I came home early the day Lencho got the metal bars off his arms. He wanted to go back to Josie's place to pick up a few things, and he wanted to go during the day when Mayra wouldn't be home to see him still wrapped up. He expected Josie to be there, and he asked me to go along because he was afraid he might kill her. I couldn't tell if Lencho was serious or kidding when he said this because his face had the same grimace it was locked into for the last few weeks. So, just to be sure, I told Georgie I felt sick and punched out at about one o'clock.

I drove my car so that Mayra wouldn't recognize the Regal on the off chance that she wasn't at the afterschool care program Josie had enrolled her in. Lencho used his key to open the door, and, when we went inside, Nick was sitting at the kitchen table, the same kitchen table where Lencho had been burned. Nick was in his boxers and lighting a Camel for Josie who was wound up tight in a pink robe. Lencho didn't say anything. He barely blinked and walked straight past Nick to the bedroom like he expected Nick to be there. I told Nick hi, and he answered with a blank look and a flick of his cigarette.

"What are you doing here?" Josie said. "You can't come back."

Josie followed Lencho to the bedroom, yelling with each step. But Lencho still didn't say anything, not a fuckin' peep, and this seemed to make Josie even madder.

"Oh, now you're not listening to me?" she said. "Well, listen to this. I'm with Nick now because he actually cares about me."

I looked at Nick after Josie said this. He shifted uncomfortably in his seat.

"It didn't matter that you were in that boy prison, Lencho. Every day I waited for you while you worked. I made you dinner. I did your laundry, and all I asked for was that you be there for me when I get home. And then you expect me to wait while you sweat over the stupid fuckin' numbers in that book? Well, you're wrong. Go ahead. Take your things."

Lencho came back to the front room carrying a small pile of clothes, mostly underwear and socks. His mouth was quiet. His face looked like all the blood in his body had been squeezed into his head. On the way out, he pointed at a frame full of Mayra's baby pictures that hung on the wall above the TV. I took it down, and put it under my arm, and told Josie good-bye.

It's Saturday night and Lencho has the air-conditioning running in the Regal. We're on the strip, and we stop for tacos at the same place. The lady remembers me from last night. As I eat, I try to remember the story behind the bump on my head, but I can't, and when I ask Lencho, he looks at me and smiles.

"Yeah, Manny," he says, wiping his hands. "We can't go back to that place tonight. We'll check out the Rosarito Beach Hotel instead. The bar there is usually pretty busy on the weekends."

The lady asks if we've been to a place called Casita Bamboo, and we both say no. It sounds a little lame, but the lady hands me a plate of tacos and winks as she says, "Allí hay muchas chicas, joven."

Casita Bamboo is five minutes away, and it has a dress code that we don't meet. Lencho's got a black sweatshirt and blue Dickies on. I'm wearing jeans and a gray T-shirt. Lencho looks tougher than the doorman though. The doorman's a tall guy, but he isn't big in any other way. Lencho scowls as he gives him ten dollars for the five-dollar cover, jerking his thumb and telling the doorman I'm with him. The doorman thinks this over for a second, then stamps our hands.

The inside of Casita Bamboo is actually made of bamboo. The walls are covered by cheap bamboo fencing with fake tropical stuff, plastic parrots, leis, and straw hats, stuck all over. Lencho walks right up to the bar and orders a double shot of Bacardi from a Mexican bartender wearing a grass skirt. I order a Tecate and turn around to see who else is here.

The lady at the taco stand was wrong. There are people at the tables, but they're mostly navy guys in white sailor outfits, or couples huddled over their drinks. The only girls here are at a table off to the left.

I ask Lencho for the time, and he says it's still early, around nine-thirty.

"Man," he says, "we should've gone to the Beach Hotel." The tone in his voice is flat, stiff and serious. Lencho plays with a handful of pretzels, counting and recounting them like he's using them to keep track of a long number in his head. He finishes his Bacardi, then orders a Corona, and watches the slice of lime bob inside the bottle before taking a drink.

We have a few beers and don't say much to each other. Lencho's sitting next to me, but his mind is off someplace else. It's definitely not listening to the music playing, a light soundtrack of crashing waves and reggae. There are two girls at a table off to the left, and the one I'm looking at has blue eyes and black hair. She's dressed in a short green dress and stacked high heels. I point her out to Lencho, and his eyes pop up in a half-hearted wow. When I walk over to her, Lencho's reluctant to get up with me. I take a seat next to the blue-eyed girl and Lencho stays standing. I introduce myself and Lencho, and we shake hands as she says her name is Eileen.

I ask Eileen if she's in school, and she starts talking about some place called SDSU. After a few minutes, I figure out that it's San Diego State. She's an economics major, a junior from El Cajon who likes salsa dancing and banana daiquiris. I buy her another. She asks about me and I start by telling her about Rio Hondo, lying when I say I want to go back in the fall but, with work, things are kind of hard.

"What do you do?" Eileen asks.

I tell her I'm in auto repair. The gleam disappears from her smile.

Eileen's friend is into Lencho. She's not as pretty, but she's pretty enough. Still, Lencho seems put off. Eileen's friend asks him questions but he's barely paying attention. She puts her hand on Lencho's and tells him to sit down. He flinches and pulls his hand back. The edges of his tattoo are poking up from his collar and the girl asks what's underneath it.

"It's nothing," Lencho says.

Now Eileen's interested too. She leans over and presses the issue. "What's 'Cruz' stand for?" she asks, her friend pulling at Lencho's sweatshirt.

Lencho knocks the friend's hand away. It hits the table, rattling the bottles and glasses, and he leaves without apologizing.

THE FRAME OF A CAR is like its spine. You fuck up the frame in an accident, and you can pour thousands of dollars into repairs, spend hundreds of hours tightening down every last bolt, and the car still won't run right. The doors will stick or they won't close tightly. New seals and gaskets leak. The car pulls to the left or to the right as if a ghost were yanking on the steering wheel. I told all that to Georgie the day this guy had his gold Cadillac Coupe DeVille towed in. The driver side looked like it had been ground against a center divider, and I could just imagine the damage underneath the bent hood and wrecked body panels.

"I know, Manny, I know," Georgie said, nodding. "But the guy says the car has sentimental value and he wants it running again. He says money is no object."

Lencho had started hanging around the shop that week. Not working. Just watching. Except for his right hand, his bandages were all off. Still he wouldn't show us the skin, and he kept pulling his long sleeves down over his hands like a nervous kid. He sat in the shade as I started work on the Caddie, taking the wheels off to get to the backsides of the body panels, Lencho telling me what to do, what tools to use, the shelf where I would find them in the toolbox.

Lencho had just moved into the room on Delnice the weekend before. Between bursts from the air gun, I asked Lencho how things were going with the old lady who owned the house. Lencho said she liked him. She said that having him around was the same as having an extra guard dog, like he should have given her a sign to put in her window that said: Beware of Lencho. I stacked the wheels off to one side and pried apart the fasteners for the front driver-side fender. It should've come free, but it held tight because of the accident.

"There's one fastener left," Lencho said. He pointed at the edge by the door. "You forgot one."

"Sure," I said. I hadn't forgotten anything. I yanked harder and harder until the fender popped off. As I moved on to the rear one, I asked Lencho how his rehab was going. He said it was okay, that it was strange having to learn how to pick things up again. Lencho talked about a rubber ball they had him grip, and how he thought his physical therapist liked him. She touched his skin with needles to test his sensation, and when Lencho didn't feel things in certain spots of his right arm, he felt embarrassed and naked.

The other fenders came off easier than that front one. After removing all four, I pulled a Marlboro from the pack I left in the toolbox and leaned against the Caddie. Lencho asked me for one, and I lit his cigarette before handing it to him. I took a few drags off mine while I looked for a 5/8 socket, then left my cigarette to burn on the edge of the toolbox. The Caddie's front end was next, and I groped under the bumper for the first nut of its four attaching bolts.

"Over more," Lencho said. "Go more to the left and farther back."

I crawled around under the car and found the nut. The bumper was bent in such a way that I'd have to attach a universal joint to the socket to get the bolt loose. I shimmied back out and found Lencho tapping my ratchet with his shoe. His right hand was twitching, the left one taking the cigarette from his lips, holding it carefully as he practiced flicking the ashes with his new fingers.

I LEAVE CASITA BAMBOO and find Lencho in the Regal, staring at the steering wheel. "What the hell was that?"

Lencho doesn't answer.

He starts the car, puts it in gear, and guns the engine. We roar up the short sidestreet and turn onto the strip without braking. The Regal does a little fishtail before straightening out and Lencho pulls the knob that turns on the headlights. We ride down the road with the smooth rush of the tires on the asphalt, the blue light of the moon mixing with the green glow of the dashboard. Lencho won't answer my questions, what's wrong, what's the matter? His eyes are focused on the road, and I start watching the white stripes going by for a clue, for the combination to the safe Lencho's face has become.

Lencho barely taps the brakes when he turns off into the darkness toward Hector's place. The tires squeal and the car rocks. "I'm sorry," he says. "I'm sorry I fucked up your action back there."

I tell Lencho not to worry about it. He takes his foot off the gas and the car slows until it rolls at idle speed, making its way past the sad houses, going over each bump and dip in the road.

When we get to the open gate, I ask the same questions again. Instead of answering, Lencho parks the Regal in the driveway and reaches under the seat. He pulls out a flashlight and shines it in my face. "You hungry?" he asks.

I tell him no.

"You will be," he says. "The reason you don't like fish is because you've never had it prepared right." Lencho gets out and empties one pot of radiator fluid and heads toward the ocean.

I follow him. The moon is full, bright as a high beam. There are some people throwing heavy nets at the water. When I get closer, the sand firm and damp under my shoes, I see that the waves hitting the shore are shiny with wriggling fish. There are thousands of them.

"I knew there'd be more grunion tonight," Lencho says. "They're coming to bury their eggs in the sand. It has something to do with the moon being in the right place and the water being warm enough."

For the next few minutes I stand with Lencho, quiet as the tide sweeps jackpot after jackpot of bright and shining fish onto the sand. Lencho pulls off his shoes and socks and yanks his sweatshirt over his head. "When we go back to El Monte," he says, "I'm not going to stay."

"What are you talking about?"

"I can't stay there, Manny. You know there's nothing for me to go back to."

Lencho says this without turning away from the water. I look over and see him thinking about each word he's about to say, considering them like wrenches, looking for the right size that will loosen what's holding his ideas in place.

"Mayra," he says. "When we get back, I'm going to take her. I'm going to take Mayra and bring her here. I never told Josie about this place. She wouldn't know where to look."

I can't imagine Lencho would do something like that, but he tells me he's got money saved, that he's going to stay in Hector's house until he finds a place of his own. "I'm giving you the Regal after it happens," Lencho says. "Sell it for parts. Scrap it and make it into a cube. I don't care."

He hands me the flashlight and walks to the water. The beam shines on his back as he gets on his knees. The waves rush over him, and he turns and smiles.

"You're the one person who knows where I'll be," he yells. He grabs at the grunion and they slip out of his fists and slide back to the ocean.

I walk a few steps forward and ask Lencho if he believes what he's saying.

He holds the pot on its side to scoop up some of the flipping fish. "It's the best plan I got."

Soon after, Lencho stands up. He holds the pot with both hands and calls me over, the cold sea water filling my shoes and rushing up my pants legs when I do. Lencho shivers as I point the light inside the pot. There are fish swimming inside, six or seven of them bumping blindly against each other.

I tell Lencho there's no chance his plan will work.

"Yes," he says. "Yes it will."

He walks away, his strides kicking up loose sand. As we leave the beach, I pick up his shoes and socks and sweatshirt, my wet clothes sticking to me. They make it harder to catch up, to match strides with Lencho as he carries the meal that awaits us.

GINA AND MAX

1 9 8 8

Max has figured out two new ways to annoy me. He found a pair of chopsticks on the sidewalk, and quickly became skilled in using them by picking every cellophane wrapper, cigarette butt, and bit of paper around the bus stop, placing them in the trash can to his left. When Max tried to pick up an empty beer bottle, it slipped from the sticks like I told him it would, falling and shattering, and I could feel the stares from the people nearby. Now Max is playing the drumbeat to "Bela Lugosi's Dead," a song he's always hated, one he's teased me for liking. Once, when we first started going out, Max stole a set of fake vampire teeth from somewhere and chased me around my parents' house, singing the song through clenched plastic fangs until I let him catch me and kiss me on my mother's couch.

The time schedule posted next to the bench shows that the number 20 bus stops running after midnight. It's almost nine now, and I tell this to Max, and he tells me not to worry as he picks at one of my earrings with his stupid sticks. I get up to read and reread the different schedules. I run my fingers across the map, tracing the red lines marking the

20's route. I try to judge where we'll get off, how far we'll have to go to this Christmas party, and how long it might take us to walk there. When the bus comes, I shield my eyes from its bright headlights. The doors swish open and I'm positive that our last chance to catch the 20 back from Benny's house will be at 11:35.

Max lets me get on before him. I hold the steel rail and look out the broad windshield while he asks the driver if she can break a five. The woman is wearing brown leather gloves with peepholes for her knuckles, and she seems more interested in adjusting her grip on the steering wheel than answering Max's request.

"Sorry honey, I don't make change," she says.

Max's five is all that he has, so I pay for the bus with the change in my purse, the last of my money until Friday, the day after Christmas, when we both get paid. Max drops the change in the cash box, and the driver yanks the lever that closes the doors.

The bus pulls away from the curb, and we take seats near the back. Max sets his backpack on the ground and tugs at the window, trying to get it closed. It won't budge. He groans and zips up his leather jacket.

"How do you plan on getting us home?" I ask.

"I'm sure someone at the party will give us a ride. You cold?"

Max puts his arm around me before I can answer yes. My coat is long, but it's thin, and my tights are too full of holes to make any difference. I sit with my feet up on the seat, knees together, rubbing the chill from my legs.

Benny is throwing this Christmas party. Seeing as how my mom hung up on me the last two times I called, being with Max at Benny's party sounds better than spending Christmas Eve alone. I start to shiver under Max's arm, and we stay quiet and watch the street go by. Max's tattoo equipment is in his backpack. He's going to get some work done tonight, make some money, which is fine by me, so long as it's not

Benny he's working on. Benny's the reason Max is so careful about who he tattoos these days, the reason he hasn't worked his machine in three months.

BENNY WORKS WITH MAX at the paper tube plant. He's a big guy with six kids by four different women. Each kid's name is tattooed on his chest, and the afternoon he came over, he wanted Max to add the name of his most recent baby, a girl named Suzana. As he unbuttoned his shirt in our kitchen, he said that if he kept up this kind of pace, he'd have to start lifting weights again so his chest could fit more names. I was making a sandwich for my break while they were getting started. Benny folded his shirt carefully and told Max that he had only seen Suzana once, shaking his head as he told him that she had fat lips and a wide nose like her mother. "Ten days old," he said. "Already she's got a nose the size of a Coke bottle."

Suzana was to go under her sisters Abigail and Gabriella, next to her brothers Joseph and Raymond and Moises. The pair of lists on Benny's chest was tattooed in black script, the boys on the right side, the girls on the left. Benny caught me looking at him and he tapped his chest. "They help me remember who belongs to who," he said.

Benny's tattoos reminded me of pictures my dad's cousin has of the plane he flew in during the war, of the little white bombs stenciled by the cockpit that marked the number of cities the crew destroyed. Later on, Max told me that Benny works at three different jobs—the paper tube factory, the go-cart track, and a paper route—but only sends money to two of the mothers at a time. Sometimes he switches off, and some months Benny's women don't get any of his money. That afternoon Benny asked me if I'd make him a sandwich too, something to keep company with the beer in his stomach. I spread some peanut butter and some jelly on two slices of bread, and Benny ate the sandwich as if it was the last chore on his long list of things to do. He sighed as he watched Max shake a small bottle of black ink. "Let me tell you, Max," he said, "life is so much easier when you keep your dick in your pants."

Suzana was to be spelled with a Z, but Max didn't know this, and after he figured out how to imitate the style, he drew out the name as SUSANA. He showed it to Benny, and Benny didn't say that anything was wrong. Afterwards, Benny stood in front of our bathroom mirror. He examined the raw rectangle on his chest and came out crazy. He started calling Max names, saying this was bullshit, that he wasn't going to pay. Max was cleaning his tattoo machine, and Benny knocked it from his hand. The motor chattered loudly against the floor as the needle sprayed the last of the ink onto my leg. Benny punched Max twice, once in the stomach and once in the head. That night, the swollen bruise on Max's forehead looked as if someone glued a prune above his eye. He said the second punch broke one of Benny's fingers. Two days later, Max assured me that things between him and Benny were okay.

MAX WAS SO EXCITED about my Christmas gift this year that he gave it to me before we left. I shut my eyes so that I wouldn't see it. The things I bought Max were next to the bed, unwrapped and buried under a pile of my dirty clothes. But he insisted, kissing my eyelids until I opened them, handing me a large envelope made of blue metallic paper. Its tag was cut in the shape of a cartoon bat, TO GINA preprinted on one of its extended wings.

"For you," Max said. "Open it. Come on, open it!"

I peeled tape from the blue paper and found a brown manila envelope underneath. I took my time with this until Max pulled it away. He tore the envelope open and poured the contents onto my lap. There were official-looking papers and forms. A thick pamphlet. Some kind of certificate. I looked among them all and found a bumper sticker that read BATTY ABOUT BATS.

There was also a large glossy photo that made me jump. It was a rat with wings. I've always feared these kinds of creepy animals. Last August, a spider in our bedroom had me sleeping on the living room floor, wrapped head to toe in a sheet so that I was practically suffocating. I'd done this for three nights until Max found the spider and brought it to me crushed in the folds of a napkin. When I asked Max what all the papers in my lap were, he seemed slightly disappointed that my face didn't look as happy as his.

"It's a bat," he said. Max took the picture from my lap and held it before me, the excitement shifting from his face to his hands so that photo shook. "It's your bat Gina."

Max explained that when he visited the doctor for his aching feet, he saw an advertisement in a magazine. He said he tore the page out and sent them a money order, adopting a bat in my name.

"Somewhere in Texas," he said, "there's a huge hole in the ground where twenty million of these things live. One of them is yours."

I didn't know what to say. I told Max thank you and kissed him and hugged him and made sure to hold him a long time before letting go. I put all the papers and forms back in their envelope, telling Max that I'd read them later, knowing even then that I wouldn't. Max left the room and I finished getting dressed. I brushed my hair, parting it on the left, and made faces at myself as I shaded my eyes the way Siouxsie's were on Request Video, purple and black, sexy and threatening. I buckled my boots and was rummaging through my jewelry box when Max came back.

He sat on the bed and spoke to me in a soft and quiet voice. "It's supposed to be a girl. A female. The lady I talked to said they'd make sure and give you a female." Max took out the bat photo, apparently inspecting it for telltale girlie traits. "Anyway, it's a Mexican free-tailed bat." He slipped the picture into the envelope, and put the envelope with the bills on my dresser. "She's supposed to be like you," he said. "She's Mexican and she's Goth."

THE BUS LURCHES AWAY from the curb and Max rocks into me. My hands are cold, and I rub them together, but nothing changes, so I tuck them under my thighs. Max's hands never get like this. His entire body is always warm, and I miss this most when one of us gets an odd shift at work. On those nights I sleep alone under thick, woolly blankets, but the cold still manages to creep into my hands and feet.

I rub my hands some more and Max asks if I'm nervous.

"No," I answer. "Are you?"

Max shakes his head and says that Benny's friends will probably just want name tattoos, gang stuff or girlfriends in Old English. "Easy money," he says. "As long as they aren't bleeders, it shouldn't take all night." He shrugs and picks at the rubber molding around the window. "It's no big deal," he says, "just some easy, easy money." Max presses his fingers to his right temple and rubs the skin in small circles. As long as I've known him, he's done this when lying. I take his hand away and hold it in my lap with the two of mine.

Last Sunday I was folding laundry, when I noticed Max's green mug of markers and pens in its spot on our table, their caps fuzzy with crowns of dust. He hasn't drawn much since the day Benny hit him, and, looking at his dusty collection of pens, I wondered if Benny knocked something loose inside Max. The bus crosses Valley Boulevard as I think of a school film I once saw on the nervous system. The filmstrip showed our insides as a bunch of sockets and electrical plugs. There was one for the heart that kept it beating, one for the lungs that kept them breathing, one for the legs that kept them walking. Max pulls the cord to get the bus to stop, and I lose the image of a plug dangling in his head.

We get up and step off, and outside the air's been replaced by the odor of wet duck.

I've smiled that smile before. This is our third Christmas together, and as much as I love Max, he hasn't gotten any better at giving me gifts. We'd been together five months and three days when our first Christmas came around. Max gave me a pack of multivitamins and a jar of iron pills because I was always tired. His mother said that I was probably anemic, that there was no iron in my blood. Besides the pills, she suggested that Max make me eat more steak. His grandma told him to prepare some longaniza, but I've seen other members of Max's family get sick, and that bloody pork sausage seems to be her answer to everything.

When Max and his sister were still talking, he gave me a used camera that she sold him. I was taking a photo class at the time, and the only camera my family had was a Polaroid that refused to spit out its slow-developing squares. We spent ten bucks on gas and took the camera to the beach on the last day of Christmas vacation. I snapped pictures of dogs chasing Frisbees, and old homeless guys passed out on benches, and surfers in black rubber suits running out to ride the water. The car overheated on the way home, and I shot an entire roll on the side of the freeway while we waited for the radiator to cool down. Max posed, the engine billowing steam behind him, and it wasn't until a week later that we found out Evelyn's Kodak didn't work. Every picture I took that day looked as if it had been dipped in milk.

Max has Benny's address written on a scrap of paper. He puts his arm around me as we follow the directions, the smell from the duck farm staying with us while we walk. Max covers his nose. As bad as it is now, the stench of wet duck shit is worse in the summer with the sun and heat. We go under the bridge and cross Garvey, ending up on Exline, where every house is next to the freeway, fake snow sprayed in the windows and Christmas lights draped over the wrought iron. The street turns into a cul-de-sac and we come up on a small house with no twinkling lights. A car blocks the driveway and one sits on the sidewalk. Behind them, parked on the lawn, is a light blue pick-up that Max recognizes as Benny's.

The address tacked up on the eave has lost its last two numbers, but the front door is wide open. Max knocks before we step inside and find that Benny's Christmas party isn't much of a party. There are two guys sitting around, drinking beer, one tapping his pack of cigarettes against the table. They look up. In the second where nothing is said I can hear a TV and some oldies playing low. The guy closest to us stands and tucks his cigarette behind his ear. He's tall, thin, and wears only a tank top, like we're in the middle of July. He's definitely not our kind of people. I stand behind Max as he asks for Benny.

"I'm a friend of his from work," he says. Neither of the guys respond. "I'm here for the tattoos."

The smaller guy still sitting nods like this is something profound. "Benny's in the bedroom," he says. "At the end of the hallway."

The hallway is dark, and I follow Max, a giggle coming from an open door on our left. The streetlight comes in through the window, shining dimly on a bed where two blue bodies are pressed together. A second giggle turns into a low moan, but the cholo in the kitchen tells us to keep going. There's a second door on the right and a third one up ahead. Max walks up to the one with a stripe of light at the bottom. He knocks lightly.

"Come in." We step inside and find Benny sitting at the edge of a large bed, signing his name to Christmas cards. A bunch of oversized red plastic stockings are piled behind him, and, when we get closer, I see that they're filled with hard candy and cheap plastic toys. Benny puts a card in a red envelope, and licks the entire flap before sealing it shut. He and Max say hello. I wave. Benny sets the card on a dresser, next to some twenty-dollar bills.

"Straight from the bank," he says. "Every year I get my kids new money. It's like they got a copier in the back of the bank just for me." Benny holds one of the bills out to Max, and he inspects it, then passes it back so I can see. The paper's thin and crisp, so crisp that the bill feels phony.

Benny signs one last card and says he'll do the rest later. "I won't see my other kids until tomorrow," he says. Max asks if any of them are here, and Benny says, "Not yet, but Marie is supposed to come by later with Gabriella, Raymond, and Moises." Max nods like he knows these people. Benny gets up and we stand behind him as he flicks off the light switch. We follow him back to the kitchen and the low murmur of talking in the other bedroom stops as we walk by.

TWO YEARS AGO, I had five hundred business cards made for Max's birthday. They were printed in glossy red ink, the Misfits' skull grinning in the left corner, Max's name and his parents' phone number below the word TATTOOS. Max gave some to his friends at a party that Friday. I gave some to mine. On Saturday we took the rest to Melrose and walked up and down the crowded sidewalks, handing cards to people who looked cool. We did this until it got dark, then Max got the idea to head up to Hollywood Boulevard. Both sides of Hollywood were jammed with cruisers, their cars bursting with bodies and bass-heavy music. Between green lights, we mixed with the traffic, cutting through the idling cars and handing out business cards. We gave some to cholos who drove their low riders by hanging out their windows, and we gave some to disco chicks in convertibles who waved at cute guys like queens in the Rose Parade.

Max expected calls in the weeks afterward, but there were none, except for one freak. According to Max, this guy first called on Tuesday around one in the morning, but soon after, their phone was ringing five or six times a night. The guy would yell the same thing every time— "GREEN HELL! GREEN HELL! WE'RE GONNA BURN IN HELL! GREEN HELL!"—and one night Max let me answer when he called. The voice is hard to describe, the calls over as soon as they began, but it did seem muffled, like someone screaming with a hand over their mouth.

None of this was funny to Max's mom. She would hold the receiver at arm's length and stare holes into Max long after this guy hung up. Max swore that the caller wasn't anyone he or I knew, and his mother made him swear on every precious object he owned. Max was still tattooing in secret then, and just in case this guy gave his mom an excuse to go through his stuff, he packed his equipment into a pair of shoe boxes and gave them to me. These stayed in the back of my closet for the month before Max's parents gave in and changed their number. Things had gotten to the point where their telephone would be off the hook for two and three days straight. During one of these times, Max's tío in Guaymas died, but his family missed the call and didn't find out until a year later.

One night, alone in my parents' house, I sat with Max's boxes and took out his tattoo machine. Even then he kept the odd-looking contraption in the maroon T-shirt, the material soft and faded. Max had gotten the job at the factory with this machine specifically in mind. It had taken him half the year to save up over three hundred dollars to buy it through the mail. Sitting on my bed, I held the binding post like an iron pencil, and examined the simple machinery above it, the polished steel base plates and chrome contact screws. Several times I had witnessed Max take the machine apart the way a soldier in boot camp would dismantle a rifle. I knew that the two silver cylinders were tiny motors, that a thick copper coil inside each of these motors made a needle snap in and out of the skin ten times per second, that some machines worked faster, but that for Max ten was good enough. After a while, I put the machine back and folded the shirt around it several times. I imagined the power one would have when using it, the sudden ability to change a person's body forever, and it seemed inconceivable to me that Max could inspire that kind of trust in anyone.

BENNY INTRODUCES EVERYBODY. Frank is the guy with the cigarettes, and next to him is Harvey, who's sucking on his crucifix like cheap gold was a rare and precious vitamin. Max nods and shakes their hands before sitting at the other side of the table to unpack all his things. First he takes out his doctor stuff—bandages and medical tape, latex gloves, cotton swabs and rubbing alcohol—then he lays out an assortment of long steel needles next to a half-empty bottle of black ink. The needles are individually wrapped like Band-Aids, and Max arranges them thinnest to thickest, liners and shaders on the left, the thicker magnums on the right. The maroon bundle with his tattoo machine makes a small thud when Max sets it down. He carefully unwinds the cord to his power supply, smoothing out the kinks, plugging the small generator into the socket behind him.

I take the seat next to Max and look out the sliding glass doors that must open to a patio. The backyard is dark and the doors look like they're made of black glass.

"Did you bring your pictures?" Benny asks.

Max says yeah, handing Benny one sketchbook, though there are many more at home, pages and pages full of Max's designs. Frank gets up and looks at them over Benny's shoulder, but Harvey stays put.

He lets the chain fall from his mouth, and says, "I'm ready. I know what I want."

Harvey takes a folded piece of paper from his shirt pocket and hands it over to Max. "You can do this, right?" I recognize the drawing from Nativity's church bulletin, two hands praying, a rosary draped around the wrists.

"Yeah," Max says. "No problem. I've drawn more of these than the pope." Max laughs at his own joke, but when no one else does, I force a supportive smile. Max asks Harvey where and how he wants it. Harvey puts down his beer and holds his hands about four inches apart. He then rubs the back of his neck and says right here. Max nods. "That'll be fifty bucks."

When Benny says okay, Max smoothes the sheet with the praying hands and starts drawing on a section of transfer paper.

I'm thirsty, and I ask Benny if he has anything to drink, a glass of water maybe. Benny says sure. He gives the notebook to Frank, hands me a glass from the cupboard, and points to the refrigerator. "The tap tastes kinda funny," he says, "but there's some bottled stuff in the fridge."

I go into the kitchen and find the jug of water behind a Styrofoam container and a six-pack of Bud with two cans missing. I'm by the stove, filling my glass, when I notice a bunch of bullets on the tiled countertop. There's eight or nine of them just thrown there, plain as car keys, ordinary as pocket change. No gun. Just bullets.

I stare at them a few seconds, then take a deep breath and ask Max if he wants some water, trying to sound as normal as I possibly can. He looks up from his drawing and says no. Frank goes into the patio and

Harvey takes over the notebook. Benny comes into the kitchen and gets too close to me.

"You need anything else?" he asks.

I tell him no and put the water back in the refrigerator. Before sitting down, I look back at the spot on the counter, and the bullets are gone.

MY FIRST MEMORY is sitting in a high chair, my tío shaking his head at how much I resemble my abuelita. I've heard it my entire life. Same eyes, same cheekbones. The same pout when we get mad. Hanging in the hallway of my mom's house is an old brown-and-white photo of my abuelita with her two older brothers. She's just turned seventeen. In two months, she'll be married. In two years, she'll leave for California with my mom kicking inside her. This is who I look like now, and the old woman now living down in La Paz is who I'll be when I get old. I can't imagine my abuelita with something printed on her skin, the letters sagging and misshapen after forty years, the image faded and blotchy. That's why Max has never worked on me.

Not that he hasn't tried. When the Cramps played the Palladium, I drank too much beer in the parking lot, so much that Max left me in the car when the band started. I woke up the next day, startled when I saw my leg. It was covered with a dragon, a wild-eyed Aztec monster that clawed its way from the small knob of my ankle up to my thigh. Its head stretched under my panties and its thin tongue flicked at my pubic hair. I felt my skin carefully, expecting scabs and soreness, but it was a drawing done in black marker, not permanent. I licked my thumb, and as I rubbed my thigh, Max came into the room.

He sat on the bed, chuckling because my spit couldn't take off the ink. My head pounded and my stomach shook from the night before. I thought about the show, about being sick and alone, the smell of barf that's more bubbles and water than barf, about the cool glass of the window against my cheek. My jaw clamped down and my eyes narrowed. Then I thought about what Max had done to me without my knowing, and before he could say anything, I punched him. I aimed for his face and hit him in the neck, but I punched Max all the same. It was the first time I ever hit anyone. I called Max an asshole and stumbled into the bathroom, locking the door, leaving him holding his throat and coughing wildly. I rinsed my face with cold water, and, as I stared at the shiny faucet, the anger came off me in shuddering waves. Max apologized, and I yelled.

"Go draw on your own fuckin' body," I screamed. "And when you're done, go fuck yourself."

I called Max all kinds of things as I undressed. I said he was a worm of a boyfriend for leaving me behind. I got in the shower, grateful for the hot water as I began scrubbing. I worked on the dragon with a soapy washcloth until Max left for his shift. The marker wouldn't come off cleanly. Instead the ink was only willing to fade, especially in the tougher sections, my inner thigh and the patch behind my knee. There it looked like Max had done his work with gray marker instead of black. Alone, I dried off, swabbed nail polish remover on those spots, and spent the rest of the afternoon with my leg splotchy and red.

In truth, it was a good-looking dragon, but I still didn't talk to Max for a week. I slept in our bed and he slept on the couch. We came and went like mismatched roommates. And then one day Max came home from work with his left hand wrapped in a bandage. I was heating some leftover spaghetti at the time. Max sat at the table, and, when I asked, he told me he'd had a small accident, that just before his coffee break, he reached for a quarter he'd dropped, and got the tip of his middle finger sliced by a conveyer belt.

"I'm just lucky it wasn't my right hand," Max said.

He looked tired and sad. He nodded his head when I asked if he was hungry. I gave him my bowl and asked if he wanted some Parmesan, then sat down to listen about the rest of his day.

When Max starts working on Harvey, I take my glass of water outside, where Frank's in a lawn chair, cigarette in his mouth, a lighter sparking in his fist. He's sitting between two girls, a thick one who looks familiar and a thin one who doesn't. As I slide the door closed, he whispers something in the thick girl's ear. I make eye contact with her as she giggles, walking past them toward the edge of the yard as she jabs Frank's arm. I take a big drink of water and remind myself that Max knows Benny better than I do, that those bullets definitely don't have anything to do with us. I check the kitchen and everything appears fine. Benny's talking to Max, and Max is dabbing Harvey's shoulder with a paper towel. This will all be over in a few hours, and the best thing I can do in the meantime is stay out here, smell the dirty ducks, and focus my attention elsewhere.

Benny's backyard looks out over the San Gabriel river. There's a half moon out, a moon that casts enough light on the riverbed to let me see the tall stalks of bamboo that rustle in the breeze. The river is dry, and the small pools of still water shine like oil. Beyond this is the 605, tiny red taillights streaming down one side of the freeway, tiny white head-lights racing up the other.

Both girls start laughing again, and this time they laugh for real, the thin girl covering her mouth with her hand. Both girls are a few years older than me. They're sharing a cigarette and their bangs are teased, sprayed high and stiff with Aqua Net. The thick girl's named Delia, and she was the only junior in my math class when I was a freshman. Delia reminds me of my cousin Ana, the one who played football in the street and taught my little brother to burp like a bullfrog. Delia looks old, not older, like fifteen years have passed in the four since her graduation. I wonder if she's one of Benny's girlfriends, or if he's seeing them both and they just don't know it. She passes the cigarette back to the thin girl and checks her hair in the glass patio door. Delia nods as she does this, and for a second I think she's nodding at me.

From the freeway comes a sudden screeching of tires. I wait for the thud of an accident, but there's nothing, and the lights continue uninterrupted.

"That'll happen once or twice a night."

I turn around and Benny's standing behind me.

"Some nights I'll be out here, and I'll hear three or four accidents. You can always tell the bad ones by the number of cars that plow into one another." Benny punches the palm of his hand as he says this. "Bam-bam-bam-bam-bam."

"I know about the accidents," I tell him. "My parents live not too far from here."

Benny says really, then asks why I'm spending Christmas Eve here.

"We haven't spoken in a while."

"Why?"

"Maybe we should change the subject."

Benny smiles. "I'm sorry," he says. "What'd you get Max for Christmas?"

I tell him that I got Max a pair of Winos from the supermarket, but I don't mention that I stole them, the thin-soled canvas shoes jammed inside my purse as I bought groceries last week. I also got Max two pairs of Dickies, one blue pair for work, one black pair for going out. Max has three pairs of pants and the thighs are all worn from the conveyor belt he leans against at the factory. I also spent twenty bucks on a four-ounce bottle of black tattoo ink, Onyx Black, the darkest shade the company makes.

Benny asks if I know what Max is getting me, and I roll my eyes and explain the adopted bat. Benny smiles. He points to the dark riverbed and says, "Max should have told me. I'd have given him a net, and he could've gone down there and brought you the real thing." Benny drinks his beer and shakes his head. "They're in there, but you probably already know that. When we were kids, we'd throw M-80s into the storm drains. The boom'd echo like we'd chucked a stick of dynamite, and once in a while out would come this mess of bats and smoke."

Frank and the girls go back inside as I ask Benny if he got Marie anything. He says no. "Tomorrow's going to be a bitch," he says, "running around to see all the kids, eating fifty bad tamales before I get to the good ones at my sister's house." As Benny talks, he seems to lose interest in his own sentence. He comes close, puts his arm around my waist and guides me toward a dark corner of the yard. I look back at the window as we move. Max touches the needle to Harvey's neck. Harvey's face squinches up in pain and the girls howl and point.

Benny leans down and his beard scratches against my chin. He kisses me hard on the mouth. Both of Benny's hands clamp my wrists to my waist, and I know I should scream, yell and fight back as our lips touch, but suddenly it isn't in me to do so. I turn my head away and Benny whispers in my ear. "Whatever you saw in there, it doesn't have anything to do with you two. It won't unless you think you saw something. Understand?" I keep quiet and Benny grips me harder. "Remember how easy it was for me to do this, how I could have done more if I wanted to."

THE NIGHT WE WENT TO HOLLYWOOD, Max and I picked up the business cards that people tossed aside, but most of them were crumpled or ruined with tireprints. Max found three that were in good shape, and on the bus ride home, he talked about making enough money to finally quit the factory. He slid these last three cards into his wallet, where

I'm positive they are still, since Max is superstitious about the number three, and he also never gets rid of anything. It was late when we changed buses downtown, and, as we waited for the 176, Max said this starting set of business cards was the first real step to opening his own shop. He said thank you. I sat on his lap as he hugged me, and we stayed like that for a long time among the dark and empty skyscrapers.

MAX IS TEARING A STRIP of medical tape with his teeth and Harvey is holding a patch of gauze over his shoulder when I go back inside the house. I keep my head down in case my lipstick's messy and ask Delia if she knows where the bathroom is, brushing past her friend when she points to the door at the end of the hall. I find the door locked. The person inside says it's busy, sounding startled after I knock. "Use the other one in Benny's bedroom," he says. I think twice, then open the door to Benny's room. I flick the light switch and take my compact and lipstick from my purse. My mouth looks like a smashed grape. It comes off with a Kleenex, and my hand paints a jagged line as I reapply my lipstick. I give up and wipe it away. I sit at the edge of the bed and call for Max.

When he comes, I tell him we have to go. I want to tell him that Benny kissed me, about the bullets on the counter, and the bad things that will happen if we stay here. Max sits next to me and it's as if I'm seeing him for the first time. He's skinny. His chest is flat and the bones in his arms stand out more than his muscles.

"What's the matter?"

I lie. I tell him that I'm sick, that I feel like I'm dying. "We have to leave."

Benny comes into the room and stands at the door. He asks Max what's wrong and looks at me.

"She's sick," Max says. He tells Benny that he'll take me home, that he'll walk me to the bus stop then come back to work on him and Frank.

We get up and Benny moves aside to let us leave. I grab onto Max's arm and we go outside.

"What's going on?" Max asks. We get to the curb and walk under the streetlights. I grasp at other excuses. I tell Max to come home, that I can't wait to give him his present, that I want to spend my Christmas with him and not a bunch of thugs. I tell Max that we should leave, but he says he wants to stay.

"Besides," he says, "my pants aren't even wrapped yet." He smiles. "It's okay. I don't care." Max tells me that all this with Benny shouldn't take too long. "I mean, we need the money, and I need to get you something good. Let's face it. My gift's kinda lame."

"That's not important."

"It is to me."

I tell Max that the bat was a lovely idea, and I kiss him to show what I mean. When he holds my neck, his fingers feel slippery from the powder left by the latex gloves. I hope that he's right about him and Benny. Max walks me to the corner, to the bus stop, and we sit and smell the ducks until he puts his five dollars in my hand. "Go home and wrap my presents. Tie them with ribbon, and in three hours I'll be there to help tie the bow."

"What's the use?" I tell him. "The surprise is ruined."

Max pokes at the holes in my stockings and says that the surprise isn't ruined, not if he keeps his eyes closed and pretends.

When the Greyhound stops in El Monte, Jose Luis has trouble getting off. The aisle is crowded, too crowded for him to pass with his guitar case and bulging sack, so he waits. He stands as the other passengers bump and jostle one another, his sack's thin handles cutting into his bony hand. A bead of sweat slips from the inner band of his Stetson. He tries to imagine Rubí waiting for him outside these stuffy confines, but her image escapes him yet again, and the anxiety at the back of his mind spreads wildly. When Jose Luis moves forward, he's like a thermometer whose mercury has no room to rise.

He thanks the driver before exiting, and ducks so that his hat doesn't hit the top of the door. It's late, about eleven-thirty, but the bus terminal is still busy with people. The Greyhound pulls away, replaced immediately by another rumbling bus. The air thickens with gray exhaust and Jose Luis coughs. He makes his way through the people milling around and finds the escalator that descends to the street. Downstairs, he rests on a concrete bench, happy to set his things down.

The plastic sack is made of a red-and-green mesh. It's the type that women use to shop for groceries in the mercado, and he feels silly carrying it, as if he's traveled from Chihuahua to El Monte with a purse instead of a suitcase. In the sack are three small bags of carne seca, the other half of a sausage sandwich, some clothes, and two soft apples that Jose Luis bought from a girl after crossing the border into El Paso. Underneath the sack is his guitar case. The case appears older than the guitar inside it, the thick black leather scuffed and scratched with nearly fifty years of wear. In places, the leather is cracked, and in one of these splits he has stowed his carefully folded money.

When he left this morning, the sack fit neatly under his seat, the first bus from Ciudad Chihuahua empty enough so that his guitar case rode on the seat next to him. After a lengthy inspection at the Juarez border, he asked for directions to the second bus station, his green card snapped securely in his breast pocket. The bus from El Paso to Phoenix was so full that he was forced to ride with the case upright in his lap, hat on his knee, face pressed to the window. It was twilight as they crossed the desert, a storm forcing the sun into quick remission. The sky darkened quickly, lightning jabbed the expanse of sand and cactus, and thunder thumped the sides of the bus.

Jose Luis is sixty-five years old, and he hasn't left much behind him. His second wife died some time ago, and the last decade of his life in Chihuahua has been a sad and solitary stretch of time. His daughters from his second marriage, Paula and Lourdes, are both married. They have families of their own, and work at jobs that pin them to the American factories on the Mexican side of the border. Lourdes makes circuit boards for IBM, and Paula installs door handles on an assembly line for Ford. Once a month they both send Jose Luis money orders, the total averaging thirty dollars. He makes the rest of his money playing for Mexican tourists visiting the cathedral in the plaza. Up until this summer, Jose Luis's life had been a meager one, but he was content getting by with enough for a few tacos de buche and a few cervecitas on Sunday night.

But last August, Paula enclosed a letter along with her money order. The letter was a brief one about a young girl named Laura who had begun working at the Ford plant in the spring. Laura was assigned to the same assembly line as Paula, and when the two women talked on the bus ride home, the subject of family arose. They talked about their parents getting older, and Laura told Paula she felt lucky that only her tío Jose had died, a distant uncle in California whom she hadn't seen since grade school. In the course of the conversation, Paula recognized the name of the man's wife, along with the name of the city from which she came. Paula asked more about this woman, and by coincidence she happened to be who Paula suspected, Rubí Navarro Santiago, her father's first wife, the woman she remembered her parents arguing about all through her childhood. Laura brought an address to Paula, who, out of curiosity more than anything, told her father it might be nice if he passed on a few kind, comforting words to his former spouse.

Instead Jose Luis spent the summer revisiting a time he had long forgotten. He could no longer picture Rubí perfectly, and he went through his things in search of old photographs, only to come up empty-handed (his second wife had burned them all long ago). The summer wore on with all the humid stickiness of Chihuahua in August and vague recollections arose with increased frequency from the depths of Jose Luis's memory, smells and tastes and sounds he once knew well. When tourists requested the occasional bolero of Jose Luis, he played the ballads with Rubí in mind, singing with his eyes closed, and soon enough she began making fuzzy appearances before him. When the weather cooled, Jose Luis played only these requests, and most of the money he had made began going to an adjacent group of Tarahumara Indians, three grubby girls wrapped in swaths of paisley whose songs were composed of horrible squawking noises made by reedy wooden flutes. By November, snow falling in the plaza, the city around Jose Luis alive with his past, he convinced himself that every day he awoke in Chihuahua was a wasted opportunity to make amends and win Rubí back.

IN 1941 ONLY JOSE LUIS and his mother knew he was seventeen, a pounder of copper pots in the pueblo of El Morrion who played a borrowed guitar for his friends at night. News of an opportunity with the Mariachi Orosco came from a dealer of kitchenware who sold the burnished goods throughout the state. The Mariachi Orosco's old guitarist had been crippled in a car accident, and, though the capital city had its share of promising musicians, Casimiro Orosco believed his group would be more interesting to the local public with an infusion of outside talent. Soon after, Jose Luis arrived in Chihuahua a newly formed man.

To the world there, Jose Luis was twenty years old, especially to Casimiro Orosco, founder of the mariachi group bearing his name. Casimiro was a broad man who could fill a room with his voice. He had large hands with surprisingly nimble fingers, and when he played the guitarrón, the large bass guitar bobbed like a toy in his beefy arms. To get the job, Jose Luis insisted he was old enough to belong, old enough to have lived the lie of playing the guitar professionally for five years with a group in the far-off township of Casas Grandes.

Casimiro's younger brothers, Juanito and Arturo, were lesser versions of their older sibling. They played violins in the group, while their cousin Joaquin played the harp, eventually abandoning the bulky antiquated instrument for the trumpet. The vihuela was played by Don Cisco, an old-timer on the undersized guitar. He hailed from Delicias and also happened to be Casimiro's father-in-law. Don Cisco was the group's poet, the one who wrote most of their lyrics. Juanito told Jose

Luis that his brother would have married one of the horses left over from the revolution to get the elder composer in the group, and when Jose Luis met Casimiro's wife, Imelda, he discovered that Juanito's statement wasn't far from the truth.

Don Cisco had earned his reputation by being one of Villa's rebels during the revolution. He had been a corridista for Villa, a spy who infiltrated enemy camps by posing as a peasant fresh from the countryside, a vagabond musician happy to pick his guitar for a meager share of the army's rations. Don Cisco gathered information regarding the government's movements and reported directly back to Villa's shifting outposts in the rugged foothills and sandy plains of northern Mexico.

Don Cisco called Jose Luis El Solterito because he was the only bachelor in the group. With the exception of Don Cisco, who was a widower, the other men were all in their late twenties or early thirties, with established marriages and young families that would attend the group's rehearsals at the Orosco estate. Besides their regular engagement at the beer gardens adjacent to the Hotel Marina, the Mariachi Orosco practiced four times a week. It was common that Casimiro have the men play through the night, sometimes happily exploring every nuance of Don Cisco's latest composition, sometimes learning to painstakingly recreate a song Casimiro overheard on the radio.

Casimiro ensured that the Mariachi Orosco looked their best, and the days that Jose Luis visited the tailor for measurements and fittings were the first and only times an article of clothing was made expressly for him. The tailor was a specialist who worked solely with trajes de gala. He wore a monocle as he tugged at the black chamois jacket and pants hanging on Jose Luis's bony frame, marking careful alterations with a nub of waxy chalk. Buttons were sewed to the pants, two sets running parallel down each outer seam, the silver shaped into pentagons inlayed with horseshoes, the intricate designs stamped by hand.

The buttons were then connected by small lengths of thin chain, the links a quarter-inch wide. These were in need of repair on the night, much later, when Jose Luis inspected the suit with the intention of selling it, his decision to leave Chihuahua made. Every silver piece had been darkened with tarnish, and many of the connecting chains had come apart. Jose Luis had forgotten about this. He went to his small collection of tools—a hammer, a hacksaw with no blade, three screwdrivers of varying lengths—and found his pliers. The tool was discolored with patches of rust, and before working on the suit's broken chains, Jose Luis decided to get the pliers clean with silver polish and a rough rag.

When Jose Luis played for Casimiro Orosco, the music and lyrics to hundreds of songs lived in his mind. He once made a list and the different titles stretched on for five pages. Rancheras about horses and gunplay. Rancheras about drinking and dying. Corridos for every state in the Mexican union. Boleros of men among many women, and women among many men. Of brilliant love and brutal loss. As Jose Luis poured polish on the rag, he could recall knowing the songs, but not the songs themselves. Many had abandoned him over his career and many more only existed in fragments. Jose Luis could sing small clusters of words, and his fingers could play different parts, but these felt unfamiliar and disconnected. Upon finding Rubí, he planned to serenade her with boleros from the few fragile pieces of music that he recalled distinctly. Jose Luis polished the pliers with his rag and saw himself playing for Rubí—on the street below her window, on the steps in front of her door, wherever she may be. He worked the rag into each groove of the pliers' iron jaw, and sang the first song slowly and quietly. Jose Luis did this to reassure himself of the song's existence inside him, rehearsing in secret as if a penalty existed for practicing aloud.

In February of 1942, Casimiro contacted XEW, a radio station in Mexico City. He managed to get the Mariachi Orosco a booking on *La*

Hora Ranchera, a weekly program that spotlighted the best talent Mexico had to offer, and that spring the group traveled south to the capital in a rented bus. The morning was dark when the men left the Hacienda Orosco, and, despite the bumpy roads that led to the highway, many of the men were fast asleep before they reached the city outskirts. Arturo drove and Casimiro rode near him, sipping coffee and looking alert. Bandits still lurked in the desolate stretches of highway between the towns and villages, and Casimiro sat with a shotgun in his lap, both barrels loaded, ready for the first sign of trouble.

The loose sounds of rehearsal began to fill the bus as the day went on. The men tuned and retuned their instruments, and Don Cisco showed Jose Luis a few of the corridos he had written while serving time in jail as a young man: "El corrido del prisionero," "Las paredes de mi corazón," "Sin tequila, sin ti." Joaquin practiced on a borrowed trumpet, running through his parts of the seven songs the group was contracted to play. The telegram confirming the Mariachi Orosco's appearance had asked that Casimiro's ensemble include a trumpet, as the brass instrument resonated more clearly than the harp in the studio's microphones.

The Mariachi Orosco was the first group from so far north to play on XEW, and the pressures of the event sat on Casimiro's shoulders like gold and silver ballast. The public attention. The chance at regular appearances on the program. The success past performers had in movies. The opportunity to record the group's compositions. At that moment, all these were within reach. As twilight came on, the other men passed the time smoking cigarettes and playing cards and telling stories, but Casimiro sat in his seat, his brain complicated with thoughts, his brow furrowed with worry. He unloaded and reloaded the shotgun. He fidgeted with the loose threads on his shirt until he undid three buttons and part of his pocket. When the bus stopped for dinner and gas, Casimiro lumbered out with the shotgun. Jose Luis and the other men were busy joking and stretching as Casimiro walked to a man-sized cactus at the edge of the lot and shot it, scattering pointy needles and chunks of slimy green flesh.

Afterward the men kept to themselves, eating a noiseless dinner, tacos de pollo, sharing a liter of 7-UP. The men steered clear of Casimiro, and when they returned to the road, Don Cisco hastily composed a song for the moment, scribbling lyrics on a scrap of paper. Eventually Don Cisco would switch these lyrics to a bird's point of view, where the bird came home to find his nest and life destroyed, and, in a few years, the song titled "El corrido del pájarito sin hogar" would become a crowd-pleasing favorite in and around Chihuahua.

They continued on through the night, the younger Oroscos driving in alternate shifts. XEW was located on the outskirts of the city, the studio and transmitter perched atop a high ledge with steps carved into the mountainside. Other stations throughout Mexico received XEW's broadcasts. *La Hora Ranchera* was heard in Guadalajara and Veracruz, as far south as Acapulco, and regular listeners were rumored to the north in Tucson, El Paso, and Laredo. Casimiro had the men change into their trajes on the bus. When Juanito protested, telling his elder brother that it was radio, no one was going to see them, Casimiro glared. Jose Luis thought of the blasted cactus and carefully adjusted the ruffles in his tie. There may be photographers, Casimiro said, there might be reporters. He picked up his weighty guitarrón case and told his brother that the group must be prepared for anything.

The men hiked up to the studio, where anything didn't happen. There were no reporters, no cameras. The only celebrities were in the framed black-and-white photos of Marco Negrete (not Jorge, but impressive to Jose Luis nonetheless) and Lucha Villa, Pedro Infante and Las Hermanas Huerta, each softly lit portrait autographed with phrases like "XEW—El Centro del Mundo" and "¡Gracias por todo!" The studio was empty with the exception of a pretty receptionist who told them the station didn't broadcast between ten in the morning and five in the afternoon out of respect for the many masses said on Sunday. It turned out Casimiro had planned on arriving at one-thirty for a show that wouldn't air until six. He confessed to Don Cisco that he envisioned disaster when he was planning the trip, smoking engines, long walks with an empty gas can, wheels spinning in mud. But none of this had happened, and so the men waited. They paced the checkered tile floor and vied for the two metal fans blowing cool air, and Jose Luis tried to get the receptionist to bat her eyes in his direction.

Twenty minutes before *La Hora Ranchera* was to start, the group was greeted by Javier Cornejo, the station's primary host, programmer, engineer, and owner. Cornejo was a small man, a fast-talker with a bushy mustache and a receding hairline. The session with him took place in a small room enclosed by glass windows on three sides, one for the control booth, one for the lobby, one overlooking the broad expanse of Mexico City. Cornejo set up three microphones, one for the violins and the brass, one for the guitars, and one for Casimiro's booming voice and bass. He instructed the men on the signals he'd use from the control booth and Jose Luis stared at the equipment, at the pretty woman typing out paperwork, at the largest city in the world, and could only imagine people in Chihuahua gathering around their radios. When the time came, the men played intently. Casimiro sang the way a big and eager man should, and Jose Luis played his guitar in the face of stardom with all the concentration his young mind could muster.

JOSE LUIS REMAINS ON THE BENCH at the bottom floor of the bus station. He is tired and he is hungry. No one knows where he is. He didn't tell his daughters, for they would find the idea crazy. A beat-up car, its tailpipe smoking, stops before Jose Luis, a Vietnamese couple arguing fiercely inside. They sound as if they're yelling with tongues made of rubber and the unfamiliar sounds remind Jose Luis of how far he is from home, of how far he's come to find Rubí. Esto es una locura, Jose Luis thinks, este viaje entero es una locura. He stays seated, and as the car turns wildly back in the direction it arrived, Jose Luis wonders if he's made a terrible mistake in coming here.

He opens a package of carne seca and puts the largest morsel of dried beef in his mouth. He chews and picks shreds from his gold bridgework with his tongue. Jose Luis has told his daughters not to bury him with this bridgework, to have the mortician remove it when he dies. He refers to it as their inheritance, and says that the small golden horseshoe holding his bottom teeth together are all he has to leave them.

Jose Luis swallows when he sees a young man who looks like he speaks Spanish. He asks the young man if he knows of a hotel nearby, and the young man gives him directions to one on Valley Boulevard, about five or six blocks away. Jose Luis thanks him and the young man sprints up the escalator, obviously late for something. Jose Luis picks up his things and walks through the bus depot's parking lot to Valley Boulevard, where he makes a right and walks some more. Jose Luis is tired, old-man tired, too tired to rehearse yet again what he'll say when he sees Rubí. All he knows is that he'll see her.

He has brought three hundred and twenty dollars to El Monte, a little more than a hundred and ten thousand pesos. Two days previous, Jose Luis sold his mariachi suit to Marco, a teenage musician who made the money shining shoes on the southern side of the mercado. When Jose Luis had mentioned the suit before, Marco expressed interest in buying the pants and jacket, both men being roughly the same size. Marco had told Jose Luis he hoped to pick up better work with one of the more renowned groups playing along Calle Carranza, the strip of seedy bars and nightclubs where the city's musicians wait to be hired. Calle Carranza's ragtag groups never match. The designs of their suits will differ—the pant seams embroidered with an assortment of patterns or colors, the buttons and buckles done in varying motifs.

In July, Marco offered Jose Luis a hundred and forty thousand pesos for the suit, half of what a new one would cost. Jose Luis rejected the offer, but by November things had changed. The afternoon that Jose Luis went to Marco, every shop in the mercado was either closing or closed. A cold wind bustled and spun through the stalls and stands. Marco was busy rearranging his brushes and dull tins of polish. The men said hello, and when Jose Luis asked Marco if he still wanted the suit, the elder musician stood with his hands in his pockets, the hair on his arms bristling with chill.

"Pues cómo no," Marco answered, "pero no tengo las cien mil quinientos que quieres." Jose Luis slowly rubbed his boot on the cobblestones under him, then asked Marco how much he did have. Marco sighed and climbed into one of his chairs, twisting the rag in his hands while he performed some quick accounting. "Se me hace que tengo un poco mas de cien mil."

For a moment, Jose Luis wore a face of careful contemplation, but just for a moment. A hundred thousand pesos was like winning the lottery. Jose Luis would have agreed to sell the suit if there were only twenty-five pesos in Marco's bank account, just as long as it was enough to get him across the border, anywhere relatively close to Rubí. "Estará bien," Jose Luis said. They made arrangements for Marco to come inspect the suit the next morning, and even though Marco's fingers were grimy with polish, Jose Luis made it a point to shake the young man's hand firmly so as not to curse the occasion.

AFTER THEIR PERFORMANCE ON *La Hora Ranchera*, the men returned home to heroic fanfare. Strangers greeted Jose Luis in Chihuahua's streets, shaking his hand and patting him on the back. In bars, they bought him shots of tequila. In restaurants, dinner was free. For the Mariachi Orosco, their reception couldn't have been greater if the capital was overrun by seven vicious dragons, the musicians each coming home with a slain head and new boots made of shiny exotic scales. But after the initial fanfare, nothing of real consequence occurred. No contracts were signed afterwards, no important men drove into town seeking their services, and the group returned to their routine of playing the beer garden four nights a week.

Casimiro tried to arrange for a second appearance on *La Hora Ranchera*, but his telegrams went unanswered. He began to curse the groups that played the show in the ensuing weeks, to glare at the radio with contempt, and, after hearing the cactus story, his wife hid their radio under their bed. When the fifth telegram received no response, Casimiro drove two hours west to Cuauhtémoc to use the telegraph service there. He wondered if his messages were even reaching Mexico City, and he imagined slips of paper bearing his name blown down an alley in the capital or caught on a branch somewhere in the countryside.

In the telegraph office, he met a farmer named Humberto Santiago. Don Humberto owned two apple orchards in Cuauhtémoc, one on each side of the highway dividing the town. He made his money selling his harvests to American buyers, and he drove a new American truck, a Chevrolet. He had four daughters: Ofelia, Mónica, Rosalía, and Rubí. His third daughter, Rosalía, was to be married at the end of the month. Don Humberto explained to Casimiro that her husband-to-be wasn't a man of the land, that he was a flojero who went to the university and had his head full of fancy ideas about the Mexican way of life. Don Humberto told Casimiro that this was a man who couldn't plant a tree or slaughter a chicken, this little man who wanted his daughter. Don Humberto apologized for putting all this upon Casimiro, and told him it would be an honor if the Mariachi Orosco would play at the reception. A price was agreed upon, on top of which Don Humberto added another hundred pesos for the short notice, and Casimiro wrote the date and location on the receipt for his telegram.

On the day of Rosalía's wedding, the men drove to Cuauhtémoc in Casimiro's old pick-up. The sky above them was a drafty quilt of ominous gray, and Don Cisco was suffering from a flu. Because of his infirmity, the elder guitar player rode up in front with Joaquin and Casimiro, while the other men sat among the instruments in the cold. Jose Luis's fingers felt frozen. He kept his hands tucked under his arms and scowled at his knees to keep his teeth from chattering. Once the truck veered off the highway, it lurched and pitched over the bumpy dirt road leading to the hacienda Santiago.

Don Humberto's home was fragrant with white apple blossoms, and the farmer greeted each member of the group in his best and only suit. Firm handshakes were exchanged all around. The men dressed quickly in the kitchen among servants carrying steaming pots of menudo and stacks of fresh tortillas. There were vats of bottled beer in ice and three kinds of tamales had been prepared—tamales de chile rojo, tamales de chile verde, tamales de dulce—dozens of each steaming outside in clay tubs suspended above pits of glowing coal.

The Mariachi Orosco performed in the patio for an appreciative group of nearly one hundred people, and the group did their best to fulfill each request made of them. The bride and groom were unremarkable in their seats at the center of a long table, but there, seated in the last chair on the left side of the wedding party, was the girl who stopped Jose Luis's heart with a sudden spike of amorous panic.

Rubí Santiago was sixteen the first time Jose Luis saw her. Her wavy black hair was drawn back with a white ribbon, her lips painted red only for the occasion of her sister's wedding. A necklace of pearls graced her thin neck, and she wore a dress of deep-blue satin, the thin straps sliding off her shoulders when she whispered to her date, a teenaged, uncouth farm boy by the looks of his unkempt hair and his tight-fitting pinstriped suit. The men played a ranchera called "El remolino fuerte," and Jose Luis's eyes followed Rubí and her apparent disinterest in the music. She seemed busy with her fork, picking at the empty corn husks on her plate, while the bride prattled on about something in her ear. This disinterest made Jose Luis play harder, too hard, so hard that he broke the top string on his guitar.

After an hour, the band took a break, and Don Humberto looked pleased even if his daughter and her new husband did not. The groom seemed more interested in talking to the guests about the war overseas and the happenings in Europe, but soon enough the two of them were off to the train station for a honeymoon in Mazatlán, the bride pulling her dress up to keep it off the ground as she stepped into Don Humberto's truck. Jose Luis ate his menudo quickly as all this happened, and when the guests returned to the patio he saw his opportunity to catch the girl alone. He went over without thinking about it. Had Jose Luis given the matter much thought, he would have never looked into Rubí's black eyes as he introduced himself, would have never noticed the small mole on her cheek or felt her small hand in his as they said hello. The girl gave off a floral scent. Jose Luis couldn't tell one flower from another, but, as he breathed Rubí in, it was a wonder that God would have bothered to create additional fragrances.

"¿Hay alguna canción especial que te gustaría oír?" Jose Luis asked, and Rubí told Jose Luis that she had always enjoyed listening to "Dos sombras sin cuerpo." She laughed a small laugh that suggested the bolero was a matter for embarrassment. The song was one of the two Jose Luis had composed that kept a regular rotation in the Mariachi Orosco's performances. His pride swelled accordingly, though he tried to keep this to himself. He told Rubí they'd play it, and Rubí giggled then said good-bye, each little bit of laughter a bright bubble of joy.

As the band reconvened for their second set, Don Cisco told Jose

Luis, "Esa muchacha está bien chula," nudging the young musician with his elbow. Jose Luis told him that Rubí was more than just cute, more than just good-looking, and as her date tugged at his coat sleeves and walked Rubí out to the dance floor, El Solterito felt himself flooded with a new sense of purpose.

After Rosalía's wedding, Jose Luis didn't return to the hacienda Santiago for another two weeks. In that time, the girl hid in the scenery of his every waking moment, laughing her wonderful laugh. Jose Luis would imagine the farm boy with her that night, that mannerless pendejo, that mule in man's clothing. The thought made him sick with jealousy for twelve days, and on the morning of the thirteenth, much in the manner of the songs he played nightly, Jose Luis awoke from a restless sleep ready to tear out his own heart. He showered and dressed in his best gabardine shirt and spent ten pesos on a bus ticket to Cuauhtémoc.

After arriving in town, Jose Luis walked along the highway, his stride brisk for another half mile. He waited at the iron gates until he was allowed in by a field hand. Jose Luis asked to speak to Don Humberto, and he was pointed to a small woman in white serving clothes. Jose Luis repeated his request to her and found himself ushered into a small, dim study room with a framed map of the state and shelves of seeds and pesticides and thick tomes on horticulture. The seeds were kept in jars on one side of the study, the pesticides on the other, in dark bottles marked with skulls and crossbones, near the window, the toxins' acrid odor of death found faintly in the room. Jose Luis stood between a broad oak desk and a pair of fat leather chairs, gathering his courage about him like a flimsy cloak.

When Don Humberto did arrive, the farmer was dressed in grimy work pants, his tan shirt flecked with mud. Jose Luis quickly revealed the feelings he had toward the man's daughter, that with his permission he'd like to see her socially. Don Humberto took this in, rubbing a patch of mud on his elbow, seemingly giving his shirt the bulk of his consideration. Like a boxer after throwing his best punch, Jose Luis stood for one terrible moment after another, waiting for some type of crushing retaliation. If she is interested, Don Humberto said calmly, you may see her. He told Jose Luis she was in town with her mother for the afternoon, and things would be best if the young musician went home.

Jose Luis returned to Chihuahua, to the room he was renting on the Orosco estate, where he spent the night awake. He thought no, no, no, she will say no. He tuned and retuned his guitar, yet every note twanged awfully regardless of how he varied the tension in the strings. Then Jose Luis remembered her request of his song, and he began to believe yes, yes, yes. The girl will say yes. With this, Jose Luis wondered where he might take her, and suddenly his adopted city became much too small, every attraction childish and petty. The next afternoon a telegram arrived that roughly read: "Rubí Santiago requests your presence at her home next Sunday at 4:00 P.M." Jose Luis sent a message back that he would be there, and this was the beginning of the end for El Solterito.

While the men in the group were happy for Jose Luis, the young musician's attention lapsed during the week's rehearsals. His nimble fingers frequently slipped along the neck of his guitar, and complex parts that had demanded only Jose Luis's slightest concentration became impossible. When Saturday came, Jose Luis ironed his clothes twice, starching the creases in his pants until they looked capable of slicing bread. He bought a bouquet of pink campanillas and a bag of mangoes with orange, unblemished skins. He took the afternoon bus to Cuauhtémoc, and Rubí met him at the iron gate, along with her mother. The girl was wearing a white dress imprinted with tiny oranges. She wore pale stockings and round-toed red shoes with thick and modest heels. They all shook hands hello, and after Jose Luis passed the mangoes to her mother, he told Rubí she looked beautiful, and Rubí glanced off into the apple trees lining the drive and said thank you.

Jose Luis sat opposite Rubí and her mother in the same patio where the wedding had been, servants interrupting the awkward conversation by bringing them glasses of Pepsi with ice, and tacos of shredded goat meat, and a tray of sliced tomato, avocado, and fragrant queso fresco. They covered the expected topics: school, movies, and music, though Doña Filomina seemed at all times removed from the conversation, and, at six o'clock, Rubí wheeled out the radio so that they could listen to *La Hora Ranchera.*

"Mi padre casi nunca se pierde una programa," Rubí told Jose Luis, explaining that even if he's out among the apple trees, Don Humberto stops his work and returns to the house to enjoy the program. This week seemed to be an exception, as Don Humberto never arrived. The featured artists on the program were a pair of high-pitched sisters from Durango. They began, and Rubí asked Jose Luis if the Mariachi Orosco had plans to return to XEW.

Jose Luis explained the trouble that Casimiro was having, tempering the information with a declaration that something was bound to happen soon. "Asi se hace todo," he said with a shrug.

Gradually the conversation shifted to the songs the group played, Rubí inquiring if any of the ones she had heard were his.

"Pues, 'Dos sombras sin cuerpo' es mía," Jose Luis admitted. Sheepishly he added that he'd since written six other songs with the help of Don Cisco, and he accidentally held up five fingers to represent his total, and both youngsters burst into a shared moment of laughter. Later, it would be this moment that Jose Luis would recall in his El Monte motel room, the exact words to the song irretrievable in the depths of his memory.

On the following three Sundays, the Santiago family met Jose Luis and his mother for the morning services at the cathedral in Chihuahua. Jose Luis always greeted them with gifts. There would be a flower for Rubí. If it matched the girl's dress, her mother would twist off the stem and tuck the blossom in her daughter's hair, and Jose Luis always gave the florist in the mercado a substantial tip in hopes that the extra money might help create the coincidence. Besides this, Jose Luis usually purchased a cigar for Don Humberto and brought a small box of cajeta or some other handmade candy for the farmer's wife.

Rubí and Jose Luis spent the afternoons in the plaza, followed by her parents. They fed pumpkin seeds to the pigeons, and sometimes they caught matinees at the Cine Chihuahuense. Her parents preferred the comedies, and over the course of the summer they saw three movies with Chaplin and one with Cantinflas where the skinny Mexican comic played a wrestler. Don Humberto always argued that Chaplin was the better comedian since he conveyed so much emotion without relying on words. Jose Luis would nod yes, of course, and Rubí would laugh into her napkin as he tapped her under the table with his foot.

It wasn't unusual for the Santiagos to visit the beer gardens when the Mariachi Orosco was playing. Rubí would always request "Dos sombras sin cuerpo" and the group would sometimes play it three times before the night was over. Once in July, Rubí asked that Jose Luis sing it. While Jose Luis had been practicing his singing in private for some time, and he'd been urged forward by the other musicians in their rehearsals, he politely declined out of respect for Casimiro. Don Humberto left their table and placed a stack of pesos in Casimiro's hands. "Deja que cante el joven," Don Humberto said, and Casimiro took two steps back, leaving the spotlight empty so Jose Luis could make his public debut.

Jose Luis approached the white circle on the stage and stood in its center. He looked out into the crowd and was blinded. He sang and his voice was timid and meek. Don Humberto pounded his empty shot glass on the table. "¡Con ganas chavo!" he cried and Jose Luis sang louder. Though he couldn't see Rubí, Jose Luis pictured her smiling and this made him sing with ardor and zeal until his voice strained at its limits. Soon it was over. Applause came and Jose Luis stepped out of the spotlight to watch Rubí clap, though he couldn't differentiate her clapping from that of the people around her. This is what Jose Luis would love from this moment onward, the feeling that from him something could spring forth that was worth other people's approval.

JOSE LUIS BEGAN TO GET the Mariachi Orosco regular bookings in Cuauhtémoc. The group played at two quinceañeras, one for a friend of Rubí's, the other for a daughter of Doña Filomina's comadre. The group played at a feast day for Cuauhtémoc's small church, and spent two weekends at a local cantina (by this time Jose Luis's visits to the town were frequent enough that the woman at the marble counter would punch his ticket before he reached her).

Occasionally Jose Luis would bring his guitar to Cuauhtémoc when he wasn't playing and occasionally he wouldn't. On the days that he did, the couple sang together even though Rubí didn't have much of a voice. After each song was done, Doña Filomina would applaud, and the romance of the moment would be broken by her clapping. That summer, Jose Luis and Rubí often talked about his guitar playing, about the aches the boy sometimes got in his fingers. Before he developed calluses, he sometimes felt compelled to play until his fingertips bled. He tried to explain this to Rubí, along with the awful guilt that came in the days he couldn't play because he was healing. Once the young couple managed to catch two minutes alone on a bench overlooking the northern orchard. Rubí massaged the calluses on his fingertips, making the hardened skin warm and soft, and at that moment Jose Luis felt connected to the young woman holding his hand, joined to her by a wildly joyous love.

Because of the continual supervision, they still had not kissed in July, but Jose Luis was certain that Rubí was in love as well. She told him once among the trees that she had been practicing her kissing, her voice hushed. She gave Jose Luis's hand a squeeze and admitted to kissing her hand mirror, telling him she felt silly pressing her lips against the cold reflective glass. Sometimes she made a fist and kissed her curled index finger, and that seemed to work best. Jose Luis asked what she saw in her future, and when Rubí didn't have an answer, Jose Luis wondered if a life spent with him might be a strange and alien concept.

It was acceptable for Jose Luis to hold Rubí's hand, but one day in August he put his arm on her shoulder while walking to the highway. Doña Filomina tossed a fallen apple and hit Jose Luis lightly on the leg, reminding him that this type of contact was not acceptable. Slowly the summer became unendurable. Jose Luis imagined what Rubí's lips might taste like, and while he had heard of sex, had pieced its machinations together from the jokes and stories he heard from other musicians and patrons of the beer gardens, he lacked any firsthand knowledge of what the act involved. He began having wild dreams where he hugged Rubí and they twisted back and forth, naked under the sheets, and Jose Luis would awaken, his body damp and musky with sweat, his underwear wet with milky fluid.

As the fall drew close, Jose Luis got the idea of a wedding. He talked to Casimiro and asked if he did get married, could he and his new bride stay with the Oroscos, the Orosco hacienda being expansive as it was. Jose Luis offered to pay Casimiro an increased rent, adding that the young couple would be no bother. It would be until things with the group took off and they could afford a place of their own. Casimiro considered the matter until Doña Imelda put her hand on his knee and it was agreed that they could stay. Jose Luis had been saving money, enough for the most expensive ring in the more reputable of Chihuahua's three jewelry shops. The 24-carat gold was extracted from the southern mines of San Francisco del Oro, cross-hatched in an elegant design, set with a stone that would cost Jose Luis an extra month's work, the credit extended once Casimiro vouched for the young musician.

Don Humberto inspected the ring closely and, after an arduous few seconds of quiet contemplation in his study, nodded his approval and his permission was granted with a firm and welcoming handshake. On the last Sunday in September, Rubí and the Santiagos were invited to dinner at the Orosco Hacienda. The other mariachis were present, and Jose Luis's frail mother was sent for. After a meal of fried fish and toasted ears of white corn, eight months since Don Humberto's third daughter was married, the ring was bestowed on his fourth girl and the matter was settled. Before their families, their esteemed friends, and the watchful eyes of God, Rubí Guadalupe Santiago del Valle would give Jose Luis, El Solterito, the honor of accepting her hand in marriage.

THE STREETS ARE EMPTY as Jose Luis goes past the Salvation Army, the post office, the Tres Hermanos with its glass storefront full of shoes. Jose Luis has walked and walked and walked, past closed business after closed business, his feet swollen and achy, his arms heavy with fatigue. There isn't a hotel in sight. After half an hour, Jose Luis begins to wonder if the young man who gave him these directions is somewhere laughing at the cruel joke of a viejito lost in this darkened part of town.

The moon is full and high in the sky, and by its position Jose Luis figures the time to be past midnight, one in the morning Chihuahua time. He continues under a freeway overpass, and walks by a McDonald's, its windows dim, the aroma of greasy beef still hanging in the air. He stops by a Pontiac dealership, the smell from the McDonald's making his stomach grumble. Jose Luis reopens the package of carne seca and puts another good-sized hunk in his mouth. Even though he hasn't driven in almost twenty years, he looks with interest at the aisles of shiny cars as he chews. The meat begins to break down in Jose Luis's mouth, and a rich saltiness rewards his tongue. He gets another piece of meat, chewing carefully, slowly, working the carne seca on the other side of his mouth.

Jose Luis picks up his bag and guitar, switching them in his hands to vary their weight. He moves on, and after two blocks he notices a blue-and-white flashing neon sign. When he gets close enough to see that the sign doesn't say HOTEL, the surge of hopeful energy in him vanishes as quickly as it appeared. But Jose Luis recognizes the words COLD and BEER and he proceeds to discover, painted on the side of the building, large horse heads encircled by horseshoes. The door's small window is a diamond of the light inside. Jose Luis swallows his second piece of carne seca, then walks into the Horseshoe Club.

The empty bar is bathed in blue light, the television on too loudly for so small a room. There's a young man talking with the female bartender at the far end of the bar, and a couple occupying one of the three booths in the back corner. Jose Luis sits on a stool and lets his worn body rest. When the bartender asks what he'd like to drink, she does so in English, which Jose Luis doesn't comprehend. His inability to understand clogs his brain with desperate thoughts. He looks at the black-haired woman before him, at her bright green blouse and the dangling gold bracelets that cover both wrists, and he wants to ask if she knows this damned hotel, if she can help him find a beautiful woman named Rubí, if she can make Rubí's heart murmur with anticipation as his does. But Jose Luis shoves all this down. He's been in plenty of rooms like this before. He knows what the woman is asking and in response he stammers out, "Cerveza."

"What kind?" the woman asks, and Jose Luis smiles and says the word again. The woman points to the red-and-white handle of the Budweiser tap. "Is this okay?" she asks, and Jose Luis nods. As she fills a mug, Jose Luis figures that since he's in America, he might as well enjoy it while he can. He raps his knuckles on the bar to get the woman's attention.

"¿Me das un whisky también, un Jack Daniels por favor?" The woman says sure, reaching under the counter for the bottle, taking her time to pour the drink.

"Five even," she says and Jose Luis looks at her five fingers and understands. He gives her a ten-dollar bill, then looks at his brimming glasses of gold and auburn liquid, grinning halfheartedly at the smallness of these luxuries. Jose Luis drinks the whisky and sips his beer. When the woman returns with his change, he asks her if she speaks Spanish. She tells him no, but Jose Luis asks if there's a hotel around here anyway.

The woman nods, apparently recognizing a word or two. "Oh yeah," she says, "the Eight Palms Inn. It's just a few blocks down, across from Crawford's Market, on the left-hand side." But it's clear that her instructions don't make much sense to Jose Luis. "Look, I don't know how to tell you," she says, "but he does." The bartender points to the young man at the end of the room. She calls him and he doesn't respond. She puts two fingers in her mouth and whistles, and the young man perks up from the television and comes over.

He sits next to Jose Luis. He's wearing dirty blue work pants and the bulging muscles in his chest strain against his tank top. Because of the poor light, Jose Luis can't make out the word tattooed on his neck, but it's clear that both of the young man's arms are covered in dark black ink. To Jose Luis these markings are markings of trouble, and when the young man extends his hand, it's as if Jose Luis has been asked to shake hands with an oversized coil of barbed wire. The young man keeps his hand out and says, "Lencho Cruz, a sus órdenes."

Jose Luis introduces himself, and shakes his hand.

"¿De donde eres?" Lencho asks, and Jose Luis tells him he's up from Chihuahua. Lencho motions to the guitar case between their stools and asks what's inside it. "¿Eres mariachi?" he asks.

"No," Jose Luis answers, "soy músico, pero no soy mariachi." He grins a private grin, and shakes his head at the beer before him.

"¿Pues qué buscas aqui?" Lencho asks, and Jose Luis tells him that he's only looking for a hotel, someplace to set his things down and get a good night's sleep.

Lencho says okay, and taps his shoe against Jose Luis's guitar case. "Tócanos una canción," Lencho says, and Jose Luis tells him that he's too tired to play. Lencho picks up the guitar case and sets it on the counter. "Órale hombre, tócanos una canción." He asks Jose Luis to play again, and this time he sweetens the offer. Lencho tells him that if he grants them a song, he'll not only give Jose Luis directions to the hotel, but he'll drive him there personally.

"Just give the old man the directions," the bartender says.

"But baby, I'm in the mood to hear some music," Lencho says. Without looking away from Jose Luis, Lencho raises his voice, throwing it to the couple in the booth. "Hey Manny," he yells, "you feel like hearing a song?"

"Why the hell not?" Manny yells back. "The jukebox hasn't worked in over a year." The girl with Manny laughs.

Jose Luis doesn't want to play. He truly is tired, and at this point he feels more annoyed by the young man than threatened. Still, he has to get to this hotel somehow. He flips open the latches to his guitar case, and Lencho yells "All right!" He claps his hands, and has the bartender climb on a chair to turn down the sound on the television. Jose Luis takes the guitar from its bed of faded red velvet and scoots away from the bar a bit so that the instrument has room. He adjusts the bridge so it's clipped to the correct fret, and asks Lencho what he wants to hear. "Toca lo que quieras," Lencho answers. Jose Luis fiddles with a tuning screw until the top string resonates cleanly, and then he plays the first song that comes to his mind.

Jose Luis sings, but he doesn't allow himself to get lost in the music. His voice comes out flat, more a recital than a song. He figures his small audience won't know the difference, won't care enough about the music to notice, and this is true until Lencho stops him. The young man wraps his hand around the neck of the guitar. He tells Jose Luis to play it like he means it, or he isn't taking him anywhere.

"Está bien," Jose Luis says, taking his guitar back. He takes a second drink of his beer, more to seem calm than to seem thirsty. He starts the song a second time and goes right back to the verse where God dresses the land with blankets embroidered with sun, where sombreros are molded from sky, where spurs are carved from the moon and stars. Jose Luis looks at the dank ceiling while singing as if the images would all be there. Manny puts two fingers in his mouth and whistles, and Lencho pounds his hand against the bar in approval as Jose Luis lets the song flow from him in earnest.

FOR HER WEDDING, Rubí wore Ofelia's dress, certainly not because her family was poor, but because the Santiago daughters had worn it for three generations. The ceremony was small, practically austere compared to Rosalía's. From girlhood Rubí had always believed she'd be married in Cuauhtémoc's modest hillside chapel, and for this reason the site was chosen over the opulent cathedral in Chihuahua. Behind the kneeling bride and groom, the old pews creaked under the weight of the guests—the parents, the sisters and their husbands, the Mariachi Orosco and their wives. The chapel walls had been decorated with the few flowers around Cuauhtémoc that were in season, apple blossoms mostly. At one point in the ceremony, the croaky priest lost his place in his reading, and Jose Luis glanced over at his shining bride. Rubí's expression, the calm and content smile on her lips, told him that he was a fortunate man.

The newlyweds spent their honeymoon in Mexico City. This was against the wishes of Rubí's father, since the Santiago sisters had all honeymooned on the sandy white beaches of Mazatlán. Rubí and Jose Luis traveled by train, a two-day journey over sloping, erratic landscape. Their compartment consisted of four narrow bunks, two on each side, along with a window and a small shelf under which was a basin for washing. Casimiro's wedding gift had been to reserve all four bunks in the compartment, ensuring the newlyweds some privacy for the duration of their trip to the capital.

On board the train, they sat side by side, Jose Luis wondering how they should begin their life together. They drank Coca-Cola spiced with shots of Puerto Rican rum, Rubí keeping the soda cool by padding the bottles with one of Jose Luis's shirts, placing them in a sack and hanging it outside their window in the cold mountain air. They talked, awkwardly at first, starting at the same time, interrupting each other's plans for what they might do upon reaching the city. Rubí wanted to visit the museum, to walk the length of Chapultepec Park, while Jose Luis had a letter from Casimiro to deliver to the XEW. Rubí snacked on pieces of tamarindo cajeta that her mother had given her. When the newlyweds kissed, Rubí's mouth tasted of the bittersweet fruit, and, in the coming months, the taste, the smell, the smallest hint of tamarind would stir Jose Luis's loins. Their actions were gentle and tentative that night, for it seemed to Jose Luis that Doña Filomina might burst through the heavy woolen curtain to steal her daughter away at any time.

Jose Luis and Rubí kissed slowly and deliberately until the sun began to peek over the blue canyon walls. They undressed for bed, and Rubí forced Jose Luis to look away as she made her way out of her new green travel dress, though he kept a careful watch on her reflection in the window. Jose Luis was anxious to consummate his marriage, but outside circumstances made the matter an impossibility. They pressed into the tight space of one bunk, but the train pitched on the rails in its descent to the Mapimí Valley, and Rubí was tossed to the ground. Still, Jose Luis was reluctant to sleep alone. He suggested that they take the blankets and sleep on the compartment's wooden floor, but Rubí shook her head and pointed at the ankles of foot traffic just outside the curtain. They eventually spent their first married night apart. The train rocked and weaved through the block mountains and bolsónes of the altiplano, Rubí in the lower bunk, Jose Luis in the upper.

The newlyweds stayed four days in the capital. The marriage was consummated upon arriving at the hotel, though the sex was nothing like Jose Luis had imagined it. They kissed and gradually undressed, and, naked, they kissed some more. Rubí was hesitant to proceed, and she bit her lip when Jose Luis entered her. He finished quickly the first time, their brief motions clumsy and rhythmless, like a machine on the verge of breaking down. Jose Luis would push Rubí away right as he finished, and afterward they held each other. Jose Luis kissed Rubí's brow and dabbed at the wetness he left on her stomach with the sheet. She gave him a meek smile and they napped, pressed together, the overhead fan creaking above them.

That afternoon they attended a bullfight, a first for them both. They spent twenty pesos for seats close to the ring, where Jose Luis was awed by the event's majestic spectacle and Rubí wept quietly when the tragic wobbling beast was finally ended. They slept late the next day, drinking beer with their afternoon lunch, Jose Luis finishing three bottles to Rubí's one. They bought a pack of Fiestas and a book of matches from a street vendor and passed each cigarette back and forth, Rubí taking two puffs before handing it to Jose Luis. They saw strange animals in the museum, and spent time in Chapultepec Park, where Jose Luis fed Rubí wedges of mango spiced with powdered chile, and she read him gossip from a magazine devoted to stars of the Mexican cinema.

Twice the newlyweds tried to have dinner at a nightclub named Guadalajara de Noche, but because they weren't American tourists or people of local importance, because their pocket money was limited, there was no way they could see El Mariachi Marmolejo. The group was billed in red neon out front as the best in the world, and Jose Luis felt eager to judge this claim for himself. Instead Jose Luis and Rubí ended up at a restaurant called El Sonido Famoso, where the food was bad, but the entertainment was worse.

On the small stage at El Sonido Famoso was a group of mariachis. Awful, awful mariachis. Sloppy in every sense of the word. When one violin player worked his bow across the strings, Jose Luis could see the man's white shirt where his sleeve was frayed at the shoulder. The same musician yawned incessantly as the group strolled through the restaurant, bored with the music he played. Both Rubí and Jose Luis caught the guitar player making the unforgivable mistake of checking his pocket watch in plain view of the clientele. Rubí even recognized when the musicians would miss their entrances, the trumpet player being the worst, so that at times the music sounded as if members of the group were each playing their own song.

"Debes de ir a tocar con ellos," Rubí said. She shook Jose Luis's arm enthusiastically and her lips brushed his ear as she spoke. "Enséñales a cantar."

Jose Luis shrugged off Rubí's suggestions, though his hands ached for his guitar and he felt that his voice was richer, weightier with emotion. They finished their dinner, and a second group took to the small stage. It consisted of five boys in tiny cream-colored trajes, each appearing no more than ten years old, with faces round as apples. It was immediately clear that the novelty of their ages was their basis for performing. While Rubí enjoyed the vocalist's overwrought, anguished cries, Jose Luis found the act distasteful.

"Es una cosa indecente," Jose Luis said. He told Rubí that the young vocalist was years away from knowing any kind of heartache.

There was rain the next morning, the newlyweds' last in the city. The showers ceased at midday, and Jose Luis and Rubí took a cab to XEW. In his shirt pocket, Jose Luis carried a small envelope with business cards and a letter encouraging Javier Cornejo to consider the group for a second appearance. Rubí took each step up the mountainside carefully, and halfway up she stopped.

"Tengo miedo," she said sheepishly. Her grip on Jose Luis's arm was tight, her legs wobbly, and it was then that he discovered that his wife had a fear of heights.

Jose Luis put his arm around Rubí's waist. He spoke assuring words, and they continued slowly, arriving at the summit only to find the lobby empty, the studio dark. The station was temporarily off the air, and there was a handwritten sign taped to the door that simply read, PROBLEMAS ELÉCTRICAS. Jose Luis had Rubí kiss the envelope for good luck, and she made the sign of the cross as he slid the letter under the door. The morning showers returned as they made their way back down, the rain increasing steadily, so that Jose Luis and Rubí were drenched upon reaching the street. Jose Luis had planned on calling a cab from the station, but now he stood with his wife, wet and stranded. Rubí's stockings and shoes were ruined by blotches of gummy, orange mud, and the newlyweds spent the final hours of their honeymoon searching for the comfort of their dry hotel.

THE SMALL WOMAN IN THE OFFICE at the Eight Palms Inn speaks Spanish, and at this Jose Luis is relieved. Lencho stands behind him like a bodyguard, arms folded, face stern, when Jose Luis pays for his room. Jose Luis tells the young man that he can find his room by himself, but Lencho picks up the sack, following Jose Luis upstairs to a room overlooking the parking lot. Jose Luis thanks him and Lencho says, "Por nada." They each say good-night, and Lencho stomps down the stairs and gets into his car, a blue Buick Regal. He waves and Jose Luis waves back as though the two acquaintances were old friends. The room is a motel room, plain and simple, and, once he's inside, Jose Luis's boots come off and he lies on the bed where sleep descends upon him like a thick black blanket.

The next morning is a thirsty one. Jose Luis drinks in gulps from the faucet and brushes his teeth. He showers and stays under the warm water for a long time because he can. Today he will see Rubí. He shaves according to this expectation, leaving his skin raw and smooth. He pulls on his dark jeans and a thin undershirt. The phone book on the nightstand has a map of El Monte and its neighboring communities, and the next half hour of Jose Luis's morning is spent eating his other apple and searching for the street in Rubí's address. He hopes her home will be nearby, within walking distance.

The map isn't a good one. It only has the city's major streets, and it seems more concerned with El Monte's position in relation to the bordering freeways than with specific details. It's of no help to Jose Luis. He sets the book aside and chews his apple. Jose Luis returns to the phone book and searches the White Pages for Rubí's name, for a confirmation of her existence, not a phone number. What Jose Luis wants to tell her shouldn't be said over the telephone. He looks under Navarro, her second husband's last name, but there is no Rubí between Romulo and Silvia. He looks for her under his name, but she isn't between Roxanna and Rudolpho Chavira either. He flips to her maiden name, but there is no Rubí between Romeo and Rufino Santiago. Jose Luis goes back to the N's and finds six different Jose Navarros, but none of the addresses in these listings correspond with the one in his hand.

At that moment it occurs to Jose Luis that Rubí may still be grieving.

He doesn't know exactly how long Jose Navarro has been dead, and this uncertainty is a terrible thing. Jose Luis thinks of what he'll have to say, what songs he might play if at this time Rubí isn't exactly eager for romance. Jose Luis still knows a ranchera called "El abandonado," but its lyrics lament the loss of a loved one after a lifetime of drinking and gambling in the arms of other women. It's a song for an audience of young cowboys, not a tender widow. "Mi vida solita" is a sad bolero that feels more appropriate. Jose Luis vaguely recalls a few lines of "Mis manos mojadas," another song that is sadder still. He unpacks his guitar and plays each tune twice, making a few hasty notes on a sheet of motel stationary, getting the notes correct in his head. Jose Luis has played all these songs before, dozens of times after dozens of funerals. He knows when to overpower every sound in the room with his voice, how to make it seem like the suffering of others exists inside him.

Jose Luis packs up his guitar and brushes his hair with a wet comb— up and to the side, up and to the side. He dresses in a fresh blue shirt with short sleeves and white pearl snaps. He packs up his guitar and gets his key and puts on his Stetson. When he passes the office, he looks for the woman from last night, but she has been replaced by a young man, a chunky kid playing loud rock on a boom box, and this makes Jose Luis want to brave the city on his own. There are no taxis the way Jose Luis had anticipated, the way that they clog the narrow avenues in Chihuahua. He walks down Valley Boulevard, toward a large intersection. There will be a taxi there, he thinks. Jose Luis is impressed by the city now that it's daylight. The streets are wide here. Room for four cars, not just one. The sidewalks are smooth, and the buildings are set back from the streets. There is nothing but open space here, and it comforts him to know that Rubí is somewhere inside it all. Today I will see you, Jose Luis thinks. Today.

Upon their return to Chihuahua, Rubí's things had been moved into the Hacienda Orosco. The room they shared was in the rear of the house, its closet full of Rubí's bright dresses. The movers had also brought her radio and her dresser, and, besides the fact that they were placed in the wrong corner of the room, she was dismayed at a small scalloped chip on the top of the dresser's mirror. Jose Luis enlisted the help of Joaquin, and the two men dragged the piece of furniture near the window. Rubí bought new sheets and she smoothed lumps from the mattress, but instead the lumps seemed to trade sides from night to night.

The newlyweds went to Cuauhtémoc for dinner one Sunday, where the story of their rainy afternoon in Mexico City was told differently. Rubí spoke of the incident with annoyance and scorn, while Jose Luis's version sounded as though he'd sneaked a note under God's door. Jose Luis and Rubí also met the latest addition to the familia Santiago, Ofelia's third son, Samuel Bernardo Chavez Santiago. Samuel contentedly spent most of the evening in Rubí's arms. There were winks and nudges as the chubby baby was passed around, and Jóse Luis's brother-in-law asked if soon Rubí would begin to curve with signs of motherhood.

At this Jose Luis shrugged, clasping Rubí's hand tightly. "Cuando Dios piense que estemos listos," he said, though he secretly worried that God would deem him ready for fatherhood much too soon. Jose Luis's income as musician was enough for him and his wife, but it wouldn't be ample for the family she leaned toward. He thought of Rubí pregnant and saw himself headed back to the foundry where he'd trade his guitar for the mallets he once used to render pots from heavy sheets of copper.

One afternoon Rubí returned from the mercado with a small shrub of Spanish jasmine. The plant took quick root, climbing the lower rungs of the trellis outside their window, unfolding its pink and white blossoms in just a few weeks. Jose Luis soon recognized the scent from their first encounter. Rubí trimmed blossoms selectively, and often she attended church with one or two in her hair. The chosen flowers were kept on her nightstand in a wooden bowl filled with water until they shriveled into wrinkly brown heads. Occasionally, when Rubí was bathing, Jose Luis stood over the bowl and breathed in deeply, because the smell reminded him of a different time, a period not so long ago where they'd wanted the same things. He'd stir the dead blossoms among the fragrant water, and, rather than dry his hands with a towel, he'd suck the homemade perfume from his fingers because it seemed such a shame to waste it.

ON THE THIRD FRIDAY OF MAY 1943, a man named Cipriano Olivares returned to Chihuahua. His arrival was no secret. Don Cipriano was a short, big block of a man. He had boxy feet and boxy hands that gave his body the appearance of a statue that forsook the artist's refining chisels before opting to walk into life. Don Cipriano had made money, much money, producing Mexican movies, comedies mostly. Upon reaching the city from the train station with his mousy wife, his daughter, and a small squad of assistants in tow, Don Cipriano went directly to the Hotel Marina, where the entire third floor was reserved in his name. His personal suite happened to be one of the three with balconies overlooking the beer gardens, and that night Jose Luis spotted the red point of the producer's cigar during the Mariachi Orosco's performance.

Since that first request made by Rubí and her father nine months ago, Jose Luis had begun to regularly sing "Dos sombras sin cuerpo" at the beer garden performances. Along with a few other standards that were invariably requested, the songs were considered his to sing. Jose Luis relished these brief minutes in the spotlight. He regarded the songs as important possessions, and their words occurred to him while in bed with Rubí, scrubbing in the shower, or while riding the bus out to Cuauhtémoc for dinner with his in-laws on Sunday afternoons. Every last word was his, and Jose Luis considered each song like a coin in a small but precious piggy bank.

That night in the beer gardens, Jose Luis sang "Dos sombras sin cuerpo" with a shaking voice, and his guitar-playing became tentative, as if the instrument in his hands had been replaced by one blown from glass. With Don Cipriano's connection to the movies, Jose Luis knew that his performance was an audition of sorts. The crowd was thin, more empty tables than full ones, and Jose Luis did what he could to guard against his encroaching anxiety. He focused his attention on the people there, the group of drunk and laughing students, thin Padre Zamora and his half-eaten tostada, Fernando the bartender polishing glasses with a gray rag. From time to time, Jose Luis could make out applause coming from the balcony, and his nerves relaxed a turn each time the faint sounds of Don Cipriano's clapping managed to reach his ears.

Afterward, the men were packing up their instruments when one of Don Cipriano's assistants came calling for Casimiro. The assistant was a wiry man with wiry glasses, and Casimiro shook his hand, happily agreeing to walk over to the Hotel Marina to talk business with the small man's boss. Juanito wished his brother good luck, and then the Mariachi Orosco went their respective ways home. By this time, it was late. Jose Luis made the moonlit walk back to the Hacienda Orosco alone, his tie undone, his damp shirt chilling him now that he was away from the stage lights' warm glow.

Though he was tired and cold, Jose Luis wondered about the deals being talked about in the Hotel Marina. The image of the two giants bargaining kept his mind lucid with fantasies: Jose Luis in the XEW studios once again, recording "Dos sombras sin cuerpo"; Jose Luis cradled by a plush leather chair, a nice glass of American whisky in his hand, his voice soaring from the radio; Jose Luis in the front row of El Cine Chihuahuense, a full house watching him sing on the broad movie screen. In this fantasy, Jose Luis stood in a fine traje made of a blue material as deep and dark as the sky above him. There was a golden revolver at his hip and a sturdy guitar in his hands. Jose Luis was singing for Dolores Del Rio, and he was playing with hard, quick strokes, making the heart of every woman within earshot beat fast.

The Hacienda Orosco was dark when Jose Luis arrived home. He latched the iron gate and stepped lightly through the yard, so as not to stir the sleeping chickens. In their bedroom, Jose Luis set his guitar next to Rubí's bureau. He proceeded to hang his traje carefully, placing the jacket on a heavy wooden hanger. Before hanging the pants, Jose Luis brushed the dust from the cuffs, and Rubí stayed fast asleep, dead to the world even as the empty legs jingled lightly. Jose Luis changed into a dry undershirt and shorts and slid into place beside his wife. Rubí stirred a bit, twisting in the sheet, and Jose Luis kissed her on the neck and promptly fell asleep.

Soon after, Jose Luis found himself awakened by Casimiro. He jostled Jose Luis's arm and whispered in his ear. "Ven a la cocina. Tengo algo que decirte."

They sat at the kitchen table, Casimiro wearing only his underwear and the thick odor of cigar smoke. Jose Luis's eyes adjusted to the bright bulb hanging above him. Through the kitchen's screen door, he saw Casimiro's traje hanging on the clothesline, its silver glinting in the moonlight. Doña Imelda came in from outside wearing a pink robe. She kissed Jose Luis on the head as though he were her son, and stood behind Casimiro as he spoke.

"Estamos contratados para una recepción," Casimiro said, his wife's hand tightly in his.

A reception? "¿Para Don Cipriano?" Jose Luis asked.

"Sí," Casimiro said. "¡Va hacer un recepiónazo!"

He explained that he had quoted Don Cipriano an inflated rate, and the producer agreed to it without batting an eye. Casimiro produced a wad of bills from his lap. He passed it to Jose Luis, and it dropped into his hand with unexpected heft. Jose Luis had never seen so much money at once. He flipped through the bills, looking at portraits of Hidalgo and Morelos and the other national heroes printed on the larger denominations.

"¡Don Cipriano esta encantado con nosotros!" Casimiro exclaimed. He clapped Jose Luis on the back and told him that Don Cipriano was impressed with the group, that he liked Don Cisco's songs, and that he found Casimiro's voice to be bold and brash, but, all that aside, Don Cipriano couldn't stop talking about Jose Luis.

JOSE LUIS FEELS AS THOUGH he's walked up and down every street in the city except the one he's looking for. He's outside Crawford's Market, on a bench, eyes throbbing from too much sun. His fingers are sticky from the snack he bought off a street vendor, a soft mango made of sweet orange glue, and, for the past half hour, Jose Luis has worked on a Budweiser tall boy, taking sips from a paper sack, his worry upon him like a heavy coat worn in the summertime. Customers leave the store with their shopping carts full of groceries. They load up their cars and they drive away to their homes, to their loved ones, their lives. Jose Luis has yet to see a single taxi today.

He begins to ask these people for help with directions, but the first woman he approaches seems to mistake him for a solicitor. The woman wears a blue business suit with matching heels that click on the pavement. She pulls a pair of dark sunglasses from her purse and takes Rubí's address from Jose Luis's hand. Without breaking her brisk stride, she says, "Sorry, I'm not interested." The paper goes into the trash.

Jose Luis retrieves the address and tries again. This time he stops a round woman holding a spiky green piñata and asks if she speaks Spanish. Thankfully, she says yes. The woman's with a boy, the boy still wearing his school uniform, blue pants, a dirty white shirt. This woman reads Rubí's address and tells Jose Luis that the street is unfamiliar. She also tells him that he's in the wrong part of the city. The zip code's in South El Monte, not El Monte. She rubs her son's brown hair and tells Jose Luis that the zip code's the same one as the boy's school.

"Do you know where this is?" she asks the boy. The boy is busy plucking pieces of silver fringe from one of the piñata's many coney legs. The woman smacks his hand away. She passes him the slip and asks him again. The boy barely glances at the paper, mumbling and shaking his head, and Jose Luis thanks them for their time.

Jose Luis next gets the attention of a young man in a sailor uniform, a case of beer hanging from each of the sailor's hands. The sailor sets them down when Jose Luis hands him the slip with Rubí's address. The sailor rubs his thumb over the writing, looking as though he has suddenly been asked to translate Braille. "No," he says, shaking his head. "No lo conozco." He tells Jose Luis it might be over by the freeway, but he can't be sure. Jose Luis asks if the freeway's near South El Monte and the sailor says yes. He gives Jose Luis some general directions and the musician listens intently. "Derecha en la Garvey," the sailor says, navigating with his free hand. "Pasarás como diez o once bloques. Cuando llegues a Santa Anita, se me hace por ahí debe estar."

The sailor wishes Jose Luis good luck. Jose Luis thanks him. He breathes deeply, as preparation for the hours of remaining daylight. Before tossing the tall boy in the trash, he pours the rest of the warm beer into the bushes and stretches his feet inside his boots. He runs his comb through his hair and pulls his Stetson down tight. He tucks his guitar case under his arm and walks to the edge of the parking lot, wringing the mango's stickiness from his hands.

AT THE BASE OF CHIHUAHUA'S NORTHERN FOOTHILLS was an old distillery, and it soon became public knowledge that Don Cipriano planned to overhaul the four-story building in hopes of opening a brewery. The distillery's tanks were still sound, and his team of engineers had promised that whatever repairs were required would be minor, that most of the machinery could be converted without extravagant expense. Don Cipriano had contracts with grain farmers in Monterey and Saltillo, the coming season's crops already purchased, so that the brewery could be up and running as early as June or July, bottling up to four hundred cases of beer in a day.

The public announcement was made outside the distillery on a Sunday, just after the cathedral's noon service. A crackly microphone was set up on the back of a flatbed truck, and Don Cipriano gave a speech before using a ceremonial saber to cut the red ribbon stretched across the wide doors. The beer was to be named Cerveza Olivares. Don Cipriano promised better things for Chihuahua. New business for the city. Forty new jobs. He said the brewery would mark the state's first step into a modernized future. He referred to the townspeople as his guests, and invited everyone to sample the provided refreshments. Besides soda and mineral water, corks were popped off bottles of French champagne. The state's prized beef was shunned for shrimp cocktails and ceviche made of abalone and octopus, the mariscos packed in ice and flown directly from the coast in dripping wooden crates.

After Don Cipriano's speech, the Mariachi Orosco performed on the makeshift stage. Don Cisco had written two songs for the event, "Ay mi cervecita" and an up-tempo handclapper sung by Jose Luis titled "Burbujas bien borrachas." The townspeople responded wildly when Jose Luis feigned drunkeness, dropping the microphone and stumbling around the stage. Those who didn't dance clapped and stomped, and soon every foot outside the distillery kicked up dust.

Rubí attended with her parents and her sister Rosalía. Rosalía danced with her husband, Francisco, while Don Humberto alternated between his wife and Rubí. Eventually Jose Luis sang the tune about stumbling, drunken bubbles seven times. By nightfall, his throat was raspy, his voice rough and raw.

Jose Luis spent the evening with Rubí and her family outside a local café. His brother-in-law talked of America, and Rubí and her sister recounted stories of the trips to El Paso they had taken as girls. Rubí shook Jose Luis's arm and mentioned that it might be nice to go back. Francisco had heard reports of good work in Texas and California since the United States had entered the war, opportunities with more promise than the local mines or apple orchards. He thought it a good place to start a family. Don Humberto looked annoyed with Francisco's last comment, but the conversation never fully turned Francisco's way. Every two minutes they were interrupted by someone congratulating Jose Luis on his performance. The young musician's chest was swollen with pride, and he acknowledged each moment of praise with a heartfelt thank-you.

When Jose Luis arrived at the beer gardens with Casimiro for that Thursday's performance, Brenda Olivares had been sitting at a table in the back all afternoon. Every bottle cap and label, every logo associated with Cerveza Olivares, was to have Brenda's face on it, and to this end the producer's daughter was posing for an artist commissioned from the capital. Jose Luis had heard rumors from Arturo and Joaquin about the stunning young woman going around the city, but he had yet to see her up close, and up close Brenda Olivares was indeed beautiful. Her brown eyes were radiant. Her hair fell in perfect brown waves across her shoulders. The expression she wore seemed informed by an awareness of this beauty in the same way that queens know the crowns atop their heads are rare and valuable.

"Mi nariz no es tan grande," Brenda said. She appeared frustrated with the outcome of the session, particularly with the shading of her face in the painting. She stroked the bridge of her nose to emphasize her contention. "Me has pintado como un perico."

The image of Brenda in the painting had a nose that looked nothing like a parrot's. This Brenda wore a bright blue sombrero embroidered with white flowers, a bouquet of tiny yellow blossoms in her hands, her gaze fixed on a serious point in the distance. It was a fine rendering in Jose Luis's untrained opinion.

With their trajes draped across an empty table, and their instruments at their feet, the two men went about the usual business of eating dinner before performing, quesadillas and carne asada and plenty of agua mineral. During this time, the rest of the group arrived. Juanito came ten minutes late, and his brother chastised him publicly—What if you put us all behind schedule? What if important men were waiting for you?—until Don Cisco calmed Casimiro down. One at a time, the group changed in the bathroom, and they took to the stage for their first set promptly at seven-thirty.

The artist had been sent away, but Brenda remained to see the Mariachi Orosco. Three songs into the performance, the beer gardens began to fill with people. Five songs into the performance, Jose Luis saw a large, handsome man take a seat at Brenda's table. This man appeared to be some sort of an assistant or bodyguard, and the two of them moved from their table in the rear to one near the stage. Brenda took a seat and crossed her legs, one swaying to the beat of the song in a motion that gave Jose Luis rhythmic glimpses of her stockinged thighs.

That night, Brenda requested "Dos sombras sin cuerpo" five times, paying ten, then twenty, then thirty pesos for each successive performance of the song. Casimiro would collect the money, and the stage's flimsy boards would bounce when he'd pound the floor with his boots and the entire group would yell, "¡Otra!" Each time Jose Luis looked down to his guitar, Brenda's eyes were fixed on him, and he responded to her flirting by singing to the night sky, to the thick clouds stretched across the moon.

Jose Luis sang his song like a child. He sang without romance, pretending that the words didn't speak of a new lust deep inside him. Casimiro left the stage midsong, playing as he made his way to Brenda's table. The other men followed, and Jose Luis was the last one to leave the safe distance of the platform. It wasn't unusual to serenade a member of the audience, but serenading Brenda Olivares could be a dangerous matter. Jose Luis continued singing to the sky, and, when he got too close to ignore her, he focused on the candle flickering in the middle of their table, on the cigarette butts in the ashtray. He could detect the piercing scent of Brenda's perfume, and as the group finally finished playing the song for the fourth time, she reached out and stroked his hand with a light touch. "Tócala otra ves," she told him, three gold coins in her other hand.

"¡Otra!" the cry came, and Jose Luis struggled to keep his anxiety from showing.

Later, Jose Luis retreated to the bar in back. He ordered a beer and drank it in three quick gulps. His hands were trembling, partly with fear, and it was this that kept Jose Luis from responding to the applause he received. Before leaving, Brenda waved good-bye to him. Joaquin tapped Jose Luis on the shoulder and he turned in time to catch the brief flicking of her fingers as she slipped away.

The whole affair didn't escape the notice of the wives who were present, namely Doña Imelda. Casimiro didn't say much as the three of them walked home that night. He jingled his share of the coins in his pocket and talked of maybe buying a new coat in time for the winter. Rubí was asleep when Jose Luis came home. Though he couldn't rest, his mind full of ideas for new songs that would certainly bring volatile consequences if he wrote them, he lay still, his body rigid as he did his best to pretend he was sleeping.

Early the next morning, Jose Luis went out back with the twenty-peso coin, flinging his cut from the previous night's work into the dirt behind the hacienda. He threw the coin as hard as he could, but he saw where it landed, just to the right of some tall green spears of aloe. Not having the coin but knowing where it was seemed twice as bad, so Jose Luis tramped out among the thistley weeds. He found the coin and, keeping his eyes closed, he flung it again, farther, he was sure. At breakfast, Jose Luis couldn't discern if Rubí had become distant, if he had somehow betrayed himself in his sleep or if he was being irrational in his guilt. They ate quietly, fried eggs and potatoes with coffee, tortillas and bottled chile instead of the fresh salsa of onions, tomatoes and chile serrano that Rubí would often dice up for her husband. She asked about the money Jose Luis made last night and Jose Luis said he planned to deposit it in the bank. Rubí offered to do it, for she had some business with Rosalía in Cuauhtémoc, the bank near the bus station, and Jose Luis swirled a bite of his last tortilla in the thin red sauce and told her to take what cash was in his billfold. Rubí nodded, and soon after she left, and Jose Luis spent the day alone with his thoughts.

Rubí arrived halfway through the beer garden performance that night, sitting at the corner table reserved for the group. She sat among the other wives, her knees pressed together, her smile demure. The other wives cast glances across the patio, trading barbs about Brenda's beauty—she wore a wig made from the mane of a horse, her feet were too big for her shoes, she wore bright makeup that colored her face like a whore's—but the Hotel Marina's balconies remained dark, and Brenda Olivares never arrived.

With two songs left, Rubí emerged from her dim corner and asked that the group play "Dos sombras sin cuerpo." She made the request of Casimiro, not of her husband, asking that they play her song, slapping down a handful of heavy gold coins, each one worth fifty pesos. There were six of them. Six individual performances. The wives clapped, and the band complied. Rubí borrowed an empty chair from a nearby table, one of the few unfilled seats that night, pulling it up to the stage. She ordered a beer and drank it from a small glass in incremental sips.

Jose Luis sang. He sang loudly. The songs sprung from him in a quick and reckless manner. At times Jose Luis forgot about his guitar, and the music proceeded without him. Jose Luis felt that he had done nothing wrong. He'd fulfilled a request that was made of him. That was his job. It was what he did. Between verses he'd look at Rubí with a hopeful smile, but his wife's lips remained taut, and this caused Jose Luis's heart to sag with a leaden, childish guilt.

JOSE LUIS SITS ON THE EDGE of his bed in his motel room. He's soaking his feet in an ice bucket filled with warm water, one foot at a time. The television is on, the sound off, and Jose Luis watches a news report. The day's fruitless search has left his head dizzy. It took him an hour to find Santa Anita, and, once he did, he was soon lost among the many factories in the area. If he was close to Rubí, to Galax Street, he sure didn't know it. The security guards he approached either didn't speak Spanish or chased him off the property. Twice he was frightened by guard dogs who thrashed viciously at the chain link fences keeping them from him.

Jose Luis gets up for a towel. He's rubbing his damp feet on the bath mat, wondering what he might eat for dinner, when there's a knock at his door. He opens it to find Lencho standing before him. The mechanic looks out of breath and Jose Luis lets him inside.

"Me tienes que ayudar," Lencho says.

Jose Luis asks what the problem is, and Lencho says that he's in a bit of a situation with Josie, his girlfriend. Last night, after he returned to the bar, he made a comment about the woman with Manny. He used the word "perfect" to describe her heart-shaped ass, and Josie overheard.

"Mi vieja está bien enojada conmigo," he says. Lencho tells Jose Luis that after Josie's shift they rode home in silence. When they pulled up to the house, Lencho went to the neighbor's to pick up Mayra, Josie's six-year-old daughter from a previous boyfriend, only to find that Josie had locked them out of her house.

"¿No tienes una llave?" Jose Luis asks. Lencho explains that Josie had borrowed his keys to get in the house. When he arrived with Mayra, the girl sleepy, Josie let her inside and shut the door on Lencho. She slipped the chain on inside the door and Lencho yelled, but he stopped so as not to scare Mayra. When it became clear that Josie had no intention of letting him inside, he checked the windows, which were locked, and stayed on the porch until this morning when he was let in by the little girl. Lencho asks Jose Luis if he wouldn't mind doing him a favor, and the old musician says yes, though he's not exactly sure how he might help.

BRENDA OLIVARES HAD BEEN ENGAGED for some time. She was betrothed to a promising actor named Salvador Herrera, and the ceremony was to be performed on an island seventy kilometers west of Puerto Vallarta. In the days before the wedding, Don Cipriano sought the Mariachi Orosco's services for his daughter and the guests of her wedding party on the two-day train ride to the coast. Casimiro was called to the Cerveceria Olivares, where he spoke to the producer over the telephone on one of the few reliable lines in the city. Don Cipriano told Casimiro that Brenda insisted on his group and his group only. Brenda being his sole daughter, how could he tell her no? Don Cipriano would pay Fernando for the time the group would miss at the beer gardens as well as for the income they brought to his establishment. Over the brewery's clanking machinery, arrangements were made so that each member of the Mariachi Orosco would net a thousand pesos.

That night when Casimiro arrived with the news and a case of Cerveza Olivares, Jose Luis and Rubí were eating dinner with Doña Imelda. Casimiro announced that they were to leave in the morning. Upon hearing the details of the plan, Rubí took her plate to the kitchen, where Jose Luis found her tearing cold tortillas into strips for the chickens.

"No puedes ir," Rubí said. She looked up from the work in her hands, her eyes steely and cold. "No te voy a dejar."

Jose Luis told Rubí that he would go despite her protests, that he would be gone for four days, and that he would be back and that all between them would be well. She was his wife, and he would do what he thought was best for them. Jose Luis repeated the amount of money he would make, and he reminded Rubí that this was without tips. He promised that, when he returned, they'd take a trip of their own, maybe a visit to El Paso or a weekend on the coast when the weather turned warm. He told her the trip would be nothing in light of what they could gain.

"No es nada," she said. Rubí set her plate on the counter. "Ella no puede comprar a mi esposo."

This exchange quickly turned into an argument, one where Jose Luis had to contend not only with his disapproving wife, but with the truth of what he had felt for Brenda. Still, Jose Luis's decision was made. He packed, throwing his toothbrush, two pairs of pants, two shirts, and two pairs of underwear into one of Casimiro's suitcases. His traje remained on its hangers. Jose Luis wrapped it in gray butcher paper, taping it carefully closed to keep away the elements. The next morning, when he went to tell Rubí good-bye, Jose Luis found her curled in a chair on the back porch, her chin resting atop her knees, a cigarette in her hand.

"Regresaré pronto," he said, to which Rubí responded by flicking the cigarette's ashes and watching them fall to the floor.

The group met at the station, where they traveled to Torreón to meet Brenda and her fiancé. In Torreón, they found the right train, but Don Cipriano and his daughter were nowhere in sight. Instead, Salvador Herrera introduced himself to Casimiro. Brenda's husband-to-be was short enough that he seemed as though he were built on a slightly smaller scale. Jose Luis recognized him from some of the films he had seen with Rubí at the Cine Chihuahuense. In one picture, the diminutive actor played a bumbling stooge, in another, a dashing doctor. Salvador shook hands with each musician, thanking them for agreeing to come along on such short notice, bringing them on board and showing them to their respective compartments.

Jose Luis stayed on his bunk until the train left the station. The last six cars consisted solely of people related to the bride and groom, along with several guests Brenda was taking with her to the coast. Beginning at seven-thirty, the Mariachi Orosco played for five hours straight. Not once was "Dos sombras sin cuerpo" requested. There was much to drink. Along with the guests, several of the musicians, Jose Luis included, drank more than usual, and the evening proceeded as though a high quota of empty bottles had been placed on the trip. By midnight, Joaquin's trumpet had left his lips swollen, and, rather than quit, he traded Arturo for Arturo's violin, and the Mariachi Orosco squawked and stumbled through five more tunes before taking a break. Afterward, the men shot pistols at the dark shapes of trees as the train rushed onward, and, when Jose Luis bumped into Don Cisco, the old man bragged about being the best shot among everyone present. He challenged Jose Luis to a duel in the morning then hobbled off to bed.

Jose Luis didn't see as much of Brenda as he had anticipated. Over the course of the two days, she and Salvador seemed to spend much of their time shut away in their compartment. When she was around, the group was busy playing for the other passengers, sometimes crowding into a compartment, sometimes taking up the dining car at the rear of the train. When Jose Luis did manage to see Brenda, she was always attached to Salvador. She would sit with her legs in his lap, pecking him occasionally on the cheek as he related an incident on the set or told of his trips to New York and Hollywood. Brenda seemed attentive to her fiancé, and this made Jose Luis wonder if perhaps he had misread what happened at the beer gardens, if perhaps it had all been blown out of proportion.

The train rolled on through the second night, and, though the Mariachi Orosco were done much earlier in the evening, the party continued. Jose Luis found the drunken mirth and laughter oppressive, and the young musician sought relief from the lively atmosphere in the open space between cars. The icy air felt refreshing, the train's steady chugging a comfort from the unruly racket inside, but soon the cold became too much. Jose Luis found a chair in the empty dining car, and there he spent the early morning hours fixed as a tree stump, his head against the window, watching the shapes his breath made as it fogged and evaporated on the chilly black pane. It was close to six when Jose Luis finally returned to his compartment. Joaquin was lying with a wet rag over his mouth, his blanket in a heap on the floor. Jose Luis took the blanket and slept as the dawn frosted the landscape with light shades of orange and pink.

When the train arrived in Puerto Vallarta, Jose Luis could smell the salt in the breeze even though the station stood several kilometers from the coast. He had awakened late and was hardly prepared to disembark. The group had ten minutes to switch to the train that would take them directly back to Chihuahua. Joaquin reminded Jose Luis of the track number and left the compartment, his trumpet case jingling with coins. Jose Luis had lost the hanger for his traje, and he became so involved in folding and refolding the suit to avoid wrinkling that he didn't notice

Brenda Olivares when she entered the compartment. She wore a pale blue dress, her hair pulled back and covered by a white scarf. Jose Luis said hello, and Brenda responded by kissing him hard on the mouth. His lips relaxed. His hands enjoyed the fullness of Brenda's trembling body. When they came apart, Brenda took the scarf from her hair and rubbed the smear of lipstick from Jose Luis's mouth before wiping her own lips. She held Jose Luis's arm and stepped over to the window, tossing the scarf out onto the tracks. She said good-bye, and Jose Luis fumbled for words, and with that Brenda Olivares was gone.

THE LATCH GIVES ON THE SMALL TOOLBOX, spilling tools all over when Lencho tosses it to the back seat. Jose Luis recovers some vise grips and two thin hacksaw blades, but Lencho tells him to forget about the tools. Lencho puts the Regal in reverse, and Jose Luis holds his guitar case tightly. The men turn onto Valley Boulevard, and, when the car stops at the first of many red lights, Lencho taps a fast beat on the steering wheel. Jose Luis has no idea what songs he should play. "¿Cuales canciones le gustan a su novia?" he asks.

"Se me hace que Josie no ha escuchado mucha música mariachi," Lencho says. He tells Jose Luis that his song selection won't matter much, that he has no preferences himself as long as he plays something romantic, something that will get him back in good standing with his old lady.

Jose Luis doesn't consider sharing the three songs he has secured in his mind for Rubí. He asks Lencho if he has a pencil and some paper. Lencho plucks a black Magic Marker from his sun visor, then leans over and opens the glove compartment, unaware as the car curves into the right lane. Scraps of paper and crumpled maps tumble out onto Jose Luis's feet, and from them Lencho gives Jose Luis an old envelope.

Jose Luis does his best to think quickly, but his thoughts are unwieldy. A line surfaces, and the Regal travels two blocks before Jose Luis figures out the verse containing its title, "No tengo rosas." He knows that every good serenade consists of three songs, sometimes four if the intended is surly or shy. He scribbles down what he knows of the ballad, his fingers stained by the tip of the marker. Jose Luis caps it and licks the spots, vigorously rubbing each one as though the blackened grooves of his skin might ruin his hold over his guitar.

Four blocks later, Jose Luis knows he can fake his way through the hazy parts of "No puedo ir solo" and "Me tiraste al mar." He writes these titles on the other side of the envelope. A fourth possibility occurs to him. Even though he prefers to play material that he feels some owner- ship over, and even though it is far from midnight, Jose Luis can remem- ber Jose Alfredo Jimenez's "Guitarras de media noche." With this written down, Jose Luis asks Lencho to pull over so that he might pre- pare.

"¿Tienes que prepararte? ¿Para qué?" Lencho asks. He runs the Regal through a yellow light, then turns back to Jose Luis. "Ahí está tu gui- tarra."

Jose Luis reads the look of worry on Lencho's face, and he tells the mechanic that he needs a few minutes to practice the songs he has in mind. Lencho asks him what he plans to play. Jose Luis states the titles on the envelope as if each song is a key ingredient to a long-lost recipe, but the old musician doesn't mention that he needs the extra time to see if he can actually remember each song in its entirety.

Lencho stops the Regal near a movie theater and the marquee's red light fills the car. He leaves the motor running. Jose Luis removes his guitar from the case, knocking the bridge against the rearview mirror. He apologizes, but Lencho seems more concerned with getting his tools back in his toolbox. Jose Luis exits the car, taking the envelope and the marker. Standing on the sidewalk, sliding the strap over his shoulder, he notices that the Regal has turned purple with the marquee's light. Jose

Luis plays the first few verses of "No tengo rosas" and he sings in a whisper to the beautiful women in the movie posters outside the theater. The words to each tune arrive freely, the places for inflection obvious, the emphasis artful. "Me tiraste al mar" comes easily, as does "No puedo ir solo." "Guitarras de media noche" is a bit more challenging, and Jose Luis is tinkering with the opening lines when Lencho lets out a sharp whistle.

"¡Ándale, ándale!" Lencho calls. Jose Luis feels insulted at being rushed. He should leave Lencho alone with his angry woman, but, after his experience today, he fears not being able to find Rubí on his own. What if the city's too big? What if there is no one else who will help him? If things go well with Josie, Lencho could take him to see Rubí tonight. It's possible that he might be with her in a few hours, and it is this possibility that gets him back into the car.

It takes ten minutes to drive to Josie's house. A young girl plays on the sidewalk under a streetlight. She has drawn squares on the sidewalk with white chalk, and she's wearing shoes of green plastic that look a size too big and clack loudly against the concrete when she hops. When the car stops, she runs over and greets Lencho with a hug before he can remove the keys from the ignition. Lencho tells her to get out of the street. He locks the doors and gives the girl a kiss on the forehead, picking her up and bouncing her on his arm. "Esta es Mayra," he tells Jose Luis. "Mayra, say hello to Lencho's friend."

"Hi," she says. Lencho whispers in the girl's ear and she smiles a bashful smile. "Hola," she says before turning toward Lencho's chest.

Jose Luis smiles back and tips his hat hello. The girl reminds him of his own daughters when they were children. He slides his guitar over his shoulder, and the two men walk up to the porch. There's a screen door whose screen is torn. "Is your mother home?" Lencho asks the girl. Mayra's eyes are trained on Jose Luis's guitar, and she says yes without looking away. Through the gap in the door Jose Luis sees the flickering blue light of a television and, beyond that, part of a kitchen lit in yellow.

Lencho leans against the stair rail with Mayra in his arms, nodding at Jose Luis. He begins playing. Jose Luis starts with "No tengo rosas" because it's fast and because it's funny. His guitar rings loudly, and his boot taps the floor, keeping the beat. When Jose Luis sings, he sings loudly. His voice fills the porch. Mayra smiles and covers her ears and Jose Luis smiles back. The old musician feels constrained by the small area and he begins to pace. Halfway through the song, Jose Luis walks back down the stairs. Mayra squirms out of Lencho's arms and follows Jose Luis, clapping her hands.

Jose Luis walks around to the side of the house. The grass is dry under his feet, and he steps carefully in the dark, walking to the window glowing with yellow light. A woman is sweeping with her back turned to him, and when she finally acknowledges the presence of music, she comes to the window. Jose Luis recognizes the bartender from the previous evening. She says something, but even if Jose Luis knew English, her words would still be muffled by the glass between them. She leaves the window, and Jose Luis walks back to the front of the house where he finds her with Lencho, waiting. A pink bandanna's knotted above her forehead, and she carries the broom as if the men are a pair of stray dogs she's about to beat away. Jose Luis notices this, but he continues undeterred. He's drawn Josie out, and, if it's anything, it's a good sign.

Jose Luis closes his eyes. He sings louder and harder—there's a saddle in his stable, but no horse to bear it, there's a revolver on his pillow, but its six chambers are empty, there's a clean glass, but no water to fill it. The song continues, and Jose Luis has a woman, but he doesn't have the right roses to keep her. All Jose Luis has is his voice, and this is pure and warm.

While singing to Josie, Jose Luis does his best to picture Rubí. When his attempts fail, he imagines his music as light. Lencho's porch, his house, everything and everyone within the reach of his voice and guitar will be bright with sound. The louder and harder he sings, the brighter the gleam. Jose Luis believes if he sings loud enough, if his voice is rich with lustful vigor, that his light will dispel the fog surrounding Rubí's memory. He finishes "No tengo rosas" and jumps directly into "No puedo ir solo."

"Real nice, Lencho," Josie says. "This poor guy's lost and you have nothing better to do than bring him here."

Jose Luis opens his eyes. Lencho has no answer to Josie's angry gaze, so Jose Luis continues to play. He lets out a grito, and the loopy, joyous cry echoes down the block. Mayra's hands clap little claps, and Josie steps away from Lencho and comes down the porch with her scowl and her broom. Although things aren't going well, he will make them right with music. Broom or no broom. Scowl or no scowl.

"I have no idea what he's singing about," Josie says. She turns back toward Lencho. "You dumbfuck. I don't even like this mary-a-chee stuff." Josie pitches the broom into the grass. "Stop," she says. "Stop-stopstop." She walks up to Jose Luis and takes a hold of both wrists, stopping his right hand from strumming the strings. Jose Luis looks Josie in the eye. "Look, mister," she says quietly and carefully. "Save. Your. Music." Josie takes Jose Luis's hands from the guitar and sets them at his sides. Jose Luis allows the guitar to dangle off his shoulder. He stares, helpless as Josie smacks Mayra on the behind, the girl bounding up the stairs and disappearing into the house, the woman right behind her.

JOSE LUIS RETURNED TO SILENCE in Chihuahua. Casimiro held his distraught wife as she explained that she hadn't seen Rubí in two days, since yesterday morning when the older woman left to take an elderly neighbor some eggs. Jose Luis's laundry was on their bed, his white shirts and underwear folded and arranged in short stacks. Jose Luis changed out of his dirty clothes and noticed that some of Rubí's dresses weren't hanging in her closet. Her jewelry box was opened and empty. The dried jasmine blossoms were in the waste basket, the wooden bowl on her dresser dry. Jose Luis went through Rubí's dresser and found that her birth certificate and her passport were missing. He pushed the laundry aside and sat on the bed and looked around him. Except for those important items, everything else was in its place—the framed picture from their wedding, her radio atop her dresser, her shoes paired at the bottom of the closer—and for a moment Jose Luis wondered if he'd been robbed by a neat and tidy burglar.

Jose Luis's first impulse was to check the telegram office. Perhaps Rubí had gone on a trip. Maybe she was visiting one of her sisters and, upon reaching her destination, she had forwarded a message explaining everything. The man behind the counter adjusted his thick glasses and told Jose Luis no, no telegram had arrived, not for Jose Luis, not for anyone the young musician or his wife knew. From there, Jose Luis jogged the twelve blocks to the bus station. He approached a taxi rather than wait two hours until the next bus headed to Cuauhtémoc, for it was there that he expected to find her, cutting onions with her mother; sitting beside her father before the radio; strolling alone in the orchard with a basket of apples to be baked with cinnamon for dessert.

The taxi driver laughed at first, but when Jose Luis pulled out the bankroll from his trip, the driver's laughing stopped. He said he'd have to fill his tank, but that he'd return shortly. Jose Luis paced the length of the depot for the next ten minutes, thinking that she may even be there, and from a distance every woman looked as though she might be his wife. He asked a porter if he had seen her suitcase, and the uniformed teenager just shrugged. Out front the taxi was soon honking. They agreed on five hundred pesos, and Jose Luis gave the man two hundred up front just to get on the road.

At first the drive seemed endless because the driver mistook Jose Luis for a tourist. At every curve, every dip in the road, the driver pointed out a place where Villa had fought historic battles against both the American and Mexican armies, sometimes engaging both at once. He believed that much of Villa's pirated gold was still in the hills, that bullion raided from banks and rich landowners was free for the taking, and Jose Luis eventually succumbed to sleep with these words in his ears.

The afternoon had turned dark when Jose Luis awoke at the outskirts of Cuauhtémoc. He directed the driver to the Hacienda Santiago, where he paid the chatty man the balance of his money. From the gates, no light showed in any of the large house's windows and so Jose Luis let himself in. A brisk wind rustled through the evergreens lining the drive, and the musician wished he had thought to bring a jacket. He knocked on the door, only to receive no answer. He then waited for an hour, guessing the time by the position of the rising moon. Finally a pair of yellow lights stopped at the front gate. He shielded his eyes from their shine, remaining seated as though the approaching headlights on Don Humberto's truck radiated warmth rather than light.

Don Humberto parked and emerged with a pot containing a melon-sized bundle wrapped in pink paper. He didn't seem surprised at finding Jose Luis at his doorstep.

"¿Dónde está Rubí?" Jose Luis asked.

The sadness on Don Humberto's face was clear, for his eyes were red with grief. Don Humberto put his arm around Jose Luis's shoulders and told him everything would be explained in a few moments. He led the young man inside, and Jose Luis stood alone in the dark entrance, holding the heavy pot while Don Humberto went to the bedroom. Moments later he emerged with a small lamp and a letter in his shirt pocket.

In short time Jose Luis would learn that Rubí had left him, that she had followed Rosalía and her husband to the United States with no intention of returning. Jose Luis would find that Rubí had come to feel differently about him than she had let on, that the more success Jose Luis achieved, the more women like Brenda he would encounter, and Rubí was unwilling to sit home and wonder about her husband's actions with other women. Rubí would explain in plain, simple language that her future seemed clear in Chihuahua, and that the promise of this future seemed less than it might be elsewhere. She wanted a husband who would assume this position without reservation. One day, she wanted a family. She had fled in the night to be in America with people who cared for her. There was no address, no hint of where she might be. In a short time, Jose Luis would curse Rubí's name, though she hoped he might come to wish her well, and because he was a poor reader, Jose Luis's heart would crumble slowly instead of breaking into clean, even pieces.

Don Humberto called Jose Luis into the kitchen, where he was busy unwrapping a cooked calf's head. Its jawbone gleamed a long white smile, its sockets were a pair of grizzled pits, its flesh dark and steaming. Don Humberto heated some tortillas and picked some meat from the skull with a fork. He asked Jose Luis to light a few candles on the table while he took the plate to Doña Filomina who was ill with grief in their bedroom.

Jose Luis would eventually mend. Eventually he would meet another woman, a quiet widow who would bear him a pair of daughters, and these daughters would also float north to the border the way hungry fish rise to the surface of a lake. Eventually Jose Luis would go on to minor success as a mariachi. He'd be known for his slow, sad corridos, and eventually he'd cease playing all together, but all of this would come in due time. For now, Jose Luis waited for Don Humberto. The farmer trudged slowly to the kitchen, burdened with the shame of his two lost daughters. He set an envelope on two plates along with a pair of small forks. These he carried to the table with warm tortillas and a small jar of chile. Don Humberto offered Jose Luis a seat, and the men sat down to eat and to talk about what course their lives might take from here.

Lencho drives aimlessly after leaving Josie's until he finally stops at Magaña's taco stand. He drives the car under one of the lights in the parking lot and cuts the engine, the flooding light white and harsh. Jose Luis smells the food coming from the stand, but he's nervous enough that food no longer poses any interest to him. Lencho digs around in the backseat and comes up with a book of maps. Jose Luis reads him Rubí's address, but Lencho is busy flipping through the index, so Jose Luis reads it again. Lencho takes the slip from Jose Luis and slides his finger down the long list of streets.

"Galanto, North Galanto, Galatina, Galavan. Okay," he says. "Here's Galax." Lencho finds the right page and points his finger to a spot on the edge of the multicolored map. "Aquí estamos," he says. He moves his finger to a place near the center. "Aquí está tu esposa."

Jose Luis nods. He tells Lencho that he needs some time. Lencho pulls a cigarette from a pack on the dashboard, and says that it's all right. He's got nothing but time now. Both men climb out of the car, Lencho leaning against the driver door, Jose Luis getting his guitar. The musician hasn't felt stage fright in decades, but here he is, wandering to the edge of the empty lot, trying to stretch the worry from his hands. He takes off his Stetson and removes the folded slip of motel stationary. He reads and walks a loopy circle and strums stray notes on his guitar. He doesn't sing. He talks.

The drive to Galax is a short one, and, along the way, Jose Luis recognizes some of the places he passed earlier in the day. When they turn the final corner, Lencho points out the small blue street sign. Galax lies behind a park, and this park is behind some factories. Jose Luis is thankful to be here. Lencho drives slowly, both men straining to find the numbers on the fronts of the houses. 2021 Galax is near the end of the block, one away from the corner. It's a small green house with white trim. A low wrought-iron fence leans crookedly, bordering the patch of grass between the sidewalk and the door. The men park across the street and sit for a while with the ticking sounds of the cooling engine.

Jose Luis gets out, leaving his guitar case open on the roof. Lencho follows him up the driveway. Jose Luis knocks, then rings a shrill-sounding doorbell when he finds it. He rings it again. When the door opens, Jose Luis is met by a young boy. A television blares inside and its racket escapes from the house. The boy keeps his hand on the doorknob, and Jose Luis hopes he can speak Spanish.

"¿No se encuentra Rubí Navarro?"

"I don't speak Spanish," the boy says. "Go away."

Lencho comes up and repeats Jose Luis's question in English. He puts his hand on the door, keeping it open.

The boy looks at Lencho's hand, then at Jose Luis. "Who are you guys?"

Lencho explains that they're old friends of Rubí's. He points to Jose Luis and says that this man has come a long way to talk to her.

Jose Luis examines the boy's face. His eyes are black, and, in the second before they turn hard and mean, Jose Luis recognizes something from long ago.

"My Grandma Ruby's dead," the boy says. "She's been dead a long time now." With that, he leans his weight into the door, and, when it doesn't move, he punches Lencho's thigh. Lencho backs away and the door closes with a firm thud.

Lencho looks back at Jose Luis, who understands the key words without translation. Things go quiet for the musician. There is his pulse in his ears, but there is nothing else. Lencho rings the doorbell again and again. He holds it down in long bursts, but no answer comes. Jose Luis walks back to the car, where he puts his guitar away and sits with his head in his hands. Lencho pounds on the door until people start coming out from the neighboring houses, and then the men drive away.

Lencho asks Jose Luis if he wants to go to the motel. Jose Luis doesn't answer, and Lencho says that he'll buy him a drink instead. When they park outside the Horseshoe Club, Jose Luis gives Lencho a questioning look, and the mechanic tells him not to worry, Josie has Wednesday nights off. Lencho hops out of the car, lighting another cigarette and tossing the match onto the street. Jose Luis will have his drink and then he'll head to the motel. He remembers the way. He opens his door and takes his guitar with him.

Inside there are more people than the night before. The booths are full, and Lencho lets Jose Luis take an empty seat at the bar. He orders two Budweisers and two shots of Jack Daniels. When the drinks arrive, Lencho pays. Someone calls Lencho's name from the back of the bar. Lencho excuses himself, which is fine because Jose Luis wants to be alone. He barely touches his drinks, but when he does, he opts for a sip of the whisky over the beer. Jose Luis sits for a long time. He gets jostled by the people next to him, and his guitar case slides to the floor. Jose Luis picks it up and is close to leaving when Lencho calls his name.

"This is the guy I was telling you about," Lencho says when Jose Luis comes over. Lencho's speaking to men wearing the same grimy blue uniforms as he is. Some are with women. Some are alone. One of the women asks him to play something. She tells Lencho to tell Jose Luis how he'd been bragging about him all day, but Lencho doesn't hear her. He crosses the floor and yanks the plug for the television and tells the people at the bar to quiet down. He drags an empty stool over to Jose Luis, and slowly the room's attention converges upon the old musician.

One of the men in the booth tells Jose Luis to play what he played last night. There are people before Jose Luis who want to hear his voice, and he recognizes that their interest is genuine. He flips open the latches on his guitar case. He breathes deeply and adjusts his hat, and then Jose Luis begins to take requests.

LA FIESTA BRAVA

1 9 8 9

A second lemon knocks Guillermo Quintanilla's band hat crooked and he looks over at Sal Torres and tells him this is bullshit. Sal laughs, and Irma Barraza and Yvette Valdez scream and break formation as another fat lemon lands between them and bursts into a wet yellow mess. Guillermo stops playing his trumpet. "Maintain your composure, people," Mr. People says. Mr. People is Guillermo's band teacher. He's a little man whose whistle bounces around his neck as he jogs alongside and tells the children to continue marching. "People, let's keep going."

The entire band has been doing dress rehearsals after school for the last two weeks, everyone marching down Fineview, up Parkway to Klingerman, then back down Bunker. Last week saw them continually bombarded by things from different houses on this street. On Thursday it was tangerines, and on Friday it was walnuts. Today it's lemons. The houses on this block are old and set away from the street. They're all hidden by fragrant, overgrown fruit trees and high rows of untended bushes. They're all connected to the world by long driveways that slope down to the curb. Guillermo can hear faint laughing behind the bushes, the laughing of little kids, and more lemons fly up in the sky and splatter in the street. Guillermo can see a bright orange T-shirt shifting back and forth behind the thick screen of branches. "At all times we must remain professional. At *all* times," Mr. People says.

Guillermo is sick of this, sick of being fucked with and not being able to do anything about it, and the sickness boils over inside him and soon after he's sprinting up the nearest driveway, his band hat bobbing on his head until he pops the clasp under his chin and tosses the oversized hat aside. Mr. People blows his whistle. "Get back here. Get back in formation!" the teacher calls, but, as Guillermo crosses the lawn, his body is filling with an anger that easily surges through anything Mr. People might say. Guillermo slips, getting green stains on his white pants and the gold braid of embroidery that runs the length of his leg. Grass sticks to the wet bell of his trumpet.

The giggling is still in the bushes, and Guillermo plunges through a gap in the thorny branches to find three kids. They look about ten or eleven, and two of them have skateboards with wheels that roar as they roll down the driveway. The third boy dashes toward his bicycle with one last lemon in his hand. The boy is chubby, round and soft as a dinner roll, and he's the one Guillermo catches. The boy pulls at the knobby buttons on Guillermo's uniform and wails before Guillermo punches him. The boy loses his balance and stumbles over his bicycle, and Guillermo collapses with him.

Guillermo swings his trumpet, striking the boy once on the head, once on the shoulder. The boy covers his face with his hands and kicks blindly. Get off me, he yells in Spanish, get off me. But Guillermo has gone deaf to his cries, deaf to the laughter of the band in the street and the shrill chirps of Mr. People's whistle. Guillermo persists in pounding the boy with his trumpet. He misses more often than he hits, and, when the trumpet clangs against the bicycle frame instead of the boy's body, vibrations shiver up Guillermo's arm.

"THIS IS SOMETHING FOR WHICH most students get expelled," Heavy Duty says. She taps the file on her desk. "Do you understand what I'm saying?"

Guillermo nods. Heavy Duty flips through Guillermo's papers, and he drums his fingers under his seat as the principal dials his telephone number. Guillermo's been suspended for the rest of the week. Tuesday to Friday. That much has been decided. He leans down and tugs at his shoelaces to hide his smirk when there's no answer at home. Heavy Duty calls Guillermo's father at his repair shop, and Guillermo holds his breath. He's been in this office before, but always for offenses that now seem inconsequential as the phone rings on his father's desk—a scuffle in the lunch line, three ditched classes, and two missed detentions. Again there's no answer and Guillermo breathes a sigh of relief.

"Do you know where else your father might be?"

Guillermo has a few ideas, but he's not about to offer up any of them. He shakes his head and checks the clock above Heavy Duty's desk. It's getting late in the day, and Heavy Duty seems to know this. She sighs and takes a sheet of stationery from her desk. She drops the paper into her typewriter, an electric IBM, and watches Guillermo as the stationery winds through the rollers. After a minute of quick typing, her fingers stop moving. Heavy Duty takes a second look at Guillermo, lowering her bifocals as if they might blur her intuition.

"Are you sure you don't know where he is?"

Guillermo knows by the tone in the principal's voice that he's caught a few breaks this afternoon. The IBM hums as he weighs the consequences of being honest.

"No," he lies. "Maybe he's out doing house calls."

Heavy Duty nods and finishes her typing, signing and folding the letter, sealing it in an envelope that she gives to Guillermo before setting him free.

The next hour of Guillermo's Monday afternoon is spent at Road Runner Liquor playing Defender. The boy Guillermo beat up was Joel Barraza, Irma Barraza's younger brother. Joel's in the fourth grade, and, under the shade of the walnut trees, between sobs, he apologized and explained to his sister that the whole time he'd been aiming for her. Irma dabbed at the blood on Joel's head with his T-shirt, ruining her band uniform as she spoke comforting words in his ear. Guillermo remembers this in vivid detail as he smacks the buttons on the video game's console. According to Heavy Duty, Guillermo's extremely fortunate that the Barrazas were reluctant to involve the police in any way. (While their children are all American citizens, Mr. and Mrs. Barraza are in El Monte illegally. Apparently the threat of attracting attention from any government authority prevented them from pressing charges.)

Last year, Guillermo heard from Sal, who heard from Violet, that Irma had a crush on him, that Irma *liked him*. Guillermo found Irma cute, but her hairy arms and her lazy eye were fatal flaws, especially in the seventh grade. Now in Guillermo's typing class, Irma sits toward the corner, near the flag. She sometimes looks as though she's watching flies land on her nose. He's caught Irma gazing at him with one eye and it gave him the chills, her left eye looking in his direction, the right one following Clack-clack's pointer across the diagram of typewriter keys taped to the chalkboard.

When Guillermo runs out of quarters, he buys a handful of penny bubble-gum and walks back toward his school, because being there is better than going home. Near the cafeteria, a yellow bus idles at the curb, and Guillermo remembers that Kranz's basketball team played Baker's this afternoon. He's got a few friends on the squad, Jimmy Ramos and Rico Mendoza, both of whom look sweaty and tired as he calls their names. The boys shake hands and Jimmy tosses Guillermo his basketball so he can pull on his sweatshirt. Guillermo dribbles the ball, working it between his legs as he recounts the day's events, a goofy pride in his story until Coach Cooper steps off the bus.

"You're suspended?" Coach Cooper asks.

Guillermo nods.

"Well, go home then. Suspended students can't be on school property." Coach Cooper is Guillermo's favorite teacher at Kranz, and Guillermo assumes that the coach is joking until he steps in and grabs away the basketball, holding it with two hands like the rebounding drill he teaches in gym class.

GUILLERMO'S WAITED UNTIL TUESDAY MORNING to tell his father about Joel Barraza. Mondays are always hard on the old man. Sunday's the day he takes off, even if taking off simply means closing the shop a few hours early. After a quick shower and a change of clothes, most of Sunday for Guillermo's father is spent in church. Guillermo once attended regularly, but last year his father quit forcing the weekly services on him as though church was an old pair of jeans Guillermo had simply outgrown. While Guillermo doesn't necessarily miss the stern lectures about the importance of being honest and the glory of God, there have been a few Sunday afternoons where he's missed riding along with his father and his godmother, Marta, afternoons where he longs for the small sense of importance he received from filling out the back flap on the collection envelope: Eduardo Quintanilla and Family.

After mass, there's always food and music and dancing, the folding chairs and tables arranged neatly in the church basement. Marta comes home early, but Guillermo's father stays late. Sometimes Guillermo snoozes through the noise his father makes when he arrives drunk and hungry at one in the morning, two if the old man's had a good night, and sometimes he lies awake in the stillness of the night and listens as his father fixes a bowl of cereal, eating only two bites before finally heading to bed.

Guillermo planned on telling the old man that he didn't throw the first punch. Technically, he'll explain, the lemon hit him first. He waits in his room a few more minutes, sorting the facts in his head, arranging the falsehoods like the key playing cards in a very elaborate magic trick. He won't mention that Joel's in the fourth grade.

He jams the letter from Heavy Duty in his back pocket and finds his father in his bedroom, sitting at the foot of his bed, putting on his shoes. Guillermo stands at the door. "I'm not going to school today," he says.

"Sure thing," his father says without looking up from the knot he's busy tying. "Let me give you fifty bucks for lunch."

"No. Really," Guillermo says. "I can't go." He explains about the suspension and his father sets down his shoe. He shrinks a little as Guillermo talks, like the air inside him has started to escape. Guillermo's account of the fight is vague, and he stares at the clay mariachi lamp on his father's nightstand when he arrives at the part about his trumpet. Right now, the trumpet's in Heavy Duty's office, its tubing bent every which way.

"I'll pay for the trumpet," Guillermo says, but after a dismissive wave of his father's hand, all the cards in Guillermo's mind flutter out of sequence.

"Lemons?" his father asks. "Some kid throws lemons at you and you ruin your trumpet?" Guillermo's father pulls on his other shoe, and quickly it gets tied. He puts on his baseball cap, QUINTANILLA ELECTRONICS REPAIR screened across the front, the brim bent in the middle. He stands before his mirror, making sure the cap is straight.

"You have to go in for a conference with my principal," Guillermo says. "I won't get my trumpet back until you do." Guillermo knows that his father must get to work, that his day doesn't allow him time for things like conferences. Time away from the shop means money out of his wallet. "She wants to speak to you today," Guillermo says.

"You know I can't do it today," his father says. "Check with Marta. See if she can go to this thing."

Guillermo nods and his father brushes past him.

"Come by the shop today around lunch time. You're free, right?"

"Sure," Guillermo says. The word seems small to him, and he feels stupid saying it, and he doesn't move until he hears his father's keys turning in the last of their three locks.

Deep down, Guillermo hoped his father would say this. Because she's only twenty-one, Marta's always been more of an older sister to Guillermo than an aunt or a godmother. Still, this moment of relief is fleeting. Last night, over the phone, Guillermo heard a few of the many rumors that have whirled into circulation, and the one about three lettermen who stopped by Kranz wearing cleats and asking about him by name seems like the most sensible and worrisome. Marta lives in a small guest house behind the Quintanillas, and Guillermo crosses the yard with quick steps, his hands curled into tight little fists. He knocks on Marta's door and checks the fig tree and the trash cans and the wash hanging on the clothesline for anyone who might be waiting. Guillermo knocks again and wrinkles his nose at the stink around him, for on days like this, days where the sun's working hard at nine in the morning, his whole backyard smells of boiling leaves and dying fruit.

Marta tells him to come in. Guillermo finds his godmother in her uniform, sitting at her dresser, applying eyeliner. "Wait a second," she says without turning her head from the mirror. Marta's house is one room. A tall paper screen covered with Chinese characters acts as a wall, separating her bed from a kitchenette with a hot plate and a tub of dirty dishes. A fan whirs at half speed in one corner, the windows and drapes shut, the room covered in shadows thrown by the lamp on her dresser.

Marta had lived in San Diego until about five years ago, when her brother's wife was finally taken by a chronic and debilitating leukemia. Through Eduardo's church, Marta was accepted by a community outreach program, and for the last four years she's been working at a dentist's office in San Gabriel, making appointments and typing them into a computer. For work she wears nurse shoes, light blue pants with a lighter blue top, a name tag pinned to her chest, but Marta's face always looks the same no matter what's going on. Her eyeliner is applied thick, so that on some days Marta appears to Guillermo as if she'd worked with a chunk of charcoal.

"What's up?" she asks, and half the story falls out of Guillermo like a stack of telephone books. He tells her it wasn't his fault, but he omits the lettermen and Joel's age, because they'd tip Marta off to the seriousness of the situation. Marta's only finished her left eye and she puts down her pencil before starting on the right one. She shakes her head when Guillermo gets to the trumpet and the hitting. Marta's darkened eye looks bigger than its partner, and her disapproval gives her head the impression of being heavy and lopsided. He tells her about the conference and his father being busy, and Marta's sour face turns even more sour.

"Oh, I don't work too?" she says. Guillermo shifts his feet and Marta sighs. She checks the time on her alarm clock and picks up the thin black eye pencil. "Who do I have to call?" she asks, and Guillermo produces Heavy Duty's letter.

GUILLERMO'S FATHER IS THE LAST PERSON in his family to be born in Mexico. He's also an electronics repairman who doesn't make house calls. Not yet anyway. Guillermo's father is saving up for a van to hold all his equipment, and then he can take the show on the road. When Guillermo was small, his father attended night school for electronics repair and soon after found himself employed by Sony, repairing radios and stereo equipment still under warranty. Before Guillermo's mother passed away, she convinced her husband to quit and go out on his own. Eduardo Quintanilla rented out a space between a tile shop and a barber who's deaf in one ear and gives Guillermo fucked-up haircuts. The parking lot there is sad, full of cracks and potholes, the speed bumps with deep gouges across the tops from cars rushing over them to get out. Sometimes, both the barber and the tile shop get more customers in one day than Guillermo's father does in one week.

It's not that Eduardo Quintanilla is incompetent. Guillermo is firm in his belief that his father can repair just about anything. Once Guillermo did a report about space, how the astronauts' capsule broke down and they were stuck spinning around the moon.

"If I was up there with my toolbox, they'd be back in twenty minutes," Guillermo's father said. He pointed his finger to the side of his head. "Brains, mijo. All it takes is brains."

Guillermo believed him. Even after his mother passed away, he thought that the answers to everything were inside his father's head, waiting to be used, the words swimming around like fish crammed into a glass bowl.

The framed diploma that makes Guillermo's father a certified ELEC-TRONIC REPAIR SPECIALIST hangs on the wall behind the counter, between a calendar from La Dulzura Bakery with an Aztec goddess, and a sign that says WE RESERVE THE RIGHT TO REFUSE SERVICE TO ANYONE. Guillermo's father doesn't notice the bell when Guillermo comes in. The old man's wrapping and unwrapping a piece of copper wire around his finger. He grabs a pair of needlenose pliers and sits on his stool behind the open backside of a television gone haywire with static. Guillermo isn't sure what to expect. His father's never been really mean. He doesn't scream or get crazy when he drinks anymore. Instead he plays old mariachi records and listens to them in the green light of the stereo. He stares at the record going around and around like he's the one drawing the music out of the black grooves in the vinyl, so deep in concentration that Guillermo gets the impression that everything will stop if his father looks away.

Guillermo's been in other fights in the past. His father would yell at him, then afterwards pat him on the shoulder and wink when his mother left the room. However, because of the trumpet, because Joel's only in fourth grade, this time is different. Guillermo can feel something coming, though he's not sure what this thing might be. He tells his father hi, and the old man looks up, the people in the program bending into snakey shapes before the picture returns to crackling snow.

Guillermo's father leans over the set and looks at the screen and slams the pliers on the counter. "I thought I had it," he says.

He asks Guillermo how it went with Marta, and Guillermo tells him she's going to do it. The old man nods. "That was nice of her," he says. He walks to the calendar on the wall and moves his finger across the days. "Now you owe her something nice."

"What?"

"You know the dresser in her room, the one that used to be your mom's?"

Guillermo nods.

"Well, that dresser was handmade in Morelos by your great-grandpa on your mom's side. He gave it to your bisabuela as a wedding present when they got married. I forget the guy's name, but I know he was a carpenter. Anyway, you've seen how it looks now. Your tía's been wanting to repaint that thing for a long time."

The dresser Eduardo speaks of is from the forties, copied by his wife's grandfather from a photo in a Sears catalogue, six drawers, a big round mirror, and a desk space for Marta's makeup. Varnish flakes off the sides, and three of the drawers are missing their flat, triangle-shaped knobs. "You're going to paint it for her," Guillermo's father says. "It'll give you something to do."

The old man then starts in on the lecture about right and wrong that Guillermo expected, but a woman enters the shop, a VCR in her arms, the cord dragging behind her. She sets it on the counter and says in Spanish that it doesn't work right, that the machine records pictures but not sound. Guillermo's father forgets about him and tells the woman he can fix it. He says, "No problem," in English and he and the customer both laugh. He tells her it'll run fifteen dollars for an inspection, plus parts as he needs them. She agrees, and he takes the pen from his shirt pocket and reaches under the counter for a carbon slip. He ties a numbered tag to the VCR cord and takes down the lady's information.

"¿Para cuando lo necesita?" Guillermo's father asks, and the woman says she wants it back by Friday. She starts talking about her novela coming to an end, that she wants to tape it for her comadre. Guillermo wishes the woman would just go away so he could talk. He wants to tell his father that he wasn't thinking on Monday and he doesn't want to wait to do it. He would've only hit the kid with his fist if the trumpet hadn't been in his hand. If things were different, he might not have hit him at all.

"I'm sorry," Guillermo says with the customer as witness to his regret. His father looks up from the pink paper, smiling a smile that leaves Guillermo with the distinct impression that he'll be on the other side of the counter for quite some time.

WHEN MARTA GETS HOME, Guillermo's making dinner, macaroni with spaghetti sauce. Marta's mad. Guillermo's father won't be home for another hour, but Marta doesn't wait to tell Guillermo about her talk with Heavy Duty. She yells at him for the trumpet and calls him a coward for hitting a little boy. Guillermo tries not to react. He stares at the bubbling pasta on the stove. "What about my trumpet? When will I get it back?"

"You'll get it on Monday, after you apologize to Joel and his family."

Marta lets Guillermo know that he's to write a letter expressing his sorrow to the Barrazas. Heavy Duty's arranging things so he'll read it to them in person.

"This is a suspension," Marta says. "Not a vacation. I'm going to call you every day to make sure you're here. To make sure you're doing your work."

"What work?" Guillermo asks. Marta tosses Guillermo's algebra book on the table, along with a sheet listing the problems he's to do, a thick packet of definitions, photocopied chapters of science he must study for Miss Fishsticks class. In addition to this, Clack-clack's supplied Marta with a laminated keyboard handout that Guillermo's to have memorized by the coming Monday.

ON WEDNESDAY MORNING, Guillermo's father helps him move Marta's dresser outside. The mirror's been removed and the drawers have been emptied and taped shut. Marta's clothes—T-shirts and sweatpants and a few pairs of faded jeans—are piled by the blue milk-crate crammed full of soap opera novels which she uses as a nightstand. Guillermo's father lifts one end of the dresser and Guillermo lifts the other. The dresser just barely fits through the doorway, less than an inch between Guillermo's fingers and the doorframe. They take small steps out toward an old sheet under the sick branches of the fig tree. Guillermo thought the tree's shade would be worth its smell, but he can still feel the sun as though its rays have purposely curved around the branches to find him.

The old man silently watches Guillermo pull the masking tape from the drawers. Some of them have circles gouged in the wood where loosened knobs once turned. Guillermo twists the remaining knobs free with his bare hands, shunning the pain of the angular metal pressed into the meat of his fingers in hopes of producing an acknowledgment, some sign of approval from the old man. Each knob comes away with its flaking gold paint stuck to Guillermo's fingers and thumb, the exposed metal bright and clean, each of Guillermo's small efforts unnoticed. The old man walks back toward the house, in all likelihood to make a fried-egg burrito, and, before he slips out of earshot, Guillermo thanks him for his help.

"Sure," his father says without turning around to say it, his voice calm and effortless.

The old man isn't talking about yesterday. He isn't talking, period. The only other duration of silence that Guillermo can compare this to occurred last winter, when the shop's yearlong lease was set to expire, and Guillermo's father was on the fence about signing the annual contract. The decision seemed to weigh on the old man, his fears for success or failure pressing him into a week of quiet and spooky contemplation that was finally broken the night he penned his name to the lease.

"This is it," he told Guillermo. "This is the year that we get big."

The document crammed with long words in little letters was spread across their table. Guillermo's father spoke of the van he still speaks about now, that it would be red, then blue, then red again. He said their name would be in huge letters on the side. QUINTANILLA ELEC-TRONICS REPAIR. Guillermo guesses that his father imagined all these people in their homes, turning on their televisions only to see the picture disappear, nothing before them but blackness and a white speck shrinking in the center of the screen. Guillermo's father probably saw nothing but ghetto blasters eating tapes. Radios that solely received static. Answering machines that wouldn't answer.

That night, the old man talked about going back to school in hopes of learning about computers. How they work. How to fix them.

Guillermo said that nobody he knew owned one, that there were only four in his school, and a couple months ago somebody broke in and smashed two of them.

"There are no computers in El Monte," he said.

"You have to see bigger things besides El Monte," the old man responded. "There's Pico Rivera and Montebello, Baldwin Park and La Puente. Plus all the businesses in City of Industry and the rich hueros in Arcadia too."

The old man snapped his fingers and winked, then flipped through the papers of the lease and, at the bottom of the last page, quickly signed a big squiggle attached to an oversized Q. Now Guillermo wonders if similar decisions are being made about him, if pros and cons are being weighed, if there's anything he can do to halt the silent machinery he's set into motion. Guillermo checks the screen door at the back of the house, and, after finding nobody there, he grabs a sheet of fifty-grit sandpaper, creases it into quarters, and gets to work on the dresser.

ON HIS WAY TO ANGEL'S HARDWARE, Guillermo passes a junkyard over on Durfee, a small one full of old pipes and busted appliances. There's no rush in getting to the hardware store, so Guillermo goes inside. Rusty water heaters line one wall on the right, doors are piled ten feet high to the left, and a small, windowless building, nothing more than a shed, stands toward the back of the lot among an assortment of old stoves, the appliances like giant molars randomly plugged into the damp and oily earth. Cluttered before Guillermo is an array of bathtubs and refrigerators and toilets, twisted lengths of gutted plumbing, leaky car batteries staining the ground, their puddles shimmering with rainbows as he steps over them. Even though he is twenty feet from traffic, the lot gets quieter the further inside it Guillermo ventures. He taps the debris about him with the length of a broom handle he's been carrying.

Guillermo hasn't seen the lettermen, but he should be careful, though, for the moment, he delights in the sharp pings and low thuds made by the different appliances he strikes.

To the right of the shed, hidden by the water heaters, is a small assortment of furniture: some sad couches and armchairs, some desks and a dresser with its feet in the air. The dresser drawers have glass knobs, the glass scalloped and carved in intricate detail. They remind Guillermo of diamonds, big diamonds, the kind worn by kings in comic strips. He nudges a damp armchair aside to afford himself a better look. There are six drawers, and, more importantly there are six knobs. He sets down the broom handle and yanks out one of the drawers. He turns it over and works on the knob, but it's frozen in place and slightly greasy so that it slips in his grip. I could take them with me if I had a screwdriver, Guillermo thinks.

This discovery occurs before the lot's owner appears. The man is thin and looks as beaten as the objects around him. He wears gray overalls splattered with brown and orange paint, and his white beard is streaked with yellow. A wad of something is plugged in his mouth, so that it looks as though he's chewing a ball of rubber bands. He takes off his cap, tucks the wad into his cheek, and says that the dresser Guillermo's inspecting goes for a hundred dollars. "But if you're really interested in quality, young man, I got a better one comin' in tomorrow," he says.

"What if I just want the knobs?"

The man steps back and kicks at the dirt like a horse that's been trained to count. "The knobs," he says. "Well, those are what makes the whole piece special. I'd hate to part with 'em, but I guess I can let you have 'em for fifty."

"Fifty?" Guillermo asks. "Dollars?"

The man nods. "That's for the whole set."

Guillermo picks up his broom handle and tells the man to forget it. The man nods and tells him that's what antiques go for these days. As if that matters to Guillermo. By the looks of him, this man's an antique, too. Fifty bucks. If that's what he really wants for the knobs, Guillermo figures the man's been around all this junk way too long.

MARTA COMES IN THE BACK DOOR wearing tight black Levi's and a purple shirt. She checks her hair in the hallway mirror, then starts looking for her house keys. It's six-thirty on Wednesday night, and Guillermo's father isn't home from the shop yet. Part of Guillermo feels good. He's gotten Marta a birthday card, filled it out two days in advance, stuck it under his algebra book. But part of Guillermo feels slightly disconnected. Marta has a dinner date with Benny, the guy she's been going out with on and off for the last year or so. Most Wednesdays Guillermo goes with them, but now with things the way they are, he's not sure if he's still invited.

Marta talks to her keys, trying to coax them from hiding by whispering come out come out wherever you are. If Guillermo's right, they're probably on the rim of the bathtub, right next to the toilet. Marta's place has no sewage connection, so she uses the bathroom in the house and forgets her keys there all the time. Guillermo checks and they are where he expected to find them, and soon enough he's standing before Marta, the keyring with the metal lettering off a Mustang (a gift from Benny, representing the car Marta wants one day) dangling in his fingers. Marta takes the keys. "You ready to go?" she asks.

It takes twenty minutes to walk to the go-cart track where Benny works as a mechanic. On the way, Marta tells Guillermo that the sanded cabinet looks good, that it's going to come out nice, then she says nothing else. Guillermo tries to think of things to say, but he's certain Marta won't want to hear about how he hates his homework, and, besides that, Guillermo's afraid any talk about school might lead to a discussion about the letter of apology he's to compose, a task that Guillermo's not fully committed to completing.

Marta takes Guillermo to the track on Wednesday nights because then it's not busy and Benny can get him onto the track for a few free races if he wants. If it's really a slow night, Benny will race too, but Benny's so big that the go-cart's engine grinds and sputters under the weight. In these weekly races, Guillermo wins sometimes, and sometimes Benny cheats and tries to stop him from speeding by. Benny will ride with one foot on the gas, standing on the seat, yanking the big bricks of hay that line the turn walls onto the track.

When they arrive, Benny's in the pit, working out with the tank for the blowtorch. He holds the tank with both hands and curls it toward his chest, scowling at the iron tube like it's been insulting him all afternoon. When Benny spots Marta and Guillermo coming across the gravel parking lot, he sets the tank aside and walks up to the chain link fence. He plays with Marta's fingers before kissing her. Then he checks his watch. "I'm off in a few minutes," he says twice, a race starting, the squeal and rattle of the engines drowning him out the first time.

Marta and Guillermo head inside. They say hello to Lyle, the elder mechanic whose primary job it is to make sure everyone's taller than forty-eight inches. Marta and Guillermo find seats at the end of the bleachers closest to the pit area, two cars zooming into turn one as they sit down.

Soon enough, Benny stomps up the bleachers drying his hands with a paper towel. His gut hangs over his weight belt so you can't see the buckle. KING SIZE is written in black marker on the broad leather in back. He gives Marta half a hug because his clothes are black with grease spots. Still, he manages to lift her off the ground with one arm. Guillermo's noticed that Benny's always lifting things and moving them, or throwing them so they disappear in the distance, he guesses because Benny can. When they play football, Benny quarterbacks for both teams, and the spiral on his passes is so tight and hard that you don't catch the ball. The ball catches you.

The three of them leave the track and Marta asks Benny where he wants to eat.

"Joey's," Guillermo says, but Benny rubs his panza and makes a sick face.

"I had cheeseburgers for lunch," he says. "Besides, when I ate there last week, I got sick."

They get to Benny's pick-up truck and decide on Taco Miendo because it's only a few blocks away. Benny owns a Toyota with no radio, and Guillermo sits in the middle, his legs folded against the gearshift, since Marta has yet to let him ride in back. She drives (she usually does on Wednesdays), and, as they pull onto Valley, Benny stretches. He puts one arm out the window and the other around Guillermo's shoulder.

"I heard about what you did," he says without turning away from the road.

"Don't encourage him," Marta says. She checks the rearview mirror and flips on the blinker before making a right on Peck. "My godson's not growing up to be a hoodlum." There's a snarl in her voice and it makes Benny smile and look at his feet like his shoes have suddenly become important.

Taco Miendo has three orange tables in front, and the people at the middle one leave right as Marta pulls into the lot. Benny hops out to grab the table, and, after locking the passenger door, Guillermo walks over and sits across from him. The people have left their trash, and Marta picks up their box of half-eaten food, their napkins and plastic cups of salsa. She walks off to throw them away, and Benny moves forward and motions with his hand for Guillermo to come closer. Guillermo leans across the table, grains of salt pressing into his arms as Benny's hand grips his neck.

"I've been in plenty of fights before," Benny says. "Big ones. One even cost me my job. But you listen to me. You did the right thing beating up that kid." Benny taps Guillermo on the back of the head. "I don't wanna sound like I'm trying to be your dad," he says, "but you don't need to take no shit from nobody."

THE STORY GOES THAT on the day Guillermo was baptized, after the service, Eduardo Quintanilla threw the party to end all parties. Guillermo's seen the pictures that Marta keeps in the photo albums under her bed. The old man ordered homemade carnitas, a whole pig butchered, split down the center, deep-fried and wrapped in sheets of foil. According to Marta, nothing so disgusting ever tasted so good (friends of the Quintanilla family still talk about it fourteen years later). Guillermo's mother had made beans, and there was fresh salsa and a never-ending stack of steaming tortillas. There was ice and, of course, there was beer. Guillermo's father borrowed a table from one neighbor and a stack of lawn chairs from another. And the entertainment. Eduardo had hired two groups of mariachis, so that one group would play under a spotlight hanging from the branches of the fig tree, and, after an hour, the other group would take over. Eduardo insisted that there be no break in the music.

When Guillermo's mother told his father that she was pregnant, the old man quit his drinking cold turkey and saved his beer money for the next seven months. A picture of Eduardo holding a small and pudgy Guillermo is framed in the hallway, the baby in one hand and, in the other, a roll of twenties thick as a bundled newspaper. That afternoon, the sun began to set, and the musicians had had practically no time to work on the phone numbers of single women or to fill up on beer and pork. People continually called out requests, songs everyone knew, songs that were improvised, songs only the shriveled old men remembered from a time when they were strong and bright, the notes hummed from memory into the mariachis' ears. Finally, the moon high in the night sky, the mariachis ran out of things to play.

Men in both groups began talking about going home, about other engagements and getting up early the next day for their real jobs. In the family photos, the mariachis are tired. Their bow ties hang limply from their necks. The violinists appear as though they're using their instruments as pillows, the lips of the trumpet players noticeably swollen and thick, the other musicians lost in the shadows cast by the broad brims of their sombreros. But Eduardo Quintanilla wouldn't let them leave. He'd peel bills off his roll and the mariachis would sigh and take their instruments from their red velvet cases.

The two groups merged into one, and the same songs were replayed, only now Eduardo took the spotlight, makeshift as it was. Eduardo Quintanilla had seven months worth of beer money and he planned on making the most of it. He sang even as his audience dwindled around him. In one picture, Guillermo's tía Rocio, having made a rare public appearance, is patting Eduardo's shoulder on her way out. Guillermo's father sang as the older women cleaned up and formed take-home plates from the scraps and leftovers. A few of the mariachis said the money now wasn't worth their effort, and, by ten, Eduardo had doubled their price, tripling it an hour later, his voice raspy and scoured. He didn't quit until there was no one left to hear him, until his wife had taken Guillermo away, moving Guillermo's crib to the room that would later be his, the place in the house farthest away from all the old man's racket.

WITH ITS FLAKING VARNISH REMOVED, the dresser's wood is nearly white, the color of bones bleached by the sun and long forgotten by whatever dogs left them there. Guillermo mixes the paint slowly, carefully, the way the attendant at Angel's Hardware instructed him so that the bubbles will rise to the surface. Guillermo's using "Hunter Green," though he thinks it should be called "Robin Hood" or "Peter Pan" because they're exactly who this shade of green reminds him of. The word "Hunter" brings images of army men and camouflage to Guillermo's mind. This green is too bright, too festive, to let him imagine soldiers hidden among the lush growth of a jungle, waiting for something to kill.

It's hot again, and Guillermo wonders if the paint will dry in the can before he can use it all. He'll have to work fast, which may prove to be difficult, since his hands are tender from the sandpaper, and his forearm and shoulder are sore from the repetitive motion of sanding. He paints the right panel first, going up and down, trying to be smooth so the paint won't drip all over the place, and, after an hour of dipping and brushing and brushing and dipping, the dresser is covered with green. The drawers are next, and Guillermo begins work on the first one even though the paint is low in the can.

Two drawers later, Guillermo's interrupted by the telephone, and he sets his brush aside and jogs to the house to catch it before the third ring. It's Sal checking if Guillermo wants to do something, maybe play some Defender at Road Runner Liquor, maybe check out the drill team girls as they practice walking in straight, organized lines.

"Right now I'm busy with the dresser," Guillermo says. "Later I'll be busy with homework."

"Are you sure?" Sal asks.

Guillermo holds the phone with his shoulder and picks at the paint under his fingernails. "Yeah, I'm positive."

"Well," Sal says, "you better not be busy on Saturday." Saturday is Sal's fifteenth birthday. There will be a party, and Sal's invited everybody he knows, which is a lot of people since Sal was voted Most Popular Seventh Grader in last year's yearbook. Sal keeps telling Guillermo that his cousin's going to DJ.

"Plus there'll be girls," he says. "Ones that are still talking about you at school."

Sal passes on some of the stories that continue to go around, Violet telling people that Guillermo beat up three kids at once, Yvette saying he was expelled. After a while, Guillermo quits listening. He switches the phone to his other shoulder and busies himself by picking away his green skin. He still has four drawers to paint. He still has homework to do. The Barrazas' letter is yet to be written.

AT ABOUT FIVE O'CLOCK, Guillermo returns from Angel's Hardware with a second tin of Hunter Green paint. Marta's home. She's standing at the counter by her window, washing dishes in the blue tub of water. Guillermos' card is opened on her bed.

"Happy birthday," he tells her.

Marta turns around, holding a glass that drips soapy water onto her floor. "He forgot," she says. "Your dad, sure, but pinche Benny forgot my birthday."

Guillermo tells Marta that it's early, that Benny's at work still. "Give him a chance," he says.

"Benny had plenty of chances this morning," Marta says. "I watched him shower and shave. I ironed his uniform and made him breakfast. When I left, he didn't say anything." Marta puts down the glass and rubs her nose. Guillermo doesn't know what to say. Marta closes her eyes for a few long seconds, then dries her hands. "Come with me."

Marta goes through her pocketbook on the way to the liquor store. Guillermo holds her driver's license, some papers and receipts, a napkin with lipstick marks so dark you'd think her mouth was made of fudge. They wait at a traffic signal, and out comes a wad of dollar bills that gets smaller as Marta smooths the bills on her hip. Before the light turns green, a car skids to a stop, and the squeal of its brakes sends a sudden rush of fear through Guillermo, which keeps his heart from beating. He feels stupid, defenseless. He pictures his broomstick next to Marta's dresser and the tin of paint. The light changes and the car speeds off, but Guillermo doesn't feel much better.

Guillermo's a regular at Road Runner Liquor. He knows the electronic beep that sounds when they walk in the store. "Go ahead," Marta says. "Get whatever you want."

When Guillermo stops by after school, he usually wants one of everything, but at this moment, the tiers of bubble gum and candy bars, the coolers of popsicles and soda, they offer him nothing. Guillermo walks aimlessly through the cramped store's one narrow aisle. He nearly grabs a Pee-Chee folder thinking it'll look good on Monday, a new folder, a fresh start, but when Marta comes to the counter with a case of Lucky Lager, Guillermo reminds himself that a folder isn't what she had in mind.

Guillermo gets a bag of Fun-Yuns and Marta tells him to grab her a bag of Fritos. She pays without having to show her ID, and they walk home, Guillermo keeping a quick pace. He carries the beer, his bag of Fun-Yuns on top. Marta opens her Fritos. She holds the first Frito in front of Guillermo's mouth and he wriggles his nose because he's always found the corn chips to smell like feet. Marta shrugs and pops the orange curl in her mouth. She crunches a few seconds, then points to the beer.

"You know," she says. "I didn't really drink before I met Benny. Beer always tasted gross to me, but the first time Benny asked me out we went to that bar over on Valley, the Horseshoe Club. I was twenty years old." Between chips, Marta explains that she tried not to act like she was too young to be there. "We sat in a corner and Benny talked about building professional race cars and I talked about maybe getting my GED. When Benny ordered me a beer, the bartender didn't check my ID either." Marta stops. "I guess I've always looked old. Anyway, the beer gave me asco, but I choked it down just to be sitting in that red vinyl booth, alone with Benny. I mean, here's this guy with so much going on in life, all these kids, and he wants to spend time with me. I guess I felt special.

"That night I dreamt about Benny at work," Marta says. "He was putting a whole car together with a blowtorch, sparks flying all around him, bouncing off his skin." She shakes her head and puts another Frito in her mouth. "Benny was different from any of my other boyfriends. He would call Art Laboe over and over, requesting different songs for me under different names, then keep me up all night on the phone listening to the dedications. He'd tell me my new name was Denise or Rosalina or Marie. I can't remember them all. They were different every time. Now, I guess it doesn't matter."

Guillermo knows he should say something, something smart, something comforting, but his mind's blank, his fishbowl empty. He nods at the Fritos in Marta's hand. "Can I have one?" he asks. Marta puts a chip in Guillermo's mouth, and by the time they get home the two of them have finished the bag.

"I'll save you the bottlecaps if you want them. I know you like the puzzles they have inside." Marta shuts the gate and they walk past Guillermo's house to hers.

"The rebuses," Guillermo says, the word popping out of no-where.

Marta nods and takes her keys from her purse. "That's right," she says. "The rebuses." She unlocks her door, steps inside, Guillermo's Fun-Yuns still on the case of beer when she takes it from him. Marta puts them on her bed. "If Benny calls," she says, "I'm not here. I'm not home." Guillermo nods and even though he sees it coming, he still jumps a little when Marta's door slams shut.

GUILLERMO DOESN'T KNOW HOW MAD he should be at Benny. After all, it's not like he can do anything to him. Still, on Saturday morning he takes his broom handle and walks to the go-cart track to find out what exactly happened. Guillermo finds the track packed, Benny in the pit area, busy with a damaged go-cart. Benny yanks the cart's steering wheel back and forth and watches the front wheels as they pivot to the left and to the right, the buzz from the engines drowning out Guillermo's voice as he yells Benny's name. When Benny finally does notice Guillermo, he sets his ratchet aside and grabs a rag from the red tool cabinet behind him.

"Hey, what's up?" he says.

"You tell me." Guillermo holds the broom handle firmly and does his best to approximate the look he imagines Marta wearing in a situation like this.

"Nothing," Benny says. He wipes his hands and works the rag around his fingers. "Just another busy Saturday. I can't get you on the track right now, but hang out and I'll see what I can do."

"That's not why I'm here. You forgot Marta's birthday."

"No, I didn't. It's next Tuesday."

"It was yesterday."

"No," Benny says. "I got it right here. Look." He takes a dirty white card from his wallet and hands it to Guillermo. It's full of names and dates: MARIE—OCTOBER 5TH. DENISE—JANUARY 14TH. JOSEPH—APRIL 20TH. ABIGAIL—DECEMBER 8TH. GABRIELLA—JUNE 28TH. RAYMOND—JULY 20TH. MOISES—OCTOBER 1ST. ROSALINA—FEBRUARY 23RD. SUZANA—SEPTEMBER 1ST. MARTA—MAY 2ND. They're sloppily written in pencil, the thick kind used in kindergarten classes or construction. The card's also smudged, so that the two by Marta's name appears like a twelve. Benny checks the days on his calendar, the same Aztec girl as in Guillermo's father's shop. "I got like nine more days."

Again Guillermo tells Benny that it was yesterday. He hands the card back and Benny examines it closely, turning from the dim light of the pit area to the sun shining over the bleachers.

"Aw shit," Benny says. He kicks the ground and runs his hands through his hair. He pats down his pockets and bums a quarter off Guillermo for the pay phone out front. Benny first calls the house, but there's no answer, just as Guillermo predicted. Marta's at work until one today. Benny gets the quarter back and thinks a minute before he dials a second number, presumably the one for the dentist's office in San Gabriel. He asks for Marta, and, before he can finish his first sentence, he's left talking to himself. "Hello?" he asks. Benny waits a few seconds and hangs up. "Listen," he tells Guillermo. "You got to tell her I'm sorry."

"Marta isn't talking to anyone," Guillermo says, relishing his role as her spokesperson. "But I have an idea."

Guillermo waits by Benny's truck, and Benny tells Lyle that he's taking an early lunch. Benny drives to Peggy's Flowers, where he orders a bouquet so large that the florist takes others apart to make it. Benny asks for it to be delivered today, and he pays extra to guarantee that it gets there right at one-thirty.

"Make sure it goes to the back house," Guillermo tells the florist. "You might have to knock four or five times, but she'll answer if you keep bugging her."

Guillermo tells Benny about the antique knobs at the junkyard. He seems to understand that buying the knobs is like signing your name on a big green heirloom of a birthday card. When Guillermo tells Benny the price, he's laughed at. "Fifty dollars!" Benny exclaims. "Come on, Guillermo. I just spent twice that on flowers."

Still, Guillermo convinces Benny to check them out. At the junkyard, Guillermo asks if Benny's got a screwdriver, and Benny checks behind the seat. He pulls out a hammer, a coffee mug, a mess of dirty napkins, and an empty box of condoms before producing a short-shanked standard screwdriver. "Will this do?" he asks.

Guillermo nods yes. He leaves his broom handle in the truck and follows Benny inside.

Everything in the junkyard has remained in its place. They find the junk man removing the faucets from a sink, and he trails them to the furniture, Benny shoving the damp armchair aside instead of stepping around it.

"Those them?" he asks. Guillermo nods and Benny turns to the junk man. "I'll give you five bucks for the knobs." Benny walks right up to the junk man, and, from Guillermo's vantage point, the junk man disappears.

"Sure," the junk man says. "Sounds real good."

Guillermo smiles. Benny tosses him the screwdriver.

SOMETIME LAST YEAR, Guillermo was in his room attempting miserably to learn his part of *The Munster's* theme that Mr. People was having the band play in an upcoming parade. Slightly winded and frustrated with the fact that the sounds he read on his sheets of music didn't match those coming from his trumpet, Guillermo set the instrument aside. He came out for something, a glass of water, a soda if there happened to be any in the fridge, and his father looked up from the mess of transistors and circuitry he was tinkering with on the kitchen table.

"Don't you guys ever play anything else besides that kind of music?" he asked. The old man mimicked a few bars of the theme. "There's no life in that mierda," he said.

The old man's soldering gun hissed as he cleaned it on a damp sponge before taking Guillermo to his shelf of records. Guillermo's father selected an album and placed the shiny vinyl disk on the turntable. Guillermo recognized the sleeve his father held before him, the matador skillfully posed in a half verónica, the bull diving at his red cape, one of the bull's horns carving a scar in the ground. The first somber measures from the speakers were from a trumpet.

"Pay attention," the old man said.

Then came the rest of the band.

"Those aren't tubas you hear. They're the pounding hoofbeats of a charging bull. Don't listen to the cymbals. Listen to the sand being kicked in the air. To the whisper of the matador's cape."

They stood, father and son side by side, and Guillermo watched the old man absorb something he didn't seem able to process. Sure, Guillermo heard the music flowing from the speakers, but the course it took with him was shallow.

"When you play," his father said, "you should feel like each note coming from your trumpet has a heart of its own, one that will stop beating when the air in your lungs runs out."

SAL'S COUSIN IS THE WORST DJ EVER. It seems as though the guy only brought five records with him because Guillermo's already heard "Brass Monkey" and "Jungle Love" three times tonight. Sal's birthday party also has more relatives than girls. It's almost eleven o'clock, and there's only five girls here, and one of them is Sal's tía and another is his cousin's fiancée. The fiancée sits on a milk crate, aloof and bored, and watches Sal's family dance goofy in the patio to the music. There's no beer or booze. Even though Guillermo isn't much of a drinker, he did expect to get his hands on more than the half-empty pint of Southern Comfort Sal found in his sister's closet. Guillermo takes a big drink when the bottle's passed around, and the liquor makes him gasp and shudder as it burns first in his throat then in his stomach.

The kids Guillermo encounters from school all want to talk about Monday, and since it's not late enough for him to leave, and there aren't enough people here for him to just disappear, he's begun nursing a small hope that the police might show up and stop the party, giving him a proper excuse to sneak back home. Guillermo goes to the front yard, and, wherever he stands, he can't get away from the flashing red light of the DJ siren coming from the black mouth of the garage. He returns to the house, to the kitchen, and feels slightly better because the kitchen is dark and the light doesn't quite reach the window over the sink. Sal's mom laid out a big spread, but at this point, even with the lights out, nothing looks good. All that's left are chips and fruit punch and a few greasy pizza boxes from Paisano's. There's macaroni salad too, Sal's favorite, but it's been sitting out all night, so when Guillermo stirs it around, the spoon in the bowl sounds like a foot being yanked from mud.

Guillermo takes the peanut butter from the cupboard, and from the fridge he takes a loaf of bread like he's done here a thousand times after school. He keeps the refrigerator door open to look for the jelly, and, out of nowhere, Irma's standing in the yellow light thrown across the linoleum. Guillermo hadn't noticed her around all night, but there she is, right in front of him, her long and black shadow stretching up the kitchen walls from the floor to the ceiling. Irma's alone, but Guillermo figures she's probably brought the lettermen with her to kick his ass, and to that end he wishes he had the thin and jagged steak knife that tonight replaced the broom handle, the steak knife that's in his wind-breaker, the windbreaker that's piled under all the other jackets on Sal's bed.

Guillermo gulps, then tells her hi. He shakes the bread in his hand and offers to make her a sandwich. Irma says nothing. The refrigerator door stays open, and Guillermo uses the light to look for any of Irma's people hiding in the shadows. Guillermo puts the bread aside and blocks his hands into fists. "Stay away from the egg salad," he says with a smile.

Irma remains quiet. Her mean face gets meaner.

"Hey, I'm sorry," Guillermo says. "I didn't mean to hurt your brother."

She still says nothing back. Her lips stay tightly shut as though she's sucking off her lipstick.

This is it. The second Guillermo looks away from her, he's sure someone will strike him. He breathes deeply and lets the refrigerator door swing shut. He wants to get this fight over with, but the beating he expects is never delivered. Instead, Irma says, "I'm sorry, I thought you were someone else," and, as she walks back outside, back into the party, Guillermo wishes that he was.

GUILLERMO'S UP EARLY ON SUNDAY MORNING. He rubs the lagañas from his eyes and waits, listening to the quiet sounds of his father leaving for the shop. His father's avoided him all week, given Guillermo only brief flashes of attention and money for paint and supplies. Guillermo pulls on some cut-offs and writes the letter of apology, a short paragraph scribbled in his notebook, three sentences that turn into four when he pecks out the letter on his mother's old typewriter. He folds the paper in three and puts it with his algebra homework. He goes to the kitchen and pours himself a big bowl of Corn Flakes and sits outside on the back steps of the house. Marta's dresser remains under the fig tree, knobless.

Marta emerges not long after. Her hair is tousled and she's wearing a purple bathrobe and matching slippers. She regards the piece of green furniture, pulling each drawer out and sliding it back. "It looks good," she tells Guillermo. "It really does."

Guillermo stirs the cereal in his bowl. The dresser really does look pretty good, even without the knobs, and in the warm morning light he munches his breakfast with a mild sense of accomplishment.

"Can you help me get it back inside?" Marta asks.

Guillermo sets down his bowl. He lifts one end of the dresser, and Marta lifts the other, and soon enough the dresser's in its old place against the wall in Marta's room. The room is dim, and Benny's bouquet is on Marta's nightstand in a wide-mouthed vase filled with water, her lamp on the ground as though the flowers were capable of giving off a stronger, fragrant light. Seven empty Lucky Lager bottles are in a line on the floor. Guillermo asks about the rebuses, and Marta reaches into the deep pockets of her robe and comes out with six of the bottlecaps, their puzzles indistinguishable to Guillermo in the darkened room. "You can put the mirror on later," Marta says.

Guillermo tells Marta to wait a minute, and he sprints through the yard and through the house to his room. He tosses the bottlecaps on his desk and gets the knobs from the pockets of the jeans he wore yesterday morning. When he comes back out, he carries three knobs in each of his fists, and he makes Marta close her eyes as he screws them in by hand. The bouquet then goes atop the dresser, the flowers heavier than he anticipated, so that some of the water sloshes onto the green wood when he sets the vase down. Guillermo throws open the curtains and the room becomes bright. He stands behind Marta. "You can open your eyes," he says. "Pretend you're looking at it for the first time."

"It looks good," Marta says. "Oh wait, those knobs. They're nice." But the tone in Marta's voice isn't nice. It sounds flat and vaguely disinterested, nowhere near the reaction Guillermo had hoped for.

"They were Benny's idea," Guillermo says, trying to be nonchalant.

"I know," Marta says, a smile developing on her face. "He told me last night."

THE APOLOGY'S WRITTEN and his homework is done, so Guillermo decides to take Sal up on his offer of video games at Road Runner

Liquor. Sal's rich with birthday money, and Guillermo tells him he'll meet him there in twenty minutes. He hangs up the phone and scrapes together some change and heads out into the world. He walks up the side streets and onto Valley Boulevard. It isn't until he passes the pawn-shop that he notices the Datsun with three lettermen.

The Datsun's driver goes slowly, staying close to the curb, and the lettermen yell out Guillermo's name. He knows not to turn around. Guillermo stops to let the Datsun pass. It coasts by and one of the lettermen hurls a greasy paper bag at him. The bag misses, though not by much. It skids across the sidewalk, the lettermen hooting and whistling, and Guillermo jaywalks across Valley. He has nothing with him. No broom handle. No steak knife. Instead of continuing to Road Runner Liquor, he heads in the opposite direction, jogging the short distance to the go-cart track. When Guillermo reaches the track's parking lot, the clattery rumble of the carts behind him, he watches the Datsun go down one block, two blocks, and then the small car makes the U-turn Guillermo hoped it wouldn't.

Benny's sitting and laughing with Lyle. Guillermo heads to the pit area, bumping the people waiting in line for nachos and hot dogs, kicking over a soda as he runs past the first row of bleachers. Guillermo calls Benny over, and Benny opens the gate to let Guillermo inside the pit crew's chain link cage. Guillermo cups his hand to Benny's ear and over the noise of the single-stroke engines, he explains the situation. He pulls Benny to the fence facing the parking lot, and together they watch the lettermen clamber out of the Datsun. The lettermen are bigger and taller than Guillermo first imagined them, and he recalls an Ensenada circus he attended with both his parents, which he'd long since forgotten. There was a skit with clowns crammed into a small plywood van much too small to house the six brightly clothed men who exited one after another after another, their makeup smeared, their relief exaggerated. Now, as the lettermen stretch and yawn in the bright noon light of this Sunday in El Monte, the curious awe Guillermo felt as a child has been replaced with a hard, cold fear.

Guillermo can make out the little gold footballs on the purple chests of the lettermen's jackets as they mill around, BARRAZA stitched in round gold letters across the back of one. Irma's older brother has a thin mustache, and, under his jacket, he's wearing a white tank top and a gold chain that glints when he moves. He's big, but not big like Benny. Benny regards all three of them while Guillermo leans against the wall next to Benny's calendar, taking deep breaths of dirty gasoline. Benny runs his hand through his hair and adjusts his weight belt.

"Don't worry about it," he says, his hand on Guillermo's shoulder. "Nobody's gonna fuck with you."

Irma's brother waits by the Datsun, and the other two lettermen enter the track. They check the bleachers and they look for Guillermo in the bathrooms. They watch the carts racing around, and, after a few laps, they return outside and wait with Irma's brother. The lettermen tell jokes and slap at each other's hair. They lean on the hood of the Datsun and smoke cigarettes. Irma's brother takes a bat from the backseat and begins knocking pieces of gravel at the go-cart track's sign.

"Hey Lyle," Benny says. Lyle looks up from his work, a piston in one hand and stiff wire brush in the other. "I'll be right back." Lyle nods and resumes his scrubbing. Benny cocks his head at Guillermo. "Let's go," Benny says.

When they see Guillermo and Benny coming, the lettermen pitch their cigarette butts toward the stand of weeds in the adjacent lot. Irma's brother lets the bat drop down to his side. He sees Guillermo and smiles.

"There a problem here?" Benny says.

"Who are you?"

"I'm Guillermo's brother."

"Really?"

Guillermo nods, Benny's declaration on him like a suit of armor, and, before either of them can say anything else, Irma's brother swings the bat at Benny's side.

There's a dull thud, and Benny clutches his ribs, and Irma's brother swings again. The second time he swings low, striking Benny in the knee, and there's the sound of one hard thing hitting another. Benny buckles. He reaches for the bat and when he goes down, he pulls Irma's brother with him.

One of the lettermen heads to the Datsun, starting the engine, and the other helps Irma's brother to his feet. Guillermo begins to run, but Irma's brother grabs him by the wrist and yanks him around. Irma's brother holds Guillermo and delivers a punch that lands square on his nose. Guillermo drops. He's on the ground and he's dizzy and for a second all he can do is lay there and wait for whatever comes next. His pulse reverberates in his ear. Guillermo blinks his eyes and leans his elbows on the rocky ground to watch the Datsun back into the street.

"Whoa, whoa! What the hell's this?"

Guillermo turns and Lyle's behind him, the piston in the old mechanic's hand like a grimy metal club. Lyle tells Benny to quit moving, but Benny can't stop rocking back and forth. His face is contorted with pain and the gravel crunches underneath him, his left shoe pointing in at an odd angle while his right one sweeps clean stripes in the dirt. He gasps for breath and takes hold of Guillermo's hand, squeezing Guillermo's fingers like he wants to rip them away, and they stay like this until the siren from the coming ambulance makes itself known over everything else.

THERE'S MUSIC COMING FROM THE CHURCH. Guillermo finds the front doors locked, but the basement windows are alive with light, the small square panes still frosted with snow in a can from last Christmas. Guillermo peers through a clear window in the corner. The basement is crowded. Tables with people eating and tables with steaming silver trays of chicken and rice are off to the sides, and tightly clustered dancers whirl in the center of the room. There are musicians on the small stage, three of them. One hugs a bass with a chipped finish; one pumps a shiny green accordion; one plays a guitar with a thin, red plastic hand holding the strings in a certain key. Guillermo's father is at the microphone. The old man's singing about being alone and leaving the door open, about being a stone in the open road. Aside from him, all the faces are unfamiliar, and, as Guillermo looks for Marta, he can't remember who he's looked at before. Guillermo spots his godmother right below him, laughing with an old woman who bounces a baby in her lap. The warm and safe feeling that Marta inspires in Guillermo doesn't come.

Guillermo walks through the alley that separates the church from the paper tube factory next door. He rubs his sprained wrist as though he might work the strained bones back into place. His nose feels heavy. At home it looked a little swollen, and Guillermo flinches whenever his face makes certain expressions. The church's back doors are open, and Guillermo steps down the dim stairway into the brightness of the basement. A new song starts, and his father lets out one of his gritos, the scream released from a happy place deep inside him. The musicians keep playing and every churchgoer watches Guillermo's father hold the note, his cheeks shaking, his face turning red. Some people in the audience let out yelps and howls of their own, but theirs are small and spotty compared to the old man's.

Guillermo walks around the dancers to Marta's table and he stands there until the old woman points him out. Marta turns around. "What a surprise!" she says.

Marta introduces him as her godson and the old woman nods and smiles. She strokes Guillermo's arm like he's made of porcelain. Marta asks if he's eaten, and he shakes his head. She gets up to serve him a plate, and they walk through the dance floor instead of going around it.

Guillermo can no longer wait. He reaches out with his good arm and tugs at Marta's shirt, but she mistakes this as Guillermo wanting to dance. Marta says something that Guillermo can't understand because of the loud music, and, a few seconds later, he's among the dancers, Marta's hand in his good one, Guillermo doing his best to keep the beat. His bad hand hangs at his side and the hurt flares up when Marta plants it on the small of her back. They turn, and the turn leaves him off balance so that he accidentally steps on Marta's toes. Guillermo looks up and he apologizes. He directs his attention to the group onstage as Marta turns them in another circle, turning more slowly this time. Guillermo watches the old man cradle the microphone in his hands, and he figures there's about a minute, maybe less than that, until he can get Marta outside and away from all this, until he can get her alone in a quiet place so he can concentrate on the right words to explain what has happened.

practice tattoo Every Night Is Ladies' Night
THE CROSSING OF HECTOR CRUZ
corporated
Riding with Larry CRUZ Media Vuelta NDA
GINA AND HER Media Vuelta RULA
Buena Suerte Airlines

BUENA SUERTE AIRLINES

1 9 8 6

Over the last two years I've dressed in the dark so Hector will have a chance at those extra hours of sleep. I stick the last pin in my hair, put on my cap, and check on Peter one more time before leaving the bedroom. I kiss his forehead just like I do every morning, and try to smooth his spiky black hair. I'm thankful that, over these last two years, I've also learned how to touch my son without waking him.

In the living room, I get my work keys, my house keys, and my purse off the coffee table, then grab my sweater from the couch. I get the bicycle that Lily was nice enough to lend me, and carefully walk it down the stairs after locking the door. My car stopped running two weeks ago. Hector says it's the starter, and when we get the money together, he'll probably have to buy a new one. He'd like to find it used. Hector's been checking the Pick-A-Part after work a couple times a week, and he's called salvage yards from Riverside to Wilmington, but he hasn't had any luck.

Hector's taken my steering wheel apart so that there's a bunch of wires hanging from under my dashboard. He's shown me which ones to connect so the car will start, but there's something about stealing my own car that I don't care for. When Lily saw him working on it, she offered to let me use a bicycle an old boyfriend left in her apartment. It's nothing great. Hector groaned when I told him I'd ride to work, but that night after dinner he must've sprayed a whole can of WD-40 on the chain and the gears, trying to get the squeaks out. So now I have to get up at four-fifteen instead of four-thirty, and my hands smell like rust from the handlebars. Still, there's something about going to work this way that makes me not miss the stalling engine of my Corolla, its springs poking through the seats.

Now I have the whole city to myself. The sky's still dark, and the air is cool but not cold. You can hear electricity humming in the streetlights. When I ride over a manhole, I can hear the water rushing beneath it, and when I pass the Happy Donut, I can smell the wonderful things baking inside. Two blocks away is Tortillerilla Bienvenida, where the fresh tortillas on the shuddering conveyor belt make the Five Points intersection smell like a cornfield. This is the first big signal that I come to on my way to work. Even though there are never any cars coming in either direction, I always press the crosswalk button to hear the faint scraping of the underground machinery that changes the light from red to green.

That's where I am, waiting to cross the street, when I remember that I didn't leave a bottle prepared in case Peter wakes up. Usually I'll boil some water while I get dressed, and leave a bottle sitting in it, but this morning I forgot. Peter started crying after midnight, and when I finally got him back to sleep, the thing between Fifi and Chelo kept me tossing and turning. The last time I remember looking at the glowing green numbers on my alarm clock, they read 2:31. I hope that Hector will be luckier this morning, that Peter will let him sleep until six, that Hector's eyes won't look like wet tea bags when he drops Peter off at Mom's. The thought of Peter kicking and twitching in his crib comes back to me as I coast slowly past the Pontiac lot, toward our sign with the big, bright golden arches. What if something awful is happening to him? What if my baby's getting sick? The bike begins to wobble, and I remind myself that pedaling keeps you from falling over.

THREE MONTHS AFTER HAVING PETER, I returned to McDonald's for the second time. Even though the circumstances were different, once again the decision was out of my hands. Hector never said anything aloud, but I could tell by the way he started conserving electricity that he wanted me to start working sooner rather than later. Somewhere around September he started making sure every empty room was left in darkness and switching off the TV if I left it for two seconds while changing Peter's diaper. Hector started saying that electricity doesn't grow on trees. We had saved some money, but it went quickly, and, with the winter months approaching, our delinquent light and gas bills came footnoted with threats. The two years I'd been out of school seemed like twenty, the pre-med student taking bio courses another person in another life. Between work and school and the baby, school lost out. I called Arielle at Human Resources on a Friday, then I called Mom, and things fell back into place.

The next Monday, Hector got up early to drop me off. I went back as morning shift manager, though now I didn't look forward to my work like I did before. I didn't need a distraction, I needed to be with Peter. Inside McDonald's, in the small rear storeroom, the metal rack with all the time cards had been covered with pink and blue streamers. A banner reading WELCOME BACK MINI was taped to the wall above the time clock, and I was so surprised by the whole thing that I didn't think of punching in until two hours later.

These were the people I was in charge of once again. Juan and a new Vietnamese girl named Fifi worked the grill and sandwich assembly in back. Patty and her cousin Chelo worked the registers up front. Patty and Chelo both pluck their eyebrows to the point where they're barely slivers, and Chelo looks mean, like she's constantly managing a mouthful of nails. Chelo still had the habit of leaning into Patty's ear to whisper things about the customers—embarrassing and ugly things, things that were just sad, men with their zippers hanging open and girls dotted with acne and viejitas whose heads wobbled from surviving strokes. Patty would suck on her teeth until she couldn't stand it anymore, and her laughter would explode wildly, turning every head in the restaurant.

My first few days back were festive. I passed Peter's picture around, and I bounced from spot to spot, from the grill to the registers to the frying vats, relearning each position before I settled into the drive-thru. Before I left on maternity leave, I could sleepwalk through an entire shift doing any of these jobs. Dreams where I was frying frozen french fries and slapping Egg McMuffins together came to me at least twice a week. Sometimes I was in our kitchen, and once I was on the Love Boat. Another time I was taking a bath, and somehow it was very important to me that I make an Egg McMuffin using only the things in our bathroom.

Besides being the manager, I was the only person on my shift with a child. From where I sat in the nook for the drive-thru, I caught glimpses of McDonaldland for the two seconds it took one car to pull forward after another had driven away. On Saturdays, McDonaldland's crowded with kids climbing over everything. They leave their toys in the restaurant, and the cubbyhole where I keep my purse became the Lost and Found for pacifiers, toy soldiers, and rattles that had been kicked across the floor all morning long. Sometimes I'd lose track of the orders flickering on my computer screen, and customers would come back looking for the right bag of food. During the slow times I'd wonder what Peter would be like in the future, who my son would be five, ten, twenty years from now, and the urge to be with him would overtake me. I'd make change from the register to call Mom from the phone out front, punching the buttons as fast as I could just to hear Peter gurgle into his end of the line.

The times that Mom didn't answer her phone, the times she was out with Peter in the El Monte Mall, shopping at the discount stores or buying caramel corn, I'd wonder if I did the right thing coming back here, if I should be the one pushing Peter in his stroller. After work I'd go straight to Mom's place and find Peter asleep, kicking the bars of his crib as my mom got ready to take tickets and make change in the parking garage at Our Lady of the Valley Hospital. Mom would be zipping up her blue pants with red ribbon running up the sides, or buttoning her white shirt, or looking for the clasp on her bow tie. This is the point in the afternoon when she stands by her mirror, shushing me with her finger while regarding herself seriously, as if somewhere in the top floors of the hospital there is a queen and it's my mom's personal duty to guard her.

CHELO DIDN'T COME IN TODAY. When I called her house, the phone just rang and rang, so I worked both the register and the drive-thru at once. Now I'm beat. I could fire Chelo for a no-call-no-show, instead of firing her for the racist joke she made about Fifi. Still, I'd hate to lose Chelo. She may have a big mouth and a bad sense of humor, but she's one of the best workers I have. Fifi, on the other hand, is one of the worst. Fifi stares and grumbles at the sausage patties as they overcook. She wraps her sandwiches so sloppily that they come apart as they slide down the heating shelf. Last month she almost had a fistfight with Juan over which station should be playing on the radio, KLUV or KROQ, even though the boombox belonged to him. To stop them, I took the radio out of the kitchen area and put it in the back room, where, if I had followed my manager's guidebook, it would have stayed in the first place.

When I get to Mom's, she's already dressed for work, pacing the living room floor with Peter and whispering in his ear. A little howl of joy comes out of Peter's mouth. He claps, and Mom makes her eyes big with feigned surprise, and Peter claps his hands some more.

"What happened?" Mom asks. She checks the clock over the stove. "I better not miss my bus."

I shrug and don't tell her the real reason I'm late. Today I found two crumpled dollar bills in the parking lot. On the way home I stopped off at Road Runner Liquor and spent them on two lottery tickets. As I scratched at the silver coating, I imagined big payments on our credit cards, a new pair of work shoes for Hector, a little pair of pants for Peter. When nothing came, I tore the tickets to pieces, feeling as if someone was laughing at me.

She gives Peter to me, and he puts his hands all over my face, grabbing at my nose. Mom gets her coat and points to some ads for Halloween costumes that are on her table. She asks if I've planned Peter's outfit this year.

"We didn't do anything with him last Halloween," she says.

"Peter's too young for things like that. He can barely walk, and I'm not going to carry him door-to-door for candy, especially with all the locos in our neighborhood."

"They'll be checking candy down at the hospital," Mom says.

"Peter shouldn't be taking part in anything where your food has to be X-rayed for needles and razor blades."

"You're too serious." Mom waves her hand at me. "How'd you get so old?"

She shows me the different costumes on sale. The children wearing them aren't Peter's age. They're grade-school kids, and all their outfits look cheap. They remind me of the construction-paper costumes that Mrs. Murphy put together for the poorer kids in my grade school, only these are going for fifteen dollars each.

"I don't know."

Mom shakes her head and sighs. "With your attitude, I'll have to dress Peter in one of your old costumes."

"The ladybug or the rabbit?" Even if I wanted Peter to go out for Halloween, even if he fit in one of my old outfits, there's no way Hector would let him wear it.

"Olvidate," Mom says, rolling her eyes and imitating Hector. "My boy isn't any bug or rabbit. He's a soldier. A cowboy. A pirate." She puts her nose to Peter's and tells him in Spanish that he's a pirate. Peter slaps at her cheeks, and she squints as if she was wearing an eye patch, growling and baring her teeth.

MOST DAYS I DON'T TAKE MY FIRST BREAK until ten-thirty. By then I'm so hungry that I just make it my lunch hour. This afternoon I have to do laundry, so at ten-thirty I get on my bike and ride down to Road Runner Liquor. Hector once gave the owner, Don, a jump-start and ever since then Don doesn't mind giving me five dollars in quarters whenever I need change. The city I ride through isn't the same at this hour. Valley Boulevard is full of people and traffic, and when I push the crosswalk button at the Five Points, all I can hear is the squealing of a bus that needs new brakes, and the rumble of a UPS truck waiting to make a right turn.

At Road Runner Liquor, I leave the bike by the door next to the pay phones. I go inside, and Don recognizes me right away. He asks about the baby, and I tell him Peter's fine, getting bigger every day. I take a five-dollar bill from my purse. Don says sure, and, as he counts the quarters out, he asks about Hector, if he's still working on cars. Don says he's got a problem with the water pump in his wife's Eldorado.

"If I buy the parts," he says, "you think Hector might give me a break on the labor?"

I tell him that I'll ask. "With the baby, things are kind of busy for the both of us."

I have Don write the problem down, because that kind of language doesn't stick with me. He tears a blank section from the roll on his adding calculator, and I look at the lottery tickets under the sheet of glass over the counter, all the past winners from Road Runner Liquor, as he scribbles. Don points out his phone number on the slip when he finishes, and even though it seems silly, I count out four quarters and ask him to give me a ticket.

Don tears one off the sheets hanging from the shelves of liquor bottles. I put the ticket, the other quarters, and the paper with his car problem into my purse. I say good-bye, get on my bike, and ride back to work, where I heat my lunch, a sandwich with the meatloaf Hector made last night. I get a cup of ice water to go along with it. According to the time clock, there are forty-seven minutes left on my lunch hour.

I take my food and sit outside in McDonaldland, in the last set of tables toward the back. They're designed to look like a boat, with Grimace as the lookout and the Hamburglar in the crow's nest. I unwrap my sandwich, and, while it steams, I take the lottery ticket from my purse. The ticket is yellow, bright yellow, with the Big Spin logo over a field of stars. I flip the ticket over and read the information printed in small letters on the back. The odds of winning any prize with the ticket in my hands are one in six. My chances of actually getting some money back or winning a trip to the Big Spin, of this ticket being one to put with the others under the glass on Don's counter, are one in fourteen. I look at the front of the ticket, at the silver stuff to be scratched away, and wonder what numbers are underneath, how close this ticket actually is to something good.

EVERY SATURDAY NIGHT MOM watches the Big Spin on the tiny black-and-white television she keeps among the security monitors in the booth. She pretends she's the one wringing the anxiety from her hands as the wheel spins, her feet bouncing as the ball springs from one glittering number to another, fifty million to one million to fifty thousand to one hundred thousand.

For years Mom's saved her change in a big glass jar she keeps in the back of her closet. When the jar fills up, she counts the change. Mom keeps the running total on a scrap of paper and divides the final amount by three. This she does three additional times, once for each of her children, and Rita has told me that Mom repeats our names—RitaRitaRita then DanielDanielDaniel then MinervaMinervaMinerva—as she does the math. The number she comes up with decides how many lottery tickets Mom can buy each day, usually nine or ten, and she keeps a lucky peso from her quinceañeara for the occasion of scratching off their coating.

After years of doing this, of buying her tickets from the same liquor store on the same corner with rolls of quarters, nickels, pennies, and dimes, Mom's luck hasn't improved any. Aside from one small payoff and fifty dollars here, twenty there, she hasn't had much to talk about, certainly no trip to the Big Spin. Mom could wear a dress made from garlic and four-leaf clovers, fingers crossed and rabbits' feet dangling from her ears, and nothing would happen. But I know she still saves her change, and I know what she watches at seven-thirty every Saturday night.

Mom's one payoff was for five hundred dollars, and two days before she got the check in the mail, we got a call that my tía Celia, Mom's sister in Torreón, had passed away. Mom's first trip on a plane was her first one back to Mexico since coming here as a teenager. It used up most of her money, and the way the travel agent booked it, she spent the entire day zigzagging up and down the Mexican border states, stopping in Tijuana, Hermosillo, and Juárez. Mom changed planes in Chihuahua, crossing the humid runway and boarding a dinky two-propeller machine with twenty seats. This second plane bounced and shifted in the sky as if the engines were unbolting themselves in mutiny. Mom said that for three hours she expected to start careening down through the clouds. Finally she landed in Torreón at ten o'clock. She kept the bag of peanuts the stewardess gave her, along with a deck of Mexicana playing cards with waving girls in orange bikinis. She kept the little bag for flight sickness, too, and though Rita and I explained its use to her, to this day she keeps the wooden rosary we all wore for our baptisms in its shiny inner lining.

After that, Mom talked of owning her own airline. It wouldn't be big, a few planes of a decent enough size, so that you wouldn't feel sick as you flew. They would go from here to Mexico, from the El Monte airport directly to the smaller pueblos where everyone we knew had family—Cumpás and Camargo, Musquiz, Gatos Güeros, and Charcos de Risa—dots on the map that made travel agents squinch up their faces and ask, "Where?" Mom wanted to call it Buena Suerte Airlines, and she wanted to be a stewardess onboard as many flights as possible, to make sure every passenger was happy, their every need attended to. No matter what the reason, good or bad, all these people going to new places or back to old ones would arrive with a smile. Mom wanted them to step forward off the plane with her voice in their ears. "Good luck to you," she would tell them. "Good luck to your family, to the time in this place your life has brought you."

HECTOR PARALLEL-PARKS IN FRONT of the Pick-A-Part on Live Oak. He backs his truck into the first open space we find, four blocks from the swap meet at the Drive-In. Peter's been good all morning, and I'm hoping that after Hector gets his new work shoes, he can check the Pick-A-Part without the baby getting fussy. I put our checkbook in the baby bag, and take Peter from his car seat. Hector gets the stroller from the bed of the truck, and I tell him that I'll carry Peter for a while. Hector locks up the truck, and we walk past the Pick-A-Part's orange metal gate, the slogan—CASH FOR YOUR CAR—painted in giant white letters over the hours the place is open. The wrecking yard is open on Sundays from ten to four, and I let out a little groan. Even though I know Hector's doing it for my own good, there's still nothing more boring than following your mechanic husband through an endless maze of junkers as he searches for a single piece to a car that probably won't ever run again.

This morning, though, the tone in Hector's voice was soft and comforting as he sat on my side of the bed. He mentioned the Pick-A-Part, then talked about the swap meet and buying new work shoes. "It'd be good to get out and spend some time together," he said. He rubbed my shoulders with his big and rough hands and gathered my hair, kissing the back of my neck. "Sometimes I can't remember what you look like without your uniform. I always picture you wearing brown pants and a white shirt with yellow stripes. Sometimes I just see your name tag." The sadness in his voice draped over me, and I turned over and said I would go.

I hadn't been thinking about the first and only time I went with Hector to look for car things. It was a long time ago, on an afternoon spent in the dusty outskirts of San Bernardino in a junkyard with no restroom and no shade. Among the aisles of scrapped cars was a sad, stripped version of Hector's truck. Hector looked back at me and smiled, rubbing his hands together, blowing on them like an athlete about to enter the big game. He leaned into the engine cavity, and after a minute of feeling around, up came a shout. It's always something with that truck. Hector had brought his tool box, and he must've figured I came along to be his assistant. He started asking me to hand him the different tools he needed, a variety of wrenches and ratchet attachments that I wasn't familiar with. I searched through the top tray, wondering if each wrench had a clearly marked label I was missing. Eventually, Hector's head popped up and he sighed as he climbed out of the truck to get the tools himself. This went on all afternoon. Each time, Hector's face would be a combination of grease smudges and genuine contempt, as if members of his family were in that little red toolbox, and after five months of serious dating I still couldn't remember their names.

As we walk down Live Oak, Hector tells me that today's the lucky day. "Today that starter will be there," he says. He points to some wrecked cars stacked high inside the yard, and says that they're new. "The new cars always come in on Saturdays," he says. "Usually it's a truckload of ten to fifteen wrecks. On the other side of that wall, there will be a '78 Toyota Corolla with a beautiful starter sitting in the base of the steering column. I know it."

We get to the corner, and as we wait for the light to change, Hector hugs me. He plays peek-a-boo with Peter, and I smell the scent I've always associated with Hector, with my Hector, the mixed fragrance of deodorant and the motor oil staining his work shirts.

We cross the street. When we get to the swap meet cashier, Hector pays the four dollars for the both of us, and helps me through the turnstile. Hector takes Peter while I get the stroller set up. I walk and he pushes, guiding the stroller toward a bright blue tarp shading a table of socks. The tube socks that Hector first looks at are white, the bright white of brand new cotton, which makes them glow in his hands. He pays for two bundles, and the vendor dumps them in a plastic bag and counts out his change.

I've been bugging Hector for weeks about his shoes because both soles on the pair he has now are cracked, split straight across from walking. These new socks are nice, because all of Hector's current work socks have black and brown stains on them from the oily floor grime that oozes its way into his shoes. His socks look like they get used for coffee filters, and they must be washed separately so they don't ruin other clothes. Now, when Hector washes his hands and face after work, he cleans his feet, too. I bought him a pair of chanclas from the TG&Y so that he wouldn't be tracking smudges everywhere. The good part is that Hector uses a degreaser made of fruit peels and lava rocks. When he picks me and Peter up at Mom's, the cab of his truck smells like a giant orange.

Peter gets fussy and Hector gives him the new socks. Peter tries to stick them in his mouth and throws them onto the ground when he discovers they don't fit. Hector picks them up, and, from the baby bag, I get a teething ring which Peter starts to gnaw on. We go up and down a few aisles and find some people selling Halloween stuff, but it's mostly costumes for adults, and Hector and I browse half-heartedly through the tubes of makeup and fake blood and plastic vampire teeth. There's one woman selling costumes for children, but Hector thinks they've all been in a fire because each one we look at smells like smoke, and the cardboard inserts are discolored and warped.

Eventually we find the vendor who sells the shoes Hector wants. Black leather with thick rubber soles and a bump over the toe, the same cheap kind he has now. I hang Hector's bag of socks from the stroller's handle while he takes the shoe from its display. He knocks it against the side of his head. "Steel toe," he tells Peter. "Fifty bucks." Next to the shoe Hector picked is a pair of Die Hards that cost a hundred and twenty dollars. They're more expensive, but they'd probably last an entire year, maybe two.

He agrees to try them both on, but I already know what excuse he'll give me so that another month will be spent with him wandering around, goo seeping from his feet as if his legs had been replaced by a pair of broken and leaky pens. The excuse won't be money. In the past, when things got really tight, I brought home leftovers from work so we could use grocery money on other things. There's no reason we couldn't do that again.

Hector sits in a chair and starts taking off his tennies as the girl laces up the Die Hards. I tell him I'll be right back, and walk out with Peter into the stream of passing people before Hector can look up. We go down a few spaces, and stop at a Vietnamese man with cages of chirping parakeets and shelves of aquariums piled around a large van. I read the labels on the glass to Peter and each fish's name makes him squeal. There are Australian Rainbows and Blue Zebras and Bali Swordtail Sharks that swim up and down, back and forth, while a pack of black eels writhes in a hunk of blue coral.

"Rubber eel," the man tells me, and I nod, hoping he doesn't expect me to buy them. I move away and watch the Hawaiian Tiger Barbs chase each other around. Fish never carry any recollections of where they're from, of the tropical islands they're named after. Once over margaritas at a Christmas party, Rita told me that fish never get bored in the tank. "By the time they swim to one end of the glass," she said, "they've forgotten about the other."

The lower aquariums are full of less expensive goldfish, orange and black Moors that drift lazily in the water, bouncing into one another like orange wedges with bug eyes and fins. Peter puts his hands on the glass. He looks at me and lets out an odd squeak, and I notice something in his mouth. I put my finger to his lips and tell him to open wide, but he turns away and buries his head in my shoulder. I try again, and he starts to whimper, and when I get back to the stroller he's holding on to the collar of my blouse with his teeth. I yank open the baby bag and get a teething cookie. It calms Peter down slightly, but I can feel his little chest heaving in my arms. He opens his mouth when I offer him the cookie, and I use it like a tongue depressor.

Peter's tongue is black on top, and the sight of it makes me so frantic that I can't remember if I fed him anything dark for breakfast. When I find Hector, he's asking the shoe girl if she'll be getting more of the cheaper shoes in soon. She shrugs and says she doesn't know, maybe in two or three weeks. I grab Hector's arm, and tell him we have to leave.

"Why?"

"There's something wrong with Peter."

I shift the baby in my arms and start walking between the vendors toward the giant white screen at the front of the drive-in. I leave the swap meet with Peter, and I'm back out on Live Oak when Hector catches up with me. He's carrying the stroller and the baby bag, and he asks what's the matter.

"Look at your son's tongue," I say. When Hector does, he doesn't appear surprised or concerned.

"He's probably been eating candy or dirt. It's no big deal," he says. "My brother Merced used to eat dirt all the time." Hector says Mom can take him to the doctor tomorrow morning or I can take him in the afternoon, but I want to go today. I want the answers now. Had I stayed in school, I'd know what's wrong with my baby. I could do something. I could tell if it's some kind of allergic reaction or if it's some kind of fungus or if it's an infection, and I would know the names of the pills, of the right antibiotic to fight the microorganisms carpeting my baby's tongue.

We get to the truck, and I wait for Hector to open my door. "Let's take him to the doctor," I say.

Hector sighs. "You're overreacting."

"Dead things should have black tongues, Hector, not our baby."

Hector points to the Pick-A-Part. "Do you want the starter or not?"

"No. Not today."

"It'll only be five minutes."

Hector opens my door. After he takes his toolbox, I put Peter in his car seat. I close the door and roll down the window. I watch Hector in the side mirror. He starts toward the Pick-A-Part, then turns back to me, then back to the Pick-A-Part. I shut my eyes and listen to the sounds on the street, waiting for Hector's footsteps to get closer, for him to come up beside me and tell me he's sorry. He'll tell me of course we'll get Peter looked at today, even though we both know we'd still be paying off an emergency room visit two years from now. But none of that happens. Instead, Hector comes back to the truck and undoes the plastic bag with his dirty shoes and socks. He takes out a rag and jams it into his back pocket. He shakes his head and picks up his toolbox. He says something to himself and walks to the opening in the orange iron door.

TUESDAY'S HALLOWEEN, and when I get to my mom's, the house is filled with the whirring and clacking of her sewing machine. I rush up her steps and leave the bag of cold cheeseburgers and french fries in her kitchen. Mom and Peter are in her bedroom. Mom's dressed for work and hunched under the light of her desk lamp, guiding two pieces of white material under the needle.

"Watch where you step," she says. On the floor all around my mom's bed are oddly cut sections of tissue-thin paper, patterns for different versions of the same costume, and there are enough of these to make costumes until Peter's in junior high.

He's on the bed, working a bottle and wearing only a bunny hood and diapers. One long ear hangs over his face, the other is bunched up under his head. I step around the patterns and sit next to him, asking Mom if he's been given his medicine yet. Sunday night I went home and looked through all my old textbooks, but I couldn't find the answer to the dark little problem in his mouth. On Monday, I lost half a day's pay when Mom and I took him to the doctor. He asked if Peter had been given Pepto-Bismol, and we both said no. He asked if Peter had been teething on anything that might be dirty, and after a few quiet moments of me shrugging, Mom nodded.

"Sometimes I give him my keychain because the jingling sound of the keys makes him happy," she said.

Most of this week's grocery money went to some drops for what I was told is a bacterial infection on his tongue, with two of the last five dollars going toward a couple lottery tickets that I bought on the way over.

"Don't worry, I gave him his drops," Mom says, holding up the half-finished costume. "Remember this?" I refused her money for Peter's prescription, and now she's turning him into a rabbit. Somewhere in one of her many albums, there's a photo of Rita and Danny and me all dressed for Halloween. I can't be more than five years old. Rita's a ladybug and Danny's a cowboy and Mom is holding me in a white bunny suit, floppy ears hanging down my back. "I knew this pattern was somewhere," Mom says. "If it was good enough for you, it'll be good enough for him."

Peter's hot. He's sweating, and the bottle he's sucking on is empty. I get his pacifier from the nightstand. "Is this clean?"

"Of course it's clean. I boiled it this morning."

I get Peter to let me switch the bottle for the pacifier, then I undo the button under his chin. Mom asks me the time. I tell her it's ten 'til two, and she sighs.

"Why didn't you tell me it was so late?" she says, asking if I can finish the costume for her. "All you need to do is sew the tail and the booties," she tells me, "unless you want to buy him some matching botines." Mom says that when she went to the yardage store this morning, she stopped by the Tres Hermanos and they had some real nice shoes in the window. "They were shiny," she says. Mom turns from the machine and jiggles Peter's foot. "Patented leather para mi conejito." Mom looks up at me. "Those are the kind I want you to get," she says.

Before she leaves, Mom tells me to go by the hospital tonight around six or seven, when she takes her break, that the church across the street is having a haunted house. She adjusts her tie, grabs her purse and her keys, and then she's gone. She doesn't ask why I was late.

Today I went into Road Runner Liquor, just like always. I walked in, bought two lottery tickets, and walked right back out. There was no line. There was no small talk with Don. It couldn't have been more than a minute. But when I came out, Lily's bicycle was gone. I looked up and down the street and didn't see anybody riding away. When I told Don, he offered to call the police, but I told him not to. Waiting for them would have made me late, which would've made Mom late. I sit down at the sewing machine and wonder if every year will be like this. Broken starters and stolen bicycles and little things that seem so impossible. New shoes. A Halloween costume.

I take out the two tickets and scratch the first one with my thumbnail. It isn't a winner. I blow the shavings onto the carpet and start scratching the second one. I get a pair of $10,000 squares, a pair for $2, and one for $20. I scratch the last square slowly and see a one and a zero, and, for a second, I hold my breath while I drag my nail across the ticket. I see two more zeros. The last amount is a thousand dollars, and I pretend to not feel surprised at losing.

I tear the tickets into pieces and put them in my pocket to flush later. I pick up Peter and tell him that somehow we'll have to pay for the bike, and he nods and paws at my face and tosses his pacifier to the floor. I lose my train of thought thinking of all the microbes on all the feet that have been on Mom's carpet. The pacifier has to be boiled before I can give it back to him.

In the kitchen, there's a small clean pot on the stove, and I put some water in it and turn the burner on full-blast. I bring Peter from the bedroom, and we do a little dance in front of the settling water until he gets too heavy and I have to sit at the table. The McDonald's bag is there, and I make up a song about hamburgers while we wait for the water to boil.

"Hamburgers for you. Cheeseburgers for me."

Peter claps his hands.

I count him the number of grease stains on the bottom of the bag. *"One. Two. One-two-three."* I stop singing and tell Peter there's no grocery money to buy real food this week. I tell him if I don't figure something out, we'll be eating these burgers the rest of our lives.

I sit and think, and then I don't bother waiting for the water to warm. Peter's pacifier stays on the table and I don't finish his costume. I pack up his things, put him in the stroller, and walk home. It takes me all of two hours. I almost call Hector from the apartment, but instead I take out the phone book, find the Pick-A-Part listing, and dial the number. A man with a deep voice answers, and I ask how much he thinks my car might be worth. He tells me to hold on. There's the thud of a heavy book falling on a table, and I can hear him flipping pages.

"What year you got?"

"It's a '78."

"How many miles?"

"A lot. More than a hundred and fifty thousand."

"That's two-fifty. Maybe three hundred dollars." He asks for three things: a pink slip, proof of registration, and a driver's license. "We close at five," he says.

It's about four-thirty now. The thought of waiting until tomorrow passes through my mind, and I tell myself no. If I don't go, I'll get tired and tomorrow I'll change my mind and this won't be what I want to do anymore. I take Peter into the closet with me. He chews on Hector's necktie as I get the shoe box that we keep all our important papers in, going through them until I find my pink slip.

I get a trash bag and take Peter with me out to the car. I sit Peter in the backseat and start collecting my things. I check under the seats and find some tapes that I used to listen to when the tape player worked. There's some change under the floor mats, an old sweatshirt and McDonald's cups, a wrapper from a candy bar I don't remember eating that's folded into a square. My registration's in the glove compartment, and I put it with my pink slip and my driver's license. I take down the faded pine tree air freshener that's been hanging from my mirror ever since I got my car.

Tomorrow I'll have extra money again. I'll pay Lily for her bike, and I'll buy my own. Tomorrow Hector'll take me to school when he gets home from work. I'll see about night classes, and if I can't take them, I'll see Arielle about changing shifts. Tomorrow Mom will take care of Peter, and she'll finish his costume, and Hector and I will go out to dinner after buying his shoes. I start to take the bag back up to the apartment, but with Peter, carrying two things at once is a hassle. I leave the trash bag on the curb and strap Peter in as best I can with the seat belts. I reach under the dashboard and take out the loose wires and they make a spark when they touch.